Acclaim for Minus One: A

"Minus One: A Twelve-Step Journey tells the intense story of a brave lesbian facing the reality of her addiction. This book clearly demonstrates how cunning the disease of addiction is through Terry's struggles with recovery and the twelve steps. After completing the book readers will be filled with hope from the examples of how applying the twelve-step principles one day at a time can produce real miracles."

Susan Murray Schopflin, MSW, LCSW
Program Director,
McCambridge Center for Women

"Only recently has the scientific and medical community recognized and seriously studied the special social, psychological, and logistical issues of female alcoholics. Certainly, few books on the market today, either fiction or nonfiction, have so completely exposed the complex and pained inner world of the female alcoholic. We highly recommend *Minus One*'s strong portrait of a female alcoholic struggling to attain and maintain sobriety. Bridget Bufford, with painstaking and believable detail, has drawn a portrait of a young woman who is alternately loveable and maddening, from Terry's fall off the wagon to her sizzling sexual encounters, a woman as addicted to the pursuit of love as she is to the pursuit of sobriety."

Sharon Robideaux, PhD, and Eleanor Agnew, PhD
Co-authors, *My Mama's Waltz: A Book for Daughters of Alcoholic Mothers*

"Meet Terry—newly rescued and returned to St. Louis, with companion cat Whacker, by friend Angela (steady, responsible, loyal) having gotten knee-walking drunk and beaten her girlfriend, unable to drive because her driver's license is suspended, jobless, and nursing a painful hangover—a lesbian not likely to win sympathetic readers you might say, unless you know her life from the inside.

But Terry has her redeeming qualities: she wears Lesbian Avengers and Queer nation T-shirts to the meetings of a mixed AA group—and looks them in the eye—but eventually finds her way to all lesbian and mixed lesbian and gay AA groups, finds an older, much wiser lesbian who becomes her sponsor, goes back to college at night, and becomes a paramedic. Her story survives its sometimes sordid and low-life events to maker her, in the end, a character who has earned her humanity and this reader's respect."

Julia Penelope, PhD
Author, *Speaking Freely: Unlearning the Lies of the Father's Tongues* and *Call Me Lesbian;*
Editor, *The Original Coming Out Stories, Lesbian Culture,* and *Out of the Class Closet*

"I wouldn't have predicted a writer could create a novel this good, and this satisfying, about recovery—let alone a story that combined working the steps with a lesbian love story. Bridget Bufford has fit these two themes together seamlessly, to create a moving and at times suspenseful novel. The reader unfamiliar with AA will get a good education in the way twelve-step programs work. The reader who has benefited from a twelve-step program will appreciate the care Bufford has taken to fill in the details of such programs."

Mcpherson, MFA, PhD
Department of Writing
Studies, Ithaca College

NOTES FOR PROFESSIONAL LIBRARIANS AND LIBRARY USERS

This is an original book title published by Alice Street Editions, Harrington Park Press®, an imprint of The Haworth Press, Inc. Unless otherwise noted in specific chapters with attribution, materials in this book have not been previously published elsewhere in any format or language.

CONSERVATION AND PRESERVATION NOTES

All books published by The Haworth Press, Inc. and its imprints are printed on certified pH neutral, acid free book grade paper. This paper meets the minimum requirements of American National Standard for Information Sciences-Permanence of Paper for Printed Material, ANSI Z39.48-1984.

Minus One
A Twelve-Step Journey

HARRINGTON PARK PRESS
Alice Street Editions
Judith P. Stelboum
Editor in Chief

Past Perfect by Judith P. Stelboum

Inside Out by Juliet Carrera

Facades by Alex Marcoux

Weeding at Dawn: A Lesbian Country Life by Hawk Madrone

His Hands, His Tools, His Sex, His Dress: Lesbian Writers on Their Fathers edited by Catherine Reid and Holly K. Iglesias

Treat by Angie Vicars

Yin Fire by Alexandra Grilikhes

From Flitch to Ash: A Musing on Trees and Carving by Diane Derrick

To the Edge by Cameron Abbott

Back to Salem by Alex Marcoux

Egret by Helen F. Collins

Your Loving Arms by Gwendolyn Bikis

A Donor Insemination Guide: Written By and For Lesbian Women by Marie Mohler and Lacy Frazer

Extraordinary Couples, Ordinary Lives by Lynn Haley-Banez and Joanne Garrett

Cat Rising by Cynn Chadwick

Maryfield Academy by Carla Tomaso

Ginger's Fire by Maureen Brady

A Taste for Blood by Diana Lee

Zach at Risk by Pamela Shepherd

An Inexpressible State of Grace by Cameron Abbott

Minus One: A Twelve-Step Journey by Bridget Bufford

Girls with Hammers by Cynn Chadwick

Rosemary and Juliet by Judy MacLean

Minus One
A Twelve-Step Journey

Bridget Bufford

Alice Street Editions
Harrington Park Press®
An Imprint of The Haworth Press, Inc.
New York • London • Oxford

Gloucestershire County Library	
992492028 7	
Askews	06-Dec-2005
AF	£9.99

Published by

Alice Street Editions, Harrington Park Press®, an imprint of The Haworth Press, Inc., 10 Alice Street, Binghamton, NY 13904-1580.

© 2004 by Bridget Bufford. All rights reserved. No part of this work may be reproduced or utilized in any form or by any means, electronic or mechanical, including photocopying, microfilm, and recording, or by any information storage and retrieval system, without permission in writing from the publisher. Printed in the United States of America.

A portion of Chapter 7 appeared as "Working Out" in *Pillow Talk II* (Alyson Press, 2000) and *Body Check* (Alyson Press, 2002).

The Twelve Steps of Alcoholics Anonymous, from *Alcoholics Anonymous*, Third Edition (Alcoholics Anonymous World Services, Inc. 1976), are reprinted by permission of Alcoholics Anonymous World Services, Inc. (A.A.W.S.). Permission to reprint the Twelve Steps does not mean that A.A.W.S. has reviewed or approved the contents of this publication, or that A.A.W.S. necessarily agrees with the views expressed herein. A.A. is a program of recovery from alcoholism *only*—use of the Twelve Steps in connection with programs and activities which are patterned after A.A., but which address other problems, or in any other non-A.A. context, does not imply otherwise.

Cover design by Lora Wiggins.

Library of Congress Cataloging-in-Publication Data

Bufford, Bridget.
    Minus one : a twelve-step journey / Bridget Bufford.
      p. cm.
    ISBN 1-56023-468-7 (alk. paper)
    1. Twelve-step programs—Fiction. 2. Recovering alcoholics—Fiction. 3. Women alcoholics—Fiction. 4. Lesbians—Fiction. I. Title.
    PS3602.U843M56 2004
    813'.6—dc21

2003001530

Editor's Foreword

Alice Street Editions provides a voice for established as well as up-and-coming lesbian writers, reflecting the diversity of lesbian interests, ethnicities, ages, and class. This cutting-edge series of novels, memoirs, and nonfiction writing welcomes the opportunity to present controversial views, explore multicultural ideas, encourage debate, and inspire creativity from a variety of lesbian perspectives. Through enlightening, illuminating, and provocative writing, Alice Street Editions can make a significant contribution to the visibility and accessibility of lesbian writing and bring lesbian-focused writing to a wider audience. Recognizing our own desires and ideas in print is life sustaining, acknowledging the reality of who we are, as well as our place in the world, individually and collectively.

Judith P. Stelboum
Editor in Chief
Alice Street Editions

Acknowledgments

Through the long journey of this book, Pat was the wind in my sails and Carole the anchor that kept me safe. Thanks to them, to Lisa, and to others who read the early drafts and gave encouragement; to my steadfast partner Becky; and to all who go to those meetings.

Chapter 1

If there's a minus [Step] *one, that's where I'm at.*

overheard at an AA meeting

Sometimes I forget this is a river town. The great stone abutments of Eads Bridge are mossy cool against my back; Memphis and New Orleans are just a brown crawl of Mississippi away. St. Louis is not where I want to be, though this town is home. I've been back three days and it still seems unreal.

The sweat is real. It drips down the back of my knees, runs into my eyes when I raise my bottle of Coke. The dry heaves and headache are gone, but I'm still sweating out the drunk.

The drive from Weston to St. Louis isn't clear to me. I emerged from a blackout, face bruised, lip bloody, and found I had dragged the more portable of my possessions to my porch. I knew someone must be coming for me, but who?

I do remember a full quart of gin, and then another half-pint of whiskey. I remember throwing up and crying. I don't remember calling Angela, but when she drove up I wasn't surprised.

The events that led to my departure remain too clear, more real than the alcoholic haze that intervened: broken promises, cocaine and gin, wounds inflicted.

Twenty-six isn't old, but I feel used up. I left St. Louis not even a year ago for a fresh start in Weston. I thought that I would leave the bullshit behind and get a job, a life. After a couple of jobs and a woman who was crazy about me, I trashed it all once again.

Sweat tickles my scalp, makes me itch.

The Mississippi's faster than I remember. The middle part races along. The sides are full of twisting eddies and trash that swirls, submerges, resurfaces to spin out of control. I finish my Coke and throw the empty bottle into the river; it follows the rest of the trash downstream. If the bottle had been glass, I would have smashed it into the rocky base of this massive bridge. I climb to the sidewalk, cross the plaza to the grounds of the Jefferson National Expansion Memorial.

A muscular black woman, six feet tall and crowned with a mass of braids, waves me over to the base of the Arch. "Girl, hold this. I got about five or six more shots." Angela hands me her leather equipment bag. She's taking pictures for a St. Louis band on the verge of a national release.

She crouches, points the camera. Gets up and moves a little more west of the structure, lies on her back. "I got a good angle, but the sun is bouncing off the top."

I offer the bag. She attaches a filter to her lens, snaps three shots. "This thing is so immense; you can get all kinds of funky takes on it."

"Monumental." I look up and wince; the sun's reflection is like a laser.

Angela hands me the camera. "Look through this."

The Arch appears to curve into a right angle and veer off into the sky. "Nice. What are they going to do with these?"

"Album cover and press release, if they like them."

"National exposure. You're on your way, girl."

And I'm back where I started. Angela has generously taken me in, once again, under multiple conditions of abstinence, employment, and attendance at the twelve-step recovery program of my choice.

Angie finishes her shoot and we go for Italian carryout. New York's got nothing on the Gateway to the West—St. Louis has the greatest deli food anywhere. The subs are the ultimate: Italian beef, Italian ham, salami ground by a dark-skinned butcher a few blocks from here. Meats that are lovingly seasoned, sliced so thin they curl, piled on thick crusty Italian bread, like sourdough without the sour.

Angela likes to eat in the tiny patio garden behind her townhouse. Evening shadows encroach on the August heat, making it tolerable. I dig into my roast beef and salami, try to disregard my cut lip. "This is incredible," I say. "I haven't had a decent sub in a year."

Angie nods, still chewing. "That pizza place in Weston was good," she finally says. "Didn't they have sandwiches?"

"It was good because the owner's from St. Louis." Angie had visited me last month. She was helping Cole, my ex, assemble a portfolio of her sketches. My throat abruptly tightens. I set my sandwich aside, look up at the clouds stained with dusk.

Angela taps my arm. "What's up with you?"

I shrug; if I say anything I'll start to bawl.

"Terry, I have seen you drunk before," she says. "I've seen you sick, maybe once. I have *never* seen you drink yourself sick for two straight days."

"Cole and I broke up. That's all."

Angie eyes my lip; it split a little farther on the sub. The whole right side of my jaw is swollen and discolored. "That Nicole is one big red-headed woman," she says. "She's about as tall as me. Hair like that, I bet she's got a temper."

"It wasn't like that. I told you I had a seizure. Goddamn it, Angie, can't you leave it alone?"

"If you're going to live here, you're going to have to tell me. You know you got to tell it at your meetings anyway."

"There's something to look forward to." I take a huge bite of sandwich, chew furiously.

"Terry." Her voice softens. "I seen this before. You come limping in like some old tomcat, bragging on how you been kicking ass. Sometime it's got to be your turn, that's all."

I'm going to fucking choke. I slap the table, finally clear my mouth. "Cole *did not* hit me! She's probably never hit anyone in her whole life." Angie's eyes are eager, fixed on me. "I was drunk. We argued, and I just lost it. I beat the shit out of her. I even—" My voice fails. I take a big drink of Coke, eyes averted.

Angie picks at her chips, casting guarded looks. Finally says, "OK, then. The thing is, you know you got a problem and now you're willing to do something about it." She forces a smile. "You need a ride to a meeting tonight?"

"No, there's one close. I'll walk." I take the trash into the kitchen, leave Angela to her little piece of backyard. I change into a gay pride T-shirt; they might as well know who I am.

At the meeting I find a folding chair, off by myself. Two old guys across the room are looking, not directly at me, but I know they're talking about me. One looks disapproving, the other is laughing. *Fuckers.*

A woman comes in: navy blue jacket, white blouse, navy skirt. She even has round navy earrings, circled in gold. She sits next to me, places her navy purse on the floor. "Hi, I'm Laura," she says. Her smile turns strange as I face her; she eyes my scabbed lower lip, the fading bruise across my jaw.

A couple of days ago, after a gram and a half of cocaine, I had a seizure in the women's rest room of a gay bar. The sink nearly took off my face.

"Hi, Laura," I say. "Terry."

She's so busy looking at my Queer Nation T-shirt that she misses my extended hand. "First time at the meeting?" she asks.

"Second."

From the podium, a man says, "Good evening. I'm Richard. I'm an alcoholic." He reads the Preamble and "How it Works," then introduces a young man named Bill.

"Thanks, Richard." Bill's voice shakes a little; when he reaches for his coffee, his knuckles knock into the microphone. "Shit. Sorry." The tops of his ears have turned red. "My name's Bill, and I'm an alcoholic."

Bill has a round face, a bit of a belly, and the clean-cut, almost-handsome look of a frat boy. He's about twenty-one, maybe twenty-two. He says he's only got ten months sober. Granted, that's ten more than me, but the guy can't have that much experience, strength, and hope to share.

Bill started drinking in high school, missed out on a football scholarship to the University of Missouri, Columbia (he calls it Mizzou), but made the team as a freshman walk-on. Once he moved into the frat, he was on top of the world, except for this one little problem: Bill wet his pants during alcoholic blackouts. Wet on himself at parties, wet his girlfriend's bed, peed on his parents' couch when he was home for the weekend. He began to wonder if he would complete his college career in Depends, but a DWI prompted a stint in treatment. His older sister, already in AA, took him to meetings and now, he tells us, everything is going great.

I sip bad coffee and try to pay attention. Bill was definitely "Billy" as a kid. He still has a baby face. He's on his way to overweight; he was probably a pudgy kid who, for about three months in high school, when he was doing two-a-day workouts for football, was really built. He'll remember that the rest of his life, how he had broad shoulders and a thirty-four-inch waist and some girls who suddenly took a second look at the fat kid. He'll go to these meetings, smoke cigarettes, go out afterward for fries and a shake and late-night bullshit. Look at himself in the mirror in the morning and that seventeen-year-old boy will still be there, mocking him. He'll swear he's going to run a couple miles after work tonight. He'll never get that body back, but he'll never stop trying.

The applause startles me. I guess Bill sobered up and I missed it. I really did go to a meeting before, when I went to treatment in Weston; it was just as inane. I've got to clean up my act, and I'm willing to try AA, but I don't see how listening to this crap will keep me sober.

The rest of the hour consists of congratulatory responses, praising Bill for his honesty. He must be a fixture in this group. After the meeting I take off fast.

Before I can make my getaway, Bill yells across the parking lot. "Hold up."

"Yeah?" I turn, let him come to me.

"I'm Bill. Are you new here?"

"Terry." I shake his hand; his eyes are on my chest. "Just moved back to St. Louis this week."

"Welcome. Glad you made it." I step back; he looks like he's going to say something else. He shifts his feet, smiles. "I hope you come back."

"I'll be here next week. See you." Maybe. I had a funny feeling he was going to ask me out. That long stare at my breasts, and he never read the Queer Nation shirt.

The half-mile back to Angela's is the best part of the evening. I lost my license a year ago, so I walked everywhere in Weston. It calms me down.

Angie is still in the garden, reading the *Sunday Post-Dispatch*. "How was the meeting?"

"The walk was nice."

She glances up, slaps the paper onto the wrought-iron tabletop. "Damn it, Terry. You don't even wear that to the bar. Why do you want to wear it around these people? You're going to scare them to death."

"At the bar they know I'm queer."

"They'll know you for a fool at AA."

I shrug. "I don't care what a bunch of drunks think."

"You better be starting to care." Angela stands, folds the paper. "I'm shooting at the Botanical Garden tomorrow. I can talk to that woman in horticulture, see if I can pick up an application for you. But if you intend to embarrass me with your bullshit . . ."

"Angie, I'm not going to wear an 'I Saw You Naked in Michigan' tank top to a job interview." Maybe to a meeting, though.

Out the bedroom window, I see Angela leaving. The slam of the door must have startled my little black cat Whacker. He woke me with a grunt; we're both disoriented from the move. Whacker stretches, then trots across the hall to the staircase.

I rub my sticky eyes, sit up. A notebook rests on the nightstand. I crumple three pages and place the paper balls on the top landing, just outside Angie's bedroom. Over the course of the day, Whacker knocks the balls down the steps and thunders after them. I hear him dashing up and down periodically. In the early evenings, he sings out a wild trill and races from the third floor all the way to the darkroom.

I chase Whacker downstairs to the kitchen. *Bless you, Angela*—she left me some coffee. I help myself to a couple of bowls of Cheerios. My jaw doesn't hurt so much today, though it's still shaded brown and green. I'm waiting for the bruises to fade before I look for work. In the meantime, I'm not drinking. It takes a lot of effort, but hardly any time.

Whacker joins me on the second story balcony over the patio. He suns himself on the rail, watches pigeons swoop and crap. I drink my coffee. The balcony is even with the roof of Angela's shed; squirrels hop up there, chase from tree to roof to tree. They stop and bark, flick their tails. Angie can bark and cluck like the squirrels. She had one lying on the edge of the shed roof one day, paws crossed and head down like a dog, moaning soulfully back to her as she clucked with her tongue.

Angela and I met at rugby. We were teammates when I broke up with my first lover, Erica; I stayed with Angela for a few months afterward. Back then she lived in a little flat behind Deaconess Hospital.

She's had this townhouse almost a year, and she loves it with the zeal of a first-generation homeowner. The old townhouses of Soulard are hot property; even the most decrepit are getting rehabbed and sold at tremendous profit. Angie gets steady commissions from the Missouri Botanical Garden and freelance jobs, but I don't know how she can afford a three-story brick townhouse. My rent money will help, once I start working.

Whacker makes a chattering sound; a squirrel just landed in a maple tree. The backyard has a couple of nice maples for shade and a big leafy tree of the type known to St. Louisans as "stink trees." The stink tree sends up so many hopeful little shoots that Angie hung a hatchet on the shed wall with orders to hack on sight.

Sitting agitates me; I slug down the last of my coffee and go back inside. At the treatment center in Weston, I attended lectures on the physiology of alcoholism. Withdrawal makes you restless, they said. Makes my skin crawl; I'm still sweaty. I wash the dishes, then start a load of Angela's laundry.

I wish I could afford to go to a gym. Erica got some dumbbells for me when we were together. She laughed when she caught me flexing in the mirror, but Erica sure liked my body. She wanted to show me off to her friends, the old dog.

It's hard to get a decent workout with dumbbells, and there's no chin-up bar or anything like that here. I start with push-ups, my feet up on the chair; I could do regular push-ups all day. Shoulder raises next, followed by dumbbell rows. Four sets of those, then I concentrate on arms—curls, reverse curls, triceps press. Last is a few sets of lunges. The focus of physical effort, pushing into the burn, stills my mind. AA's Step Eleven counsels meditation, but lifting weights works better for me.

My trunk is strong; I don't bother to count, just go for five minutes of sit-ups and five minutes of leg raises. It's hard to stay motivated in this quiet house, nobody around, but for forty-five minutes I haven't thought about taking a drink.

I pull off my shirt, check my waist: incised center line, obliques curving down to the top of my shorts. I've got some natural assets—straight shiny black hair, blue eyes, decent proportions for such a runt. The body takes work, but overall I look pretty good. So what; my bar days are over for now. Cole sure doesn't want me around. I grab a Coke, flop on the sofa and try to watch TV—fifty channels and nothing on.

The midday heat is searing, but I'm desperate. I pull on my running shoes, go a few blocks. Though the hangover's gone, I'm feeble and rubber-legged. I give up and walk the last half-mile, then peel away my soggy clothes and shower.

Alone in the house, I ponder its history. The outside looks much as it did when it was built, but it's starting over, all new fixtures. I have fallen from grace to Angela's rehab.

Before the arrest last fall, I did live in a state of grace. The things I loved, I conquered. Rugby, softball, pool, dancing—I excelled at them all. A woman once stroked her cheek down my bare belly and whispered, "You are the perfect dyke hero." Dyke knight on a white stallion. Not chaste, though, not untouchable—you could have me, if you wanted.

After two workouts, a short nap seems justified. The slam of the door wakens me; I come off the couch like a farm dog barking, I'm so glad to see somebody. "Hey, Angie. How was work?"

"Hot. We had to stop early." She sifts through the mail. "Allison wants you to schedule an interview."

"Allison?"

"Yeah. She hires for the horticulture crew. She said she prefers to get people with an associate's degree in horticulture, but I told her you were going back to school to finish up." She gets us each a Coke, pops off the metal caps on the bottle opener screwed to the frame of the kitchen door.

"You told her I'm getting my associate's in horticulture?"

"No, I said you were going to finish up. She might have thought I meant in horticulture. But check it out—there's no permanent full-time positions right now, but she could give you full-time till December, then part-time over the winter. Then you *could* go to school."

I did take a year of horticulture at Meramec Valley Community College. When I met Erica, my class work went to shit. But right now, I just want a job.

Angela persists. "It's too late to enroll for the fall, but you could take an evening class. How are you on general ed stuff?"

"I don't know, Angie. I've been on conduct suspension, on academic probation . . . I've got incompletes all over the state."

"You just take the job, then think about it." She hands me a business card—Allison Woodall.

"I can try. How do I look?"

"A lot better." She inspects my eye, touches my jaw gently. "Schedule it for the end of the week."

The Friday night meeting's interminable. Sweating unnaturally, I sit in front of the air conditioner and gulp a cup of bad coffee. The speaker is Richard, a middle-aged guy I just can't listen to.

AA has twelve Steps. They're posted at most of the meetings. "Working the Steps" is how you learn to live sober. Popular custom decrees I obtain a sponsor, someone with more experience who will guide me through the Steps and down "the road to happy destiny."

There's a newcomer here tonight, so Richard is bursting with platitudes. He talks about Step One ("We admitted we were powerless over alcohol—that our lives had become unmanageable"), and "putting the plug in the jug," and "doing the next right thing."

After the meeting, the regulars go out for coffee. Not to a coffeehouse—AA people drink real coffee, not espresso drinks. Steak 'n' Shake is tonight's venue. It's on the way to Angela's, so I accept a ride with Bill. "Alice's Restaurant" plays on the radio, an interminable paean to St. Louis radio's enthrallment with classic rock. Not a day of my formative years went by that I didn't hear "Stairway to Heaven," and The Beatles, and The Who, and the Rolling Stones. Sadly, it hasn't changed much. This city hums along to thirty-year-old songs of youth and rebellion, fresh in their time. White male heterosexuals, thinking they were making a difference.

Laura of the navy business suit and purse is at Steak 'n' Shake, along with Richard and a few other chain-smoking drunks. Everyone's loading cholesterol like that's the true key to the program: hot fudge sundaes, cheese fries, double steakburgers—a real feeding frenzy.

I sit next to Laura, at the end of the table. "Look who's here!" she says. "I'm so glad you came." Richard nods in tandem with her. Are they together?

I order a Coke; Richard urges food on me. "No, thanks."

"It'll help," he says. "In the *Living Sober* book it says that you're not so likely to get cravings on a full stomach."

"I'm fine."

"Fine?" Bill laughs. "Fucked-up, Insecure, Neurotic, and Emotional?"

Morons. I sip my Coke, catch Richard looking at my ACT UP T-shirt. "What?"

"What's that?" He indicates the shirt.

"AIDS research group." He's clueless. "Did you see the back?" I get up, face the next booth.

Richard reads, " 'We're here. We're queer. Get used to it' . . ." The waitress at the counter looks up. I give her a wink, and she turns away. Richard's red-faced. Laura's eating.

"Are you gay?" Bill asks.

"I'm a lesbian."

Laura flinches a little at that but keeps shoveling in the ice cream. Richard's looking at his watch.

"Hey, that's cool," Bill says.

"I appreciate your vote of confidence," I reply.

Richard's finished his triple steakburger already. I guess he and Laura aren't together; she gets a coffee refill while he's leaving. She talks a bit about the meeting, her job as a secretary at the utility company, her husband. Laura's nice enough, if bland. She didn't flee at the sight of gay pride attire. On my list of the meeting members (first names and last initials only, to protect anonymity), she underlines her phone number, tells me to give her a call anytime.

The Botanical Garden is the most beautiful space in St. Louis, an incredible place to work. As a little kid, I saved my dimes to buy fish food for the koi in the Japanese Garden. I've strolled the paths with more than one young lady, showing my sensitive side after a night of drinking and dancing and running the pool tables.

Can't beat the uniforms, either. I work in an off-white Garden polo shirt, tasteful little logo on the left breast, and khaki shorts. Boots with shorts is not the best look for me; I look like one of Rip van Winkle's little men, or maybe a piece of yard art. It's comfortable, though.

Allison put me with another gardener, a handsome blond man with muscled forearms. Tim prunes, rakes, and waters with a methodical, contemplative air. He's been here three years; he can show me the ropes. The first two days, Tim was quiet. I wore some fruit loops earrings yesterday; since then, he's been almost garrulous.

It's hot, even for a midwestern August. The Garden has lots of shade, but sweat is running down my legs. I take a pocket saw, a folding tool about seven inches long, and cut away dead wood from the bottom of a redbud. Tim's shaping shrubs with a long-handled pruning tool. When he nears the end of his row, he asks, "Terry, you want to rake this stuff up?"

"Sure." I trot back to the shed, slowing when I see some visitors. No one's ever told me not to run, but I've garnered some looks when I did. I get a rake for myself, and one for Tim, too. We'll be mulching later on.

Tim's half-hidden in a bush when I get back. "You could have taken the cart."

"I like to walk. I brought a couple of rakes."

He nods. Teeth gritted, he squeezes his clippers through a branch. His tan forearms glisten with sweat. He sees me looking, watches the play of sinew himself.

I drive the Cushman cart behind his work area, rake up the trimmings and throw them into the back. I don't like to drive even these little vehicles; I stay away from the maintenance trucks altogether. My application packet stated that I "must obtain, prior to employment, and maintain a valid driver's license." I should get it back in October; until then, I'm lying low.

Some branches have fallen across the sidewalk. With the rake, I sweep them into a pile, bend, and gather the bundle against my chest. I kick the rake, ineffectually; I shouldn't leave it here, but my hands are full.

I hurl my armload at the back of the Cushman. Half the branches go in the cart, half fall on the ground. I'm too damn hot and tired to care. It's an hour until quitting time. Late nights at the AA club gulping coffee and breathing cigarette smoke make it hard to get any rest. At least when I went to the bars, the beer eventually made me sleepy.

"Terry!" Tim's voice comes out of a hedge.

I address a likely row of boxwood. "Yeah?"

"Would you get the bigger saw out of the Cushman?"

"Sure." Shit—I buried the pruning saw under my leafy debris. I dump more of the trimmings on the ground, trot the saw over to Tim. I return to the mess around the cart; what did I do with my rake?

"Oh! Look out!" A twanging noise, like something from a cartoon, punctuates a shriek. I race back to the sidewalk.

Two young men are assisting an elderly woman to her feet. Her white hair hangs over her face. They sit her on a bench.

"Are you all right, ma'am?" I pick up the rake; it couldn't have been that far onto the sidewalk.

"She tripped over that." The bigger guy points, then grasps the woman's thin arm.

I set the rake well back in a flowerbed, then kneel before the woman. She's calmer than the boys, but there's a triangular tear of the fragile flesh over her shin. It's bleeding freely. "Can you walk?"

"Heavens, yes. It's just a scrape." She smiles at me, holds out a hand so I can help her up. "My nephews have a tendency to hover."

"Please, sit still a minute," I say. "I'll have to call security."

"We can take her. What's your name?" The big guy glowers.

"Terry Manescu."

"Spell that."

I do, and admit that yes, it is my rake. I trot back to the cart. Tim's cleaned up the branches.

"What happened?" he asks.

"A lady tripped over my rake."

"Oh, no. Where was it?"

I shrug. "It was over by the sidewalk; I don't think it was really on it."

"Is she OK?"

"She tore her shin a little."

Tim frowns, pulls the radio from his belt. "I'll call 5190; they'll send somebody. You stay with her." He hands me the first-aid kit. "You'll have to fill out an incident report."

I put on some gloves, self-conscious about the need for protection from this sweet old woman, then press gauze to the wound.

Beryl from Security is competent. She's an EMT, though that's hardly needed. She cleans the skin tear, applies a large Band-Aid, advises the woman to get a tetanus shot. Takes a brief account from everyone.

She offers the woman and her nephews a ride back to the Visitor Center. Beryl has wavy, light brown hair, nice teeth, great smile, a crushing handshake. "I'll need to give a copy of the report to your supervisor," she says.

"Yeah, I figured."

At quitting time, Allison is expecting me at the maintenance shed. She isn't happy. Safety first, the Garden has an impeccable reputation, we have to look after the welfare of the visitors at all times. I finish my first week of work with a warning and an extension of my probationary period.

Fantasies of getting wasted brighten the remainder of my afternoon: getting a half-pint at a liquor store and telling Allison to shove it; going to a bar, dancing, getting laid. . . . Having a place to live is a good thing, though. I dig up the AA phone list and dial Laura.

"Terry! I'm so glad you called!" Her voice suddenly drops. "Is everything all right?"

"Oh, yeah," I say. *Why would I tell you anything?* "Everything's great."

"Great," she says. "What's up?"

I cast about for something to say, finally come up with "Would you be my sponsor?"

"I would be honored," Laura says. "Do you know what a sponsor is for?"

"To help work the Steps, Richard said."

"That, and to help with the program in general," Laura says. "You can call me to talk; you can call me if you're having a rough day; you can call me if you feel like drinking. Don't call me if you've already taken a drink; I will not talk to you then."

"If I take a drink, you're through with me?"

"Until I see you at a meeting, I am. People drink and come back; it happens all the time. I'm saying that I won't talk to you when you're drunk."

"Fine. That's why I'm going, so I don't drink."

"Good. I'll pick you up for my home group tonight. In the meantime, read Chapter One and Two of the Big Book, and we'll talk about it."

"Big Book?"

"The *Alcoholics Anonymous* book. The blue one. Do you have it?"

"I got one in treatment," I say.

"OK. We'll talk more after the meeting."

Laura's home group is on Chippewa, close to where she lives. A home group is the primary meeting you attend, where you have voting privileges and a say in how the group is run. Laura brought me tonight so I could check out the Sober South-Siders.

Laura chose this as her primary meeting based on the location, as far as I can tell. The room is full of expounding old farts and used-up older women that hang on their every word. After making me suffer through a ninety-minute meeting, Laura talks in the parking lot for another twenty minutes, then drags me to Denny's.

Everyone gets coffee or Coke, a burger, some fried appetizer. Richard's here, so happy to be sober (he's gainfully employed, has a car that runs and a place to live). He orders me a Diet Coke and some fried zucchini.

I say I'm not hungry; he says I'm too skinny. Everyone with more sobriety than me thinks that they know what's best for me. AA is a conspiracy to rob me of my individuality and my intellect. AA is making me paranoid.

On the sound system, Guns N' Roses annoys me with a nasal whine. Bill is swilling a vanilla malt like beer, reminiscing about getting high to this song. He didn't even go to the meeting; he just came here afterward to hang out with us.

The waitress brings platters laden with oily delights. She hands me a plate of zucchini and a Diet Coke. "Coke," I tell her. "Regular." She apologizes. So does Richard. If he's going to order for me he could at least ask what I drink. I set the zucchini between Laura and me, tell her to help herself. She's working on some onion rings, too. Really, I like greasy foods; it's the unctuous company that bothers me.

Laura smiles at me. "Terry, I'm really glad you're going out after the meetings."

"The meeting after the meeting," Richard says. "That's what it takes."

"Right, Dick," I say.

"How's your zucchini?" he asks.

"Very good. Thank you so much."

Bill giggles; the zucchini is untouched. "Can I have some?"

"Help yourself." I set it next to him.

He wolfs a greasy length of vegetable, and then looks at me and giggles again. "Terry, you crack me up. You're so fucking hostile."

"I try."

Laura gives Bill a look like I used to get from the nuns in high school. "Who's your sponsor?"

"Barry," he says. "He's hostile, too."

Richard edges the platter of zucchini back toward me. "I've been at meetings where Barry was asked to leave because of his language."

Bill laughs. "Yeah, he's cool."

"I thought that 'the only requirement for membership is a desire to stop drinking.'"

"Terry, two points!" Bill marks my score in the air.

"I read the Traditions," I say.

Laura says, "I don't approve of Barry's language, but he shouldn't be asked to leave." She shakes her head. "We can just hope to serve as examples."

"He never actually left; they just asked him to," Richard says.

When the "meeting after the meeting" ends, I follow Laura to her Accord. She commences with her ground rules: tells me to go to thirty meetings in thirty days (she did ninety in ninety), to read the Big Book, to call her every day, and to stay out of relationships until I get my one-year coin.

What's that about? As long as I'm not drinking, who cares if I get laid? Not that I have any prospects at the moment. "So what's considered a relationship?"

Laura frowns. "Well, to be blunt, no sex. Take a year to concentrate on your program."

"No *sex?*"

"Not with . . . anyone else." Laura doesn't care to be blunt; she probably doesn't care for sex.

"Why not?"

"Because it takes your attention from your program. Getting sober is hard enough; most people can't afford to make it any worse."

We're at Angie's house. Laura pulls up, shuts off the engine. "Terry, this might be hard to believe, but I do care about you. I want you to stay sober. Behind that hostility I think there is a young woman with a lot to offer."

She's staring at me, so sincere. I've got to ask. "So you were celibate your first year?"

"I'm married," she says. "We'd been married eight years when I sobered up."

"You're granted an exemption?"

"It's a different situation. They tell you not to make any big changes in your first year, either."

"Staying celibate would have been a big change?"

"Well, we . . ." She's getting red. "It's not the same. Anyway, we're talking about *you*. You asked me to be your sponsor. It's my job to give suggestions."

"That's enough suggestions for one night." I'm out the door, up the sidewalk before she can yell, "Keep coming back."

Half awake, I crash my knees against the wall. If this room were mine, I would turn the bed so I didn't run into the wall every morning. It's not my house, not even my bed. It's Saturday, though—the day is mine.

I hope I didn't wake Angie. She was still out when I fell asleep. I roll out of bed, to the left this time, and pull on some jeans and a dark red Eddie Bauer polo shirt I stole from my brother's girlfriend. Julie's his wife now—Marius got married while I was in court-appointed treatment, before I was sentenced. I always thought the big issue would be whether I wore a dress, not handcuffs.

I lace up my black hightops, comb my hair with a little water. There's no coffee in the house, so I head to the Bread Company. When she runs out, Angie drinks tea or sometimes pop. I like Coke, but not first thing in the morning.

The street's quiet, although it's almost eight o'clock. A middle-aged guy in a jogging suit urges an elderly cocker spaniel to pee on the stop-sign post.

I ought to run, but not before coffee. I stretch my hands and wrists; they made it through my first workweek with no damage other than a blister in my right palm, a little tightness in the forearms.

The St. Louis Bread Company is pretty dead. The line at the counter is mostly rumpled unshaven guys whose wives sent them out for breakfast. Not many people are at the tables. It's like a library; everyone's reading a newspaper or a book; conversations are hushed.

I get a cheese bagel, unadorned, and a cup of coffee. At least they have free refills here. I hate coffeehouses where you pay for every single cup. Next they'll charge rent on the chairs.

The table next to me has a guy and two girls. I sip my coffee, try to figure out the relationships. The girls both look like they could be dykes, but one is awfully close to the guy. They're both blond and stocky, the guy and that girl, Teutonic. Could be brother and sister.

The girl on the other side is a babe: petite and dark-haired, a generous mouth and lively eyes. She has an orange scone, untouched. She's talking, and the other two are rapt. "Sex is a lot like writing. You experience the same things when you're writing. It's beyond an analogy—you know there's that nonverbal component to both. You know what I mean? It's not an analogy."

Hansel and Gretel both nod seriously, though neither can muster a reply. The guy chomps a bagel, his muscular jaws clenching. I'll bet he's got a bite like a German shepherd.

The dark girl picks at her scone. "This is so big. I need to slice it."

Hansel and Gretel draw from the hip. "I've got a knife," Gretel says, flipping open a red Swiss Army model.

Hansel's got a lock-back Buck. "Mine's bigger," he says. The girls look at each other and laugh.

"I'm sure it is," says Gretel. She takes the scone and slices it evenly, dips the blade in her coffee and cleans it on a napkin. Hansel is chewing furiously. Score one for the dyke.

Wish I had some friends here to gawk with me, to laugh and drink coffee. I used to have a lot of friends—too many. The phone rang all the time. I haven't even told my brothers or my mom that I'm back in St. Louis; I haven't called any of my old friends.

At the meetings they say you need to change your playgrounds and playmates. In other words, get your ass out of the bar and act like us. I can't see me doing AA the rest of my life. I would never spend time with any of those people if I wasn't in AA. Sobriety has taken away everything I like.

AA is a program of suggestions. They tell you that, then they lay down the law. I walked to the clubhouse for the Wednesday night meeting, but Laura's giving me a ride home. "Good meeting," she says.

"It was all right." The topic had been fellowship.

Laura lights a Virginia Slims Ultra-light. Her hands are slender, with fake nails painted a shade of burgundy that does not match her lipstick. Her wedding ring is one of those diamond-sapphire sets popularized by Princess Di several years back. She offers me a cigarette.

"No, thanks."

"That's right, you don't smoke."

"I smoked at the bars. I've been tempted a couple times after meetings, but I've been running—smoking doesn't help that. I quit."

"I should. I'll have two years sober in April; I might quit then. I'd have the same stop date for cigarettes and drinking." She rolls down her window; the night is humid, but pleasant. "Do you have a home group list?"

"You gave me the phone list at Steak 'n' Shake."

"Have you called anyone?"

I shrug. "Just you."

"That's good. You've been good about that, and you do go out to coffee sometimes. It would be even better if you found some other women to call. Fellowship is a big part of recovery. It helps you to feel like you're a part of the program."

"Right."

"And in case you haven't noticed, Richard thinks the world of you. You could call him."

I almost laugh—*Hey, Dick, this is your queer friend Terry.* "I don't think so."

"You could at least treat him with a little respect. He has eight years sober." She sighs. "Richard would never say anything to you, but he had a seventeen-year-old daughter that he was crazy about. She was killed by a drunk driver eight years ago—that's what got Richard to look at his own drinking. I think you must remind him of Michelle."

Eight years ago; she'd be almost the same age as me. "Laura, that's really sad, but he's not *my* father. What is it you want me to do?"

She flicks her cigarette out the window. Faces me briefly at the stoplight. "If you could just act like—I don't know. Not so hostile." She rubs her forehead with two fingers, starts again. "Everyone comes to AA with a lot of barriers; everyone thinks they're unique. But that attitude—you're so extreme, it puts people off."

"Extreme how?" My face is hot.

She plucks at the sleeve of my T-shirt, reads, "*Lesbian Avengers—we recruit.*"

I jerk away. "It's a gay pride shirt."

She snorts. "There's an *ax* on it, Terry."

"That's a labrys."

"Whatever. We all know you're gay by now." She accelerates hard at the green light. "Mostly, nobody cares. It's got nothing to do with recovery."

"So the way I dress is a 'defect of character'?"

"It's just that you flaunt it."

"It's who I am." I am walking home from now on. "If you got a problem with it, that's on you."

"Do you dress like that all the time?"

"Dress like what? Like a dyke?"

"You don't dress like that at work."

"We have a *uniform*." I'm practically shouting.

"And it looks good on you; I've seen it. Look, all I'm trying to say is that maybe you should look at what you're doing, and why." She pulls up to the curb. "Just be honest with yourself."

"Right. Thanks for the ride." I bound up the walk, jerk the door open. There's a quick shuffle in the living room. "Hey, Angie."

"Terry, this is Sharon. She came over to watch some movies."

"Hi, Sharon." They're sitting about eight inches apart, probably seven inches more than when I opened the door. Sharon's cute in a boyish way, freckled and slightly gap-toothed. Lanky; they might have met at basketball. Go, Angela.

"Is that a Lesbian Avengers shirt? Where do you even get this stuff?"

"Don't start, Angie." I wouldn't go to these damn meetings if it wasn't for Angela.

I snag Whacker from the coffee table, where he's been gawking. In my bedroom I pump iron for an hour while Melissa Etheridge bellows promises from the stereo. Angie and Sharon are still in the living room when I go to bed; I expect Sharon's staying the night.

Chapter 2

Today I took all my serenity and balled it up and threw it at one of my kids.

overheard at an AA meeting

"Hi, Terry." Laura looks at my Houston Comets jersey, smiles. I scowl, waiting for a comment, but she restrains herself.

It's a speaker meeting tonight: Preston C., some old guy with a cigar in his pocket, a nose like W. C. Fields. Preston C.'s been sober eighteen years. Must've been drunk for a lot longer than that. He talks forever, about respect for The Fellowship of Alcoholics Anonymous. "This Fellowship saved your life." He points at Bill. "It saved your ass. Don't ever forget it." Talks about how he sobered up in Cincinnati, where Dr. Bob, a cofounder of The Fellowship of Alcoholics Anonymous, started the very group that Preston C. attends. His home group has a tradition of dressing up every Friday night. Women wear dresses; men wear coats and ties. Newcomers do the first nine steps as soon as they get a sponsor.

For their Fourth Step, the "searching and fearless moral inventory," every man Preston C. sponsors gets a yellow legal pad and a No. 2 pencil. "An alcoholic can't lie with a legal pad and a No. 2 pencil," he says. "You don't need any fancy notebooks or anything special to write with. You just need to get honest."

What a bunch of shit. I look at Bill and he rolls his eyes. Laura's enthralled.

After the meeting, people line up to talk to this Nazi. I'm out the door, ready to take a slow run back to Angie's, when Laura spots me. "Terry, you need a ride?"

"No."

"Wait a minute; I've got something for you."

I follow her to her car. With a smile, she pulls out a legal pad and a pencil. "Here. It's about time you get started with your steps."

"Oh, thanks." She's heard Preston C. before. "I'd better get going, then." I take off at a trot.

At home, I toss the legal pad onto Angie's desk. I pour a Coke and sit down with a burgundy spiral notebook. I wish I had a computer; I'd type my steps and hand Laura the disk.

First Step: "Admitted we were alcoholic, and that our lives had become unmanageable." I know I'm an alcoholic. First time I went away to college, I was reading in the TV lounge when a girl came through with her parents. "This is the lounge," she said, "and this is Terry, our resident alkie." I nodded to them, blew her a kiss.

I've been drinking since I was fourteen or fifteen, sneaking it on trips with the softball team. I'd do favors for Marius, vacuum his room or wash his car, and he'd buy me beer. I don't know when I got to be an alcoholic; maybe in college. Maybe on the rugby team. I do know that for the past couple years, even when I didn't get drunk, I drank every day. I did things I'm not proud of; I quit because I don't ever want to do them again.

Last fall I was arrested for DWI. The cop who pulled me over called me a "mouthy little dyke," which surely violated a tenet of his required course in sensitivity training. He deserved to get popped, though it was not good judgment on my part. Nor was it smart to continue to struggle with my hands cuffed behind my back; Officer Jackson lifted my wrists until I was on tiptoe, then—"Oh, sorry"—tripped me. If I hadn't turned my head, I'd have no profile left.

Officer Jackson didn't press charges for resisting arrest or assault. If the whole story came out, he could be in trouble for harassment. For the DWI conviction I got probation, a year's suspension of driving privileges, and a month of mandatory rehab. I was sent to a women's treatment center in Weston. It had the first available bed. The counselor said it's better to attend treatment away from family and friends, that it gives you a chance for a fresh start.

The night I got out of treatment I ended up at the Rainbow's Edge, Weston's sole gay bar. I didn't go there to drink; I wanted to meet some women, see what there was to do. I thought maybe I'd look up a soccer or rugby team, some wholesome activity to sustain my new way of life. Then some sweet-looking babe said, "Can I get you a beer?"

I'm powerless over drugs. Doing cocaine at the Edge, when I'd had seizures from it before, now that was stupid. Cole and I were supposed to go out later that night; I told her I just wanted to shoot a couple of quick games of pool. At the bar I ran into a friend from St. Louis, and she had some blow. I thought *maybe this time will be different,* and did a couple lines. After the seizure and the run-in with the bathroom sink, I wasn't in any shape to keep a date. My buddy Jane dragged me back to her place, and I spent the night on her couch.

I knew Cole would be upset about the drugs; I knew she would be hurt that I had neither showed up nor called. I wanted to apologize in person. The next morning I called her and we agreed to meet after she got off work.

I was wrong; I was prepared to own up to it. My intention was to tell Cole how sorry I was and explain what had happened. Then I looked in Jane's kitchen for a coffee cup, and came out with a bottle of gin.

I'm powerless over alcohol. I don't even like gin, but I saw that quart, and I put just a little in some orange juice. Then I had a little more over ice. By the time I got to Cole's I had knocked off half the quart.

I'm powerless over my actions when I'm loaded. No control. I never intended to hurt anybody, ever. I sure never wanted to hurt Cole. I started to apologize; God knows what kind of bullshit I was talking. Cole got angry. I got defensive. Then she made some sarcastic remark about me being on probation, and I just lost it.

The thing is, I never told her about the DWI or treatment or any of that. I don't know how she found out. I got it in my head that she had gone behind my back, that she had been checking up on me. I remember kicking over the coffee table. Yelling. Grabbing. Hitting.

Next thing I know, Cole's beat to shit and I'm on the floor. It makes me sick. I had to get away from Cole, away from what I'd done. So I escaped to St. Louis, which I had left so that I could stop drinking. Unmanageable.

Some nights I dream of Cole and wake up haunted by her battered face. Most mornings I wake with a horrible feeling of foreboding, trying to remember what went wrong. Then it comes back to me and I hate myself again.

Twice I woke up happy and in love, just for a moment. Those mornings were the worst.

I look down at my page. It reads Step One: Unmanageability. DWI, treatment, relationship, move to St. Louis. That's enough step work for tonight.

The Handsworth boxwoods are surrounded by English lavender and creeping lemon thyme. I'm raking new cocoa shell mulch into this bed; the old wood chips, weathered pale gray, are disappearing into the soil. Cocoa shell mulch is a by-product of chocolate processing; there's a bin of it at the shed. It's finer than the wood chips and it looks better: the rich sepia color deepens as it ages, elegant against the greenery. It's heavy, though, because you have to rake it wet.

I've been at the Garden just over three weeks; I can see myself lasting for a while. My last two jobs were retail, but working outdoors is much better. When my friends were baby-sitting back in junior high, I was painting exteriors with my father.

All of us painted with Pop. My youngest brother Andrei still does. Marius, my older brother, painted all through college. He's been a chemical engineer with Monsanto for seven years now; he worked on that bovine milk hormone that's pissed off the consumer advocates.

Alecki, the brother just after me, is a terrific poet—gifted but broke. His work record is almost as inconsistent as mine. Last I heard, he was serving espresso at a Central West End coffeehouse.

I scrape a new pile of mulch from the bed of the Cushman, then get my water bottle and take a break. It's hot, very muggy today; the sky's cloudless, but hazy. My boots are full of mulch; I loosen the laces and knock the debris out.

My skills are even less marketable than Alecki's—I can juggle up to five objects, hit a softball over the right-field fence, run a pool table, sink a three-pointer from half-court. My parents are unimpressed. "You're intelligent, you have so much personality, why don't you do something with your life. So much potential." Mom won't like me working here; at least I am using my education.

My mom graduated with a degree in music education; she taught while we were in school. Pop went to college for a year, then started his painting business over break. By the end of the summer, he had so many contracts that he never made it back to school. Made a good living, though; at one time he ran four crews. Now he's only got his crew and my brother Andrei's, which is more of an autonomous unit.

I've been in St. Louis for a month. I'd better call Mom and tell her before I run into one of the boys. I should at least tell Alecki I'm at Angela's. When I left Weston I didn't disconnect my phone service; I'm sure he's tried to call me by now.

The boxwood bed is mulched; I follow the curved walk into the formal garden, a walled brick courtyard encircling an intricately planted oval parterre. Ground cover and flowers border knee-high hedges of boxwood. A few weeds peek from the edges of the thyme; I draw them from the damp soil, then plop a bucketful of wet cocoa shells into the bed and spread it with my trowel. It's too close in here to use a rake.

My partner approaches, clipboard in hand. "How's it going?" Tim keeps an inventory of every plant in our area. A computerized list tracks the vigor of every single tree, shrub, and flower in the Garden.

"Hey, Tim. All right; everything looks healthy in here."

"The west side beds look good. Me and John are going to Adriana's for lunch today. Want me to bring you a sandwich back?"

"Sure. Italian beef." I dig some damp and crumpled bills out of my khakis.

Tim hands me his radio. "We're going a little early. I won't be back until twelve-fifteen or so. I'll call you and leave it at the shed." He walks away, whistling.

I brought some leftover pizza for lunch, but I love Adriana's Italian subs. I just love to eat, really. One of the benefits of working here is that the ripe fruits and vegetables from the Home Gardening Center go to the staff. We've had tomatoes, peppers, zucchini, peaches, and plums sitting out in boxes for the taking at lunchtime. Maybe I'll have some cherry tomatoes with my sandwich.

I must be getting hungry; it's only 10:45. I try to concentrate on mulching evenly through the narrow spaces in the beds.

Tonight's meeting topic was "Facing Your Fears." Fortified with the evening's dose of recovery, I place a call to Mom.

"Finally, you come back."

"I didn't run away. I just wanted to stay in Weston awhile. I made some friends there."

"Girls?"

"Yeah, girls. I played basketball and softball there."

Mom's glad that I'm not drinking anymore, but embarrassed that I call myself an alcoholic. "Alcoholics drink," she says. "If you're not drinking, then you're not an alcoholic."

"Alcoholism is a disease."

"Then get well," she says. "If it's a disease, find out what made you sick and stop doing it. What about those bars you go to? Those girls you run around with? They drink all the time. No wonder you got to be an alcoholic. That doesn't mean you have to stay that way."

Mom drives me nuts; she thinks she's the world's foremost authority on everything. She doesn't know anything about being an alcoholic, or a lesbian, for that matter. To her, it's more of my dirty secrets, shame that I bring on the family. "Just please don't tell your grandma. It'd kill her."

Bunica's probably tougher than the lot of them. My brothers and I called her that when we were little; I still do. It's Romanian for "grandma." Bunica probably doesn't need to know I'm an alcoholic, though; she doesn't need to know I'm a lesbian.

I resemble her. She's a tiny woman, shorter than I am and very slight. When she was a girl in Romania, she worked in her father's bakery, kneading huge vats of dough and carrying the heavy trays to the oven. "Strong," she'll say, pulling up her sleeve and pointing to the stringy biceps under wrinkled, hanging skin. "Like you."

"How is Bunica?"

"I talked to her Sunday; she's OK. She asks about you every time, Terry. I tell her who knows what you do? I don't see you."

When I was little, Bunica would sit me before her in a kitchen chair and brush out my hair. It was long; I didn't get it cut until the summer after sixth grade. She'd brush until it shone and braid two long pigtails. Once my hair was secured she'd crouch before me, inspect my face. "Blue eyes." She'd shake her head. "Where'd you come from, gypsy brat? You'll be a wild one." She'd smack my butt, and I would run from the excess of care and grooming.

"I'll write her, Mom."
"She'd like that. When are you coming over?"
"Soon."
"Come over Sunday; we'll call your grandma."
"I'll see."

I planned to sleep in, but since I got here I haven't slept much. Withdrawal from alcohol can cause insomnia, muscle twitching, night sweats, bad dreams; I heard that at a meeting. God knows I have some nightmares.

It's just before seven on Saturday morning; I might as well get up. I make some coffee, then load the dishwasher and run it. When I lived with Angela before, she wasn't so messy.

I'm a little tired, a little bored, and way fed up with my life. I could start my laundry, but I'd rather not. Instead I start a letter to Bunica. Beyond letting her know my current address, though, I have nothing to say. What am I going to tell her? That I'm going to AA now? She really wants to hear that. She'd be glad that I'm not drinking, but that would require her to stop pretending that I never did in the first place. I could write about work, I suppose.

The phone rings. "Hello."

"Hey, what's up? This is . . . you're not Angela."

"No, this is Terry. Manescu." I don't recognize the voice.

"Terry! I didn't know you were back. It's Willow."

"Willow?"

"Brenda, from softball. My name is Willow now; it's more the reality of who I am."

Whatever. I vaguely remember a Brenda. "Angie's not up yet. Can I take a message?"

"Well, I saw Angie a couple of weeks ago, and I told her I was going to be moving, and she said she'd help out." Willow pauses. "I should have called her yesterday. She's not up?"

"No."

"We got a U-Haul. We've got to get it back by five o'clock," Willow says. "We've already packed everything up, we just need a hand with some of the big things—mattresses and dressers and stuff."

Might be better than laundry. "I could give you a hand. I don't have a car, though."

"I can pick you up. How soon—I mean, when would be good?"

"Anytime. Soon."

"I'll be there in a little bit."

"OK. See you later."

Angie comes in from the hall. "Who was that?" She pours a cup of coffee, holds up the pot and frowns. "Damn, girlfriend."

"I like it strong. That was Willow."

Angela sets down her cup, wide-eyed. "Is she coming over here?"

"She said you were going to help her move."

"No, I am not!"

"Relax. I said I'd do it."

"*You* are going over there?" Angela sputters. "Oh, honey, no! Call her back."

"She didn't leave her number. What's the deal? I don't mind moving stuff."

"Oh, no. You don't want to do this, Terry." Angela shakes her head, cuts the coffee with a hefty shot of milk. "I threw away that number, though. I have got to get out of here. I'll be in the shower."

Willow shows up at eleven-thirty. By then I'm done with my laundry and Angela is long gone. Per instructions, I inform Willow that Angie and I are just roommates. Angela's awfully touchy on the subject, actually. Like it would be such an awful thing to have me in her bed. I've heard otherwise, more than once.

"Willow, where are you moving?"

"My partner just bought this really nice condo, right at the edge of Forest Park. The lease is up on my apartment, so I'm moving in with Erica."

Shit. "Erica who?"

"Erica Schneider."

The bitch goddess of head games. I've avoided Erica for nearly four years. A couple of times I've seen her in a restaurant or at the bar and I've had to walk right back out. That woman put me through some serious changes, but I still get a little weak when I see her. She could get me off in ten seconds flat, raise her head and smile.

"Erica said you two are friends," Willow continues. "She's really happy that you could help us out."

"No problem." My voice breaks, and Willow looks over. Maybe I should feign an illness—heart attack? Stroke? Dysentery? I manage a weak smile, and Willow goes on about Erica and her charms.

When we arrive, Erica emerges from the moving van. "Terry, how nice to see you." She approaches for a big hug. I smell patchouli—she's the one who got me started wearing it. I used to steal hers and pour it into the little vial I still carry. Erica presses my face into her breasts and sweat starts down my sides.

She might be a little thinner, but Erica's still built, blonde, beautiful. I can't help but notice the way Willow pants after her like a dog—too familiar to be funny.

I carry boxes down the stairs and stack them in the truck while the two of them giggle and slobber all over each other. How much of that is for my benefit?

"The kitchen's empty except for the table," I yell. I'm not about to enter the bedroom unannounced.

"Good deal," Erica says. "Willow, go put the rest of the bathroom stuff in that box. Terry, give me a hand in here."

Willow does as directed. In the bedroom, Erica smiles at me. She pulls off her flannel shirt; underneath, she's wearing only an undershirt. Her nipples stretch the thin cloth.

"Getting hot," she says. "Help me take apart this bed. We started to do it after Willow called you this morning, but one thing led to another . . ."

Erica's smirk is like a punch in the gut, but I wouldn't give her the satisfaction of my refusal. I help her break down the bed, not acknowledging the brush of her hand across my hip, her body briefly pressed to mine as we pass in the hall later on.

Erica's building has an elevator; we lock open the doors and fill it nearly to the top with furniture and boxes, then send the load to her third-floor condo and race up the stairs to intercept it. I can't wait to get out of here, away from Erica's furtive touch and malicious smirk. How can someone so hateful be so hot? The woman is like a bad drug.

I lift the oak headboard and Willow rushes to take an end. Erica says, "Leave that, let the butch get it," and squeezes my biceps as I pass. In my mind, I smash it through her teeth. In reality, I haul it to the elevator single-handedly, not even gouging the wall.

We empty the van by 4:45. "You two have worked really hard," Erica says. "Terry, you drop off the U-Haul. Willow can follow you." She holds out a hundred-dollar bill. "Pick up a pizza and some brews with the change."

Willow casts me an apologetic look. "Honey, Terry doesn't drive."

"Oh, right. The DWI. I guess you don't want any beer with your pizza, then." She laughs. "Can't have you flunking your pee test."

Erica returns the moving van; I make Willow take me to Angie's before she picks Erica up.

"You got a call," Angie says. She and Sharon are in the living room, watching a movie.

"I didn't think anyone knew I was back. Except Erica."

Angela grimaces but doesn't meet my eyes.

"Terry, we have a mutual friend," Sharon says. "I work with a woman named Christy. We were talking the other day, and she said she knew you from high school. She just called about ten minutes ago."

"Christy Salerno? We were good friends."

"Here's her number." Sharon takes a folded paper from her purse.

My curiosity is strong, but the stench of the day's labors is stronger. In a hot shower I soak away the grime, the aching muscles, the day's humiliations. I don't much feel like going out, but Laura is going to pick me up for a meeting. I wolf some leftovers, then give Christy a call.

She invites me for scrimmaging at Forest Park on Saturday, followed by an informal game. The official soccer season starts in two weeks.

"Who's playing?"

"Meredith, Sue, Holly, Jeri for sure. . . . Why don't you ask Angela?"

"I don't think she's big on soccer. I'll check her out, though. Holly who?"

"Holly O'Brien. You know, from St. Thomas. You guys had French together, I think."

"*Holly?* No way. Is she a dyke?"

"She's been coming to the bar."

"She wasn't like that in high school."

"That was high school. I'll pick you up Saturday, OK?"

"Sure. See you." Holly O'Brien: the fantasy crush of my adolescence! Holly is the reason I still break into a sweat whenever I see plaid against the downy thigh of a young girl. It's a wonder I don't have a fetish for navy blue sweaters, too. Saturday can't get here fast enough. I've been so bored since I've been back, I could just about expire. Not having a car sucks, especially in the city. In Weston it wasn't so bad, but here it's like being in jail.

Friday night Angie drops me off at the AA clubhouse on her way home from work. I hang out in the snack bar for an hour, drinking Coke and eating an egg salad sandwich. Laura shows up right before the meeting and smiles, approving of my Garden T-shirt, dirt-streaked khaki slacks, and boots.

The topic is Step Three, "Made a decision to turn my will and my life over to the care of a Power greater than myself." When it's my turn to talk, I say I already turned my life over to alcohol. Surely I can turn my life over to some other power greater than myself.

Laura whispers, "I hope someday you can find a Power greater than yourself." These insinuations about my ego just chap my ass; she's the one who's always so ready to tell me what to do.

After the meeting, Laura asks me if I want a ride home. I had planned to walk, get some time alone. But I spent the day hauling shrubs and trees from the carts, unwrapping root balls and readying them for Tim to set. I accept.

In the car Laura says, "I haven't heard from you in a couple of days."

"Everything's going OK."

"You don't have to wait until you're in some kind of a crisis before you give me a call. Let me know when things are OK, too. It works both ways, you know. I always get something out of it when you call."

A pain in the butt?

"So Terry, do you have any plans for the weekend?"

"Yeah. I'm going to play soccer at Forest Park tomorrow."

"Wonderful. Are you on a team?"

"I will be. They're some old friends, people I went to high school with."

"Are these girls that you drank with?"

I used to drink with everybody. "Some of them."

"Are any of them in the program?"

"I doubt it."

"Well, be careful." She clears her throat. "Will there be any drinking there?"

"Maybe afterward."

"Maybe you should make a plan for afterward, then. Maybe you should hit a meeting tomorrow night."

"I usually do go to a meeting on Saturday nights."

She pulls up at the curb before Angie's. "Call me."

"I will." I resist the urge to run into the house; it drives me crazy that everyone is into my business. Maybe sponsors have to be like that, but I can't stand it.

I talk to Angie and Sharon for about a half hour, then jump into the shower, scrub the soil from beneath my fingernails, and hit the sack way early for a Friday.

Saturday morning I dig through my T-shirts and shorts, looking for my best soccer outfit. I've still got some cleats, black leather ones with a royal blue stripe on the side, so I pick out a loose black T-shirt and some royal blue shorts. Not bad, though the baggy shorts make my legs look kind of skinny. I hike them up higher around my waist and knot the drawstring tightly to show a little thigh, but they won't stay up. Still, the shorts bring out the blue of my eyes.

I do have some royal blue knee socks, but I don't want to look like the only one there with a uniform. Besides, I can't wear cleats all day, and the socks look funky with white sneakers. I settle for standard white ankle socks, rolled down. I'll pull them up at the field.

Angie doesn't play soccer, but she said she might drop by to watch and maybe go out afterward. She probably wants to keep an eye on me.

Christy shows up a little before two o'clock. I race out to the car.

"Christ, Terry, don't tear the fucking door off."

"Sorry. I thought it would be heavier." I hop in, drop into the seat with both feet solid on the carpet, perfect three-point landing. Dust rises alongside my thighs.

Christy smirks. "I guess you're not excited, then."

"I'm about to fucking levitate. You don't know how much I've missed you guys. You don't know how much I've missed playing."

"Missed you, too, Manescu." Christy thumps her fist on my shoulder. "I can't believe you've been back for two months and I just found out. You didn't even call Jeri."

"I know. I've been pretty low-key."

"Manescu, you may be a lot of things, but low-key isn't one of them. I thought you had a girlfriend in Weston," she ventures.

I shrug, staring at a passing minivan with a rainbow stripe decal. It's nobody I know. "So you said Jeri's playing, and Meredith, and all those guys?"

"And Holly."

"Damn. I didn't even know she *could* play."

"She's OK," Christy says. "Not too quick, you know, because she's big. She can run, though. Meredith put her on defense."

I eye Christy dubiously; she's built like a linebacker. "What do you mean she's big, behemoth?"

"Asshole." She slaps; I duck away. "I'd say she's a little taller than me; that'd put her just under six feet. Slender, though. Long legs," she says, grinning at me. "She's still fine."

Christy parks next to Meredith's old bomb; I recognize it as her mother's former car. Christy whacks me again and points. "There she is."

Holly's on the bleachers, stretching her hamstrings. She grips her heels and bends forward, her chest nearly touching her knees. When I get out of the car, she's looking my way. "Terry!" she calls, and I saunter over, grinning. Holly looks almost the same, but the modest amount of makeup she wore in high school is absent, and her long, wavy strawberry-blonde hair is pulled back into a ponytail. She smiles at me, teeth like a toothpaste ad. "Terry," she repeats. "You used to sit by me in French class."

Not by accident. I smile back. "Hey, Holly." She's still slightly freckled across the bridge of her pug nose; those high, bouncy breasts might be a little fuller than when she was a senior. I take the next bench up, slip off my sneakers and begin to lace my cleats. "You surprised me. I didn't even know you liked soccer."

"Oh, sure," she says. "I never got a chance to play at St. Thomas because of cheerleading, but I was on a team in grade school."

A greenish spider scrabbles over the edge to the aluminum riser and marches straight toward Holly. I suppress a shudder; I can't stand spiders.

Holly's telling me something about playing soccer with her brother. My eyes are on her; I try to will the spider back to its lair.

Holly glances down, then shrieks. She draws back, right against my chest. "Oh!" she points. "You see it?"

I can handle this. I grit my teeth, arm myself with a sneaker.

"Don't kill it!" Holly says.

"I won't." Of course not; I was just going to make its acquaintance. I let the spider crawl onto my shoe, then carry it quickly to the end of the riser and tap the sneaker firmly. "All gone."

Holly flashes a grin, a little embarrassed.

Just let me be your hero. "Come on," I say, "let's play."

I run to the field and Meredith sails a high one my way. I head it to the ground, dribble about thirty feet, then come to a quick stop and flip the ball up with my toe. Catch it on my left knee and bounce it up, one, two, three times, then juggle it in the air from one knee to the other.

Christy races up and smacks me on the butt. "Hot dog." She steals the ball and I chase her down the field, take it back. I love soccer.

Meredith has already assigned positions. Jeri and I are forwards, just like at St. Thomas. The opposing team has a lot of Latinas, I guess from Washington University. We'll kick butt anyway.

Maybe not. We do stay a little bit ahead, despite the long brown limbs and flashy moves of the girl from Brazil. Jeri and I played together for ten years; we can almost read each other's minds. We fall into a passing game so crisp that it could have been choreographed.

Holly's in the backfield, playing a solid, capable defense. She doesn't handle the ball that well, but she boots it long with powerful thighs, and I can get there in time to clean up the pass and make her look good.

We win, 6-5, in a fast-paced match that leaves me sweaty and elated. It's cooling off fast, and Angie never showed. I should have brought a jacket.

"Want to go out for a beer?" Jeri asks.

I hesitate, wanting it. "I can't."

Christy says, "I'll give you a ride home. I need to run by Holly's for a few minutes first, if that's all right."

"Sure." Actually, it's perfect.

"You want a Coke or something?" Holly asks.

"Coke's fine." I settle onto a love seat, notice a streak of mud with a few sprigs of grass still attached to the left side of my shorts. "Holly, where's your bathroom? I need to clean up a little."

"Down the hall; it's a mess. I forgot that Christy was coming for these shoes."

The bathroom is a mess, but a hygienic one—the white fixtures are sparkling clean. Hand-laundered pantyhose and unmentionables hang from the showerhead and the shower curtain rod. I reach for a pair of pale blue lace panties, but resist.

The wicker basket of potpourri on the back of the toilet is still scented, with no dust gathered on the contents. A little table holds hairspray, gel, mousse, and four different types of perfume, all nearly full except the Obsession. In a smaller wicker basket are a couple of sets of linked earrings, a slim gold watch, mascara, eyeliner, three lipsticks, and foundation.

This I would have expected from Holly; the soccer was the surprise. I wet some toilet paper, start to scrub the mud from my leg. The paper balls up and disintegrates. Recycled TP; she's environmentally conscious. I spot some panty liners on a shelf over the toilet tank, dampen one to blot the dirt from my shorts. The dirt and grass stains on my knees I leave as kind of a butch cosmetic effect. The panty liner works great, but looks very bad when I'm done. I start to bury it in the trash basket (wicker also), but decide to roll it up and stick it in my pocket. I wash my face and forearms, comb my hair.

In the living room, Christy has her broad feet jammed into a pair of dark red pumps. "Looks like they fit," she says, then lurches against me.

I steady her. "Those would probably go better with maroon shorts."

Christy takes two more toddler steps, nearly goes over again. "I'd like to see you try it."

"I'd do better than that."

"I'll bet you could," Holly says. "I used to watch you play soccer at school. You run like you're not quite touching the earth."

Christy rips off the pumps and holds them out, daring me.

Holly intercepts. "Christy, her feet are half the size of my big boats."

"Spared you, Chris," I say. "What's the occasion?"

"My sister's getting married. She really wanted me in the wedding party, but she knew better than to make me a bridesmaid. I'd look like I was in drag. I'll be in some of the pictures, though, so she wants me in some kind of a dress." Christy holds up a peach-colored dress with burgundy piping.

"Model it."

"It'll fit."

Holly rescues Christy again. "I'm sure it will, if you wear a fourteen. It's not a tailored dress."

I drain my Coke and stand. Contriving her escape, Christy has collected her jacket and Holly's things.

"Hold on," Holly says. She goes to a bookshelf, rummages through the very bottom shelf until she produces a yearbook from St. Thomas. Surely we are not going to look at geeky old pictures. Holly flips through several pages, then takes a folded piece of lavender paper from the book. "Terry, is this your handwriting?"

"Let me see." Sure looks like it, though it's very carefully done. It's a quote from *A Midsummer Night's Dream: I am your spaniel . . . the more you beat me, I will fawn on you. Use me but as your spaniel, spurn me, strike me, neglect me, lose me; only give me leave, unworthy as I am, to follow you. What worser place can I beg in your love—and yet a place of high respect with me—than to be used as you use your dog?*

"Where'd you get this?" I ask.

"Is it yours?"

My face is getting red. "No, it's Shakespeare."

"But you copied it."

"It appears to be my handwriting." I don't remember this at all; I must have been loaded.

"I thought so." She sits next to me on the couch, relishing my discomfort. Flips the paper over; a yellowed rectangle at the crease marks where a scrap of tape was once attached. "It was stuck to my locker door one morning before school. I thought it was from a boy at first, but the color seemed odd."

"Lots of boys like orchid."

"Yes, and Shakespeare. I'll tell you how I figured it out: do you remember that Saturday afternoon that Bobby and I drove past the stadium and you and Alecki were up in the bleachers?"

"Drinking Thunderbird. Yeah."

"Do you remember what you yelled?"

"No telling."

"It was in French, something about returning from afar with savage eyes, limbs of steel . . . something by Rimbaud. One of the optional readings at the back of the textbook. You were the only one who memorized stuff like that for fun."

"So you knew it was me?"

"Suspected it." Holly smiles; now her face is redder than mine. "All these years; I don't guess I've seen you since high school. I thought you were so hot, but you scared me half to death. You were kind of wild."

Christy leers. "There were those rumors that you might be a lesbian."

"Surely not. Just because Coach kept me after practice a few times . . ."

Holly sits up straight. "Coach Brown? You didn't really."

"No, I didn't. We talked, and she gave me some beer once. Twice, I guess. Chris, don't we have to be going?"

"This is getting interesting, but Jeri and Meredith are waiting."

Holly walks to the door, stands close. She smiles again. "Nice to see you, Terry. Thanks for clearing up my mystery."

"My pleasure," I say. "Anything else I can do for you, feel free to call."

"Spurn you, strike you, neglect you?"

"Anything."

Christy's eyes widen; she starts to speak and I hip-check her out the door.

I roll over and blink; the bedroom is dark. A disembodied shadow stretches across the carpet, black on gray, from the door to the edge of the bed. I stare at the shadow, disoriented, then look up. Silhouetted in the dim hallway light is a tall, longhaired woman.

"Cole?" My voice comes out a raspy whisper.

The figure stands with arms folded, shoulder braced against the doorframe. The stance is familiar: one ankle rolled uncertainly to the outside, hip cocked. Darkness obscures her face.

"Cole?" I ask, a little louder this time. The shadow doesn't move. "What—how did you—" I sit half up, draw my knees to my chest.

Her hip shifts to midline, arms uncross. She takes three strides and switches on a little lamp on the bedside table that is not mine. She reaches for me, her palm sticky with blood. A red drop hits the sheet and spreads. I lower my head from the sight of her swollen, battered face.

My fists dig into my closed eyes. "God, baby, I'm so sorry . . ." The bed shifts. She's sitting next to me. I draw up tighter, my knees against my chest. She looks so hurt, so bad. Cole, I'm sorry. How can you still look so bad? I feel her: close, patient. Waiting, as she always did. Her sticky palm touches my cheek and I straighten out, rigid with shame.

Smack of skull against headboard jerks me awake, ears ringing. The doorway's pale rectangle illuminates the dark bedroom. I'm soaking wet, tangled in damp sheets. Both pillows are on the floor. My muscles are taut as wire. I draw a tense, shuddering breath; I am crying.

I give in to the urge, pull a pillow up to my face and sob. Cut loose with tears and snot and ragged breaths through the clean-smelling pillowcase. God, I miss her. Surely she's healed up by now. I wish there was a phone in here—like she'd love a call at two a.m. from the crazy drunk who beat her up.

She didn't say anything, just sat close. Cole never talked much. It was a dream. That's all it was, a dream, but the pain and guilt and shame and remorse are real.

I bawl harder, choking sobs that leave me breathless and exhausted, eyelids thick. I've got to do something; tomorrow I'm writing her a letter.

I pull away the soggy pillowcase, blow my nose on a corner of it. Angie would shrivel up if she saw that. I toss the offended pillow and its cover behind the bed, scrunch up with the dry pillow and fall into a blessedly dreamless sleep, the Serenity Prayer humming through my head like a mantra.

In the morning, I can't get the dream from my mind—Cole standing in dim light, looking hurt, looking haunted. Amber eyes ringed with bruises, wrist still bleeding where she jerked it from my teeth. My teeth!

I get pen and paper, compose a letter that makes me sound like a serial killer. It's grandiose; I tear it into thin strips, start over.

> *Dear Cole,*
>
> *Every day I mean to start this letter; every day I'm afraid of it. What can I say? I'm sorry. Seems pretty lame.*
>
> *I'm staying with Angela for now. I've been going to AA meetings, and I've stayed sober for almost two months. Angie got me a job at the Botanical Garden; I work on the grounds crew. It's beautiful, peaceful on the weekdays. You'd like it, especially the English Woodland.*
>
> *I get my license back this month. I can't wait; I hate depending on Angie for rides. There's an AA clubhouse just about a mile from here, so that hasn't been a problem.*
>
> *I think about you all the time; I think about what a shit I was. I love you, and I miss you. I hate what I did, Cole; I hope you're OK. I won't bother you anymore, but I had to tell you how truly sorry I am.*
>
> *Love,*
> *Terry*

I call Laura and read her the letter.

"Terry, it's a good letter, but I don't think you're ready for amends. That doesn't come until Step Eight."

"I thought amends were the Ninth Step."

"Well, both," she says. "Step Eight is where you become entirely ready, and in Nine you make direct amends to those you have harmed. But the Steps are in order for a reason. Why don't you start your Fourth Step inventory before you tackle amends?"

"I've got to get this done. I can't handle another night like that."

"I won't tell you not to send it, but I think you'd be better off waiting," Laura says. "Have you even started your Fourth Step?"

"I go to meetings almost every night. Then I get home all wound up and I can't settle down to writing, or else it's late and I'm tired. I started it, but I haven't gotten very far."

"That could be because you're not ready to look at this stuff. It never hurts to work Step Three for awhile, either, and practice turning over your will to a Higher Power."

You are not going to talk me out of this. "I'll take another look at that Fourth Step just as soon as I put this in the mail."

"I'll see you at the meeting, then." Laura sighs. "Take care of yourself, Terry. This stuff is hard; give yourself credit for trying."

"Yeah. See you tonight." I put the letter in the envelope and walk straight out the front door, before I lose my resolve.

In the three blocks to the post office, the neighborhood changes from pricey rehabs to two-story brick flats. Big old maple and oak trees cleave the tiny front yards with layers of roots that crack and tilt the sidewalks. The concrete walks are old, rimmed green with dense moss. I imagine Cole walking beside me, her big feet catching a crack, gangly body flailing to stay upright. She was kind of oversized, endearingly clumsy. A light scatter of leaves on the ground shows edges of red and gold.

Was it Cole that brought me down? It seemed like we might be good for each other, then everything turned to shit. On a porch, a short-haired woman in a denim jacket looks at me; I don't even have the energy to smile. I can't believe I feel this old at twenty-six.

A quaking begins inside me as I walk, a rapid pulse of the low-grade anxiety that used to melt away at the very first drink. Lacking that, I develop a full-blown tremor by the time I slip the letter through the slot. Cole's got a box at the post office; I wonder if she'll open the letter right away or wait until she gets home. Probably she'll throw it in the trash.

I jam my shaking hands into my pockets, bite my trembling lower lip, and head back to Angela's. The wind blows into my eyes, bringing tears at the first stinging hint of winter's bitterness ahead. The sun is about to set and I feel like I'm going down with it, dropping into dusk, cold and alone. I don't want to mess with the Fourth Step today; I'd better hit a meeting instead.

My ribs ache from a collision, and the side of my left shin burns from sliding in coarse grass. On the field I don't feel anything, but Christy pulled me out for a breather; now I hurt all over.

If I had any sense, I'd pick up my old shin guards from Mom's. Most players forgo them, but I'm not going to take any shit about wearing them. My beat-up shins aren't likely to turn anyone on.

Christy looks my way, I nod. Next score, I go back in. We get possession; Jeri speeds the ball down the field. Damn, she's fast. I'm quicker, though, and I sprint ahead for the setup. Jeri passes, I fake left and blast the ball into the net on my right.

Jeri slams me with an embrace that's half collision. We trot back for the kickoff. Holly watches from the backfield. Defense has been underplayed this game, we're pretty much keeping the ball to the other end. Holly's had plenty of time to observe my backside.

We win, 7-2. Our opponents approach to shake hands and congratulate us. Their team was solid: experienced older players, but nobody very fast. Ten years from now, will I still be playing? Will I still have any speed? I'll be playing something, even if it's pool.

Holly claps her hand onto my shoulder. "Good game."

"Thanks." I hand her a paper cup of water, and swallow mine in a single gulp. "Good game yourself."

"We didn't do much."

"You blocked that one shot, from that long-haired woman, and deflected it to Jeri."

She blushes and smiles. God, I love redheads. "Yeah. It wasn't much of a pass."

"Come on, Jeri scored. It was a great play."

"Thanks." Holly's pulling off her cleats. "I wish I could stick around, but my sister's in town and I've got to get to my mom's."

Guess I'll be going to a meeting tonight. "Have a good time with your family. I'll call you."

"I'd like that." She knots her shoelaces, stands to leave. "See you."

"Yeah."

Jeri and Christy sit on the hood of Christy's car, watching me. I lean against a fender and pull off my cleats. "Holly asked me if you were going to play again," Christy says.

"Did she?"

"I told her nothing could keep you from it." Christy smirks. "Soccer, I mean."

"You're right."

"You going over there?"

"She said she's busy."

"Terry, you know if you—"

"So what are you guys doing?" I ask. Christy plays games; I don't want to give her a chance to take comments back to Holly.

Jeri says, "Usually we get a couple beers, go get something to eat. Want to hang out?"

I knot the laces together and stuff my cleats into my old black backpack. I did thirty meetings in thirty days, as of a week ago. I might go for ninety in ninety, but tomorrow's Sunday. I could go twice, at ten a.m. and eight p.m. "I don't have the money for both."

"Let's do sliders and Sappho's," Christy yells. She's still keyed up from the win.

Jeri hops off the hood of the car, comes up to me. "Terry. You never turned me down before."

"OK, shrimp. Let's go." She's the only adult I know who's as short as I am. "I've got to clean up if we're going to Sappho's," I say.

Christy takes her car, I ride with Jeri. "Does Holly go to the bar?"

Jeri shrugs. "I've seen her there, but we haven't really talked."

"She's not seeing anybody?"

"No," Jeri says. "She's kind of trying to stay away from guys."

"Really? I think she's been flirting with me."

"She did ask about you when we were getting the team together. I wasn't sure how Holly would do, but she's been OK. She's in shape; she's been teaching aerobics."

"Holly's an aerobics instructor?"

"I think so," Jeri says. "Are you surprised?"

"Kind of. I always thought aerobics teachers were dumb bimbo types."

"And you see a discrepancy here?"

"Holly's not dumb."

"Like you'd notice." She laughs. "Did you ever talk to her?"

"Sure, I—"

"I mean a conversation, Terry. I know how you get, you're like some guy who thinks with his dick."

"I've known Holly since ninth grade. She's not an idiot. It makes sense, as a career move; she was a cheerleader for four years. Where does she work?"

"Dynamo, I believe."

"Damn." Dynamo is in the Central West End. It costs a small fortune, and you need the recommendation of a member to get in. "She must be good."

"Wouldn't you like to know?"

We swing by White Castle and get a bag full of "sliders," tiny square hamburgers with steamed onions, forty cents apiece. They reek, but they're tasty. I wolf down four in the car before we get to Angie's. Jeri says she'll be back within the hour.

I haven't been to Sappho's in almost a year; haven't played pool since August. Jeri doesn't play much—she'd rather dance—but Chris might shoot a game or two with me. I shower fast, wincing at the hot water on my abraded leg, then dab patchouli on my throat and wrists. My shirt's already pressed, but I redo the collar and front with a touch of spray starch, get it really crisp and smooth. I like to iron, though I've never told anyone. When the shirt's cool, I slip it over my head without unbuttoning. I'm glad Jeri's driving; I can perch on the edge of the seat and not get the back of it wrinkled before we even get anywhere. This is my favorite shirt. It's an odd color, kind of periwinkle blue. Reflects in my eyes, gives them a stormy look. I wouldn't wear it without a tan, but forty hours a week at the Garden have kept me dark even in October.

I pull on my black jeans, black boots; nothing else goes with periwinkle. For my twenty-fifth birthday, Alecki gave me a bolo tie with an iridescent black-and-purple tempered glass clasp. I slip it under my collar, draw it high and snap the clip. Too severe; I undo my top button and drop the clasp a half inch. Better. I check myself in the mirror, turn my sleeves up a little more. Lean over and mime a bank shot, watching my triceps. It'll do.

I take my black and white letter jacket from St. Thomas for later; right now I don't want to mess up my shirt. In my jacket pocket, next to the wallet, is a small silver rosary my great-aunt gave me and a "60 days" aluminum coin stamped "AA" and "To thine own self be true." I place the AA medallion with my money as a reminder. My other pocket has a key ring, a leather tab tooled with a black triangle. There's also a small vial of patchouli oil and some lip balm, vanilla flavored. I put a little on; my lips stay chapped, working outdoors.

Angie just beats me to the door. Jeri nods to her, but I sidle past Angie. "Not going to a meeting?" she says.

"Tomorrow."

Christy's car is parked in a littered lot, across the street from the club. Jeri pulls up next to it. A dark figure looms in the second story of the brick building next door. I look up at the window, and a male voice screams, "Faggots! You're an abomination!"

I flip him off, but Jeri's cool hand takes mine. Her smile consoles. "Don't get too fierce, girl. We're outnumbered until we get inside."

The security guard shakes her head. "Sorry, ladies. Some drunk's been screaming over there all night."

I pay my cover charge; we enter the dark, smoky space. The crowd of women parts around my body, closes again at my passing. Luminous under the black lights of the dance floor, two young platinum-haired girls weave around each other, joined by fingertips. A swarthy girl, Middle Eastern, smiles. Her teeth glow and her hair, black as my own, has a spectral shine in the strange purple dim.

We find seats at the edge of the dance floor. Jeri points to the bar, goes to get a pitcher. I follow her, order Coke. This place is loud, but not as wired as a men's bar. A few guys are here, mostly drag queens; they have to be accompanied by a woman to get in. It's a huge place, practically a dyke community center.

Cole was shy; she wouldn't dance. She never cared if I danced with anyone else, but I wish—stop. I want to get my mind off Cole.

I take nearly as much pleasure in dancing as I do in sex. I don't like to slow-dance, though; I'm too short to lead. Next song, I ask Jeri. She's good, a joy to watch. The grade school years we spent playing, running, laughing, loving each other, fiercely innocent, must be marked somewhere in my body. Sweat beads above her lips; I touch her face, fingertips on her cheek, thumb flicked lightly through the sweat. I drop my hand, and her pointed tongue licks across her lip.

The music segues into a slow song, and I look to the table. Contact jolts me—Jeri grips my hip with one hand. Steps close, astride my thigh. I match her moves, grind slow and soft. I'm holding my breath, biting my lip. Time slows down and the colored lights reflect in Jeri's dark eyes. She dances dirty, low and easy, a tease.

"Girl, you're bad," I whisper. It comes out hoarse, a catch in my throat. I'm wet as paint by the end of the song, trembling as she turns me loose. I want that woman, and I want a beer.

I settle for another Coke. "Damn it, Jeri, you've got me shaking. At least you've got someone to go home to."

"You could, too, if you wanted." She gestures toward the door; the guard is staring at us with a slightly dazed expression.

Christy teases Jeri about the dance. I look at Jeri and remember small breasts, dark nipples, the tension of her belly as I slid my tongue along the tender skin above her hipbone. Though we were never really lovers, Jeri was the first girl who rocked her hips against my mouth, left my lower lip swollen and my chin smooth and wet. I learned moves between her knees that I've practiced ever since; the bright flecks in her eyes are constellations that guided all my future pleasures. Kneeling before her, my tongue pressed inside, I gained a universe with her hand cupped sweaty around the back of my head. I'd ride my bike home with her spicy smell on my fingers, the down still palpable against my lips.

A hand claps over my eyes and I stiffen, fighting the impulse to jab an elbow to the gut.

"Guess who?" It's too loud, I can't tell.

Fingers trail down the back of my neck, tug my hair just the way I like. I shudder. The hand drops, palm brushing my breast. I spin around and grab the front of Erica's shirt. Next to her, Willow stares at the floor.

"Terry. I didn't think I'd find you here." Erica pulls my fingers from her T-shirt, holds onto my hand too long. "Get your license back?"

Somebody ought to kill this bitch, but she's not worth the trouble. Under the black light, Erica looks as fine as ever, thick yellow hair combed into a perfect wave, teeth iridescent white.

Willow gives me a wounded look. Baby, I know. "Hey, Willow. You guys enjoying your new place?"

She shrugs.

Erica laughs. She reaches for me again, but I twist away. "It's a great location," she says. "You'll have to come over sometime." She pulls Willow in front of her and wraps both arms around her waist, fingers the button of her jeans. I think of a dog pissing on a tree, claiming what can never be owned.

Jeri moves to my side; another song begins. "You want to dance?" she asks me.

"No, I think I need some air. It's kind of close in here."

Jeri follows me to the door, then turns back. It's much cooler outside; the air smells good. Fuck, I wish I had a cigarette. Wish I had a beer to go with it. I don't know how I fell so hard for a bitch like Erica. Her looks, I guess, that great hair and a killer smile. Clean-cut turned a little bit nasty, like your favorite PE teacher after a shot or two of Canadian Club.

I was eighteen when we first met. I thought I was experienced. I'd never had a lover, just those sweaty explorations with Jeri. Erica was twenty-six, with a car, a place of her own, plenty of cash. At semester break, she took me skiing in Aspen for four days, at a resort owned by friends of her father.

She introduced me to the bars. I saw women dancing together, women standing arm in arm, women kissing without watching their backs. I loved it. I grew up with a pool table in the rec room, so I was all over that. Erica taught me to dance, watched me clean up at pool, showed me off like a prize pup. When the bartender asked her if I was underage, Erica slipped her a fifty and said, "She's twenty-one."

Like a prize pup, I panted after her. Thought I was in for a good time forever. I couldn't believe it when I caught her with Melissa. I'd heard Erica was a player from the women at Minerva's; even my starry eyes could tell that some of them despised her. She told me she was sorry, it would never happen again. It didn't, for about a week. She'd probably been at it all along, and I was too young and dumb and flattered to notice.

I jam my hands into my pockets and shiver. Leaning against the nondescript storefront of the bar, eyes closed, I let my head fall back against the bricks. I open my eyes at the footsteps.

"Rough night?" The guard lights a Marlboro Light, offers them. I hesitate, then pull one out and take her lighter. I like to hold 'em and hit 'em, but the pleasure ends there. I cough until my eyes water. She pulls the cigarette from my fingers, scuffs it on the sidewalk with a spit-shined black shoe. "Didn't you used to come here?"

"It's been about a year."

"I've shot pool with you. You're good."

I search her face without recognition. Maybe I'd know her out of uniform. "You play any sports?" I ask.

"Softball. Volleyball, in high school." She flicks her cigarette into the gutter. "I've only been working here two months. Been coming here for years, though."

I nod, like I remember now. "Right. My name's Terry. I've been out of town, living in Weston."

"Julie." She shakes my hand. "You go there for school?"

"Something like that." I stand up straight, smile off past her like I'm thinking of something I'd rather not say. Step toward the door.

"Hang on." Julie pulls a checkbook out of her hip pocket and carefully tears her address from a deposit slip. "Here's my number. I work mostly Thursday to Saturday, but I'll come here anytime. Give me a call, if you want."

"Sounds good. Thanks, Julie." I make a production out of placing the scrap in my billfold. She holds the door for me.

Christy's by the window. "Did she just—"

"We were talking." I can't hide the grin.

"Damn, Terry."

I drain my watery Coke, feeling much better now. The ex of an old rugby teammate smiles at me, and a minute later we're dancing. She gives me her number, too, on a business card. She's a seamstress. "Aren't you the flavor of the day?" Christy says.

Erica doesn't bother me again. Right before we leave, she and Willow begin to argue. Erica really does look thin, with dark circles under her eyes. Willow must be a handful.

Late Sunday morning, Jeri calls me. She got so excited when she heard I was working at the Garden, we just had to come here. She's been in the Garden Shop for an hour already, talking to an employee about the bonsai show last weekend. Angela photographed that show.

I can't believe I'm here on my day off. I got bored in the shop, told Jeri I'd meet her out at the rose garden. Nothing's over chest-high, so she'll be able to find me here.

A few hardy bushes show red, salmon, or yellow flowers, but the roses are mostly bloomed out. I climb the steps to the water lily pools. The leaves are still full, despite chilly nights; the pools are heated so the lilies linger into autumn.

The middle pool has the giant water lilies, with leaves two feet across. The plaque says these leaves will support a man's weight, but it doesn't invite me to test them. The urge hurries me past. I wish the flowers were out; I don't remember the subtleties of color implied by the names: Peach Blow, Afterglow, Midnight.

I walk the perimeter of the far pool like a concrete balance beam, eyes closed, hands in pockets. At the corner, I hop down and turn to a bronze statue of a mermaid atop a giant carp. The fish is larger than I am; the mermaid has shoulders like a Soviet shot-putter, hair like Medusa. How can a mermaid straddle a fish? At the back of the figure, I see her scaly legs are separate, with two finned feet. Something about her reminds me of Cole. Not the wild sense of movement; Cole gave an impression of stillness. She loved the water, though. Swam almost every day, year round. Cole is broad-shouldered, though not burly.

Enough of that. I turn back to the rose garden, sit by some flagging, tattered blooms. No sign of Jeri. She slipped a credit card into the pocket of her jeans before she locked the car, so it may be awhile.

Her nasty dance surprised me at the bar last night. We haven't touched like that in so long, not since high school.

Jeri and I grew up together, went through all twelve grades of Catholic school. We both were products of compromise: her family is Greek Orthodox; mine's Romanian. She attended services at the Greek cathedral downtown sometimes. There's not even a Romanian Orthodox church in St. Louis, so my family always went to Roman Catholic mass.

Our neighborhood was full of O'Haras and Reillys and Schmidts, little towheads. Manescu and Panatzopoulos kids stood out. Jeri and her brother were olive-skinned, with dark eyes. Even when I was a child, her looks captivated me: brown thin summer arms and legs, skin smooth and warm, kid sweaty. She was tiny, a month younger than me but a year smaller. We wrestled and shoved each other, constant contact. We started kicking a soccer ball around with Marius and Alecki before we went to kindergarten. Small and quick, we were natural forwards.

We'd go to my brother's fort in the vacant lot and sit there, shirtless, like the boys. In fourth grade, we kissed. Just once, but it was thrilling. Jeri's eyes shone, she pushed me and laughed and ran off without a word. In fifth grade, we cut our palms and became blood brothers. Sisters, I guess.

In sixth grade we had a terrible fight, black eyes and bloody noses, goose eggs on the forehead, bites and scratches, after I took an ID bracelet from a boy. The boy moved at the end of the school year; a week later, Jeri was sitting on my porch with her ball glove and bat.

At St. Thomas we played soccer and softball. Coach Brown had me try out for basketball. Jeri was just too small, even for a point guard. I had started to drink, when I could get it. One night at her mom's house, with everybody gone, we took a six-pack from the garage and had three warm beers apiece. Burped like frogs and laughed ourselves prostrate on the carpet. Then we went to her room and kissed like in fourth grade. Didn't know what to do, tangled in clothes and arms and legs. We were awkward and embarrassed and too hot to care. We didn't talk about it for weeks, but I thought about it every night, alone in my bed. I started dating Danny, a guy on the basketball team. I slept with him, much sooner than I would have if I had not just seduced my best friend. To my relief, everything worked. I decided I was straight, and that I should not drink again.

Within the year, I had a huge crush on Coach Brown. Next year, in French class, it was Holly. I decided I might as well drink, and I might as well hang out with Jeri.

When we were little, I called her "Pan." For Panatzopoulos, initially, but also for her nimble physicality. She was "Pan" all through elementary school and most of high school. When things changed between us, I began again to call her "Jeri." It threw me, how I felt; we were intimate but distanced, a little more formal after that. We were so close as kids; there was no room to get closer without something pulling back.

"Manescu!"

Finally. She's toting a big brown bag, probably full of miniature trees. Though I'm drawn to redheads and blondes, I've always found Jeri so pretty. She's petite, dark, a violet among roses. For all the rolling around in high school, we've never dated. Our covert activities were more training than romance. We'll always be friends, though.

"Check these out." Her three bonsai are small, but well formed.

"Nice. Were they expensive?"

"Terrible." She fits them back into the bag. "This one's a boxwood; you can help me keep it healthy."

It's getting cloudy, looks like rain, so she takes me to a coffeehouse on South Grand. The place is full of dykes. I nod to Beryl, the EMT from work.

Jeri asks what I've been up to this past year. Not much I care to say about that. I steer her back to movies she's seen, books she's read. The woman she's seeing, Rita, is a cop, and so closeted that Jeri won't tell me her last name. That can't last.

"We better get going," Jeri says finally. "It's after five."

"Damn." I finish my last refill, grab my jacket. "I'm so glad to see you again. I've been kind of lonely since I got back."

"You see Angela every day."

"I appreciate Angie's help, and she means well, but between her and AA—" I shudder. "I need the support, I'm sure. But it is nice to have a conversation finally, instead of listening to someone tell me what to do."

Jeri smiles. "Not my job, Manescu."

Allison, my supervisor, has been under the mistaken impression that I am taking classes this semester. I never said that I was going to finish the horticulture program; Allison got that idea from Angela. Allison called me into her office this morning, and then she ran into Angela at lunch. By the time we are on our way home, Angie's had several hours to prepare her lecture. "I've got a reputation to protect. People at the Garden know me and like me, and they know we're friends. Some of them know you live with me. I just want you to act like you got some respect for yourself. You got a chance here, another chance, and you're gonna let it slide on by."

"Angie, I'm glad you got me the job. I'm grateful. I thank you for letting me stay with you. But I'm not going back to college for another year and a half so that I can water plants and cut dead limbs from trees. I don't get it."

"You got to have the degree to keep the job."

"Allison's not going to fire me. I do a decent job. Shit, they're only paying me six thirty-five an hour."

Angela pulls up in front of the house. I get her equipment bag out of the backseat. "Thanks. But I went out on a limb for you, getting you this job. You said you wanted to work at the Garden, and I told you then that you'd have to finish your horticulture degree."

We trudge up the walk to the house. I hear a squeak from my bedroom, and Whacker thunders down the stairs.

"Terry, I know you've only been sober two months. I been trying to make allowance." She sighs. "You haven't changed. You still sneaking around, coming in at all hours, hanging out with drunks. You don't go to meetings half the time, and you lie about it."

"I don't lie about it. I just don't tell you where I'm going every damn time I walk out of the house. Just because you *think* I'm going to a meeting doesn't mean I am." I get a Coke for me, one for Angela. "I'll hit one tonight. I've been to a meeting every night, except when I play soccer."

"Or when you go to the bar."

"One time, Angela. *Once*."

"Whatever." With a dismissive gesture, she turns on the TV.

"Not *whatever*. One goddamn time I've been to the bar since I got back. I danced and had a Coke. Big fucking deal." Tired of waiting for my attention, Whacker launches himself onto my shoulder. I carry him upstairs, sprawl on the bed. He pounds my chest with his hard little paws, thumps his head into my chin.

Bitch. I really do like Angela, but this mother trip has got to stop. I know where she's coming from: her aunt was an alcoholic, in and out of AA for years. She lived with their family while Angela was growing up, but she ended up on the streets, finally died of liver failure. That's not about me, though.

Maybe dinner will mellow her out. After a shower, I rummage around the kitchen and whack up some zucchini, mushrooms, and chicken breasts into a pretty decent stir-fry. I serve it to Angie in front of the TV. We don't talk, but she seems more relaxed. When I'm done, I stack the dishes from the coffee table and carry them all to the sink, including the orange juice glass and the coffee cup crusted with the little globs of undissolved dried cheap creamer that Angela had left from breakfast. Angie lounges in front of the TV, expecting dishes to get up and trot themselves to the kitchen.

I run water in the sink, add the soap. This is the first meal I've eaten here since Friday night, and I always rinse my coffee cup and put it in the dish drainer before I leave in the morning. Look at this nasty shit. Stuff's been festering here in the sink for going on three days, getting moldy and sour. The cold, smelly water from the bowls feels slick when I dump it out. Angela tells me to act like I have some self-respect, but I swear the woman lives like a pig.

I rinse everything under the hot tap, then plunge the dishes into the soapy water of the left basin. The right basin I scrub out with cleanser, so that it's clean enough for rinsing the dishes. A foul stench wafts from the garbage disposal; I've disturbed some culture down there. I squirt a bit of detergent into the slimy hole and flip the switch, praying for the absolution of my soul for whatever kind of genocide I just committed.

Whacker hops onto the cabinet and settles in, his tail around his haunches. Angela doesn't like him on the counter, and normally I don't either, but I swear he's the cleanest thing up there. I let him stay, for company.

I wash about a dozen bowls and dump them loudly into the other side for rinsing. Whacker lays his ears back and narrows his eyes. How many people are eating here? "Are any of these yours?" I hold a plate before him; he sniffs, but doesn't claim it.

In the living room, Angie's laughing at a sitcom. Having a good time, now that I've cooked you stir-fry, put away the leftovers, and washed your damn dishes from the past week? You get to play savior to my sorry drunken ass, and you acquire a maid in the bargain.

There must be a commercial; she's getting off the couch. She rummages around upstairs, slams her bedroom door. "Thanks, Terry," she says, dumping another armful of dishes into the sink. "These were in my room. You mind?"

I shrug. Not at all; I enjoy groveling for a place to live.

"By the way, dinner was good. A little spicy, but good."

"Thanks," I mutter. A napkin comes unglued from the bottom plate and reaches nastily to the surface. I watch in disbelief, fish it from the water and carry it sopping to the trash. I'm beginning to shake.

"Count to ten," I tell Whacker. "Breathe."

The program's back on; Angie's busting a gut in the other room. I pull up a glass dotted with little islands of mold, grassy centers ringed with white foam. "Terry, this is hilarious," Angela yells. "You're missing it."

I watch the glass fly into shards against the wall.

Whacker smacks head first into Angela's shin, escapes around her feet. She stands in the doorway, looking, as I twist the dishtowel in my fists. "You going to a meeting?"

"Uh . . ."

"Come on, get your jacket. I'll give you a ride."

I get to the meeting forty minutes early. It gives me a chance to walk a little, smoke, cool down before it starts. When I get home, the dishes are done and put away.

Chapter 3

Getting lost in my head is like talking to an asshole in a bad neighborhood.

overheard at an AA meeting

The day dawned cool, but by 8:30 my sweatshirt hangs over the handles of the wheelbarrow. Gorgeous weather—low humidity, sky so clear and blue that it looks more like Colorado than Missouri. There's not much I'd rather be doing than hanging out at the Botanical Gardens and getting paid for it.

My throat hurts, though, and I'm tired, and I've got an attitude. That scene with Angie last night still bothers me. Before the meeting I bummed two cigarettes, and I haven't smoked since last July. The cigarettes, coffee, and rage wrecked my sleep.

The boxwoods north of the parterre are growing fast, getting wayward and straggly. I take the short clippers from my belt holster and snip at them. A kid squeals somewhere down the path. It's a school day; usually we don't have children here so early. Sneakers slap the pavement.

I shouldn't have lost it like that. I shouldn't have thrown the glass, but goddamn it, she makes me mad. Angie needs to get off my case, and she really needs to quit promising Allison that I'll go back to school. This is a great job, but I can't see getting a degree for it.

I check the shrub for symmetry, move to the next one. Prune the top, step back and compare the two. A vine is coiling into the lower branches of a nearby cedar. I step into the foliage to trim it away. A fit of coughing nearly brings me to my knees. Smoking—that was stupid. I clear my throat, spit.

A branch cracks. Startled, I turn around. A little boy runs straight into me. He's looking back, giggling; my hands fly up to catch him and my clipper jabs his left shoulder. He's got a jacket on, thank God.

"Randy, where are you?" A young woman pushes a stroller up the path. I holster my clippers. Randy is chalk-white, holding his shoulder.

"Randy!" That does it. The kid screams and falls to the ground; he's only about four. Mom comes running. "What happened? Is he all right?"

"I think he ran into this branch." *Good one, Terry.*

"Randy, honey, let me see." She sets him on her lap, removes the jacket and pulls his shirt away. There's a small cut, oozing blood, in a swelling bruise already faintly blue.

Randy wipes his eyes, hitches in a breath. "She stuck me."

"What?" Mom ceases her gentle palpation. "The tree?"

He shakes his head, points. I shrug, hold out empty hands. "I caught him when he stumbled."

She buttons his shirt. Randy moans, clutches his shoulder again.

"Hey, big guy. You're going to be all right." He jerks away from my touch, leans against his mom.

She stands, lifts him to her hip. He's a hefty kid, big to be held. "He's never had a tetanus shot. I'm going to have to take him to the doctor."

"Noooo!" Randy wails.

"Yes, ma'am. You'd better." *Fuck.* I can't believe this is happening again. "I'll call Security. They'll treat his injury and fill out an incident report." Once again, I radio 5190; Beryl's on her way.

Mom's taken Randy back to the sidewalk. His brother is hopping up and down. "Come on, Jeremy." She shifts Randy awkwardly, reaches for the stroller.

"Want me to get that?" I ask.

She hesitates. "No, I've got it."

Jeremy stops skipping. "Mommy, what happened to Randy?"

"He hurt his shoulder. I told you two not to run off like that."

"Is that how come she hit him?"

"I didn't hit him." My face flushes. "I caught him when he stumbled. He startled me."

Mom looks at me, starts to push the stroller.

"Ma'am, I need you to stay here until Security arrives. He's going to be all right; it doesn't look bad. Just bruised." God, let me shut up.

"He'll need a tetanus shot. Jeremy, come on."

"Yes, ma'am. But I need you to stay."

Beryl's Cushman pulls up to the five of us; she steps out and blocks the way. "I'm an EMT. Can I be of some service here?" As before, Beryl is capable and quick, pacifying the child and his mother. She assures the woman that the tetanus shot will be reimbursed, gives her an envelope for mailing the bill to the Garden.

I fill out my brief report, head back to the boxwoods. All morning long I wait for someone to call me in. By noon I'm a nervous wreck. I eat about three bites of my sandwich, toss it in the trash and take a walk with my Coke.

AA is a program of rigorous honesty. Things won't get any better if I can't tell the truth. Next time I will; I'll remember this.

At 3:30 I finish pruning, go back to the shed for some mulch and a rake.

"Terry, could you step in?"

I blow out a long breath. "Sure, Allison. What's up?"

"Let's go in my office." Allison walks briskly away. Wiping my hands on my pants, I follow. I start to sit, until I see my check on her desk.

"I've been really pleased with your work, Terry. You're always on time, you're not afraid to get dirty, and you work hard."

"Thanks."

"You're welcome. But this is the second incident, Terry, on your probationary period. I don't have any choice."

I can't even answer her. I sign a form, take the check, and start walking. If I had a joint I'd smoke it. Angela is in the Visitor's Center; I tell her I don't need a ride home, that I'll be going with someone else. She looks worried, but says OK. She's right to be worried.

I scuff along the sidewalk, block after block, banging my heels down hard. It must be a five-mile walk home, but I'm going to need every inch of it to chill out. The wind's picked up; it stings my ears, burns my cheeks, even with my head low. This was a stupid fucking idea. I don't know what I was thinking—I just know that if I don't keep moving I'm going to get loaded. It's getting dark, and colder by the minute. I've got a jacket, but my sweatshirt is still on the wheelbarrow. Faint stars appear in the east; my eyes blur from the whipping wind.

The neon light of a diner catches my eye. Inside, it's warm. The place looks like it's been here fifty years—worn black and white linoleum, chrome barstools bolted in front of the countertop. The Formica pattern is rubbed away in a blank scallop before each stool. The kid behind the counter looks like a skinny Clark Kent, handsome in a geeky way, with horn-rim glasses and oiled, wavy, black hair. A Tracy Chapman song plays on the radio, and I relax a little into the familiar tune.

A pale, dark-haired girl sits behind a brimming ashtray. She lights another as I watch. It stinks, but I wish I had one. Jack Daniels smells bad, too, but I still wish I had one.

Clark Kent slaps a menu before me. The laminated cover sticks to the table. An overhead fan scoots loose ash down the counter.

I order some fries that I don't really want—my stomach's in a knot. It will take more than just coffee to keep me occupied, though. I wrap my cold hands around the thick white mug; my fingers are red and cracked around the knuckles.

"Fries up!" A plate bangs on the counter. The cook's behind a shoulder-high partition; I can see his white ball cap and apron. He's smaller and thinner than Clark, with similar dark hair. This one must be young; his sideburns look like they're combed down, not grown.

Clark slams the little plate before me, sets down the ketchup so hard a drop burps from the spout. Either he's got an attitude or no depth perception at all.

There wasn't this much chrome in the whole town of Weston. The upright coolers are chromed, chrome strips edge the tabletops, the milk dispenser's chrome. The pie safe is chrome, with a sliding glass door and tilted mirror in the back that shows the whole pies and slices, suspended in a sea of shining metal. The clock's even chrome, with a neon ring.

I roll a fry in ketchup. The table is sticky; my sleeve rips loose from it every time I reach for my coffee. "Hey, could you wipe this, please?"

Clark makes a huge production of going to get a rag, slashing it in the sink four times, holding it up and inspecting it, wringing it out. He moves all my dishes, scrubs the table so vigorously the chairs dance and the spoon rattles against my coffee cup. Don't fuck with me, boy. I am seriously not in the mood for this.

The anger swells from humiliation, clenching my guts. How many jobs have I had in the last three years? More than I can count on one hand, for sure. The only one who didn't fire me was Pop.

Clark Jr. comes out from the grill, sits at the counter next to a pack of Salems and a half-empty glass of Coke. The sideburns are definitely not attached at the bottom; the cook's a girl. She's thin, kind of severe-looking; she scowls at her matches, trying to get a cigarette going. I reach for my lighter before I remember I quit. She might not welcome the attention, anyway.

The radio's playing a Melissa Etheridge fuck-me song. The cook hits her cigarette like a joint; the ember flares brightly. She blows a long stream of smoke and frowns over her shoulder at me. "Did you play soccer?"

"What?"

"Indoor," she says. "Did you play at that complex on Pardee Road?"

"A couple of years ago. Then I switched to rugby."

"My name's Pat. I think we played in your league. We went out to Sappho's after a game once."

"Right, Pat." Good memory. "It's been awhile."

She nods. "I used to have long hair." She draws her finger across the juncture of neck and shoulder, and it clicks—brushing aside full dark curls, kissing the slender neck.

"You lived on Shenandoah."

"I still do."

I try to look noncommittal. Only hazy bits of that night come back to me: kissing her neck in the parking lot, slipping my hand under her jersey on a couch in a dark room. She wore no bra; I had wondered if she played that way or if she had pulled it off unseen.

The girl's still looking at me. "Terry, isn't it? What're you up to?"

Feeling humiliated, trying not to get drunk. "Heading home from work. Missed my ride."

"Where do you live?"

"Soulard. Off of Broadway."

"Long walk." Pat grinds out her cigarette. "Looks like it's getting cold out."

"It is."

She ducks behind the counter, brings the coffee pot and warms up my cup. "If you want to wait, I can give you a ride in about an hour."

I could use a meeting tonight, but I'd never make it on foot. "Sure," I say. "Thanks."

"You want a burger or something? On the house?"

"Yeah, I'll take a burger."

Clark says, "*Pat,* I have an order from a *customer.*"

She glares at him, heads back to the grill. Fixes a turkey club with chips for the customer and a huge cheeseburger for me.

Pat slams the sandwich down before Clark, brings me the burger and a slightly used copy of the *Post-Dispatch*. I relax with the paper and the occasional resentful coffee refill.

I ought to call Laura and tell her I can't make the meeting, but I don't want to talk about the way this day went down. Instead, I go into the bathroom and wash up. A bag under the sink holds some tampons, a tube of lotion and a hairbrush. I borrow a little lotion, smooth it on my chapped hands, brush my hair neat and shining, and spread some vanilla balm on my lips.

Pat hangs her white apron on a hook just as it starts to get busy. A stocky, Greek-looking guy has the grill and fryer sizzling. Pat pulls on a leather jacket; I follow her out to an old green Datsun. "You need to get home right away?" she asks.

"Not necessarily."

"I haven't been out this way in a long time." She turns north on Watson, heads on into Forest Park. One hand reaches into a pocket of her coat and pulls out a joint. She lights it as I watch, draws deep and slow. I'm shaking inside: thinking about Laura, thinking about AA, about my job. That's fucked, anyway.

Pat holds out the joint. I take a tentative hit. Tension melts from my shoulders as I hold the acrid smoke, then let it flow from my lips.

The car drifts to the curb. "That's not how you take a hit." She pulls so hard on the joint that the resins pop, the paper blackens and falls from the end in big flakes. She plucks a straw from a plastic soda cup, sticks it in her mouth, then leans to me and grasps the back of my neck. She shotguns the hit between my lips and I'm reeling.

My eyes gradually focus. My breath is loud, labored, as if I just surfaced from a great depth. Pat's smiling. I grasp her shirt and pull her to me, falling into a kiss. Her cold hands slide under my shirt, making me gasp. Pat rakes her nails down my back.

She whispers "Can I come over?" in my ear, then bites the lobe.

I hesitate. "It's not my house."

"Your loss, babe." Her smile is nearly a sneer.

"What about your place?" Pat looks at me, shrugs. My hand slides to her crotch. "Come on." I unzip her pants, slip my hand inside.

"OK, shit, your hands are freezing." She hands me the remains of the joint and puts the car in drive.

The pot makes my mouth sticky and dry. We stop at a convenience store, I get a thirty-two-ounce Coke and a half-pint of rum. It's sweet and wet and tastes fine; we drink it through a red straw, cruising south on Kingshighway.

By the time we get to her apartment, Pat's looking good. I'm buzzed; every time a thought arises about AA or my job, I take another drink. I'm not drunk, just kind of loose, and ready for anything. Pat leads me to the bedroom, straight off. She fires up a tiny pipe, and unbuttons her white shirt, all the way.

"You bit me," Pat whispers. She hands me the rest of the bowl. I hit it slow, remembering again long curls draped across her neck, tender skin between my teeth. "Remember? You left bruises." She takes my hand, touches a finger to her neck, her back. "Here. And here. And a little one here." My fingers come to rest across a firm nipple.

I step close, kiss and lick her throat, her breasts. She swallows hard. "I like that. Bite me again."

I drop to one knee, brush aside the shirt and bite the skin over her ribs. She's thin, the bones are prominent. Pat gasps as I bite firmly. Her nipples are hard as bullets under my palm.

I lean to her left side, nip the skin of her waist. Pat winds a lock of my hair around her finger, yanks it. I stand up, rubbing my scalp.

"You're good with your mouth." Her voice, husky with desire, makes me shiver. "Don't be afraid to leave bruises. I like it."

She pulls her shirt away. I follow suit, remove my shoes and socks, hang my shirt and jacket over the chair. Keep the khakis for now; the room's a little cold. Pat has stripped bare. She sits on the side of the bed. "Last time I didn't have my toys."

I sit down next to her. She turns away and I pull her thin back to my chest, stroke my palms over her breasts as I bite her scalp and the nape of her neck. Her skin tightens all over. Her nipples draw into points, I pull and twist them between thumb and forefinger. "Do it hard," she whispers.

I press her down to the bed, bite harder and clamp my hand firmly over her breasts. Place my forearm across the back of her neck, so she's pinned. Pat struggles a little and I squeeze a breast, clamp her elbows to her side. She squirms beneath me, making me wet. I bite the scant flesh over her shoulder blades, taste blood as she tries to pull away. The coppery taste puts me off; I loosen my grip. Pat rolls to face me, her face flushed. She twists her hand into my hair again.

"Stop it," I tell her.

She pulls. I slap her hand away, hard. "Bitch."

Pat smiles. "You are just perfect."

I retreat to the chair. The half-pint is in my jacket. I swallow the dregs, quenching a sullen rage. The day blurs into unreality, a hot frustration at the edge of my consciousness. I toss the bottle at a metal trash can; it bounces off the rim.

Pat dumps some magazines and an alarm clock from the big black trunk that serves as her nightstand. She raises the lid, sorts through the contents, and drops two sets of handcuffs on the bed. A streak of red marks her back.

She's examining a big black dildo.

"I don't need that shit." My voice sounds strange, raspy from the dope.

"But it's fun. Terry, you're made for this." Her eyes gleam in the darkened room; she's not nearly as high as I am. "You're halfway there, babe. You've drawn first blood already."

She moves the pillows, fastens one side of each cuff into brass eyebolts secured through the headboard. Draws a short flexible whip from the trunk, then slams it shut.

"Cuffs or crop?" she asks.

"You're not putting those on me."

"Fine." Pat tosses me the crop. I catch it, let it fall from my hand. "All right, your choice."

Pat's on me before I see her leap. She catches my wrist and twists it, pulls me toward the bed. She grabs a handcuff. That big cop twisted my arm like this, the night I was arrested.

Pat's quick, but slight. I roll on top, lever her arm out, clamp the cuff on her right hand. She jerks her other hand free, lunges for the crop. Cuts it across my shoulder. I take it away, and she tries to grab my hair a third time.

"Bitch, knock it off." I shove her down, press a knee in her chest. "What the fuck's wrong with you?"

"Part of the game. If you don't like it, stop me." She twists out from under me, snatches at the whip. I catch her hand, force it toward the handcuff. She relaxes as I start to snap it shut, then kicks my knees out from under me. I land heavily on her, her arm snakes around my neck. I stiffen, but she kisses me. I find her tongue, draw mine across it. Her nails rake my back, not too hard; she raises her hand to the cuff and I snap the second one around her wrist.

I'm kneeling, looking down at her. The crop is in my hand, and I tap it against my palm. It's limber, like a switch, with a little leather flag on the end.

"Go ahead," she says. "I know you want to hit somebody."

I shudder, seeing Cole fall. The cuffs rasp against their bolts and a foot catches the side of my jaw. I grab her ankle, throw Pat to her side. The sound of the whip striking her ribs seems distant. I hit her hard, four more times, feeling nothing. There's a faint smear of blood on the sheet.

As soon as I stop, Pat tries to kick again. "Crazy bitch!" I shove her down, spread her legs. Get it over with, this is too weird. Pat's ready for it; she struggles, but it's no trouble holding her down.

"Fuck me," she whispers. The crop handle's big, wrapped with leather. I stick it in, hard. That's for pulling my hair. I lean my mouth into her, circle her clit with my tongue as I shove the handle in again. That's for kicking me. Next one's for your shitty counter boy. Pat's straining, gasping something, but I'm into this. One for getting drunk. One for losing my job. One for your sick fucking games.

I don't like this. The twisted bitch is having all the fun, and all I've gotten is a kick in the face. I step away, pull off my pants.

"What're you doing?" She's out of breath. I dig through her treasure chest. There's a hot pink vibrator with a sort of fin attachment. I jerk the crop handle from her and she grimaces.

The vibrator won't go in; Pat fights it, bearing down. I stick it in her mouth. "Lick it." She gets it wet. I push it into her and switch it on, then swirl my tongue across her a final time.

"My turn." I climb across her, straddle her face. She just smiles. *"Do me,"* I tell her, and she gets on it. I press up against her, on my knees, gripping the headboard with my hands. This won't take long; I'm pretty hot, despite her crazy pervert games.

The edge of the headboard cuts into my forehead. I'm holding my breath, almost there, when Pat stops.

"Damn it, don't."

She smiles. "Make me."

"Fuck you. Finish."

"Make me."

She flinches as I scream, all the rage of this crazy day pouring forth. My fist hits the headboard, and she recoils again.

"Oh, fuck." I fall beside her, holding my wrist. I can't stand to touch my hand. The room goes dark, then gradually fades back into focus. I hear Pat's breathing, the buzz of the stupid vibrator inside her. Ragged gasps; I think that's me.

When the dizziness abates, I roll to my feet. I gather my clothes in my left hand, go to the bathroom to dress. A couple of times Pat calls out.

The phone's in the kitchen. It's not even late. Alecki says he'll come get me; he doesn't ask why.

Pat looks awfully vulnerable. It's cold in the room; she's probably freezing. The vibrator has slipped out. It buzzes ineffectually by her thigh, next to the sticky riding crop. We can hardly stand to look at each other. "The keys are on the side of the trunk, on that hook," she says.

I awkwardly set one hand free; she takes the keys and releases the other. My right hand is a hot agony; I can't move it at all. I start to tell Pat I'm sorry, but I just want to get away.

Pat wraps up in the blanket. "Is your hand OK?"

"I broke it."

She nods, staring out the sliver of window under the shade.

"I'll wait on the porch; I've got a ride."

She nods again.

I sit on the porch under misty streetlights until Alecki shows. What a fucked-up night. I don't think I've ever felt so wretched. I grip my wrist, trying not to move my hand. What am I going to tell Alecki? I'm drunk and I fucked up?

Angela is going to shit. I just lost my room, too.

The door opens, just as Lex's small blue pickup pulls up to the curb. Pat says, "You can wait inside if you want; I made some coffee."

"My ride's here." We stare at each other, and she softly closes the door.

Alecki scoops some papers from the seat. "Who was that?"

"Girl named Pat. I don't really know her." I shiver. "Don't really want to."

"Guess not. Did she get hurt?"

I ripped a leather handle from her vagina, but she may have enjoyed it. "No. I hit a post."

Alecki keeps driving. It seems that nothing I might do would surprise him.

At the ER, they don't waste much time on drunks. They check my insurance, X-ray me, wrap my hand and wrist in dark blue fiberglass. A "boxer fracture," the guy calls it.

I've about sobered up since I hit the bed frame. In AA they say, "One is too many, and a thousand never enough," and I am not nearly drunk enough. I can't even believe this day.

I wish I could call Laura, but she said to call before I drink, not after. I'll hit a meeting first, then check in with her. I don't think Laura will write me off just yet; a lot of drunks relapse before they get permanently sober. Not permanently; a day at a time.

By the time I'm casted, Alecki is asleep on a love seat in the waiting room. I step into the women's bathroom, lock the door. It's one big room with a white tile floor, toilet with guardrails in the corner.

I flip off the light and face into the room. It's absolute black; the corridors are dimmed down to emergency lights, and the paltry gleam from under the door doesn't extend into my line of vision.

I kneel on my folded jacket, cover my face with my left hand. Soothed by the dark, I start to cry. Not loud, but hard—wrenching sobs that leave me breathless, drained.

When the racking cries subside, I'm reciting the first prayer I ever learned: *Hail Mary, full of grace, the Lord is with thee; blessed art thou among women, and blessed is the fruit of thy womb, Jesus. Holy Mary, Mother of God, pray for us sinners, now and at the hour of our death. Amen.* Tears run steadily down my face. As if the prayer is saying itself, I don't remember starting it. My eyes open into blackness, soft and welcoming.

My knees are beginning to hurt, and my hand throbs. I don't hurt so much inside, though. I shift to sitting, my back against the door, my lips still moving, but now the prayer is one I learned in AA: *God, grant me the serenity to accept the things I cannot change, courage to change the things I can, and the wisdom to know the difference.* I say it over and over, gripping the rosary in my pocket.

Nothing happens—I don't see anything, or hear anything. I just start to feel better. It's all right. I'm all right. One day at a time, I'm all right. It must be Wednesday now, and all I have to do is stay sober for just this day.

I stand up stiffly, flip on the light. I've looked better—I'm pale, bangs matted to my forehead from the cold sweat in the ER. There's a scrape on my jaw, my eyes are bloodshot from crying. But I do feel better. I put on some patchouli, dab vanilla balm on my lips.

Alecki, still sprawled on the love seat, wakes easily. "Draga, you OK?"

Draga; dear one. Nobody calls me that except for Bunica and Lex. "I'm going to be," I say.

He smiles at the floor, nods his head. "Stay with me tonight."

"If you make me breakfast."

"You got it." He stands and stretches, wraps an arm around me and we go.

It's a long night on the couch. My hand throbs in the cast, my face burns where Pat kicked me. By morning the hangover's fierce, as well. I ask Alecki for the Darvocets the doctor gave to him instead of me. He parcels out two, and I doze away much of the day.

Alecki wakes me at six p.m. "I ran a bath for you," he says, "and I ordered a pizza." On the bathroom counter are one of Alecki's clean shirts and a pair of jockey shorts. My khaki pants are still stained with yesterday's labors—for the last time. After we eat, Alecki takes me to my home group.

I clear my throat; my voice still squeaks. "I'm Terry. I'm an alcoholic." Pause for "Hi, Terry."

"I got drunk last night, as you might have guessed. I lost my job, got drunk, went someplace I shouldn't have. I ended up in the emergency room with my favorite rescuer.

"I'm glad he showed, I don't know what I would have done without him. But he's not an alcoholic. He doesn't get it. My brother's seen me drunk a hundred times; he's thinking, 'what's the big deal? You just smoked a jay, had some rum and Coke.' He thought the busted hand was a big deal, but me getting drunk is like, 'so what?' Everyone knew it was going to happen sooner or later."

I'm shaking; I grip my plastic cup of cold coffee. "I guess I was the only one not expecting it. I didn't intend to get drunk. I just couldn't stop it.

"That's the funny part—I was surprised. Before, I always expected to get drunk." My hand aches. I don't know where I'm going with this. "The drinking doesn't work anymore. Late last night I said a prayer, though, and I felt like maybe I could change. Anyway, I'm here."

"Thanks, Terry. Keep coming back," the chairman says, and I nod. I don't know if I can do this, but I want to try.

All around the room, one member after another talks about relapse and return. I nod, pretend to listen. On the wall is a poster listing the Twelve Steps. Tonight I can't stop looking at them:

1. We admitted we were powerless over alcohol—that our lives had become unmanageable.
2. Came to believe that a Power greater than ourselves could restore us to sanity.

3. Made a decision to turn our will and our lives over to the care of God *as we understood Him.*
4. Made a searching and fearless moral inventory of ourselves.
5. Admitted to God, to ourselves, and to another human being the exact nature of our wrongs.
6. Were entirely ready to have God remove all these defects of character.
7. Humbly asked Him to remove our shortcomings.
8. Made a list of all persons we had harmed, and became willing to make amends to them all.
9. Made direct amends to such people wherever possible, except when to do so would injure them or others.
10. Continued to take personal inventory and when we were wrong promptly admitted it.
11. Sought through prayer and meditation to improve our conscious contact with God *as we understood Him,* praying only for knowledge of His will for us and the power to carry that out.
12. Having had a spiritual awakening as the result of these steps, we tried to carry this message to alcoholics, and to practice these principles in all our affairs.

In the book it says to strive for progress, not perfection, and it's a good thing because this all looks like a lot of work.

I read Step Two again, "Came to believe that a Power greater than ourselves can restore us to sanity." Maybe. At least I hit the headboard, not Pat. She wasn't doing a thing I hadn't signed up for. Now I'm out of work. I can't use my hand. I hardly even got a buzz on, and it was a fucking disaster. Some sanity would be good, and a job, and maybe some sleep, though I sure don't want to talk to Angie. She's had it with me.

After the meeting, I walk out to the parking lot. Laura's standing by her car. "I haven't given you a ride for awhile," she says.

"No."

"Well, I always liked our little talks after the meeting." She unlocks the door for me, takes an empty Diet Coke bottle from the passenger seat and sticks it into a small trash bag in the back. "Does Angie know what happened?"

"I haven't had the guts to face her yet. I left a message on the answering machine about ten this morning." I stifle a grin. "I said I wasn't coming in to work because I hurt my hand. I imagine she's pieced it together."

"Will she let you stay?"

"I doubt it. Maybe tonight. I'll probably get my stuff and go stay with Alecki until I figure out what I'm going to do."

"You'll be OK there?"

"It's not like I have a lot of options."

"I wish you had called." Laura sighs. "It does get better, Terry, as long as you don't drink."

"I can't tell you how weird it all was," I say. "I didn't have any intention of getting drunk; I met up with this woman I'd seen once before and we got into this really freaky scene."

"You just turned up drunk, like catching a cold."

I shrug. "I'm not sure."

"You know how to keep it from happening again?"

"Call my sponsor, read the Big Book, work the Steps, go to meetings..."

"At least pick up the phone before you pick up a drink."

"Yeah. You know what bothers me most? Of all the bullshit—my job, the busted hand—the thing that kills me is that letter to Cole. I told her I'd been clean two months, and two weeks later I'm loaded again." I turn my head, scrub my left wrist across my eyes.

"That kind of makes sense," Laura says. "Are you ready to work the Steps in order this time?"

"I'm ready to do something different."

"Good."

One story above a city should have some kind of noise, even at two-thirty a.m. I'm on the balcony at Angela's, and there's no sound at all. Angie said I could stay, last chance.

I wish I'd gotten the pain pills from Alecki. I wish I could sleep. I wish I could drink until I pass out.

A car goes by, blocks away. I wish I had my car here. If I did I'd be drunk again. My thoughts keep circling, moths around a lamppost.

St. Louis sky is an ugly color at night. Stars can hardly penetrate the glare from the street lights. When it's overcast like this, the sky's evil— a dark murky pinkish-gray.

I hate my life. I hate feeling like this. I hate feeling. I used to have friends, people to hang out with. Used to have a lover, for a little while.

I miss Cole. She was strange, intense. Pretty, though, and she had a quiet presence that made me think that we were going to last. Nothing's forever, I guess. Not in my care, it's not.

My care. I can't take care of a relationship; I can't even take care of myself. I killed off the love Cole had for me. I damn near killed myself with the cocaine.

My care. Step Three says to turn your will and your life over to the care of a Power greater than yourself. Any power is greater than me. Any Power that accepts me has some low standards, though. Whatever's out there, take my life. I don't want it.

Music drifts down the alley. I lean over the rail; there's a dim light in the bedroom window of a flat down the street. Faintly, a piano plays Gershwin's "Rhapsody in Blue." My grandma used to play the piano; I did, too. I lay my head on my arms, eyes closed, and listen to a lone instrument trying to carry this full orchestral piece. My mind fills in the missing section of horns. Finally sleepy, I go back inside.

Sunday morning, Angela takes me to Laura's with my Step One and Step Two. Laura invites me in with a smile. "David went to Sunday School without me. We've got the place to ourselves until I leave for church." She gets me a coffee, black with sugar. "How's the hand?"

I flex it against the cast and wince. "Not bad if I don't move it. At least navy goes with everything."

She gestures to the spiral notebook. "Got your steps?" I read them aloud. When I'm done, she smiles. "It's a good start, Terry. Do you think you're ready for Step Three?"

"I read it. I looked at the Big Book and the Twelve Steps book. I don't know, though; turning my will and my life over seems like shirking. Shouldn't I be able to handle it myself?"

"That's the whole point of AA; you can't do this by yourself. People in the program will help you, if you're willing to accept it, but you won't always have people available. Sooner or later, you're going to have to find something more reliable than alcohol, or people, or sex, to make you feel better."

I nod, sip my coffee. "So do you get that at church?"

"Church is important to me, but it didn't get me sober," she says. "My understanding of God has changed a lot since I got in the program. Now I'm willing to ask for help."

"I believe in a higher power. There's got to be something out there more powerful than me. But we haven't been on speaking terms for some time."

"Look at it this way—praying can't hurt you. If your prayers are answered by a loving God, then you'll be better off. If you pray because it says to do it in the Steps, and you know that's how millions of drunks have stayed sober in AA, then you're still better off."

"Descartes' wager."

"Pardon?" Laura frowns.

"Descartes' wager. Descartes, the philosopher; he said the same thing."

"Oh. Well. Did he stay sober?"

I laugh. "As much as he wanted to, I think."

"There you go." She collects our empty cups, heads to the kitchen. "Terry, don't think too hard about this. It's a matter of faith. You can't force it. There's hardly anyone too dumb to work a program, but some people are too smart to do it."

"Thanks." I hesitate before I get up, decide to speak. "I'm not sure I can be part of any program that requires me to check my brain at the door."

"I think you'll be OK with that. The hard part is checking your ego." Laura helps me pull my jacket on; it's tight over the cast. On her way to church, she drops me at Angela's, my last-chance lodgings.

Chapter 4

The nuns told me that to become a saint, you have to be a martyr or behave. By third grade, I knew there had better be a serious persecution.

                        overheard at an AA meeting

Once again, I wake to the sound of Angela leaving for work. Once again, newly sober, I wander down the stairs. The day extends before me; once again, I'm not willing to look for work until I heal a bit. The hand's better, if I keep still and elevate it. If I forget and try to use it, the pain is fierce. Alecki has my Darvocet; I'm trying to do without.

Angela and I had a talk yesterday. "I always been there for you," she said. "We been friends a long time. But I'm not doing you any favors, letting you hang out and drink."

"I never took a drink here, Angie."

"What I'm saying is you don't help yourself, I got no use for you. The only reason I let you stay is you went back to a meeting the next day. It won't happen again."

"I don't intend to do it again," I say. "It wasn't that much fun."

"I been through this shit before, Terry. My daddy threw his own sister out the house four times. She'd say she was through, come back stinking like whiskey that same night. You may be my friend, but I'm not living with that."

"You shouldn't have to. If AA helped your aunt, it'll work for me. I'm going to give it another shot. I'll go to meetings every day. I'll go twice a day until I get another job."

"I'm not saying that," she says. "You do what you got to. But by the end of this month, you're going to have a job and be going to meetings or you are out."

"I'm in total agreement."

No job today, though. By the time I fix myself some cereal and slop coffee all over the counter, I'm ready to stretch out on the couch with my hand propped on a cushion. Whacker hops onto the couch, glad I'm staying. He pounds and kneads me, bumps his head on my chin, licks my hand. Finally settles between my feet, chin pillowed on my right ankle.

I look at the want ads for about five minutes. I get my license back this week; that'll broaden my options for work. I call Mom to tell her I'm going to come pick up the car.

"Finally, we get to see you. Still short, black hair?"

"Last I checked."

"What are you doing home? Don't you have to work today?"

"I was supposed to work, but there was an accident Friday. We were taking down a tree, and I broke my hand."

"Good Lord," Mom says. "Was anyone else hurt?"

"No. It wasn't a big tree, I just caught my hand and it got twisted."

"So it's covered under workers' comp?"

I wish. "Yeah, that's no problem. I'll be off for a while, though. I'm thinking I might look for another job."

"Are you having money problems?"

"Not yet, but there's none coming in. I'm not sure what I'm going to do for money while I'm off."

Gusty sigh. "Well, you know we don't have a lot, but we've always helped you out before . . ."

Oh, please. Your sofa cost more than my car. "I'll see, Mom. Thanks. I'll talk to Alecki about a ride. He can let you know when we're coming." That'll give me a chance to get the story straight with him.

"We'll be glad to see you," she says. "Glad to get rid of that old car in the yard, too."

"Yeah. See you." It's not an old car, it's a Mustang. I drag myself from the sofa, pour a Coke. Good thing Angie has a job. I'm not going to hit her up for money, but I will drink her Coke.

The phone rings. "Yeah?"

"Terry? I'm glad you're at home." The voice is male, and uncertain. "This is Bill. From the meeting."

"Hey, Bill. What's up?" I relax back onto the couch, arrange my pillows.

"Are you going to the meeting tonight?"

I regard the cast propped on my chest. "I think I'd better."

"Do you care if I pick you up?" He hesitates. "There's someone I'd like you to meet."

"Sure, Bill. I need a ride. Who is it?"

"Listen, I'm at school. I can't talk now. You live in Soulard, right?"

I give him the address, perplexed, then call Laura to say I've got a ride.

Bill shows up early. He unlocks the car door for me, holds it open. He keeps clearing his throat. His car's a mess, full of books, papers, empty plastic soda cups. I pluck a crumpled AA flyer, stained with mud, from the floor.

"Oh," he says, "that was last week." He pitches the flyer into the back seat.

"So who's this person you want me to meet?"

He clears his throat again. Glances at me, then back to the road. "Did I ever tell you about my sister?"

"One night when you spoke, you said one of your sisters helped you get into the program."

"She's my only sister," he says. "Half-sister, really; Annie's a lot older than me."

"But she goes to AA."

"Yeah. She's coming to the meeting tonight; I asked her if she would talk to you. I think she could help you. I hope you don't mind." He looks over, his cheeks a little red.

"No," I say. "I guess not." He's so nervous; it's making me edgy.

"I don't usually talk about Annie, because I respect her anonymity. But she goes to meetings over at the Lambda Club. You ever go there?"

"No. AA club?"

"Gay and lesbian AA meetings. Narcotics Anonymous, too, and co-dependent meetings. Anyway, it's a clubhouse. I told her about you, and she thought you might want to go there. She loves it."

"Really. I would like to check it out."

Annie's about thirty-five. She's big-boned, broad-shouldered like Bill, but with short, prematurely gray hair, warm brown eyes, nice smile. Bill and I sit next to her; he warned me that she probably wouldn't want to talk until after the meeting. She teaches at an elementary school in West County.

Annie doesn't stay long; she talks more to Bill than to me, but she takes my phone number and gives me hers on the back of a Lambda Club schedule. She says her home group is Wednesdays at six-thirty; it's a small group, women only. She offers to pick me up, tells me to call her.

I couldn't wait until Wednesday. Angie had never heard of gay AA, but she was glad to give me a ride to the Tuesday eight o'clock mixed meeting. It wasn't far.

The Lambda Club is an old two-story house in a disreputable part of town, next to the lot of Lee's Fried Rice. Alecki and I ate there a couple of times. The proprietor is a wild man. Lee cooks orders two at a time in washtub-sized woks, right out in the open. He bangs at the sizzling rice and meat with a thing like a spatula in each hand, throws stuff everywhere. He hurls the food at the plate, bangs it down. There's food on the floor; rice rings the plates after they hit the counter. Lee's got rice in his hair. The place smells great and the food's incredible, but it's so unhygienic that I would only eat there when I was stoned.

The clubhouse is almost anonymous, distinguished by only the AA circle/triangle logo on the door. There's no doorbell, so I knock firmly. A plump middle-aged guy opens the door and says, "You here for the eight o'clock group? You don't have to knock. It's upstairs."

"Thanks." The stairway's lined with flyers for AA gay/lesbian/bisexual dances and conventions throughout the Midwest. The smell of coffee wafts down the stairs. At the top is a dingy lounge with a couple of beat-up sofas and easy chairs, all flanked by big ashtrays on stands. A crewcut woman nods as I pass; she's smoking. Call me traditional: I like shaved pits, not heads.

The meeting room is small and high-ceilinged, an old bedroom with water-stained ancient wallpaper. The slogans are posted: "Live and Let Live"; "Easy Does It"; "But for the Grace of God"; "Think, Think, Think"; "First Things First." Six of the members here are women, mostly in their twenties and thirties, though one could be my grandmother. Bill's sister Annie is talking to two men who arrived together. They could be a couple: both middle-aged and dressed conservatively in sweaters and slacks. A husky blonde woman gets up and shakes my hand. "I'm Portia. First time here?"

"At this group, yeah. I'm Terry."

"Welcome, Terry. Want some coffee?"

"Black, three sugars. Thanks."

Portia indicates a chair next to herself, and I sit. The smoker from across the hall gets the notebook with the meeting format. With a knowing grin, she hands me "How it Works" to read.

Portia brings the coffee for us both. I realize with a start that the shorn smoker is Beryl, the EMT from the Botanical Gardens. She begins the meeting with the preamble. I read "How it Works," then Beryl introduces the thin, gray-haired woman. "I've known this lady for four years, and she's something special. When I grow up, I want to be like Evelyn."

The voice is so raspy, I have to decipher the speech by its rhythms. "My name's Evelyn, and I'm an alcoholic."

Evelyn talks for twenty minutes, mostly about honesty. About not lying to yourself, more than being honest to others. When she's done, there's a coffee and smoke break.

"Hey, Beryl," I say. "Got your hair cut."

"I always wanted a crew cut." She laughs, rubs her hand across her head. "Finally got up the nerve to try it. What do you think?"

"It's really different. I didn't recognize you at first, street clothes and no hair."

"Terry, it looks like crap. At least it grows fast. What did you do to your hand?"

I start to tell her I hurt it at the Garden, then catch myself. "Relapse. I broke it."

Beryl grimaces. She squeezes my shoulder, says, "Glad you're here."

After the coffee break, I'm determined to talk. One of the guys goes first; he says that Evelyn has twenty-two years. Damn. She must have been something like fifty when she quit. I don't know if I could make it that far.

The room goes quiet for a moment. "I'm Terry. I'm alcoholic." My heart pounds like I'm at the free-throw line.

"Hi, Terry."

I tell about the kid Friday, how I lied about him running into the branch. Beryl's nodding her head. I tell about getting fired, and getting drunk. Nothing about Pat, though, just that I ran into some trouble.

When I'm done, Portia speaks up. "I've been a liar all my life. When I first started coming to meetings here, I didn't take it seriously. I thought I'd just stick around until I got a handle on how to manage my drinking; shouldn't take more than a couple of meetings.

"I told people all kinds of crazy stories. Said I was going to Washington University on a tennis scholarship, that I'd hurt my knee and got addicted to pain pills and that's how I lost control of my drinking."

Annie's nodding her head, laughing. Portia is red-faced, but grinning. "See, I thought I was going to Boston with this chick, as soon as I got a little legal matter cleared up. I don't even play tennis. The only time I've been to Wash. U. was to deliver pizza. The chick went to Boston by herself, and I went to a halfway house. At least I kept going to meetings. The first time I had to speak was awful. To tell the real story, I had to keep backing up. 'Wait, that really happened like this—'

"All I have is today, though. I can't change what I did yesterday, or last year. With the help of this program and the Steps, I can stay sober today, and I can start getting honest, one day at a time. Terry, glad you're here." Almost everybody there says that they're glad I came. I am too.

After the meeting, Evelyn gives me her phone number. "Call me any time, kiddo. Unless you take a drink, I mean. I'm retired; you can catch me during the day."

"Great. I'm in temporary retirement myself."

"I figured."

Beryl gives me a ride home. She knows Annie and likes her a lot. They both have five years sober. I'm actually looking forward to the next meeting. And I can't wait to tell Angie that Portia was wearing a Gay Games rainbow flag T-shirt.

Wednesday night Annie takes me to the lesbian meeting. It's a small group; the meeting only lasts an hour. The mixed meeting, like the mainstream AA groups, was an hour and a half. Four of the women from Tuesday night are back. After the meeting, some of them are going to the Coffee Grounds on South Grand. I feel like I'm back in Weston; Cole went to the Coffee Mug Cafe practically every night. I hope she's doing OK; so far, she hasn't answered my letter.

Good thing I brought my jacket. It's a pretty night, so clear you can make out some stars, but it is cool. By the time Annie and I arrive at the coffee shop, Beryl's at a table outside.

"Hey, Terry," she says. "We'll sit out here so Evelyn can smoke."

"Terry, you don't smoke?" Evelyn's coming up the two steps to the deck.

"Not anymore. I never did, really, except at the bar."

"What is AA coming to, when the smokers are outnumbered?" She pulls up a chair and drops her cigarettes on the table.

Beryl pulls out Marlboro Lights. "I'll even it up."

Annie probably never smoked. It's hard to imagine her drunk: grade-school teacher, middle-aged, quiet. There's even a tiny cross around her neck. She stands. "What does everybody want?"

"Plain coffee, black," Evelyn says.

I ask for Coke, hand Annie a buck. Beryl gives her two and says, "Surprise me, babe."

"Does she always wear that cross?" I ask Beryl.

"I didn't notice. Probably. She and her lover go to the Metropolitan Community Church downtown. Every Sunday, without fail."

"Do you go to church?"

She snorts, lights a cigarette. "I go to meetings."

Evelyn says, "You know that AA has no religious affiliations."

I nod. "It's in the preamble. Only time I ever get to a Mass is when someone gets married."

"A recovering Catholic," Evelyn says. "Join the club. Half of the groups in St. Louis are CIA: Catholic, Irish, alcoholic."

Annie brings the drinks. Beryl's is carbonated and faintly gold, like ginger ale with cream. "Surprise."

Beryl sips, makes a face. "For sure. It's kind of like . . . I don't know. Licorice?"

"Anise-flavored Italian soda."

Evelyn grunts. "Good Lord."

"It's not so bad. Definitely different." Beryl sees me eyeing it, offers a sip.

"God." I chase the weird flavor with a gulp of Coke. A short, stocky Asian woman walks by and smiles at me. I nod; we've danced at Minerva, though I don't remember her name.

Annie asks me, "How do you like Lambda?"

"It's great. I had no idea there were gay and lesbian AA clubhouses. At most of the meetings, I feel like I'm from outer space."

"It's not really an AA clubhouse," Evelyn says. "There's no such thing. It's the same with those clubs downtown—the club rents space to twelve-step groups, but you can't have an AA club."

"Why not?"

"Tradition Seven says that AA groups aren't connected with the facility where they meet, in order to avoid problems with money or control from outside influences."

Annie has to get home, so Beryl gives me a ride. I keep expecting her to say something about all the stupid shit that went down at the Garden, but she doesn't mention it.

The phone's ringing as I come in. Angie must be gone, though her car's here.

"Terry? It's Holly."

All right. "Hey, girl, what's up?"

"Erica Schneider told me you're staying with Angela. Willow gave me the number."

"I didn't know you knew Erica."

"Yeah, she was at the bar last night, being her usual charming self. She said you spent a whole day helping her move last month, that you didn't know it was going to be her stuff until you got there."

"I didn't have any idea. I wouldn't have done it; I thought I was moving Brenda. Willow."

"She thought it was funny," Holly says.

"She would. I can be a bitch sometimes, but Erica . . ."

"You're just a soft bitch. Erica's a stone bitch."

I laugh. "True."

"Anyway, I called to ask if you're going to play soccer again Saturday. Missed you last week."

"Well, Holly, last week was rough." I consider my cast—I'm not a goalie. "I'll be there this time."

"Maybe we can go out afterward."

"Sounds good. See you Saturday." I haven't time to rearrange my face before Angie's in the hallway, smirking.

"Who's Holly?" she asks.

"A friend of mine from high school."

"Really. Is she gay?"

"How would I know? She likes soccer."

"And you're going to play this weekend? Girl, you've been in so much pain, you haven't even looked for work." She reaches for my cast, and I step back.

"I'll look when I get my car. Besides, you don't play soccer with your hands." I fake an aerial kick. "What are you doing? The place is like a tomb. I thought you were out."

The hallway light comes on. "Sharon was helping me hang new curtains in my room." Angie says.

"Right." Whacker and I leave them to their privacy.

Every time I go visit Mom and Pop, I want to wear some queer T-shirt. I know better; in high school a simple gold hoop in my right ear inspired much contention.

"Why are you wearing one earring? What does that mean?"

"Nothing, Mom. I lost the other one."

"Then don't wear any. Wear some of mine."

"No!"

It's getting chilly for a T-shirt anyway; I bypass the Lesbian Avengers pile and slip on a purple and bronze striped rugby, dab on patchouli and some vanilla lip balm.

Alecki shows up with a head full of hair extensions, long narrow black braids. He and Angie look like twins; Mom won't even notice the cast on my hand. "Hurry up," he says. "I told them we'd come for dinner."

"Alecki! What were you thinking?"

"Free food, draga. She can cook."

I can't complain; at least he's going with me. And I'll get my car back, finally. Mom will ask for proof that I have my license again. The notice is in my jacket pocket.

In the car, Alecki asks if I told her about my hand.

"Listen," I tell him. "I hurt my hand at work, cutting a limb off a tree. Don't say anything about the other night." Alecki's been covering for me since he was eleven, I was twelve, and I drank four of Grandpa's beers and threw up on their carport.

At the doorway, Mom gasps. "Oh dear God, son, what have you done with your head?"

He pats his cranium. "It's still there."

First time I've been home in a year. "Hi, Mom."

She looks at the cast, shakes her head. "So can you wash your hair?" she asks Alecki.

Dinner's OK, Polish sausage and sauerkraut and fried apples. Alecki tells about his poetry reading in a coffeehouse the other night. Someone opened the back door when the place got too smoky, and a squirrel got in and ran across the stage.

"I was saying 'Sorrow clotted in my throat, sadness muted my reply' and the damn thing went for the bar stool and climbed me like a tree. I let out a shriek, threw poems everywhere. Then I couldn't stop giggling. Pretty much spoiled 'Suicide Love.'"

Pop asks about my hand. I repeat the tree limb story.

"What are you doing for money?" Mom asks.

"I'm OK for now. They laid me off so I could draw unemployment."

"That's nice," she says, and starts clearing the table. I don't offer to help; it's hard to wash dishes one-handed. Pop retires to the bathroom with the *Post-Dispatch*, so I go check out my car.

It's a thirty-year-old maroon Mustang of classic vintage, well-kept but a little worse for wear. Two small dents mar the driver's door and there's a scratch on the hood; despite consistent waxing, pinprick rust spots seep from the chrome bumpers. I have missed my car, though.

I bundle the tarp, throw it in the trunk. It's empty except for the jack and a clean new spare tire. I haven't driven since the night I got the DWI. The next day Alecki drove the car over here. It'll be strange, getting used to a car again. In Weston, I lived downtown, walked to work, to the store, to the bar. Coming back to St. Louis with Angela, with the worst hangover of my life, I felt like we were moving too fast.

When I slide into the seat, the smell takes me back—dust, oil, and a thousand coats of Armor All. The steering wheel and gearshift knob are cold, harder than I remember. The Mustang used to be an extension of me, but tonight it feels skittish. I fire up the engine; it starts right up, throbbing low out of the dual exhausts. I look to the kitchen; I ought to go say good-bye. Instead I burn out in reverse and head to Angie's.

The Mustang finds its way to the soccer fields. If I don't watch it, the car will drive habitually to Minerva or Sappho's. I doff my tennis shoes, loosely tie my cleats. Still don't have much grip on the right. Jeri and Meredith are doing a passing drill.

"Hey, Terry." Holly's stretching on the sidelines. "I'm glad to see you here. You and Jeri carry the team by yourselves."

"No way. Not without our defense."

Holly switches legs, her muscular thighs taut with the stretch. She gets up and saunters over. When she spots the cast, she frowns. "What happened to your arm?"

I shrug. "Rough week."

"Manescu!" Jeri drills one, straight at my head. I leap up, do a chest trap and boot it back. She bellows "Yes!" and runs the ball back down the field.

"Jesus," Holly says, "I thought your face was gone."

"Telepathy."

She laughs. Comes closer, touches the dark blue fiberglass. It matches my shorts.

A whack on my butt makes me jump. "Christy!"

"Come on, Killer, let's play. Nice cast." Christy takes off running; Holly and I chase her down to where Jeri has the ball.

We play a solid game. The other club is not real tight. Like us, they don't have uniforms or a sponsor. Unlike us, they must not have a history.

Once we're well ahead I get a little flashy, take some chances. Jeri passes close to the goal, too near their fullback. I dive and slide like I'm stretching for a base, kick the ball right into the goal from the ground.

The fullback leaps over me; I'd have taken her out like a bowling pin. I roll to my feet, slap Christy five. My hand throbs; it'll be killing me tonight.

"Hot dog," Jeri says.

"Not me."

We win readily, 6-1. Christy wants to go to the bar, but I talk them into pasta first. Jeri likes this little place on South Grand. They can get drinks if they want. I'll have Coke. It's not too fancy; we can go in our shorts and sweatshirts.

We ride together in Jeri's car, Holly and I in the back. Christy asks about my hand; I say I broke it at work.

"Your fingers are swollen," Holly says. She reaches across my lap, spreads my fingers gently. The middle two especially are puffy, mottled and blue. It hurts when she moves them, but I don't mind.

"I need to elevate it."

"You need to quit rolling in the dirt," Christy says.

"That was great." Jeri looks at me in the rearview mirror. "It was a shit pass. I thought 'there's no way she'll get that,' and you blasted it."

"Defense played really well today," I tell Holly.

"We're coming along," Christy replies. "You should have been there last week, Manescu. Those girls were good; they hammered on us. They made three goals, but me and Holly must have blocked twenty shots apiece."

"Because we didn't have our front line," Holly says. "I never see the ball when Terry and Jeri are there."

The restaurant lives up to Jeri's press. We get there early, a quarter to five; except for a middle-aged couple sipping wine, we're the only table. The two servers could be sisters: dark-haired slender girls with Mediterranean faces, not yet blossomed into the fullness of Italian physique. They wear red aprons over their jeans, red pocket T-shirts; they slouch and chew gum by the kitchen, then come to our table with smiles. I want to take one home—I don't care which.

The wall sports a wild scarlet mural of ancient Rome, highlighted with lurid touches of black and green. There's the Coliseum, and gladiators, chariots and horse soldiers, lions and Christians. Next to my elevated forearm crouch Romulus and Remus, unattractively nursing what appears, in this rendition, to be a jackal. Despite the barbaric display, I'm starved. I order tortellini; unlike spaghetti or fettuccini, I can eat it left-handed.

It's hard to be cool with one elbow propped on the table, hand stuck straight up. Jeri, bless her, cuts my salad smaller and pushes it back without a word.

The pasta's fresh and tender, not mushy. The tortellini comes with prosciutto and peas, the right touch of garlic. Holly has spaghetti. She winds a coil around her fork and feeds it to me: chunks of fresh vegetables, the sauce is aromatic and bold. For dessert, Christy gets a strawberry gelato; Jeri and I split a piece of cheesecake. Holly orders an espresso con panna, whipped cream to tame the bitter bite. It smells good; she gets me one, too.

Jeri's going to see Rita, her cop; they don't go out. Christy and Holly vote for the bar. I beg off, say I need to prop up my hand. The truth is, right now I feel too good to go out. These girls could get me into trouble. So could our doe-eyed waitress, with her long black lashes.

Jeri drops me off. Angie's not home. She's probably out with Sharon, who called earlier. I flop on the sofa, tired, dirty, and stuffed. I place a pillow across my chest, to raise my throbbing hand. It's still swollen, but not so blue. Whacker pounds the pillow with his front paws, purring his effusive greeting. I tell him about Holly, how she fed me spaghetti and gave me her number. I'll call tomorrow, see if she wants to go out next weekend.

That noise. Distant, but approaching—one, two, three, four. I wake with a start. The phone. What time is it? Whacker grunts and jumps to the floor. I rub my eyes, rediscover the fiberglass cast. Sit up and find the clock; it's 9:45.

I get a Coke from the fridge, take the phone back to the sofa. Bill's on the voice mail: "Just wondered if you're all right. I haven't seen you for a couple days; I thought you'd be at the Saturday meeting tonight. Laura's wondering about you, too." Shit, the meeting's over. I went to Ladue Chapel last night, but Bill wasn't there. Laura never goes to Ladue; I guess I haven't seen her since last Sunday. We're supposed to meet at her house tomorrow.

I call, but Laura's not home yet; I leave a message that I skipped the meeting because my hand was bothering me. In the morning I'll come over to discuss the steps. At least I don't have to ask her for a ride.

Sunday I get up early; I had plenty of sleep. It's a pretty autumn day, dew on the trees and maples turning gold and red. I slip on my running shoes and start a slow jog, about two miles. At first my hand aches in the cold. It's a little swollen when I get home. Still, it's good to move.

I fix some coffee and take an awkward shower, hand held high like the Statue of Liberty. If I dropped the soap, I'd just have to do without. When I come back downstairs, the coffee's almost gone. Sharon's sitting at the breakfast table in Angie's robe. "Morning, Sharon."

She smiles her shy, gap-toothed smile, salutes me with her coffee. She must have enjoyed her stay.

"There's a message for you," Angie says. She's frying some eggs. I reach behind her and pop the scorching toast. "Oh. Thanks." She begins scraping the toast over the sink; I shut off the flame beneath the congealing eggs. "You want me to fix you something?"

Sharon and I grin, conspirators. "I don't think so, Angie. I'm going to Laura's."

I'm not, though; the voice mail says she went to Sunday School this morning. "Call me later." I wonder if she's upset that I missed the meeting. She attends that home group with superstitious regularity.

I leave two messages, but Laura doesn't call back until after I've returned from a six p.m. meeting. "Hey, Laura."

"Terry. I haven't seen you in some time."

"I've been going to different meetings this week."

"How do you mean 'different'?"

"They're AA meetings," I say. "I've been going to the Lambda Club."

"Where's that?"

"By Lafayette Square. It's a gay and lesbian twelve-step club. Like the 4522 club in the Central West End, but smaller."

"I've been wondering about you," Laura says. "I didn't know whether to expect you this morning, since I haven't seen you."

"I'm doing OK. Been going to meetings; tomorrow I'll check into getting unemployment."

"You're not looking for work?"

"I picked up some applications—nothing promising. I'm not in a hurry."

There's a long pause; her lighter snaps out a flame. "But you're doing OK?"

"Yeah."

"You don't have a job, you've missed your home group for two straight weeks, we haven't talked since Sunday, and you have a week sober." Her voice is clipped. "You're going to these club meetings, some special interest group . . ."

"I like the Lambda Club. People don't look at me like I'm from Mars."

She quotes Tradition Three, " 'The only requirement for membership is a desire to stop drinking.' If you start thinking that you're different from any other alcoholic, you're just looking for an excuse for why the program won't work for you. You're an alcoholic, Terry. That's all."

"I'm a lesbian, too." My fist clenches around the phone. "At least at this place, I feel like I've got a shot at recovery. Laura, I'm not shy, but I don't like to talk at meetings. I can't relate. These people have their own stories to tell, and they weren't forged in a gay bar. I just don't think I'm in the right place. Someday soon, things are going to have to change for me. Whether that means I'm done with drinking and bars, I don't know. But I can't take too many more weekends like the last one, and I don't want to go back to treatment. I don't want to go to jail. If Lambda is going to help me stay sober, then that's where I'll go."

"OK." Another pause. "If that's where you're going to go to meetings, maybe that's where you should get a sponsor."

Bitch. "Maybe it is."

"All right. Good luck."

"Yeah. See you around." Nice. I finally get serious about the program and my sponsor dumps me. Sometimes AA is just bullshit.

It's ten o'clock Monday morning. I didn't even hear Angela leave. I walk to the St. Louis Bread Company, have a croissant and two free refills of coffee. The complimentary *Post-Dispatch* provides a copy of the want ads. I mark a couple of retail positions; I've got to give Angie some money sometime.

Down the street, Kinko's is a hotbed of activity. It looks like an anthill, with people three deep at the counter and the copy machines flaring and yawning open. I take an application, but they're not hiring.

On the sidewalk out front, right next to the newspaper machine, is a neatly rolled joint. I look around; there's no one close. Is it a decoy? Will I pick it up and get busted for possession?

Someone reached into a pocket for change to buy the *Post-Dispatch* and unwittingly dislodged this little number. I don't need this, I don't even want it, but I can't seem to leave it here. I could take it to Alecki; he smokes every so often. I could walk away.

I don't. I stare at it, wonder how good it is, what kind of leaf, what color. *God, grant me the Serenity to accept the things I cannot change, Courage to change the things I can* . . . My right foot, sudden conduit of divine intervention, strikes across the joint. The paper shreds, pale green and gold leaf spreads to the winds. Is this working a program? I hurry to the house; make some calls, get the car.

Applying for unemployment takes forever, filling out the forms left-handed. I thought about asking for help, but it's simpler to do it myself. Then I get to the interview and find out I'm not even eligible—I didn't work there long enough.

I cruise down to the Central West End, pick up applications from a record shop, gay bookstore, health food market. The ice cream place is out; I can't scoop one-handed. I don't like retail, but it's the wrong time of year to be working outdoors. I'll have this cast on until nearly Christmas.

Having gathered a few applications, I stop at a used bookstore. The musty secondhand odor brings a surge of melancholy—Cole worked at a place like this in Weston. I mess around in biography awhile, head to the fiction section. I pick up a Barbara Kingsolver paperback for myself, then get a book of Nikki Giovanni's poetry for Angela. I really do appreciate her allowing me to stay. I'll stick a chicken and some potatoes in the oven for dinner, settle on the couch with my book until she gets home.

A blonde in a ball cap is selling back some books. She looks like another friend of mine from Weston, but Jane never read much. I position myself at the end of a row to watch her.

Not Jane, but she's definitely a dyke. She scowls at the owner's offer, seizes back one book. The rest she drops onto the counter; she takes her credit and stalks out past a group of high school Goths by the door.

At the counter, I fork over $12.50. It seems high for used books. Two boys and two girls come in; the girls wear black lipstick and black fingernail polish. All four of them look like they dyed their hair with shoe polish. The owner counts my change, watching them. "I don't need a bag," I say.

"All right. Come again." He cranes his neck; I smell cigarette smoke. "Hey! You'll have to take that outside, please!" He starts around the counter. I lay my books on the blonde's, stroll out with the stack. At the car, I check my haul. One by Amy Tan, an Alice Walker that I've already read, and *Pillow Talk II,* an anthology of lesbian erotica. Sounds promising.

Angie likes the poetry, appreciates the chicken dinner, but she bitches about the stack of dirty dishes I left. I don't care. I'm not doing dishes one-handed. By eight o'clock, I need a meeting.

There's a mixed meeting at Lambda; the chairperson, Camille, has long curling chestnut hair, full lips, and big blue eyes. She's gorgeous, an effect diminished by her nasal drawl. "I was thinking that maybe I might want the topic of this meeting to be sex . . ." Long silence; it isn't clear whether she's done talking or is just waiting for someone to rescue her. "Well, I was sober for awhile, but I was living with this person, and she kept using. I knew she was, but I stayed there anyway. Then I started using, too. I've got three months now, since I moved out, but she called me the other night and I went over there. I know better. She makes me crazy, but sometimes I don't want to spend the night by myself. That's all."

Really long silence. One by one, all turn to the wiry gray-haired woman. Her dark eyes almost disappear in the wrinkles of her smile. "Is it my turn? My name's Evelyn, and I'm an alcoholic."

"Hi, Evelyn." Definite relief in the chorus.

"Sex is a tough one. It was tough when I was twenty and weighed one-twenty, and it hasn't gotten any easier since all my parts headed the wrong direction and at night I put my teeth in a glass.

"For a long time, I used sex to, if you'll pardon the expression, fill that hole. If it wasn't sex, it was booze or pills or overwork. I've never been troubled by compulsive overeating, but some people turn to that. But the emptiness persists. It's a spiritual affliction, and it requires spiritual remedies: prayer, meditation, working with others. The thing that's worked for me is the Twelve Steps.

"Having had a spiritual awakening doesn't mean you'll never feel alone or empty. It does mean you have some tools of the program to deal with your pain. I'm grateful today to have these tools at my disposal. Thanks for the topic, Camille; you're brave tonight."

The next speaker is a young guy. He went to a club two weeks ago, did some amyl nitrate with a friend, then they left together. "I didn't drink. I don't consider it a slip. I don't know if I'd do it again." He takes a quick sip of coffee; his hands shake, and it spills on his shirt.

Evelyn says, "Thanks, Jeff. Keep coming back." He shoves back his chair, stalks to the kitchen. Through the sliver of open doorway, I see he pulled off his shirt to rinse it.

I'm tense, waiting for a pause. It comes, and I blurt out my name, then take a deep breath during the response. "I got drunk a week and a half ago, the day I lost my job. I got canned and . . ." I glance up and falter; Beryl's eyes are on mine. "Then I just . . . then I . . . I don't know, I took off walking. Ran into someone I knew a long time ago. We ended up drunk, and I slept with her. It was weird. It was a mess. I never liked her to begin with. But she said 'let's go,' and I went. At least I didn't hit her. But I broke my hand. So I'm starting over. I like this meeting, though. I just have a long way to go." Shit. That didn't make any sense. I ought to keep my mouth shut.

Evelyn says, "Keep coming back, Terry." This time, she smiles.

After the meeting, Portia and Camille empty ashtrays and gather the cups from the seats and the floor. Evelyn gestures to the big silver coffee urn. "Help me out, kiddo."

"Sure." I grab one side, she gets the other. We haul the heavy pot to the kitchen and lift it into the sink. Evelyn disassembles the percolator; she hands me the grounds and I dump them in the trash. "Evelyn, do you meditate?"

She laughs, a raspy bark. "Yeah, I meditate. I don't sit cross-legged and contemplate my navel, but I do take some quiet time every so often. Probably not enough." She runs hot water in the sink, indicates a dish towel. "You on Step Eleven?"

"Not even close. I've just been thinking about it. My last sponsor gave me a meditation book, but I'm not too crazy about it. I don't like the idea of being told what to pray or think."

"You sound like an alcoholic. That's the great thing about this program, though; you can pretty much work it any way you want, as long as you don't drink." Evelyn washes the cups and ashtrays, I stack them in the dish drainer.

"I'm starting to figure out that part of it, at least. Don't drink and go to meetings. Work the steps in order."

"That's a good start," she says. "Who's your sponsor now?"

I swallow hard. "I was wanting to ask you about that. I need a sponsor."

She nods. "I wondered why you got this sudden urge to do the dishes. I gave you my number, right? You got a car?"

"Just got it back."

"Pick me up for the meeting Tuesday. It's an early one; we'll talk more afterward. Call me before then."

"Sure. Thanks."

"Got to go." She indicates Portia, in the smoking lounge. "My Monday ride."

A melancholy smell of distant burning leaves suffuses the clear night, escorts me to my car. I hadn't expected to talk tonight, and I sure didn't think I would find a sponsor so fast. I must be in the right place.

"You don't need me to tell you what to do," Evelyn says. "I can tell you what I used to do, or what works for me today, but I can't take responsibility for your decisions, and I don't give advice."

I shift in the booth, draw my knees up and cross my legs. Evelyn said she was tough. When I asked Laura to sponsor me, I got schedules and rules. Evelyn sounds more like a guide than a baby-sitter. "I can think for myself," I say. "But at some of the meetings, they act like you have to ask your sponsor before you wipe your ass or you'll get drunk."

"A lot of people stay sober on fear," Evelyn says. "They suffered a lot, and they don't want to go back. They try to intimidate everyone else, because that's their way. I happen to think there's a better way. If I stay sober, it's because I like it. I like the way I am today better than when I was drinking."

I think of a dance floor, green felt pool tables, everyone's eyes upon me. "I liked the way I was before, too. Did you ever go to the bars?"

She laughs, her smoker's rasp. "Sure I did. It was the only way to find anybody; we didn't parade around in gay pride T-shirts or hang colored rings in our ears. I liked the bars, sometimes; I just didn't like myself. If you're so happy with your life, how come you're going to AA?"

I fidget with a piece of loose Formica at the edge of the table, trying to disregard an abrupt memory of Cole. "I don't know; it just seemed like everything went to shit overnight. It's not getting any better since I've been sober, either. In the last two months I've lost my job, alienated my best friend, broken my hand . . ."

"Did you *stay* sober?"

"No." She really is tough. "I got drunk once, when I got fired."

Evelyn laughs again, that gritty snort. "Well, kiddo, it takes more than just showing up at the meetings. You've got to want it, and you've got to work at it. You've got to be willing to go to any lengths."

The length of table edge snaps off in my hand; I stuff it between the seat cushion and the wall. "Yeah. I guess I'm getting a little more teachable."

Evelyn nods, lights another cigarette. "How long since you drank?"

"About two weeks."

"You seeing anybody?"

"Sort of. This girl Holly, that I knew in high school."

"Sleeping with her?"

"This weekend will be the first time we go out alone." Here it comes.

Evelyn shakes her head. "I can't tell you what to do; I haven't been with anybody in over three years. But that will get in your way quicker than anything. You need to focus on yourself right now. Get to meetings, get involved in AA. I don't care what you do with Holly, but make sure you've got your priorities straight."

Priorities. I used to be clear on that—work a little, make enough to get by. Stay in shape, go out, spend time with my friends. "I want to make AA a priority. But the longest time I've ever gone without sex is probably two months." I reach for my Coke, but it's empty. "You've gone three years?"

"It's been as much as seven," she says. "What are you, twenty-five?"

"Twenty-six."

"You're probably sitting there wondering why I would want to have sex anyway. Let me tell you, it may slow down but it doesn't go away." She grinds out her cigarette, hard.

"I hope I've still got it going when I'm your age, Evelyn." She's going to ask.

"How old do you think I am?"

"I don't know. Fifty-two, maybe."

"Listen to that. Are you Irish?"

"Romanian."

"I'm sixty-eight."

"I can't believe that."

"Lay off, Terry. This is an honest program." She goes to the counter and gets refills on her coffee and my Coke. I must have made some points. "You know the recommendation is to forgo sex your first year. There are solid reasons for it. For one thing, getting romantically involved takes up so much time and energy that a lot of us lose sight of everything else."

"I've got plenty of energy," I offer.

"I'll bet you do. But your program has got to come first. And that brings up another good reason. A lot of us used sex to fill the empty spaces inside. It's like another drug, something that makes a difference when you don't feel good about yourself. If that's your pattern—and it was mine, when I could make it work—then you need to realize that your emptiness is a spiritual deficit. It requires spiritual remediation."

"Working the steps is a spiritual process." This is getting heavy, especially when I'm going to ask the biggest crush of my life to have dinner this weekend. "I've started that already."

"And that's good. That's where you need to be. But you don't ever get done with the steps. And sex—it's too bad it can be such a bad thing, because it can be such a good thing, too." Evelyn looks at her watch, drains her cup. "I need you to take me home. Give yourself a chance, Terry. It can't hurt anything to take it slow."

There's a message from Holly when I get home. I call her right back. Jeri was right; Holly holds classes at Dynamo, the most exclusive gym in St. Louis. Some of the Blues hockey players work out there in the off-season; the masseuse counts Rams and Cardinals among his clientele. It's owned by Kurt and Frank Hammerschlager. They were hot-shot high school wrestlers; I remember them from when my big brother Marius used to wrestle. I always wanted to work out at Dynamo, but it's expensive.

"We have free trial workouts," Holly tells me. "You could come in and talk to Frank."

"A trial workout would be great. Do we have to set it up through Frank, though? Can't you just show me around?"

"I don't guess it would make any difference," she says. I arrange to stop by the gym in the morning.

Holly teaches a nine o'clock class on Monday-Wednesday-Friday. The aerobics floor is huge, with an observation deck on the second floor. The room used to be a bank of three racquetball courts; the intervening partitions have been removed. Mirrors encase the lower half of the room; higher up, the white walls are still marked with oblique ball prints. The floor is glossy wood that ricochets the deafening blast of aerobics music.

The class is only seven women, but the modest turnout doesn't daunt Holly. She's bouncing and pumping, sweating and exhorting, just like she did along the football fields at St. Thomas. Looking good, too. When she sees me, she waves without missing a step, then cranks the housewives and second-shift workers into high gear. Droplets of sweat fly from the ends of her bangs.

After the cool down, one of the ladies wipes her flushed face with a towel. "Holy shit, Holly," she says. "What got into you today?"

Holly laughs. "I was stoked." She's looking at her reflection.

"You looked good," I tell her. "How did you get to be an instructor?"

"Lots of classes," she says. "I took a lot of aerobics before I even thought about being a teacher." She shows me around the facility as she explains the certification process, the importance of safety and intensity, how to use the heart rate charts.

Holly works the desk when she's not teaching. If I come in and show her my driver's license, she could get me through by entering her own membership number. The cast limits me, but I could use the cardiovascular equipment. Many of the resistance machines have forearm pads instead of grips; I might be able to do some light weights. I'll see how the date goes first, broach the subject afterward.

We firm up plans for the weekend. The game will be our next-to-last one of the season and shouldn't be too tough. Good thing, since I won't have a chance to clean up afterward. Holly and I will go to her place and change, then hit a Mexican restaurant down the street. She suggests "a movie or something" after dinner. Normally I'd pick "something," but I'm supposed to pray for guidance first.

Saturday I heed my priorities with a noon AA meeting. Afterward, I press my carefully selected casual outfit and hang it in the backseat of the Mustang. Ironing is my ritual; I always press my clothes before I go out. My little brother Andrei washes and waxes his truck. Alecki is the worst; he showers, shaves and dresses, polishes his shoes, and then cleans house like our seventy-two-year-old grandmother. Once I caught him using the edge of a cleaning rag to wipe between the buttons of the phone.

The game is at four-thirty. As predicted, it's a total rout. Fun, though; Jeri, Meredith and I pull off some neatly choreographed ball work. I'm always at my best with an audience, and Holly's definitely looking. Afterward Christy wants to go out, but I had enlisted Jeri's assistance in advance. She distracts Christy, and I whisk Holly away without explanation.

At the restaurant, I take Holly's jacket and pull her chair out for her. Good start—I didn't have to fight a waiter for possession of the chair.

Holly raises her eyebrows, but sits. "Thank you."

"Of course." When the waitress comes, I order a Coke and Holly gets a Busch on tap. When she's glanced at the menu, I ask what she's having.

"I think the chicken chimichanga; I love them. Their hot sauce here is great—kind of a green chili and tomatillo base."

"Sounds good." When the waitress returns, I order for us both: two chimichangas and a refill of Coke. Until my refill comes, I clutch the empty wet glass. I haven't been stone sober on a date, ever. "Holly, when did you start playing soccer?"

"Growing up, we were always kicking the ball around. In grade school, I played in gym class. I was never that good; I just play to get out with the girls."

"In high school you weren't much into sports. Not as a participant, anyway."

"I was into being what my mom and dad wanted." She heaves a mock sigh. "Go ahead, say it. I was a cheerleader."

"You were a credit to your kind." The waitress places chips and salsa before me. I wait for Holly to take a portion.

"So were you. You never came out in class or anything, but you didn't hide who you were. I always noticed when you were in my classes."

Probably because I sat so close, giving thanks for the alphabetic proximity of Manescu and O'Brien. "Was I obvious?"

She smirks. "You were Coach's pet."

"She was a big old dyke, wasn't she? We did get pretty close." I can smell Holly's beer; I take a quick sip of Coke and dig into the chips.

"How close?"

"I had a crush on her. She bought me some beer, we talked. But my social life surely didn't compare with that of the head cheerleader."

"I only dated two guys. You went out with more than that."

"I went to dances and stuff, games, with some different guys. Mostly we got loaded. You dated that basketball player, Joel. Were you checking out the foot-size theory?"

"It doesn't mean much in a high school boy. I went out because they asked me. Boys ask, you go. That's how it worked at St. Thomas."

"It worked better if one was not a lovesick lesbian, with a tendency to get drunk and bawl sophomoric French poetry at pretty girls."

Holly turns a charming shade of pink. I love to watch a redhead blush. A memory of Cole intrudes; the arrival of our order saves me from maudlin reminiscence. I get a fresh Coke. Holly's still sipping at her beer. "You're not going to have one?" she asks.

"No. I'm not drinking anymore."

"Really. You don't drink at all?"

"No. It was getting out of hand, so I quit." The chimichangas arrive, and we eat in silence for awhile. Now Holly's switched to water. Sober dating: awkward, or merely uncomfortable?

Finally she asks, "Did you play soccer in college?"

"I played softball at Meramec, softball and soccer at St. Louis University. I tried out for soccer in Kirksville, but was on suspension before I ever played. I've played rugby on and off ever since I lived with Erica."

"I used to love to watch you play soccer. You were as good as anyone on the boys' team."

"Don't ever say that in front of Andrei."

"Girl, you were quicker than Andrei, and you had all the moves." She smiles, blushes again. "You've still got the moves." She reaches for a tortilla chip, knocks over the substantial remains of her beer. Foam gushes into my lap. "Shit. Guess I don't."

I blot myself with a napkin, to little effect. It looks like I wet my pants, and I smell like the Anheuser-Busch plant. "Don't worry, they'll dry."

"Terry, they're cotton slacks. They'll be soggy all night. Aren't you cold?"

"Yeah."

"Let's run by my house and throw them in the dryer. We can still catch the show."

She abandons the soggy remains of her chimi; there's nothing that looks worse than a half-eaten plate of Mexican food swimming in beer. The restaurant is only a matter of blocks from her apartment. Still, it's a good thing the Mustang has vinyl seats.

In her bathroom, I slip off my pants and hand them out through the door, feeling silly. The dryer's in the basement. I wrap a towel around my waist, hoping it will blot the remaining beer from my silky red underpants, and sit on the edge of the couch.

Holly's back in a minute. "The dryer's in use. I'll try my blow-dryer."

"Holly, let me do that." There's a damp spot on the sofa; I sit back down, fast.

"I insist. I was the one who doused you."

The stench of hot beer fills the apartment as Holly blasts the hairdryer into the crotch of my slacks. Head in hands, I wonder if my wet panties will soak through the khakis.

"Here. Are you OK?"

"I'm fine." Cold air hits my rear. I shiver, try backing into the bathroom. A faint butt-shape marks the couch cushion.

She advances on me, brandishes the blow-dryer. "Let's get you out of those wet things."

Drunk, I would go for it. It could be charming, allowing her to solicitously warm my buns with her little apparatus, then tuck it down the front of my drawers to get me good and dry . . . "I'll take that." I clamp my hand over the blow-dryer. Holly relinquishes it with a snicker. I flee to the bathroom, blast hot air into my sodden undies.

Properly attired, we end up at the late movie. Eat popcorn, drink Coke, rub knees. Touch hands briefly, mindful of the heteros. Sobriety, insipid as a Coke. After the movie we part with a chaste kiss, then another, more auspicious. I promise to show for the last soccer game next Saturday.

Angie and Sharon are on the couch at home, with candles burning. The TV's off for once; must be serious. I wave and pass without speaking.

Next morning, I'm first up. The smell of coffee draws Angela to the kitchen. "Terry, we need to talk."

"OK." I pour myself a cup, fix one for Angie, then butter a slice of toasted raisin bread. "Want some toast?"

"Not now." Angie picks up her mug, stares into it. "I know you and Holly went out last night."

Sleep has granted a little perspective; this morning, I can smile. "What a disaster."

Angela won't meet my eyes. "I need to ask you to move out."

My toast catches in my throat. "Why?"

"Terry, you know I think the world of you. I've bailed you out over and over, and when you're sober, you're fine. But you get around girls and you drink. You come in last night just reeking."

"Angie, that wasn't mine. Holly spilled her beer on me."

She holds up her hand before I'm halfway done. "I don't want to hear it. I wish I could believe you. But this isn't good for me, and living here isn't doing you any good either."

"Angie, you don't get it. I drank Coke all night. Worst date of my life. I didn't drink at all. If that's the way you want it, I'll move out, but I swear to God I didn't drink."

"Terry, I . . . Whatever. I can't be worrying about you. I need you to go, this weekend." She fixes coffee for Sharon, walks out.

I can't believe this shit. She's kicking me out because I had a lousy date. Whacker strolls in, looks at me. My hands shake as I gather him onto my lap and rub his head. What am I supposed to do now? I pick up the phone, dial Alecki.

"Hello."

The voice is wrong. "Evelyn?"

"Yes? Terry?"

"I'm sorry, I was trying to call my brother. I wasn't thinking, I called your number by accident."

"I've done that," she says. "You sound upset."

"No. I mean yeah." Start over. "Yes, I'm upset. I went out with Holly last night and it was a drag, we just went to dinner and a movie, and she spilled her beer on me at the restaurant. Now Angie thinks I've been drinking and lying about it. She wants me to move." There's no response at first; I wonder if I woke her.

"So you're not using, she just thinks you are?"

"Right. I smelled like beer, but it was Holly's. Angela is mad; I don't know if I can convince her any different."

"You know, people get used to us bullshitting them when we're drinking. It takes a long time to get that trust back. Didn't you tell me that Angie has a new relationship?"

"She's been seeing Sharon for a few weeks."

"Things happen for a reason," Evelyn says. "Maybe she just needs some space. You might consider moving out, then talking to Angie when you've got a little more time under your belt."

"Maybe. I'm not inclined to talk to her now."

"Give it some time. Do you have a place to go?"

"I guess I'll move in with Lex, if he'll have me. He'll let me slide a little if I'm short."

"Lex is your brother, right? Does he use?"

"Espresso, more than anything. Drinks a little when he's out with his friends. He smoked some dope in school, mostly with me."

"Does he keep stuff in the house?"

"Maybe some wine."

"Do what you need to. You can't expect other people to understand alcoholism, but he's your brother, maybe he'll work with you. You tell him what you need."

"I will, Evelyn. Thanks."

"Hang in there, kiddo. See you tomorrow."

"Yeah." I hang up, dial with more attention. Whacker wakens with a grunt, hops from my lap. "Good morning."

"Terry?" Alecki sounds groggy. "Draga, what's up?"

"You mind living with a crazy black cat?" I wince at the pause; maybe I've used him up, too.

"Not as long as you come with him. You moving today?"

"You know me too well. I'll explain when I get there. I don't know when, maybe noon."

"Cool. See you."

This will be the third place I've lived this year. Not much survived the last move: my cat, two suitcases of clothes, a tackle box of hand tools, two Pevely Dairy crates of books. The dumbbells and my juggling balls. I have to make about a dozen trips, carrying everything left-handed. All my stuff fits into the trunk of the Mustang with room to spare.

I shove the toothpaste and shampoo into my backpack, spitefully—I bought the last round. The kitty kennel will go last, in the passenger seat. Angie and Sharon stay in the bedroom.

When everything is loaded but Whacker, I pour one last cup of coffee. The shower is running. Try washing your hair, my friend. On the counter, I place my key and a note—*Thanks for everything. I'm staying with Alecki. I really wasn't using. I know you have no reason to trust me, and I don't blame you for not wanting to live like that. But I was sober last night. Call me sometime. Best Wishes, Terry.*

I'm not sure whether Alecki believes me, but at least he'll let me stay. He's been considering a roommate anyway; his friend Rodney moved out in August to share an apartment with his girlfriend. Alecki unloads the car for me, provides a repainted ancient dresser for my clothes. There's the twin bed that Rodney left when he got a better offer. The mattress has no more than the usual number of stains, but I have Alecki flip it. He roots through my crate of books, snags *Leaves of Grass* and settles on the sofa.

I sit on the mattress, survey my belongings. When I lived in Weston, I got some furniture from the Salvation Army store. My drinking buddy Jane had a pickup; we loaded up the back for about sixty dollars. I found some fabric on sale, a burgundy on navy paisley print that looked like boxer shorts or neckties; bought the rest of the roll and draped it for curtains, stapled it over the ugly old sofa and love seat. It looked pretty cool when I was done. When I moved, though, I just left it—a ton of books, all my furniture, the secondhand stereo. Now my worldly possessions fit in the trunk of my car, with room left over.

I get a Coke, join Alecki. "Any house rules?"

"Whacker poops in the litter pan; you go in the bathroom." He lights a Salem, offers me one.

"No, thanks. I'm off it."

"Good. Maybe I'll quit again. How about you? Can I drink in the house?" He catches my hesitation. "Talk to me, draga. I've got to know, or I can't help."

"Right now it would be hard."

He shrugs. "I don't much anyway."

Alecki doesn't get much exercise. The suitcases did him in. I sweep the floor, take out the trash while he lounges on the sofa with Whitman.

"I haven't looked at this in ages," he says. "The guy is intense."

"Yeah. He writes too much about his dick, maybe."

"Terry, if you had one you'd be writing poems to it, too. Listen to this, though." He reads aloud from "Songs of Experience" and "Song of Myself." Soon I'm sitting on the floor, leaned against his leg, picking out pieces I love.

"This is just like being back in high school," Alecki says.

"Without the dope, though."

"I can do poetry without pot. Thanks for sweeping. You can't wash dishes, can you?"

"Not really."

"How about going to the grocery store for me? The list's on the counter; it's not a lot. I'll cook."

"Deal. Soon as I finish my Coke."

There's a big pot of rice almost done when I get back. I drop the empty grocery bag on the kitchen floor, put the veggies in the fridge and the cereal in the cabinets. When I reach for the bag, it bulges, makes a scrabbling sound. Stupid cat; I fall for it every time.

I poke the bag with my toe and Whacker bangs back with his paw. Finally he's too wound up to be further contained; he shoots into the air, a jack-in-the-box freed, mouth wide like a laugh. His rear feet strike in place three times before he gets some traction and races down the hallway.

The phone rings. Alecki gets it, but it's for me. "Turn down the stereo," I yell. Alecki just laughs, so I take the extension to the limits of its cord. I like R.E.M., but I like to hear a phone call, too.

"Hey, kiddo. How's it going?"

"Evelyn? How'd you find me?"

"I found Alecki Manescu in the phone book. Beryl knew your last name."

She had to write it down enough. "I'm OK, I guess. I didn't have much to move. I've only been in St. Louis since August."

"Everything OK with your brother?"

"Lex is cool; we get along."

"Going to the meeting tonight?"

"Lambda? I could. Do you want a ride?"

"I'd like one; thanks. Hang in there, kiddo; you're doing all right."

A sponsor that calls me; the AA police might revoke her license.

Alecki is an easy roommate. He doesn't work much, three or four days a week painting interiors with Andrei. Most days, he sleeps until ten o'clock, then reads, writes, listens to music. He doesn't even have a TV. Evenings he goes out with Susan, his on-and-off girlfriend, or stays half the night at coffeehouses, doing readings and talking with his anarchist poet friends.

Until I run out of cash, I'm not that eager for a job myself. This seems like a good opportunity to work the Steps, go to meetings, get to know my sponsor.

I reviewed the First Step with Laura, before she fired me. *We admitted we were powerless over alcohol—that our lives had become unmanageable.* At the hospital, in the women's rest room, I reached an understanding of powerlessness. I can't drink anymore; I am Mirela Theresa Manescu, alcoholic. If I don't drink, who am I?

After the meeting I ask Evelyn about it. "All the things I like about myself are linked with drinking—dancing, pool, rugby, softball. Spending time with my friends. I met almost all my lovers at the bar. Going out with Holly, what are we supposed to do? If I stay sober—and I don't see that I have much choice—it's like there's nothing left of me. I don't even know who I am."

"That I'll buy," she says. "You *don't* know who you are. You're about to find out. This takes time, Terry. Give yourself a chance. If you can't stand who you become in AA, you can always drink again. You'll get back your old self and more."

"But it wasn't all bad."

"No, it wasn't. You could get a lot worse," she says. "You don't have to, if you stay sober. And those things you miss will still be there. You may find that you can go back to all of it and not need the booze. For now, though, it would be smart to concentrate on your program."

The waitress here is such a babe, but I didn't mean for Holly to catch me eyeing her. We're having lunch at Jeri's favorite restaurant, the Italian one with the mural.

"Tell me about your last girlfriend," Holly says.

Good idea. I stuff a big wad of salad into my mouth and chew it slowly, looking apologetic. "She was nice. She was an artist." She sketched me, mostly. The dark-haired server walks by and I stop her. "Could you bring us more breadsticks, please?"

She looks at the basket, back to me. "More?"

"These are cold." She takes them. "Now I wish I'd gotten the lasagna. I'm hungrier than I thought."

"What was her name?" Holly asks.

"Nicole. I called her Cole." She's not going to drop it. "What do you want to know?"

"Anything. What she looked like."

"She was pretty. Auburn hair, hazel eyes. Light-skinned, with freckles. Tall. Everybody's taller than me." Tall, broad-shouldered, a little clumsy when she was nervous. Shy. Big hands and feet, full lips that softened against mine.

Holly smiles. "So, you like redheads. How did you meet her?"

"I'd seen her around. Weston's not that big a town. She came into the store where I worked."

"I thought maybe you played ball with her."

"No, Cole was kind of a loner. She was athletic, in a way, but she didn't much like team sports. She used to watch me play softball sometimes, though." There was a double-play Cole sketched: me at shortstop, throwing to second. A pang of loss tightens my chest; I gulp some water.

"She was athletic?" Holly asks.

"Sort of. She did play volleyball. Cole was from the Gulf Coast, and she used to surf a little. She liked to swim, and she got around town on a bicycle." Cole was from Texas, and her voice held a low thrum like waves, a warm gritty wash that left me wanting, ready to plunge.

"I didn't know you could surf the Gulf," Holly says.

"I don't think it's like Maui, but apparently it's done." The invitation of Cole Rankin's voice did not often extend to her impassive hazel eyes. I never saw her swim, her long sleek form slice the water, wet curls dark as blood about her shoulders. Around me she was awkward, a bit of a geek. It was mostly her voice that was sexy.

The waitress returns with the fettuccini and a basket of breadsticks. She sets the bread before me, pulls away the cloth to reveal steam. "Fresh from the oven."

"Thank you." Grateful for the reprieve, I take a breadstick, then gather fettuccini noodles and twirl them on my fork. I've gotten more adept at eating with the cast on.

"This is wonderful," Holly says.

"It's pretty good. Not enough garlic."

She smiles. "The fettuccini's good, but it's just nice to be here with you. I've been thinking about you all week. Last Saturday . . ." She shakes her head.

"It could have gone better."

"I feel so bad that Angela kicked you out."

How the hell does Holly know *that?* All I said was that I moved. "It was time for me to go. It's probably not a good idea to live with a friend too long. You get to know too much about each other."

"Yeah, but throwing you out; you weren't even drunk. That's totally unfair. I almost called her."

"When?" My face burns; I really detest rumors.

"Last Tuesday, after I talked to Lex. He told me what happened."

I try to quell the edge in my voice, with limited success. "What exactly did Lex say?"

"Just that Angie smelled beer on you, and she kicked you out because she thought you got drunk again, so you had to move." She shrugs. "It's my fault. I was the one who dumped beer all over you."

I shove my plate aside; I'm going to have to take the rest home. Why do all my dates with her end up so fucked? I'm pissed at Lex for getting into my business, I'm missing Cole like crazy, I've got this goddess in front of me and I could care less. "It was kind of a mess. Could you excuse me a minute?"

"Sure."

The pay phone's back by the rest rooms. I hope Evelyn's home; I've got to calm down.

"Hello," she says.

"Hey, this is Terry. I can't talk long. I don't even know why I called, really."

"OK. You're not using?"

"No." I draw a long, quivering breath. "I'm at a restaurant with Holly. I just feel like I'm going to explode. I don't know what to do."

"What's going on?"

"She said she talked to Alecki, that he told her Angela kicked me out, and I just wanted to go off."

"You're angry?"

"Yeah, I'm angry. I hate that shit, people talking behind my back. And I . . ." Abruptly my eyes sting. I bite my lip, control it. "She was asking about Nicole. My ex."

"You got sad."

To my horror, tears start down my face. I hardly cried at all, until I got sober. Now I cry in bathrooms, restaurants, meetings.

"Terry," Evelyn says, "you've spent years medicating yourself with alcohol, drinking away your feelings. It sounds like they're starting to come back, and you're not used to it."

"You got that right."

"It's hard when that happens. It doesn't feel very good. But you're OK, even if you don't feel like it. You did the right thing, calling me. We can talk for a minute, until you calm down."

I lean my forehead against the corner of the phone, hoping nobody will see. "OK."

"Feelings are tough. What you are going through happens to everyone in sobriety, sooner or later. With time, it gets easier to manage. You don't feel so raw." Her rough voice is almost tender. "Being able to feel is a valuable thing. It'll get better."

I wipe my eyes on the back of my hand, through sniveling. "I know. I'm together now. I should get back. I just walked away in the middle of a meal."

"All right. You did good. See you tonight?"

"I think so."

I wash my face at the sink, blow my nose. I was much cooler as a drunk, I think.

Holly's almost done eating. "Are you OK?"

"I got a little dizzy for some reason, but it went away. I'll get my leftovers boxed up."

"Do you need to go home?"

"No. I'm fine." I don't want to go to her apartment right now, though, and I barely have enough cash to pay for lunch. I check out Holly's shoes. Leather, with laces, OK for walking. I pay the tab, excuse myself again, and run across Grand to the St. Louis Bread Company. There's a crumpled waxed paper bag on an outdoor table. Inside, three tables are not yet cleared—I score a nearly intact roll, the crusts from a sandwich, and half a bagel. I roll the sack closed and stick it in my book bag. The bakery is crowded, especially around the counter, so I skip the register and head straight to the coffee bar, pull out the sixteen-ounce plastic coffee mug I take to meetings and fill it with hazelnut coffee from a Technibrew dispenser. Holly likes one sugar, a little shot of half-and-half. Moderation. I meet her on the sidewalk, offer the coffee. "Want to go over to the park? The trees are gorgeous there."

"Sure." She smiles. "Thanks, Terry."

It's a beautiful day, classic crisp fall weather. Low humidity; the light wind carries a faint sharp note of tannin from leaves that litter the shadowed ground beneath the big old oaks. Tower Grove Park has great trees. An achingly blue sky highlights rusty pin oaks and golden maples, brushed with scarlet.

Two fat red squirrels race across the path, dart up a cypress. One scrambles to the lowest branch. He looks down, tail flicking. The other one spins around on the trunk and looks at me. I cluck my tongue at him, the way Angela does. He jumps back, swivels his ears forward.

"Do that again," Holly says. We stop and I cluck a couple more times. The squirrel prances with his front feet, not easy to do at nearly horizontal. I step closer, and the one on the branch barks an alarm. All three of us jump.

The cypresses retain their needles, but all around us leaves spin free in random whirling gusts. By the fountain, a huge willow hangs green and gold cascades, reflected bright as coins in the shallow man-made pond. It smells damp here, mild odor of leaf mold and decay. A little willow offspring seeks a foothold at the water's edge. Up close, the prettiness of the surface gives way to the litter below: a million pennies, beer can tabs, condoms settled into muddy opacity. Wishes made and granted. I find a bench in the sun, unroll the bag of bread.

"What's that?" Holly points to a murky circle, ill-defined, like an orange manhole cover.

"Goldfish." I tear the bakery scraps into chunks. A couple of pigeons strut closer, violet heads bobbing and breasts puffed. Holly drops them a handful of crumbs, well to one side. Birds rush and flutter on the ground.

I turn to a rustle. Another squirrel, or perhaps one of the couple from the cypress, stands erect below a nearby shrub. He's got an acorn in his forepaws. He rotates it once, again, turns it at an angle and jams it into a little hole. Tamps in earth, pats and smoothes and pulls leaves across just so, pausing twice to glare at me. "Go ahead," I say. "I don't want it." The rusty tail jerks, curves into a question mark, and the dexterous little paws pat pat on the leaves.

A trio of ducks paddle over, panhandling. Four more follow, muttering and twisting their heads to see what we have. I scatter fine crumbs to draw them near, hand the bag to Holly. She teases a bold green-headed male with a bagel chunk between her thumb and forefinger, then shrieks and drops it when, thrashing wet wings, he makes a grab.

"We're on urban safari," Holly says. The pigeons finish their bounty; all twelve of them retreat to a little pedestal atop the concrete fake ruins behind the pond.

Holly shows the ducks the empty bag. They bump and hassle each other, disgusted, move away en masse. At the end the goldfish come, scavenge the debris for leavings. Wishes granted.

Our bench no longer warmed by the sun, we start back. We giggle about the duck, how Holly screamed. A low radiance of setting sun streams through ruddy foliage and dapples her cheek with gold. I'm struck with an urge to kiss her. I check my impulse and take her hand.

Holly jerks, looks over her shoulder. She gives my hand a hard squeeze, then releases it.

"I didn't mean to embarrass you."

"No big deal," she says, her cheeks red.

What's her problem? It's not like I put my hand up her shirt. My fine romantic feeling has dissipated. I shove my errant hand into the pocket of my jacket and walk a little faster through the long shadows of autumn.

I drop her off and say good-bye, promise to call. Maybe it won't be that hard to stay celibate.

Chapter 5

> *"What's the difference between a pizza and a fuck?"*
> *"I don't know."*
> *"Want to go for a pizza?"*
>
> overheard at an AA meeting

My second week at Joiner Oil, third-shift cashier at an old gas station in an old neighborhood. This is someone else's life. I never get enough sleep; I'm always cold. The little glass booth is heated, but early in the shift I constantly slide the window open to deal with the barrage of customers. I turn the pumps off and on, make change, sell cigarettes and gum—it's not hard, just tedious.

All the pumps are pre-pay after dark. Some nights no one remembers that. They stand there with the nozzle, screaming, "Turn it on!" and I bang open the window and yell, "The sign says pay before you pump!" I'm resentful; the customers are resentful; they come up to the booth and snarl, "Why don't you get a card scanner on your pumps?" Like I could change it.

It doesn't feel real. I sit in my glass aquarium all night, drink coffee from a thermos and stare down the black street, watching the traffic lights change. I wonder if they ever miss me at the bar here, or in Weston; wonder if they ever think of me at all.

After 12:30, hardly anyone stops for gas. After 1:30, nobody does—the bars close down. It's cloudy tonight and very still. I've been trying to read the AA Big Book, but my gaze keeps returning to the low, heavy sky. Clouds blot out the stars and the gray city grunge of light pollution reflects from the heavens. The cigarettes seduce me; I resist.

The Second Step is harder than the first. *Came to believe that a Power greater than ourselves could restore us to sanity.* When I took this step with Laura, she had me write about insane things I did. Evelyn has me read the Big Book: Chapter Four, "We Agnostics," and the appendix on spiritual experience. Chapter Four is about discovering your own concept of a spiritual power. In order to stay sober, you find a belief in a Higher Power, or God, or whatever works for you. I believe there are many things more powerful than me, including alcohol. Do any of them take a personal interest in what I do? I'll try not to rule it out completely.

There's room in AA for a broad array of beliefs. At regular meetings, I hear about God, and Higher Power, and the occasional quote from the Bible, twisted to fit the purpose of the moment. At the Lambda Club meetings, I hear references to Goddess sometimes, and the cars outside have bumper stickers like "Blessed Be," and "Magick Happens," and "My Goddess Gave Birth to Your God." Annie wears a cross; Portia wears a Star of David. I don't know what I believe, but Evelyn says an open mind is the key to spiritual growth.

I can't concentrate. I'm not cut out for the night shift; three to eleven would be better, except I'd miss my meetings. My arms are propped on the counter, but they keep sliding. My head drops, and pretty soon I'm dozing, drooling a little down my forearm.

Someone slides the window open, softly. I hear it, something in my brain reacts, but my eyes will not open.

A finger trails down my face, just the lightest touch, from my temple to my chin. My hand lifts to brush it away, then I realize where I am. I suck in a lungful of air and sit up, staring.

Jeri's outside the window, laughing. "This is a stickup." She points her finger. "Be glad it isn't loaded, hotshot."

"Damn, Jeri." I wipe the drool from my left cheek, then take a paper towel and dry my slimy hand.

"How long were you asleep?"

"I don't know." I sound like a whiny child. "What time is it?"

"Two-thirty."

"Damn." I just said that. "What are you up to?"

She indicates her car, by pump number three. "Hanging with Rita. I didn't know you were working here."

"Not for long, I hope."

She hands me a twenty. "I want to fill it."

I punch the code, and Jeri goes back to the pump. Rita's in the passenger seat, staring straight ahead. I can see only a mop of curly brown hair and part of her cheek. The woman is totally paranoid; this is probably the only time of day the two of them go out in public. Jeri deserves better than this; she ought to get with someone who'll treat her right. Rita's a bitch.

When Jeri comes back, I count her change. "Call me," she says.

"Sure. I'm off Sunday. You want to introduce your friend?"

She smiles. "Not today." In the car, she speaks to Rita, who doesn't appear to acknowledge her at all. Jeri pulls around the booth and waves.

I just can't help myself. I scream "Rita!" and whip up my shirt, press my bare breasts against the window. Rita never moves except her eyes, which flick toward me and go so wide I can see the whites all the way around. Jeri's hand flies up and covers her mouth, and she hits the accelerator.

There's a bang, and the entire rack of one hundred brands of cigarettes tilts. The packs rise in unison and cascade to the floor, burying my feet to the ankles. I jerk my shirt down and spin around. A middle-aged guy, very red-faced, is shifting into reverse. As he backs away from the corner of the building, I can see a crease in his fender. He departs right after Jeri.

"Hell." I have to start the morning cash drop around 5:30; until then, I'll be sorting packs of cigarettes. So much for the Second Step; at least this will keep me awake.

I try the black jeans on; Holly and I are going out again. The jeans fit snugly—not tight, but not loose by any means. I could pull them off myself, but there's something to be said for allowing a woman to slip your pants down over your hips. Struggling one-handed with a buttoned fly is not sexy, and watching someone hop around on one foot, jeans half off, interrupts the flow.

Possibly the tan pants, then; I try them with a dark green turtleneck. Not bad. But I can't wear sneakers with this, and my boots are black, and my loafers are oxblood, and none of them go with tan. I wish the strap of my Birkenstocks hadn't finally given out.

Maybe a white dress shirt and navy slacks. The pants go with the loafers (and won't show spilled beer). I still have enough of a tan that the shirt will look good with the sleeves rolled back to the forearms.

I press the shirt first, lots of spray starch and razor creases down both sleeves. Open collar, thin gold necklace with a garnet pendant. Turn back the sleeves carefully, evenly, in a thin flat roll.

The doorbell rings. Someone comes in, and I hear Alecki's throaty chuckle. He must be going out with Rodney. The door slams and his car pulls away.

I flip the navy pants onto the ironing board, line up the seams, and start creases down the legs, less sharp than those on the shirt. A pleasant steam smell follows the iron.

The door's half-open before I look up. Holly, with a dozen red roses. I'm standing here, no pants, white shirt and navy socks. Holly smiles. "Nice legs." She sets the roses on the dresser and advances. The iron hovers in my left hand, an inch above my pants. She disarms me, pulls the plug.

"I thought I was picking you up," I say.

"You were."

"You're early."

"And you are fine. You should just dress like that, all the time. Maybe lose the socks, though."

Ten years I've waited for this moment, replayed it in my mind, and never once did Holly make the advances. I'm the one who makes things happen; suddenly I don't know what to do.

Holly plucks at the crease of my sleeve. "I didn't know you were so domestic." She leans into a kiss. My hands figure it out, pull her blouse from her waistband and slide up her back.

"Let's not mess up all your hard work." Holly unbuttons my shirt, presses her hips close. It really didn't matter which pants I wore. She edges me toward the bed.

My socks are new and snug. I struggle to slip them off with my toes, but they won't go. I release the girl of my dreams, almost fall against her, jerk the socks away. Her smile mocks my effort; I kiss it into softness. Lift her shirt and brush my lips across a pale, sweetly curved belly. I want to lick her smooth white skin, but my mouth is dry and tart with longing.

Her torso is long and sleek. I run my hands under her shirt, up the curve between hips and ribs, under her arms, slide around back to her thin shoulders. Her shoulder blades slip under my hands and I dig my nails in slightly, stroke to the small of her back. Holly shivers.

I do it again, slow: fingertips up the waist, across the ribs, then scratch firmly down her back. This time the skin tightens at my touch, right before the shiver. Her nipples mark her blouse; I anticipate firm points under my tongue. I brush my lips across her breasts, inhale her scent. Obsession—from the bottle in her bathroom.

I lift the tail of her blouse, run my pointed tongue across her belly. Holly draws in a breath. I kiss, gently, again and again, waist and belly and ribs. Tug at her waistband with my teeth. God, I wish I didn't have this cast. I sink to my knees, press my face to her zipper and breathe into it. Her hands on my shoulders betray a fine tremor. I grip her hips, lean my forehead against her. Knead the muscles of her hamstrings, her calves, pull every part of her close. I see her in a crowded hallway, navy sweater, white blouse, books clutched to her breast. I wish she had that plaid skirt on now.

I unzip the slacks and spread the fly; she hooks thumbs into her panties and pulls them low. My nose burrows in red-blonde curls, I press them flat with my lips. That narrow aperture, warm and wet; I slide my finger in. Holly inhales sharply, settles her shoulders more firmly against the wall. I can't do this left-handed; the angle is awkward. I jerk her pants lower, spread her lips and circle my tongue. Her hands cup my head, guide me with subtle pressure. She strokes my hair, pulls it— I love that. I offer delicate torment, keep her on edge until she's afflicted with a desperate lust. Then I stand. "Take your clothes off."

"Goddamn it, Terry!"

I smile, put my shirt on a hanger and stretch out on the bed, waiting. Holly's ripping at her outfit, tangled in her pants. She lands on me, naked, with a panting, devouring kiss that thrills me to my toes. I roll her over, kneel between her knees and do her right.

Holly's uncertain, inexperienced. I slide to the foot of the bed, have her kneel on the floor. To give her an idea of the pressure, I circle my tongue on her palm. She fumbles a little, but I'm so hot it doesn't take me long. I come with a roaring in my ears, my knees against Holly's shoulders.

She smiles, comes to rest beside me. "Was that OK?"

"You were fantastic," I lie. "Incredible." I twine a lock of her hair around my index finger, admire its sheen. "I love red hair."

"Do you? I like having it, but I could do without the freckles."

I touch them, one by one, sprinkled across her bare shoulder. "They're kind of cute, I think." We lie in silence a moment longer, my head on her chest, her arm around me.

"Let me finish your pants," she says.

"My pants?" I barely remember having any.

"Iron them. I got here too early, sneaked into your bedroom, caught you in your underwear. . . . Let me at least do your pants for you."

"OK." I roll to my back, watch her breasts move as she leans over the slacks, pressing. "What did you do with my brother?"

"Five-dollar gift certificate to The Coffee Grounds."

"That works."

While Holly finishes my pants, I put the roses in a pickle jar of water. Both of us are starved. We go to a Chinese buffet, so we don't have to wait for an order, and have a happy, tranquil meal during which nothing is overturned. *This* is how a date should go.

Get a No. 2 pencil and a yellow legal pad, Laura said, and it would keep me honest. AA superstition irritates me. I scrounge around the apartment, collecting a Coke, my Big Book, a mechanical pencil and the spiral notebook with the burgundy cover that I used for all my other steps.

The notebook opens to the next blank sheet. Tapping the pencil against my front teeth, I stare for a long time. Maybe the No. 2 pencil is so you'll have something to chew. I letter "Step Four" across the top, and "Made a searching and fearless moral inventory of ourselves."

Should I use columns with headings ("Fear," "Resentment," "Lust"), or make new sections as transgressions occur to me? Maybe I should use two notebooks. No, keep it simple.

I tear out a separate page for notes and write "Honesty" at the top of both the pages. That should be "Dishonesty," instead—I'm not writing about what an angel I have been. Anyway, "Dishonesty" would equate with "Resentments" and "Fears." There's "Sex Relations" versus "Lust" to consider. I could go with "Sexual Misconduct."

Perhaps I should consider "Procrastination."

Honesty. *To thine own self be true, and it must follow, as the night the day, thou canst not then be false to any man.* In your own words, please. A lot of little stuff comes to mind, especially from old jobs where I've helped myself to sodas or gum, or had dinners I didn't write down. At A Step Beyond, the new-age store I worked at in Weston, I slipped a few crystals and stones into my pocket. I gave them away at the bar—"I saw this today, and thought of you . . ." I presented three crystals to Cole in a little woven pouch. She threw that back in my face, later. She didn't throw it, exactly, but she sure didn't keep it.

I stole when someone pissed me off. I worked at a Texaco station where the manager was always making faggot jokes, then coming on to me. One night after he left, I scratched $500 worth of lottery tickets. I got a few winners, not as many as you'd think: a $10 and two $25's, one $50, a handful of $1, $2, and $3 matches. I gave them all to a homeless guy in the alley when I took out the trash, and told him not to come around for a couple weeks. I quit right after that.

Will I have to make amends for that? I'm sure the asshole doesn't work there anymore. They weren't *his* lottery tickets. I'm getting ahead of myself; this is just the Fourth Step. Amends don't come until Step Nine.

What else? I stole for fun, and not long ago; I picked up those three books at the used bookstore in the Central West End.

The shirts: my collection. I'm surprised I've been able to hang on to the suitcase, as much as I've moved around. I haven't even opened it since I moved from Weston. I drag it out from under the bed.

On top is a sleeveless basketball jersey from St. Thomas, souvenir of Danny Stegmann. Lucky boy, the only male to grace this collection. I've slept with a few other guys, but never stole their shirts. This one is from Erica, a royal blue polo shirt with a logo on the breast. There's a shapeless tie-dye that Carmen brought back from Michigan. The Harley-

Davidson tank top is from a girl whose name I don't remember. She had long, tangled hair, homemade tattoos on her knuckles, professional tattoos on her arms. She was in town with a carnival, a thin girl with haunted eyes, prominent veins. She snorted crank until I thought she'd explode. We spent one strange weekend together and I slept for twenty-eight hours when she left. She gave me a cheap gold chain and her sister's address; she didn't know I had the shirt.

There's a rugby shirt, big enough for a scrummy; it would hang to my knees. It belonged at one time to Nicole Rankin. I had thought this might be the first shirt I would give back. I guess not.

I gather the shirt to my face. It just smells musty, like every other shirt in the bag. My Fourth Step resolve has faded. I fold the shirts up and put the suitcase back under the bed, stretch out on top of the covers and stare out the window. The sky dims. The stars grow bright, and still I stare. I wish I had a drink. Wish I had a beer, and a pool table, and a bunch of my friends around, and some girl's eyes on my ass as I stretch for a shot.

The closet door thumps, slides slightly open. Whacker's head wedges it aside and he slips through the crack. He hops onto the bed, stretches his paws toward me and trills a greeting. "Hey, buddy." I rub his head and he stretches alongside me, purring. Kneads the air slowly. His alternating paws spread his toes, extend his claws. He looks near-comatose, but suddenly he twists around and bounds to his feet. Gold eyes stare into mine. He parts his lips, white fangs glinting, and says, "Call your sponsor."

I sit straight up; Whacker nearly falls from the bed. He glares at me, ears back. "What did you say?" I ask. He huffs, runs off. I fall back to my pillow. "Work your own program." I will call Evelyn, though.

The only great advantage to working at Joiner Oil is that I get so many opportunities to work on my "searching and fearless moral inventory." I hope to get through "Honesty" tonight and start the sexual history.

Besides the lottery tickets, shirts, and other outright thieving, I've used and manipulated people. I certainly took advantage of my parents: I had no business going to college. I majored in PE, recreation, education, horticulture, and literature. School was just an excuse to read a little, party, get wasted and get laid, and not worry about money.

Catholic education should have made me studious, respectful, disciplined. Catholic discipline was all external, though. I graduated from St. Thomas with a great love of books and an even greater love of the look of plaid on a young girl.

Meramec Community College: I met Erica. She was older, taking another shot at college after a time out. She'd nag me to keep up my grades, until I'd run a hand up under her shirt, uncover the flat, soft belly I loved to lick. She made passing grades that semester; I didn't. She dumped me after the brawl with Melissa.

I got a job at Texaco, devoted my life to the Mud Sharks and the muddy battlefields of rugby. Mom and Pop said that I couldn't stay at the house if I wasn't going to school. Fine; they were getting in the way of my drinking. I moved into a big old house with Meredith and Christy. It was Angela's place, initially, but when it got too wild Angie was the first to leave. The rent was practically nothing, split four ways, and we had parties almost every night. Eventually we lost the lease and I resumed my higher education.

St. Louis University: I was living at home, constantly fighting with Andre and my mom. My parents thought it might be better for me to go away to school.

Truman State at Kirksville: dorm indiscretions were my demise; Kirksville was not ready for this lovesick lesbian. After my second conduct suspension, I left for a year at Mizzou.

University of Missouri at Columbia: a party school. I stayed so drunk I failed half my classes. My parents retrieved me and suggested I try community college again.

Forest Park Community College: I got through one semester before the DWI and a stint at the treatment center in Weston.

How do I make amends for five years of dissolution? I can't pay back the tuition. I can confess, apologize. More important, I can focus on the Fourth Step inventory and worry about amends later.

Honesty. I've stayed with friends rent-free, but I always tried to contribute or to keep moving. I can't think of any overt financial amends there. Erica did get my car out of the shop once, to the tune of $320, but she's never asked me for the money. The bitch knows better, I guess.

Erica will make a guest appearance on the Resentments page.

What about Cole? I hate the way we ended, but I don't know that I used her. I really did love her. She's through with me, though.

I must have dozed; a line trails off the edge of the page. That's enough on honesty; the notebook goes into my book bag for tonight. It's not even two; I have five hours to go.

I prop my elbows on the counter of my glass cell, stare down at my Big Book and try once more to read page 69. "One school would allow man no flavor for his fare and the other would have us all on a straight pepper diet." This is the AA wisdom of the ages regarding sex. Sounds like my grandmother's kitchen. Every time I read it, I think of Holly.

An extended fantasy drifts into a doze, until a knock at the window jerks me awake. A seedy older guy with a worn book, the gilt pages interspersed with indexed indentations, offers a twenty. "Sixteen," he says. "On two."

I stare at this apparition, then look to the monitor and take his money. "Four dollars makes twenty, thank you and come again."

"Have you heard the Good News tonight?" He holds up his book, a maroon leather Bible.

I nod, hold up my Big Book. He smiles. "God bless you." He pumps his gas, then makes a notation in a small binder and drives away.

Two forty-five in the morning: I give up on Chapter Five. I lay my head on my folded arms, scoot forward on the stool and dwindle into a dream. A man at a gas pump tells me the hose won't run.

"It's kinked," I say.

The man pulls it and a flood of words gushes from the hose, pooling into black tangled letters at his feet. A few consonants have splattered up onto his pants; I offer him a paper towel. "Blot them. If you rub them, they'll smear."

A horrendous noise yanks the breath from my body. The stool crashes over. I land on my feet, stumble back. What the fuck?

A semi is almost against the booth. The gas truck; the driver pulled up close and blew his horn. He's bent over the steering wheel, shaking with laughter. I've got to get a life.

The dishes are done, dried, and put away. The kitchen floor has been swept. I've scooped the litter pan and taken out the trash. Lex vacuumed already on Saturday. Would I rather clean the bathroom or keep my date with the Fourth Step? With a sigh, I pour myself a Coke, gather my notebook and my Big Book.

Sex Relations: Have I been "selfish, dishonest, or inconsiderate?" I used women to get me off, for sure, but there weren't too many who didn't have a better time than I did. That sounds egotistical, but I never had any complaints. I pissed off some ladies by not coming back, not calling, not sticking around, but I never promised them anything. Is that selfish? I don't know; that's just the way we did things at the bar in St. Louis, in Columbia, in Kirksville, in Weston. Women gave me presents, gave me money, took me on trips, let me stay on the couch for a month. They've given me flowers and books and patchouli oil, sports tickets and concert tickets, bought me dinner, cooked me dinner. Photographed me. Drawn pictures of me—playing softball, playing pool. One of Cole's drawings of me hangs over the bar at The Rainbow's Edge in Weston.

I miss Cole. I miss her, and I feel so bad about it that I can't fucking stand it. I knock the notebook to the floor, lay my head down and bawl for about ten minutes. Get up snotty, eyes swollen. Blow my nose and dial my sponsor.

"Evelyn? Did anyone ever get drunk over a Fourth Step?"

"Not if they picked up the phone. What's up, kiddo?"

"Every fucking piece of this comes back to Cole. Honesty, and fear, and sex, and anger—" My voice sounds whiny. *Butch up.*

"The Fourth Step is tough, Terry. It brings up all that stuff we don't want to look at. When we're drinking, and we love someone, sometimes there's an awful lot of regrets. It's going to hurt.

"The important thing is that you called me. You didn't drink, you did the right thing. The steps are an opportunity to become aware of our actions and start making better choices. You're only on the Fourth Step, but you're making better choices already."

I'm using a speaker phone, so she won't hear me cry. I take my hands from my face and mumble, "I guess."

"You are, Terry. You're getting better all the time. Maybe you need a break right now, though. Why don't you go do something physical? It's not too cold out; if it helps you, go run."

Good thing I don't pay for this. "Right. Thanks."

"See you at the meeting, then."

"I guess." I hang up and pull on my sweatpants. Start at a fast walk; the sidewalks are cracked and heaved until I get to Forest Park. I break into a jog on the smooth asphalt trail. When I reach the cottonwoods that line the golf course, I lengthen my stride to a run.

Damn Evelyn; the old heifer's right. My shoulders loosen; breath builds, shaping my torso. Rhythm shapes my discord into energy. I pass three girls on skates, struggling against the grade, and my stride is smoother than their glide.

The wind gusts; I slit my eyes against blowing dirt. Two little boys on ten-speeds race toward me. I smile at them.

"Hey, bitch!" One sticks out his hand. The stinging slap leaves grime across the shoulder of my jacket.

I recoil, then spin and race at them. "Motherfuckers! You little bastards!" Grab a rock and heave; it falls short. I turn and smack my fist into a big old tree. The pain drops me in a whirling yellow light; I lay on the ground, moaning.

When my vision clears, I don't much feel like running anymore. A chunk of fiberglass hangs from the back of the cast, but my hand seems OK.

Up the hill I plod; a couple of tears leak out, probably from the wind. What the hell am I doing wrong?

A bath and a sandwich calm me down. At the Lambda Club, I chair the meeting. Originally my topic was the Fourth Step, but instead I vent about every miserable thing that went down today. Everybody has something to say: that it's a hard step, at least I didn't drink, and that I'm doing the right thing. Annie says that doing what's right doesn't necessarily feel good, but in the long run sobriety does get better. I damn sure hope I'm in this for the long run.

Afterward, I help stack chairs. Evelyn and Beryl clean the coffeepot. I have to work tonight, so I can't stick around. Evelyn asks me for a ride home; in the Mustang, she's uncharacteristically quiet. "Good meeting," I venture.

She lights a cigarette, cracks open the window. "I don't know what happened between you and Cole. Whatever it is, it's messing you up.

You can't think about her without losing your mind; you can't talk about her at all."

I glance at her, then stare back at the road. My throat tightens.

"Terry . . ." Evelyn shakes her head. "I wish I could tell you how many people have come through these doors with stories just like yours. I wish you knew just how common this stuff is. You're not unique, and you haven't done anything that can't be reconciled by applying yourself to the Twelve Steps."

I shake my head. "Evelyn, I make myself sick. I can't even stand to think about it."

"Then don't. Grab a sheet of paper, get it down and forget about it until you do your Fifth Step. Ask your Higher Power for help. You can do this, Terry," she says. "You *will* do it, if you want to stay sober. If you don't, then you'll be doing the same thing and worse down the road."

"It just seems like so much shit."

She smiles. "I was forty-six when I got sober. Think how much shit you'd have in twenty years.

"Everybody's got their own pain, kiddo. You'll hear stories around the tables that'll curl your hair. They'll make you grateful. Woman lets her sick baby die because she's too drunk to get off the couch and check on her. Guy kills his best friend in a blackout, and doesn't remember a thing. There was a woman in that room tonight whose sister's in a wheelchair for life because of a wreck they had when they were drunk. I don't know what you've done—I don't care. I only care that you get past your fear, and past that ego that keeps telling you nobody is as bad as you." She flips the butt out the window, turns to face me. "Are you willing to go to any lengths to stay sober?"

"Yeah. I want to change."

"If you want to change, there are Twelve Steps that will help you do it, and a whole fellowship behind you," Evelyn says.

"I will work on my Fourth Step tonight." As much as I can stand, at least.

"I sit here and tell you what to do like I know it all." Evelyn sighs. "I don't, you know. I know how I stay sober; I know what works for me. I did what I had to, to save my ass when I got here."

"Did you do your Fourth Step right away?"

"I should have," Evelyn says. "It would have been better if I did."

"Oh, yeah?"

"I got a sponsor right away. She was an easy choice; twenty years ago there weren't that many women in AA. The meetings I went to, there were a couple women about my age, but one of them was sponsoring too many already, and the other one was shaking worse than me.

"There was one younger woman, though. She had four years sober. I asked her, and she accepted. Her name was Belinda; she was from Sauget."

"Sauget? That's just a bunch of factories."

Evelyn nods. "It was factories and liquor stores, and the people that worked in them. Belinda moved to Maplewood when she got sober." She stares out the car window, pensive.

"So, she said take it slow?" I prompt.

"We did the steps. Belinda took sponsorship very seriously. We met twice a week before meetings and talked about the program, and where I'd been, and what I needed to do to change. She was a real Big Book-thumper. But she listened to me, too. She listened with everything she had. I wasn't used to that. You know the kind of shit you sling in bars—they can't have changed that much. It's all about image. I wasn't used to being heard, and it seemed like I couldn't get enough of it.

"I don't know what Belinda thought of me, exactly. She shared with me about her drinking. She was married, but she didn't talk about it much. She was thirty-five, married to a guy in his late forties.

"When I got sober, I was forty-six. I used to look sharp, but by the time I got to AA I was pretty dissipated."

"I bet you weren't," I tell her. "Girlfriend, you still look good. I didn't think you were but fifty when I met you."

"Spare me," she says. "You can't bullshit a bullshitter, Terry." She goes on about her and Belinda; I study her face by the light of the traffic signal. The red blush softens her wrinkles, and I can still see a fierce beauty in the fine prominent cheekbones, broad forehead, strong line of nose and chin. She really has a great profile.

"She was just looking at me," Evelyn is saying. "I don't know how I knew. I told her 'I want to tear off your panties with my teeth' and away we went."

"Jesus, Evelyn!" The woman wears dentures, for God's sake. She points, and I put the Mustang in reverse and back up a little; I passed her building.

"It wasn't worth it," Evelyn says. "She ended up drunk and back in Sauget within two weeks." She looks at me and laughs. "Don't look so shocked. I'm no angel, but thank God I'm sober. Call me."

"Good night."

Joiner Oil, after midnight. Business is slow for a Saturday. "Anger" is my next Fourth Step heading; this should be fruitful. I've rarely handled anger in any sane and appropriate fashion.

I popped Melissa in the mouth at rugby practice, because I'd caught her with Erica. At least I had justification for that. I've kicked, hit, and jumped on other women, just because I was hacked about a play. Rugby is a license to be aggressive, but I would hit too hard. I got childish about it, sometimes—hit officials, loud-mouthed spectators. Sometimes I got kicked out of the game, and the Sharks would have to play short.

The sad thing was, I played basketball the same way. Last year, in Weston, I played in a Parks and Rec League, just some women trying to stay in shape and have a little fun. I tripped and shoved and threw elbows like a paid assassin. Fouled out twice; that's not easy to do in Parks and Rec.

When Officer Jackson stopped me for the DWI last fall, he did grab my shirt; he called me "dyke." I should have quit mouthing, though, and I should not have hit him. I'm surprised he didn't beat the hell out of me. He took me to the ground rather hard, but if he hit me, I don't remember it.

Speaking of cuffs, there was that weird night with Pat. I got mad, did things that hurt her. How specific does this Fourth Step have to be? I'll just put down that I used a whip on her. She gave me the whip, and I was the one who went to the ER, but it was not an appropriate expression of anger.

Cole. I wish I could remember—What did she say to me? I was just enraged.

I went over there to explain why I had stood her up the night before. All afternoon I drank gin and rehearsed my apology. As soon as she showed, we got into a fight.

She got sarcastic; said something, but I can't recall . . . "Another few drinks and you'll be out of commission anyway." Cole's voice. I remember.

Fuck. I didn't want to remember; not really.

I had just made some crack about my busted lip not putting me out of commission. Nice; I start off with "I'm sorry," then make some drunken, smutty remark.

It made Cole mad; she got up from the couch, started pacing in front of me. "Shit, Terry, what possessed you?" She was pissed off; Cole hardly ever cursed. "You had seizures before, and you did it anyway? Are you insane? You're on probation."

That was it—"You're on probation." I never told her that, or about the DWI. I never even told her that I was in treatment. Someone had been talking to her, or Cole was checking up on me. Furious, I kicked over the coffee table. I can hear the crash, hear myself screaming at her.

Cole started to cry, and I grabbed her. She let me do it—let me shove her, hit her in the face, kick her. Then she tried to push me away, and I bit her wrist when it knocked into my face. When I came at Cole again, she grabbed my shirt and swung me past her, into the wall. I remember that, too: the face-first crash, sparkling yellow lights that swirled around me and the harsh, far-away sound of my own rasping breath. I came to on the floor, the fight knocked out of me, but I was still full of rage. I hated Cole right then, hated what she had brought out in me.

Cole never even hit me back. Like the cop, she finally just knocked me down. I don't know how much I hurt her; she put ice on her face, or her head, right before I left. That was the last time I saw her.

My stomach tightens. I can take only shallow gasps of air, and my head feels like a siren's going off inside it. I'm in a cold sweat, as if I might pass out. I cannot take the pain of knowing that I can't trust myself, of knowing the rage and insanity that lurk within me, waiting for the next drink. I can't stop seeing Cole fall, can't stop the sound of my fist pounding her head. God, I wish I had a joint, and enough whiskey to make me pass out. If that picture flashes through my head again, I may just go insane with self-loathing, remorse, grief.

I lay my head on my arms, then slide the window open so that cold air washes over me. My head still reels. I stare out into nothing, breathing hard.

A car pulls into the lot, then another. The bars are letting out. I get up, mechanically make change, flip the switches by rote. The muscles still twitch in my back and arms, but I no longer feel like I'm going to pass out.

One young guy pays, pumps his gas, then returns to the booth. Just what I need. "What time do you get off, babe?" he asks. "Let me buy you some breakfast. I could just wait here, if you let me in there with you."

"Sorry, sir, I can't let anyone in the booth." Like I'd have breakfast with this loser. Through the open window I can smell the whiskey on his breath.

A dark green Lexus misses the turn into the driveway, bumps down into the ditch and then climbs back up to the lot. It nearly hits a pump; my hand hovers over the emergency shutoff until the car jerks to a stop. Usually a cop parks down the street on weekends; he's missing his opportunity tonight.

A nice-looking woman in a black leather jacket fumbles the nozzle into the port. "It's prepay after midnight," I yell. The sign is on every pump. The woman bangs the switch off, then back on. When she looks up, I recognize Willow. Shit. I yell "Pay before you pump!"

Willow raises a hand in reply, then raps on the window of the Lexus. The passenger door swings wide; Erica falls to one knee. She slaps Willow away, steadies herself on the quarter panel, then walks stiffly to the booth. Somebody kill me now.

Erica looks ghastly. Still got the killer blond waves, but she's gaunt and pale, with dark circles under sunken, bleary eyes. She's so trashed, she may not know me. Willow's almost as gone, leaning her forehead on folded arms atop the car.

"Ten dollars," Erica says. She doesn't even look.

I take her bill, set the pump.

"Nice car," the drunk says. Erica just looks at him. "Her and me are going to breakfast," he says. "Aren't we, babe?"

Erica squints into the booth. "Hey, Terry. I almost didn't see you in there. Weren't you going to say anything?"

"Hello, Erica." I rip open a carton of Winstons and turn away to place them in the rack.

Erica slumps against the ledge, folds her arms. "Would you check my oil?"

"This is a self-service station."

"Is this guy bothering you?" she says. "'Cause I can take care of him, if you want."

"I'm not bothering her," the drunk says. "We're just gonna go to breakfast when she gets off. Right, Terry?"

"Is that right?" Erica says. "You doing dick again, Terry? Or do you want me to get rid of this guy for you?"

I just want to leave. I watch Willow hang up the hose, screw in the gas cap.

"You don't need me." Erica grabs the guy by the shoulder. "That's a dangerous dyke there, man. A one-punch wonder. She'll knock your teeth out if you mess with her."

"Get off me, bitch." He shoves her. "Dyke? You a dyke?"

As little as I like Erica, as much as she deserves it, it pisses me off to see this asshole push her. I slam my hands on the counter and shout, "Get out of here! Both of you! Just get the fuck away!" My cast cracks again, through the palm.

Willow's come for Erica, she's pulling her to the car. Erica jerks her arm free and gets in on the driver's side.

The drunk is leaning in my window. "I'm gonna have to say something to Marty, because you are not friendly to customers. I don't know what he's thinking, hiring some dyke to work here."

"If you don't leave right now, I'm calling the cops."

"I'm not doing nothing. All's I said to you was do you want to go to breakfast—"

I dial 911, give my location and the plates on the drunk's car. Down the street, red and blue lights flash. The dispatcher says, "There's a unit right there." The little pecker takes off in the opposite direction, still hollering. My hand aches.

When the sun comes up, I see a dark green Lexus just down the road.

The orthopedic surgeon seems loath to hear how I broke the cast across the knuckles as well as the palm; he only asks if I'm having any pain. After an X ray, his assistant cuts the cast. Emancipated, I try to make a fist. The skin is red, dry, and sore. My wrist feels like it will crack if I turn it too far. I'll get over that in a couple of days.

When the films come back, the doctor shows me the thickened callus that bridges the fracture. "Whatever you've been doing, it's healing well." The cast was supposed to come off in two weeks anyway, so he leaves my hand free except for a Galveston brace, a goofy device that fits over my hand like an outsized clamp. It relieves stress on the affected bone, he says. Actually, it sticks out so far that I can barely use my hand.

I get home after noon, too wound up to sleep. I flip on the radio, stretch out on the sofa with a copy of *Curve*.

The phone rings. "Hey."

"Terry? Andrei tells me you're living with Alecki."

"Hi, Mom."

"You move and don't tell me? When was I supposed to find out?"

"When did you find out?"

"Last night. Andrei was over. At least I get to see *him*."

"Well, he works with Pop."

"If it wasn't for Andrei I would never know what's going on. So you're still not working?"

"I've got a job."

"You don't work Mondays?"

"I work nights. It's a gas station."

"A gas station." She sighs; I can almost feel it through the phone. "What are you doing this afternoon?"

"Lying on the couch. Trying to sleep."

"That's not good for you, to lay around like that. You're depressed."

"I'm not depressed."

"No, listen, this girlfriend of mine had no energy, just wanted to lie on the couch all the time, and she was an intelligent person. She went to see her gynecologist and he said she was depressed. This stuff he gave her is like a miracle. I've got his name," she says. I hear the clasp of her purse. "I want you to go see him."

"I'm not going to see a gynecologist; you're starting at the wrong end. Anyway, I'm not depressed. I work night shift; I just need some sleep."

"Why don't you work for your dad and Andrei? You could keep decent hours, at least."

"I don't want to paint again. Pop and I would both be happier if we don't work together."

Another draft blows through the phone lines. "Well anyway, Terry, I called to see if you were really living there and also to see if you and Alecki could come for dinner after Mass on Sunday."

"Probably. I'll check my schedule at work."

"You're working nights at that place? What if there's a holdup?"

Didn't I just say I worked nights? "Then I'll give them everything in the register. I don't care. I have to sleep, Mom."

"See you Sunday, then."

"Mom, I didn't say—" She cut me off.

Depressed. I'm not depressed; I'm just sober. Happy, joyous, and free. I must not be to that part yet. I turn off the phone's ringer and retire with Whacker to my bed.

Four hours sleep—this is going to be another long night. In a daze, I bang the cash drawer open and closed, hand back change without counting aloud, try not to yawn in anyone's face.

I brought my juggling balls for a little hand therapy. They're woven cotton, brightly colored, all different shades and designs. I have five, but three is plenty for now. At one-fifteen I step outside into a blast of cold air. I dread dropping the balls on this greasy pavement, but the booth presents too tight an arrangement for juggling inside.

The air is bracing. It cuts through the taint of petroleum and exhaust with brisk December purity. I start easy, a simple two-ball pass. Can't quite get my right hand turned so the palm is up, but it's close. I ditched the brace as soon as I got to work.

I drop two balls right off, then slip into an easy rhythm. My coveralls constrict me at the shoulder. I unzip them to my mid-chest, draw the third ball from my pocket and begin a three-ball cascade. I work it, eyes flicking back and forth, hands rolling smoothly from catch to toss. Twenty passes, then one falls. Start over. Forty, sixty, I lose count. I love this; it's like flying a kite, meditating, a frame-by-frame focus in the present.

Eventually the cold seeps into my consciousness; my hand has started to throb. I return to the marginally heated glass compartment and contemplate the Fourth Step. My notebook opens to the page I wrote last night; I flip past without reading it, unable to suppress a shudder. Evelyn said to get it down and forget about it until I do my Fifth Step. What next, then? I think I'm done with anger.

Little stuff comes to mind, stuff that was so long ago that it should be insignificant, but it must still bother me. The more I write, the more I remember. I turn back to the section on "Honesty."

The suburban wastelands of West St. Louis County presented few opportunities for employment; strip malls divided subdivisions dotted with golf courses and pristine new public schools. The summer I was fifteen, I watched a baby boy every Tuesday and Thursday afternoon. Really, I watched HBO and the couple's small selection of triple-X videos, and sampled their expensive liqueurs (Cointreau was my favorite, but I liked the Amaretto and Kahlúa, too). The baby lay on a blanket on the carpet, where he couldn't fall. I changed him right before his mom got home, or if he really started screaming, but he was such a quiet baby I left him wet for hours.

What else? This is trivial, but I cringe at the thought of telling it. Meredith caught a knee to the face at a rugby match in Springfield, lost a front tooth and broke her nose. Nothing serious, but she was sick from the pain. She got a Demerol shot in the emergency room and a prescription for Tylenol with codeine. While Meredith lay in the backseat of the van with an ice pack, I went to the pharmacy. The prescription was for sixty pills; I smudged the label and kept half. I told Meredith I only had enough money for thirty. Meredith would never use all that codeine.

A searching and fearless moral inventory. I ransacked the medicine cabinets of friends and their parents, scored everything from paregoric to Ritalin. Some of this petty stuff is harder to face than the big deals; I hit that cop with some bravado, but I'm not proud of stealing from a little boy with an attention-deficit disorder.

Alecki sets a huge bowl of raw shrimp in front of me. "Two months," he says. "It doesn't seem like it's been that long."

It's nice to have two hands again finally. I begin to shell the shrimp. "I can't remember the last time I had sixty days sober. Well, October. But before that, it must have been since I was fourteen or fifteen."

"Save those shells. I'll use them to make stock for bouillabaisse." Alecki flips me a quart Ziploc. He's pushing a pile of imperceptibly toasting flour around a small cast-iron skillet. A huge pot of finely diced onions, peppers, celery, and canned tomatoes bubbles on the stove. Alecki stirs and stirs the flour with a wooden spoon.

"Lex, it's not doing anything. It's not even hot."

"It takes patience to make a roux," he says. "That's why you're pulling shells."

The shrimp are bad enough, like trying to unfold wet toilet paper. Holly's coming for dinner; we're having romaine lettuce salad with artichokes and hearts of palm, gumbo, and cornbread. Later, after my meeting, we'll share the leftovers of the yellow sheet cake with chocolate icing Alecki baked this morning. I don't think he cares so much that I have sixty days sober; he just likes to put on a dinner party.

The flour's finally approaching the smooth tan color of his hands. He cuts off the heat, drizzles a tiny bit of peanut oil and keeps stirring until it cools. "Does it feel any different, sixty days?"

"I sleep better. At first I prowled around the house all night eating cereal and reading. Whacker liked it, but it made me crazy."

"Do you miss getting loaded?"

"I get pissed off or frustrated or bored, and I think about drinking. I really miss going out and dancing."

"You could, though."

"Yeah. I went once with Jeri, last September. The whole time, though, I had this awareness that I'm not drinking. I talked to Evelyn about it, and she didn't think it was a good idea yet."

He frowns. Unwraps the crab legs and claws, snaps them apart. "When you're done with the shrimp, you can fry the andouille. Make sure it's well broken up. So do you have to do what Evelyn says?"

"No. Usually I want to do what she says. She's been sober twenty-two years; she knows how to do this."

"Twenty-two years! She's been going to AA that whole time?"

"More like twenty-five years, I think. She was in and out for awhile."

"If she's been sober twenty-two years, why does she keep going?"

"So she can stay sober. Alcoholism is progressive. You get better, but you don't ever get over it."

"Yeah, but twenty years of AA . . . She's old, though."

"In her sixties." I pause, then ask, "You think Evelyn goes to AA because she doesn't have anything else to do?"

"Well, she's older, and she lives alone. She probably likes the company."

I rinse the shrimp in the sink and drain them. Alecki drops chunks of crabmeat into the bowl.

"Evelyn's not some loser that comes to meetings just so she'll have a place to go," I tell him. "She's cool. She knows a lot."

"I'm sure she is. But look at you—you're only twenty-six. I can't see you going to AA another twenty years."

"Can you see me staying sober twenty years?"

"I don't know." Alecki grins. "Not really."

I stare at him, astounded. "Lex, this shit can kill you. People die. Alcoholics don't get better; I sure didn't."

"You'll settle down," he says. "One of these days, you'll figure out what you want, and you'll be all right. You're about the smartest person I know. I don't think you're really alcoholic."

"I'm so glad you didn't tell me that two months ago." My voice trembles.

He snaps a leg, hard. Faintly fishy drops hit my cheek. "Why?"

"I *am* an alcoholic, Lex. I'm not proud of it; I'm not even too happy about it. But you tell me I'm not . . . That's like signing my death sentence."

"You're a little dramatic, maybe." He shrugs. "You drink too much and do stupid things. Who doesn't, if they're drunk? But once you're away from that scene for awhile, you'll learn to control it."

His assurance infuriates me—addiction isn't something you just outgrow. I stab the spatula into the crumbling sausage. "You don't know what you're talking about, Lex, so you might as well shut up. Here, this is done. I'm going to go run before Holly gets here."

"I don't know why you're being so pissy."

"I'll cut the salad when I get back." I go to my room, grab my shoes and change them on the porch. Take off fast and run until it hurts, until my lungs burn and my nose seeps from the wind and the rage begins to recede. I'm still pissed, but not so ready to go off. I slow to a jog, then stop at a pay phone three blocks from the flat.

"He doesn't get it, Evelyn. The one person I thought I'd always be able to count on. He's always come through for me, no matter what, and now he's saying I don't need AA." I swipe at my nose with the back of my hand. I'm sweaty, and the wind is freezing.

"Why should he get it?" she says. "He's not an alcoholic. He may never understand. You're his big sister; he admires you. He's making you and your girlfriend dinner. He doesn't want you to have some fatal, incurable disease. It probably just sounds like so much drama."

"Lex *is* a great guy. He's a great brother, but it seems like when it comes to sobriety, he doesn't believe me."

"Give it time. He may come around. He may not. The important thing is that *you* know you're an alcoholic. You don't need to convince anyone else."

"We've always been so close." Sadness overtakes the receding self-righteousness; I don't want recovery to come between me and my brother.

"And you still are. You just don't agree, and that's all right. You're doing OK, kiddo. You didn't hit anything; you didn't throw a fit. You didn't get drunk over it. You did something constructive."

"Yeah. If I keep losing it, at least I'll be in shape."

"Are you coming to the meeting?"

"Of course. Got to get my coin. Holly's going to stay and clean up after dinner; she's bringing a movie." My teeth are starting to chatter. I relax my jaw with an effort. "So I'm not sticking around long afterward. I'm bringing a cake, though. Lex made it this morning."

"See, he's trying. He'll come around, he's just got his own denial to face. Alcoholism touches those you're close to; they need a chance to recover, too. Are you outside?"

"Yeah."

"Go home and have some gumbo, get warmed up. I'll see you at the meeting."

"OK. Thanks."

When I return, Alecki's setting the table. The salad's already in a serving bowl, cornbread's in the oven. The place smells warm and wonderful.

"Pardon me, sir, is this Bourbon Street?"

"No bourbon for you. Did you have a good run?"

"Yeah; I'm soaked, though. I better get cleaned up."

Alecki nods, not facing me, and aligns the silverware alongside a plate. That aloof avoidance is a signal; his feelings got hurt.

"Lex, this is great. You're a hell of a cook. You're a hell of a brother, too." I grab him from behind, hug his waist.

"Christ, you're cold!" He grins now. "Go get ready."

Holly brings a bottle of alcohol-free champagne; the dinner is excellent. Alecki and Holly get into reminiscing about high school. I hate to leave for the meeting, but I want to pick up my two-month coin.

When I get back from the meeting, Holly has the kitchen cleaned, the food put away. Alecki went out to The Coffee Grounds; said he'd be back late. Holly makes coffee and I slice a piece of cake for her, a little one for me. I already had one at the meeting.

"What movie did you bring?" I ask.

"*Go Fish.*"

We get on the couch, get close. I've seen the movie before, but Holly hasn't. It's fun to watch. At the end, though, when Max says, "The girl is out there," I see Cole's face before me. Then Holly leans over and I give her a long, hard kiss.

Chapter 6

Only an alcoholic can regret the future and fear the past.

overheard at an AA meeting

The kitchen light is on; Alecki's at the table, drinking coffee and reading. I drop my gym bag on the floor and slam the door. "It's getting cold out. The temperature's dropped all afternoon."

"Looks cold," Lex says. "You been to the gym?"

"My third initial trial visit."

"What do you do, wear a disguise?"

"Holly tells me what time to come in. Dynamo's a huge place; the staff doesn't know all the people who train there. What's cooking?"

"Tuna casserole. It'll be done in about fifteen minutes." He sets down his coffee and reaches behind his chair. "Terry, Angela Johnson dropped this off while you were at work."

"Thanks." It's a long, slender tube, marked with UPS stickers, from Nicole Rankin, Weston, Missouri.

Alecki is watching me, his eyes gentle. "That the girl you lived with?"

"Cole. We just dated; we never lived together." Never will. "She was pretty," I tell him. "Long auburn hair, hazel eyes. Tall." I rip open the brown paper, shake a rolled sketch from the tube. It's the picture of me playing softball.

"Let's see." Alecki lays it flat on the table, weights the corners with clean coffee cups. "Hey, that's you."

"It's called Double Play. I was playing shortstop. The batter hit a line drive way over my head, but I snagged it somehow and threw to Jane at second. Cole was in the bleachers. She drew this that same night."

There's something else: a handmade Christmas card, about three inches high and fifteen inches long, slightly curved from the tube. In the picture, a pine forest surrounds snow-covered rooftops. Santa and eight reindeer soar over the village, lit by the Star of the East. I lay the card on the table, across the sketch; my hands are trembling. I wrote to Cole so long ago—October? It was before I drank again. I didn't think she was going to respond.

Alecki turns the card. "Awesome." He points out a tiny stork on a chimney, the Grinch and his dog lurking in the pines. "It's like an Advent calendar with all the doors open."

"Cole's good. Really talented. Kind of reminds me of you." The picture's funny, but my smile doesn't quite deter the brimming tears.

"Let me fix you some coffee, draga. Sit down and read your card. I've got to get this casserole in the oven."

I inspect the card more closely. A black cat sits in a miniature window—Whacker. Inside it says:

> *Dear Terry—Sorry it took so long to get back to you. I was glad to get your letter, happy to hear you're working and going to AA. Your job sounds great; do you work all winter? I'd like to see the Botanical Garden sometime.*
>
> *What do you think of the card? I made some others (more conventionally scaled) in a linoleum block print. They're selling pretty well at the bookstore and A Step Beyond.*
>
> *I want you to have "Double Play." This picture is so much the essence of you. Consider it a Christmas present.*
>
> *I'd like to hear from you again. I'm still at the same address. I don't hate you, Terry. I know you were drinking a lot. Things got out of hand. I'm glad that you are staying sober now.*
>
> *Tell Angie I'm still using that portfolio. You guys really helped me out. I've got pictures up at The Mug and also in the lobby of Weston Community Savings and Loan.*
>
> *I miss you; I think about you a lot. I'd like it if you stayed in touch.*
> *Love,*
> *Cole*

The quaking has become a coarse tremor by the time Alecki sets the mug in front of me. I leave the sketch, take the coffee and card to my bedroom. In the early dark I sprawl on the bed. Whacker curls at my side. Tears run into my mouth; I chase them with gulps of coffee, and read the card over and over.

Cole says she doesn't hate me. She should. I wrote to her about my job and my sixty days sobriety; a couple days later I got drunk and fucked some skanky trash with a whip. How would Cole feel if she knew *that?*

She misses me, wants me to stay in touch. She thinks I've been staying sober, though. Sixty days; I've only got a week over that now.

She misses me. I miss her, too, but I hate what I did, and I don't know if I will ever be able to think of her without seeing first her pain, her bewilderment at my attack.

By the time Alecki taps on the door, I'm all cried out. He says that dinner is ready, and I'd better eat if I'm going to make the meeting tonight.

I sigh and trail behind him to the table, weary and not the least bit hungry. Still, Alecki makes a mean tuna casserole, and I manage to force down two small helpings. He talks steadily, evenly; tells me about a subtitled German movie that he and Rodney saw, and about a really bad poet they heard at a coffeehouse in Webster Groves.

"Thanks for dinner, Lex. I'll wash dishes in the morning."

"No problem," he says. "Are you going to the meeting?"

"Yeah. Definitely."

Alecki smiles, squeezes my shoulder before he gets up to clear the plates. He worries, sometimes.

"I'm Terry. I'm an alcoholic." I pause for the response. "I got a Christmas card today, and a package, from the girl I was seeing right before I got sober. She's an artist." I draw a shaky breath. "Cole sketched a picture of me making this great catch in softball last summer. It's pretty good; she called it 'Double Play.' She sent me that picture, said she wanted me to have it.

"I haven't seen Cole since August. I got drunk one afternoon and just beat the shit out of her. I wrote a letter a while back, but I haven't . . ." I drop my face into my hands. The women wait silently. "How do you make amends for something like that? I beat her up and just left town. I didn't mean to get into all this. I'm sorry."

Portia rubs her hand across my back. "Thanks, Terry. Glad you're here."

The women say they're glad I spoke, and that I should forgive myself. I'm different now, they tell me. I wish I could believe it.

After the meeting I go to coffee with Beryl and Evelyn, then get to work a little early. Customers come and go until past midnight; I try not to yawn right in anyone's face. About 12:45 I take my jump rope from my backpack and step to a dark corner of the lot. The night is freezing, but I break a sweat eventually. I can jump on one foot, two feet, skip, or do doubles and triples. As a kid I did crossovers; I can still do them, but not without stopping.

I practice doubles and crossovers until I'm breathless and sweaty, then settle into a steady rhythm, sustained by singing along to the beat of my sneakers and the staccato whip of the rope.

A car slows; the passenger window rolls down and Alecki yells, "Hey, Rocky!" He's with Rodney; they don't stop.

After thirty minutes I'm wide awake. A customer pulls in, and I run back to the booth. While the register's open, I take a pack of orange bubble gum and drop in a quarter. I think better of it, ring it up and pay the rest. A light snow is falling, the first of the year.

I pull on my coveralls. The snow is pretty, but it's hard to see through the dirty glass of the booth. I take some glass cleaner to the few areas of window not plastered with a cigarette decal.

The flakes get fat and heavy, swirl in gusts. I turn the radio low, to the "Classics 98" station. I rarely listen to this; it reminds me of Cole, a night we relaxed in the dark and listened to Rachmaninoff and Chopin on her CD player. We were on the couch. I lay back against her chest, just feeling her breathe. I wonder if she's sold any of her paintings.

Pachelbel's "Canon in D Major" is playing. Snow blankets the asphalt outside the booth. It's almost two on a Thursday morning; nobody's out. I shut off all the overhead lights except the row by the street and the Joiner Oil sign. Backlit now, the snow blows against the glass like I'm traveling some back road through a blizzard. I pour coffee from my thermos. Sitting on the safe with my feet kicked up on the counter, I'm content to watch the falling flakes, savor quiet music in the night.

Tires crunch on the snow; I hop to my feet. It's my supervisor Marty. He pulls up at a pump and sticks the hose in his car. He looks up pointedly, and I switch the lights back on, unlock the booth.

"Hey, Marty. You out late or early?"

He flings the door wide. "What the fuck is this?" Slams it shut, stamps snow from his boots.

"I was just watching the snow." I point. "I left the sign on."

"Terry, you don't turn off the lights. Ever. This is a twenty-four-hour station." He rings up his sale himself. "Goddamn it. I got idiots working for me. My wife's sick, she's been puking all night, I got to take her to the hospital, and I come by here and you're watching the pretty snowflakes."

I shut off the radio. "What's wrong with your wife?"

"I don't know; am I a doctor? Have you started your inventory?"

"No."

"Your shift report?"

"It's not even three o'clock."

"Shit." Marty jerks a form from the drawer. "I might as well get started. People will know the place is open, at least."

"Marty, I'll leave the lights on. Why don't you go get some breakfast or something?"

"No, go home." He looks at my half-finished coffee, throws it in the trash. "Sitting here in the dark, Jesus Christ. Stupid dyke."

"Excuse me?"

"Well, what the fuck's wrong with you, anyway? How's anybody going to see you're here with the lights off?"

"What the fuck's wrong with *you?* It's the middle of the goddamn night, slowest night of the whole fucking year, there's a blizzard out there, dickhead, and we haven't even made eight hundred dollars all shift—" I shove my fist into my pocket, lower my voice. "You don't need to be calling me a stupid dyke. I'm sorry I said all that, but you—"

"Go home. Now. I don't want you in my store." He sits down at the window, takes a pen. "I was going to get rid of you anyway. There's lots of *guys* that would love this shift."

"Oh, sure."

"I got applications." He writes the date at the top of a shift report. "Come by at noon, I'll have your check by then."

"Asshole." I cram my book, jump rope, and thermos into my backpack. Snow stings my face as I cross the lot to my car.

The living room's chilly. I put on my denim jacket, sip my coffee. In the jacket pocket is the small leather pouch that holds my rosary. It belonged to my great-aunt, who came over from Romania with my grandfather. The rosary itself probably isn't Romanian; our family was Romanian Orthodox. They converted to Catholicism after they got to Chicago. But I like the rosary; I've kept it with me since my First Communion. It's been in the pouch since that night with Pat. My sobriety date; I took my last drink that night.

The aroma of fresh coffee lures Alecki from his room. He rubs his head. It's free of the braids now, but at the moment his thick black hair looks like it was styled in a blender. "Rodney's in the bathroom," he says. "Where you going?"

"No place; I'm just cold." I pull myself farther down into the jacket, like a turtle.

He stares, scratching his chest, then goes to the kitchen. Returns with the irregular brown mug his last girlfriend made, and sits next to me on the couch. "Looks like you've been sleeping."

I nod.

"So you came home early," he says.

"That's right."

"What happened?"

"Marty came to the station around two-thirty. He was pissed off because I had turned off the overheads and the booth lights, to see the snow better." I scowl. "I left the sign on; people could tell we were open. There weren't any cars out anyway; it was the middle of a fucking blizzard."

"Tell me you didn't lose your job because you wanted to watch it snow," Alecki says.

"Marty's not supposed to show up at two-thirty in the morning. His shift starts at seven. I left the station lights on; you could tell we were open. We only get maybe two or three customers from then to five-thirty anyway."

Alecki buttons his shirt, goes to rummage in the fridge. "Want some breakfast?"

"I've got nothing else to do." I follow Alecki in, sit at the table.

He bangs cabinet doors, ruptures a tube of biscuits. "What was Marty doing, checking up on you?"

"Something was up with his wife," I say. "He took her to the emergency room; she was sick. So he was in a pissy mood anyway. Then he swings by the station, probably to see if I'm sleeping." Alecki cracks eggs into a bowl. "I wasn't doing anything. I just turned off the overheads so I could watch the snow fall. It was pretty. Nothing to do, so I put on the classical station and watched the snow swirl around."

"Then Marty comes in and busts you."

"Exactly." I take another long pull at the coffee. Alecki has a Salem going; I pick it up. How can he smoke that menthol? I set it down, temptation deferred. "You know what I think it was? A couple of weeks ago, a guy came in and wanted to hang out until the end of my shift, take me to breakfast. I told him no, I don't want to—What?"

He's laughing. "You went off on him."

"Not really. I just told him 'You're not my type. I like girls.' He wouldn't leave, so I had to say something. Anyway, the guy said he's a friend of Marty's. I think Marty's been gunning for me ever since."

Alecki had to go to work then. I called Evelyn, told her about getting fired right before Christmas. Evelyn said that every time my Higher Power closes a door, another one's going to open. Said she would meet me at the five-thirty Rush Hour AA meeting. I went back to bed until midafternoon, got up in time to apply for unemployment.

I get to the meeting a little early, take a quick walk around Lafayette Park. The dull gray sky is clearing; lingering clouds are backlit, pierced by bright shards of sun. At the corner I grope in my pockets, remember again I don't smoke. I touch the pouch with the rosary; take out the beaded chain and slip it around my neck, tucked under my shirt. A luminous indigo darkens the east, where a single star burns with cold fire.

I reach the church where Rush Hour meets. The failing light burnishes the clouds pink and gold. Maybe Evelyn's right, there's a door somewhere with my name on it.

At the meeting, I pour out my fresh tale of woe. There's a lot of commiseration—sobriety does not necessarily make one more employable, at least not right away. At the coffee break, a social worker suggests I check out Vocational Rehabilitation. He tells me where the office is, and which of the counselors he'd worked with. Beryl has been trying to talk me into checking out VR; that's how she got her EMT training. It's the perfect job for a jock, she says. At least the timing seems right.

It took three calls to get set up with a counselor, but when we finally meet she tells me Vocational Rehabilitation will pay for books, course work, and my state license. Unless I work full-time while I'm in school, they'll even give me a ten-dollar daily stipend for attending classes, an extra $200 a month. I could get paid for being a drunk.

At the community college, I drive through three parking areas before I find a free space that isn't designated for staff or handicapped. Parking problems—there's a luxury of sobriety. I take my Voc Rehab packet to a series of offices, conveniently located at opposite corners of the campus, and then to the bookstore. Three hours later, I'm a college student again. Classes start the second week of January.

Six months of classes won't be too bad; that's about as long as I ever lasted, anyway. I've managed to complete a semester here and there, generally with some measure of disgrace.

I stop by Holly's with the news. She had a long lunch with some friends from the gym; she's a little tipsy.

"I can't see you in a medical profession," she says.

"I wouldn't want to be an EMT forever. Beryl's only making seven eighty-five an hour at the hospital. But I wasn't even making six at the station. I can draw unemployment until the session starts, and Voc Rehab will pick up my expenses."

"Sounds promising," she says. "Let's celebrate." She gives me a deliberately sloppy kiss, then sticks her hand right down the front of my pants.

Her fingers buckle my knees. Holly presses, I lurch, the wall smacks into my back. My lip breaks against her teeth, her throaty chuckle inflames me. My fingers, nimble again, release Holly's buttons and her blouse relinquishes its treasures. I savor her taste, the texture of nipples strained against damp sheer lace, smooth skin flavored with lotion like bitter slick flowers and a tinge of my own blood.

Holly's busy hands undo my slacks; her fingers flirt around my crotch, slip and stroke. I stand in precarious balance, my shoulders awkward against the wall. Her slippery explorations notwithstanding, I grip her wrist and lead her to the bedroom. Turn her palm up, circle it with my tongue, suck her finger into my mouth. "Girlfriend, you can do whatever you want to me, but watch those fingernails." The polish is pretty, but they look lethal.

"I'll be careful." Her voice is husky. I kiss her freckled shoulders, nip her long smooth back. Seized by urgency, we finish undressing ourselves.

I finish first, fling myself onto the bed. "Kneel over me." I bunch the pillow behind my head. She straddles my face, grips the headboard; I cup her ass, pull her to my hungry tongue. My favorite position: I like to make it last. I dally with her clit, ticklish, curbing my fervor. Holly catches the rhythm, rocks against my face. I slow down, feel the swell and throb. Flatten my tongue for a firmer stroke. Glimpse the tension in her belly; her thighs are trembling.

I switch back to fast and light, barely touching; slow fire spreads from this delicate flick. Holly's biting her lip, palms against the wall. Muscles show in her arms. Subtle and precise, I urge my tongue. I slide my hand from Holly and reach for myself. I love this. Eyes closed, concentrating above and below, I take my time. Holly begins to tremble and I speed up, just a little, then go for a sudden pressure. Holly's thighs clamp down, her hips crush into my face. I gasp against her, keep the rhythm with my hand.

Thickly pungent joy explodes within me and I'm off into some dark and starry place. I surface with Holly sprawled upon me, my right hand trapped between us. Holly rolls away, eyes damply closed. A flush is fading from her cheeks and throat. Drift of red-gold hair across the pillow reminds me for a moment of Cole. I curl a strand around my index finger and lean into Holly's warm, bare side. Skin touch is companionable, but she's just not here. What place does she go when we make love? Why doesn't she want to come back? Cole's pleasure was so much my own. Making love, we crested dark waves of ecstasy, her heart as open as her body. We rounded corners, tumbled into chasms, went so far into each other.

A shadow flickers on the ceiling. It must be getting windy out. I can't tell through the drawn blinds. Holly's staring at the flicker; looking up, stretching those long fine legs. Erica called me a "pussy hound." Cole made me a lover. With Holly, I can penetrate and still not connect.

Holly gets up, comes back with two sodas. She pulled on her blouse to go to the kitchen; it hangs halfway open, reveals creamy slices of breasts and a hint of abs. She slips it from her shoulders, slides under the covers next to me. I prop pillows against the wall, sit halfway up with my Coke. Holly lays her cheek on my belly, and I absently wind a strawberry-blond curl around my hand, then gather her hair into a single ponytail. She shakes her head, pulls it all free. Sits up next to me and pops her Coke.

"Thanks," I say. She looks puzzled. "For the Coke. For the afternoon, too."

"You're welcome. You're welcome in my bed anytime, Ms. Manescu. Christy says you're all brag, but I'd say you deliver."

"Christy wouldn't know."

Holly pulls the sheet down to my thighs, traces my torso with her fingertips. "So pretty," she whispers. "So perfect. I knew you were going to look like this."

"You're the pretty one. I sat by you for three years in French class, dying to know what you looked like under that white blouse and navy sweater."

Holly leans over and plants a kiss, right above my navel; turns to her side and faces me. "Nobody's that perfect. Show me your scars."

"My scars?"

"You never tell me anything," she says. "You flatter and flirt and brag about what a jock you are, but you never show me anything real. Where have you been hurt?" Holly started with a little pout, but now she's serious.

"I really don't have any scars." I look down at my body, treacherously whole. "Just these, I guess." I hold out my right hand. The middle and ring finger knuckles have thickened white creases: tooth marks.

"That's all?" She takes my hand, plants a kiss on each tiny mark. "Were you fighting?"

Pat's headboard broke my hand. I hit Cole, three or four times; it might have been a dozen. I punched Melissa in the teeth; that's where these scars came from.

"Terry?"

I'm staring at my hand, still thinking. "No, not really. It happened at rugby practice. Melissa had the ball and I caught her in the mouth with my fist. It was an accident." It was a cheap shot. When Melissa turned, blood dripping from her lip, I popped her again. Christy grabbed her before she could retaliate. It turned into a real free-for-all. I never did get hit, just these two little cuts where her teeth scored my knuckles.

"Melissa who?"

"I don't think you know her. She didn't live in St. Louis for long." I cannot believe I fought her over Erica. Erica threw me out, right after that, because I was "too immature." Maybe I was.

"'Rugby practice.'" Holly's swirling her Coke, killing the fizz before she drinks it. "'An accident.' You never tell me anything."

"No scars, babe. Just lucky, I guess." I inflict scars. "What about you?"

"See this tiny one?" She touches her upper lip, a pale notch in the red. "I got that when I was in kindergarten. My mom baked a cherry pie. I leaned over to sniff when she took it out of the oven, and I burned my lip on the pie tin." She shifts in the bed, uncovers her knee and points to a jagged mark, says something about high heels and a car door.

I'm drifting again, imagining a child's grief. Enticed by an aroma, you expect something wonderful, then a searing pain: you're burned. I must be tired; it almost makes me cry. I sigh, sit up and gather my clothes. "Holly, I better get going. I want to hit a meeting tonight."

Holly pulls the shirt back on, follows me to the door. "Call me after."

"That would be great." My coat sleeve brushes a pile of mail on the telephone table, knocks everything to the floor. Bills, looks like; I scoop them up and set them back. "Holly Lamont?" I didn't intend to say it aloud. The return address names an attorney.

Holly's cheeks are blazing. "That was my married name," she says. "It's O'Brien now. I've been divorced seven months." She takes the mail.

"So you did get married." And she thinks I never tell *her* anything. "I always thought you were straight."

"I always wanted to be," Holly says. She's looking out the window, tapping the letters in her palm.

"So what are we doing?"

"I'm sorry. I'm just in a weird mood." Expressionless, she stares at branches agitating in the rising wind. "Call me later."

"If I get a chance." I dawdle with my coat, but she doesn't look back. "See you."

Holly nods.

I get to the clubhouse well before the meeting, rifle through the cupboards and set up the big silver coffee urn, then stretch out on the sofa and flip through my new textbooks, *Emergency Medical Management* and *Transporting the Ill and Injured Patient*. The class meets twice a week in the evenings, from five to nine-thirty. Tuesdays are lecture, Thursdays are the weekly exam, followed by the "psychomotor objective" in the lab. We'll have units on body mechanics and lifting, taking vitals, maintaining the airway, patient history and physical exam, all kinds of medical emergencies: diabetes, poisoning, cardiovascular, respiratory. Lots of stuff on trauma, and a unit on obstetrical emergencies.

Someone's barreling up the stairs. A happy "Yes!" comes from the kitchen; Annie pokes her head around the corner. "Girl, you're a lifesaver. I was running late, and it takes about thirty minutes for that coffee pot."

"No problem."

"You want to help me set up?" she asks.

"Sure." I begin to arrange the folding chairs.

Annie sets out the literature, then distributes ashtrays. "I'm going to announce this after the women's meeting on Wednesday, but I'll ask you now," she says. "Jean and I have a cabin down by the Meramec; every year we throw a New Year's Eve party there. We've done it for a long time, but now it's a sober party. I'd like for you to come. We have a bonfire, and some nonalcoholic champagne to toast in the year."

"Sounds good," I say. "I didn't have any plans."

"Will you be bringing someone?"

"I don't know." I bang a chair open, set it down hard. "Depends."

Annie frowns at me, but only says, "That's fine. Let me know by next Friday."

I consider calling Holly after the meeting. Instead, I go to The Coffee Grounds with Annie, Evelyn, Beryl, Portia, and a newcomer. Her name, she claims, is just Indigo. She's costumed in a Stetson and a tan duster that hits her at the midcalf. Faded Levi's frame long narrow legs, and of course she's wearing cowboy boots. She wore her hat all through the meeting, and in the coffeehouse as well. I can't see her eyes.

Indigo stays through only a cup of coffee, no refills. When she leaves, I say, "Just Indigo? Like Cher, I guess, or Madonna."

"Tolerance, Terry. She's just scared," Evelyn says.

"That outfit is so affected. I can't deal with the pose."

"I've seen disguises more outlandish than that. Give her time." She eyes me. "It's easier to take someone else's inventory than your own. How's the Fourth Step coming?"

"I think I'm about done. I want to read over it one more time, but I've covered all the bases. Every so often, though, I remember something else."

"That'll continue," Annie says. "Indefinitely. Maybe infinitely."

Evelyn asks, "When do you want to schedule your Fifth Step?"

"Anytime. Thursday."

She looks dubious. "I could do it Thursday, but that's Christmas Eve."

I shrug. "I've got no plans."

Chapter 7

It takes several Steps to get from medication to meditation.

overheard at an AA meeting

I merge onto Highway 40 and flip on the radio. Christmas stuff is everywhere; even the classic rock stations are playing versions of Christmas songs. All this forced gaiety irritates me, and this year, once again, I didn't have enough money for gifts. Alecki rescued me—he bought a bunch of tins and together we made fudge and Christmas cookies for our numerous relatives.

The relatives gather later this evening, though, and until I turned on the radio my mind had been entirely occupied with the Fifth Step. *Admitted to God, to ourselves, and another human being the exact nature of our wrongs.* Evelyn initially said to come over around one o'clock today. I watched the clock all morning, resisted the temptation to look at my Fourth Step. That could have stopped me from ever leaving the house. At 11:45 I finally called Evelyn.

"I've been thinking about you," she said. "Come on over. Give me about twenty minutes to grab a quick lunch." I took the notebook and my Big Book and made a run for the Mustang.

Once in motion, I'm a little less anxious. Last night Beryl told me the best thing about the Fifth Step is that it doesn't take very long. Driving to Evelyn's flat will take eighteen minutes; reading through the burgundy notebook shouldn't require more than that.

I say the Serenity Prayer all the way to Kingshighway. At Evelyn's street I pull up to the curb, grab the notebook, and mutter one last "God, grant me the serenity to accept the things I cannot change, courage to change the things I can, and the wisdom to know the difference."

Evelyn has coffee ready. She indicates the couch, settles herself in a recliner. Her eyes are half-closed; surely she won't go to sleep.

The telling is hard. My voice gets shaky, but I steel myself to keep reading, no matter what. My guts knot up when I read about stealing Meredith's codeine and taking the Ritalin from a friend's little boy. I sip my coffee and envy Evelyn with her cigarette, then pick up the notebook and continue. During the part about the relapse and that bizarre night with Pat it's an effort to keep my tongue from sticking to the roof of my mouth—it's so dry. My hands are like ice: I set the open notebook on the coffee table and clutch my mug for warmth, then press on.

Evelyn watches me, her narrow face impassive as stone.

The disclosure about beating Cole I wrote separately, more as a narrative; I save it for last. My voice is strained, raw; I force each word from my throat, then fall silent.

Evelyn stubs out her half-finished butt. "It's tough, isn't it?"

I nod.

"Anything on that list, you could do again tomorrow; anything and more, if you take another drink. Remember that insanity is what is waiting for you. Stay sober, and you have the choice—you may never do any of it again. You may do some foolish, crazy, hurtful things in your sobriety. Lord knows I have. But today you can learn from your mistakes. Every day you stay sober, you get a little better."

I nod again, too overwhelmed to talk. It had taken more than eighteen minutes to read through a lifetime of my insane behavior. Echoes of it spin through my thoughts.

"Do you remember the day you called me from the restaurant?" she asks. "The day you got mad at Alecki because he told Holly that your old roommate kicked you out?"

"I remember."

"This seems like a pattern," Evelyn says. She kicks down the footrest of the recliner, leans toward me. "You lost it with Cole because you thought she'd been talking to someone behind your back. You got hacked off with your brother for basically the same reason. Anything like that ever happen before?"

DYKE. Black permanent marker, the word slashed diagonal across the door of my locker. It spilled over just a little, the bottom bar of the capital "E," onto Jamie Dudenhaefer's locker next to mine.

Permanent marker, and not a damn thing I could do about it. St. Thomas was small, our graduating class just 183 students; everyone knew whose locker that was with "DYKE" slashed across it. No point in going to the principal; he'd know about it soon enough. I couldn't say the word "dyke" to a nun.

I threw my jacket inside, grabbed my books, and took off for first period history, conscious of the steps that slowed behind me, of the whispers. In class, I saw eyes cut sideways at me, heads leaned together after a backward glance. I saw a note passed under a desk.

Someone must have seen me with Coach Brown the night before. But it was nothing—we just started talking after practice, and I missed the bus. She gave me a ride home; on the way she asked if I was hungry. We went to her apartment. I called Mom and said I was out with a friend. Coach ordered a pizza, and she let me have a beer from her fridge, but that was my fault—I practically begged her for it. Then she brought me home.

That had to be it. Coach was a big old dyke, for sure, but everybody liked her. I thought so, anyway.

First period seemed to last forever. The teacher kept writing on the board, oblivious to my life in ruins behind her. My hands shook too badly to take notes, and all I could hear was the faint repetition of "Manescu. Locker. Dyke."

At the second period bell I bolted from the room. I walked fast, head down, to the far stairwell and the long way up the first floor hall where the freshmen and sophomores had their lockers, so that I didn't have to pass mine.

No sooner had I thrown my books under the bench in the girls' locker room than Jeri stood before me. "The janitor is washing it off with alcohol," she said. Her voice was low, tense. Clenched on the strap of her backpack, her hand looked bloodless.

Ten years later I can still picture that—Jeri's white knuckles; her rapid, urgent whisper; the yell from the next aisle—"He can wash it off, Manescu, but everybody knows that you're a dyke." In the PE office, Coach frozen with one hand in midair, holding her plan book. Miss Johnson, who taught gymnastics and dance and drilled the cheerleading squad, storming out tiny and blond and red-faced, shrilling, "We will not tolerate that kind of language—that kind of *attitude*—" The rest drowned out by my bellow, "Who the *fuck* said that?" and Coach Brown still frozen as Lot's wife, a pillar of salt.

"Terry?" Evelyn's voice startles me; I realize I trailed off, probably some time ago. I lift my cup, but it's empty.

"Need some more?" she asks.

"Not right now." I take a long breath, relax my shoulders, and lean back into the couch. "Jeri tried to grab me, but I punched a big dent into the locker and pushed her away. I ran out of the locker room. Coach just watched me go.

"I walked around all day, went home at the regular time. Mom was waiting; the principal had already called. I got a two-day suspension."

"*You* got a suspension?" Evelyn is outraged. "What about the kid that marked up your locker?"

"It was a Catholic school," I say. "I got suspended for using foul language and for leaving the grounds without permission. Nobody ever got accused of defacing the locker.

"Mom was furious. I spent the whole day walking around, thinking up excuses as to why someone might call me a dyke: because I was a jock, because I grew up with all brothers, because I was smarter than most of the boys. For hours I defended myself against all these imaginary attacks, but never once did anybody ask if it was true. Mom acted like I had written on the locker myself for the sole purpose of embarrassing her. She screamed herself hoarse at me, and when Alecki asked her to stop, she smacked his face."

"What about your dad?" Evelyn asks.

I shrug. "He never said a word. He hid behind the paper when my mother started screaming. The two days that I was suspended, he told me I needed to come paint with him, but I got paid for the hours."

Evelyn sighs. "You hear about the prevalence of suicide for gay and lesbian kids. It's a wonder any of us ever makes it."

"That's the truth. I'll say one thing for Jeri, she always stuck by me. All my other friends—before the locker thing, I was always popular, but afterward it seemed like everybody was afraid to be seen with me."

"Queer by association," Evelyn says.

"That sucked." I remember how alone I was those days, how Christy and Meredith and even Coach would sometimes look my way with fleeting apologetic smiles, but never again would I go to someone's house to study. Never again did I get picked for a team in PE class, even though I was the best athlete at St. Thomas. Nobody but Jeri and Alecki ever talked to me. It was around the end of senior year, and I started drinking a lot. I was out then, no sense denying it, but I was awfully alone. "I don't really blame them, especially Coach; she had a lot to lose. It hurt, though."

Evelyn briefly massages her temples with her thumbs. "Darlin'," she says, "it hurts to hear it. No wonder gossip sets you off. It may always bring up some of those old feelings. But now you know it's a pattern for you, and that can help you to handle it differently next time."

"I hope so." I shudder, thinking of Cole.

"You've made changes already," Evelyn says. "Last time you called me when you got upset." She stands up and stretches. "You made it through Step Five; ready to move on?"

"You bet." I turn to the bookmark in my Big Book and read aloud: "'We then look at Step Six. We have emphasized willingness as being indispensable. Are we now ready to let God remove from us all the things which we have admitted are objectionable? Can He now take them all—every one? If we still cling to something we will not let go, we ask God to help us be willing.'"

"So, are you entirely ready?" Evelyn asks.

"I think that ego still gets in my way," I say. "I had to pray for willingness to do Steps Four and Five."

"You got it, hon," she says. "These Steps don't have to be worked perfectly, though, you just have to do your best. Six is 'We're entirely ready to have God remove all these defects of character.' Seven just says 'Humbly asked Him to remove our shortcomings.' If you are willing to let go of those defects of character, then you are ready for Step Seven."

"I think I am."

"Good enough." Evelyn puts one hand on the coffee table, eases herself to her knees. "Let's do it."

I kneel as well, and we remain silent a moment. Evelyn looks like she's praying. Then she hands me her beat-up old Big Book, open to page 76, and I again read aloud. 'My Creator, I am now willing that you should have all of me, good and bad. I pray that you now remove from me every single defect of character that stands in the way of my usefulness to you and my fellows. Grant me strength, as I go out from here, to do your bidding."

Evelyn smiles at me. "That's it. You did Five, Six, and Seven."

"Cool." I give her the book. "The next big challenge: Christmas Eve with the family."

Evelyn hands me a pencil and scrap of paper. "Write down your mom's phone number."

I comply. "Here you go. What for?"

"About seven-twenty tonight, expect a call from an old lady with no family who is desperate to attend a meeting." She grins. "It's up to you, kiddo. If you aren't ready to go, then don't."

A slow smile overtakes me. "I'll be there for you, Evelyn."

Except for last year in the treatment center, I haven't spent a sober New Year's Eve since I was twelve. Annie's cabin is out of town. I have to keep checking the directions by the light of the moon; there are no streetlights on these country roads. It's warm for January, foggy. The snow has all melted away. Finally I pull up to the little A-frame, three miles into some heavy woods.

The voices inside are loud; I knock hard. Warm smells of coffee and food greet me, and Evelyn flings her skinny arms around me. "Terry, welcome. Wasn't sure you were coming." She clasps my hand, leads me to the kitchenette. "There's stew, vegetarian chili, some biscuits. Coffee's in the big pot and there's cider in the refrigerator."

"Great." I help myself to stew and two biscuits, join the group around the fireplace. Eight women are here already, including me. Seating is at a premium; some of the ladies are perched on bedrolls they brought. We talk program, exchange war stories of New Year's Eves past. From time to time more women drift in. Most I know from Lambda; some are spouses or friends. Full of stew, I mostly listen and relax in the easy humor of the evening, a visit with family in lesbian utopia.

At ten o'clock, Portia picks me for the bonfire crew. "You look like you can make a fire."

"I can handle it." I join her and three others. Behind the cabin is the fire pit, ringed by broad stumps cut for seats. In the quiet clearing, the moonlight is sufficient for gathering twigs and pulling splits from the cord wood by the back door. Though the fog is rising, it's still damp; the wood won't catch at first. Portia goes to the shed and produces a bottle of charcoal starter. I pile more twigs over our expired first attempt, and Portia douses them. A woman in a ski jacket flicks a last lit match to gratifying effect. The explosion would launch a small spacecraft. We put on the split wood and finally a couple of logs, making a bright blaze.

I get coffee orders from the crew, fill and season the cups as requested, and bring them back out on a tray. The fire's appeal has dwindled for me; the chili caught my eye when I went in, and so did Beryl. Her hair's grown out over the winter; it softens her features. I go back in the cabin and ladle up another plate of food. "Hey, Beryl. Can I join you?"

"Sure. How's the chili?"

"Awesome, with a little Tabasco. I liked the stew, but this is great."

"You just like to eat," she says.

"I have monumental appetites." I flash my most suggestive smile.

"How do you stay so thin?"

"I work out a lot, and I play soccer. I like to stay in shape."

Evelyn interrupts this promising interchange. "Who needs a meeting?"

Everyone refills cups with cider and coffee, then trails outside to the fire. We sit on the stumps and upturned logs, and Evelyn hands Beryl the Big Book. "Take it, kid."

"I'm Beryl, alcoholic."

The meeting topic is gratitude. Beryl speaks about how AA has become her family.

My turn. "I'm Terry; I'm an alcoholic. This is so mellow; it's not even like New Year's. Beats last year, though. I was in a treatment center with a bunch of other resentful drunks. We were issued paper cups of grape juice and a big bowl of popcorn, then ordered to celebrate. We didn't even try. I'm grateful to be here instead of on my way to detox somewhere."

At the end of the meeting, we hold hands and say the Serenity Prayer. Evelyn produces a chilled bottle. "Sorry, Terry, all we got is grape juice this year too."

"At least it's sparkling white. In treatment it was that purple syrup."

Annie's partner, Meg, brings out champagne glasses for everyone. "One of the remnants of my marriage."

At twelve o'clock we toast and hug, yell to the silver moon. Some of the ladies settle in with their sleeping bags, fearing the seasonal traffic. Drunks in recovery refer to New Year's Eve as "Amateur Night." I hang around the fire a little longer, then head home around one, feeling good. Maybe this will be a better year.

It's been over a year since I was in school; this will be my fifth attempt at postsecondary education. I push that out of my mind as I find a parking place, right in front of my building. Parking is not as bad for evening classes.

"You'll do great," Evelyn told me this afternoon. "The Terry who got kicked out of all those other schools is not the same Terry who's enrolled in EMT school." I was never nervous about going to school before, but before I never cared how I did.

With twenty minutes to spare before class, I drop my backpack at a front-row desk and go off in search of a Coke.

Near the stairwell is a student lounge with vending machines. I get a soda. The lounge is littered with papers, flyers, chip bags, and candy wrappers, but no students. A pay phone hangs above a ripped yellow vinyl couch. Chrome and plastic chairs stand askew around four orange Formica tables.

Six months of training begins tonight. I pop the tab on my Coke and start down the hall. That's more than a semester; we go for twenty-five weeks, total. The midterm and final are both on Saturdays. Other than that, I only have to show up from five to nine-thirty Tuesdays and Thursdays from now until June and I'll be an EMT.

I step through the doorway, imagining myself in a navy blue uniform, but the sound of rushing liquid seizes my attention. "Evening, fellows." I smile at the two backsides and hurry to the classroom next door. You'd think guys would have the decency to close the door to the john. I think the stocky guy with the crewcut is Mr. Carr, our instructor.

It is; he returns to the room with his face redder than mine. Fortunately, he couldn't see me from his vantage point, and there are seven other women in the class.

We begin with a brief review of the syllabus, then begin a lesson on body mechanics. After two hours, we have a twenty-five minute break. A lot of the students brought dinner in a paper bag, and a couple of the guys make a McDonald's run. I ate at home.

The class has eight men, eight women. A few students went outside to smoke, but almost everyone else is in the lounge. I get another Coke and sit by Linda, broad-faced and amiable. She took the first twelve weeks of class last winter, then dropped out to have a baby. "Nobody's going to hire an EMT that graduates eight months pregnant," she says. "I thought it would be better to just start over." She shows pictures of her little girl, a blonde cutie with a big head. "I want to get a job on second shift," she says. "Her daddy works days."

After body mechanics, the unit progresses to personal safety and the ethics of emergency care and transport. Mr. Carr stresses the need to take care of ourselves psychologically as well as physically. "You don't see EMTs and paramedics rock-climbing or jumping out of airplanes," he says. "You'll get all the adrenaline you want on the job."

By eighty-thirty I'm ready to go. On Thursdays we have just an hour of review and a quiz; after break we go to the lab and do simulations. That will go quickly. Every Tuesday night we have lecture, and we have to write a three-page research paper pertaining to one of the units. This should be easy, as long as I make it to class. Attendance has never been my strength, but Evelyn says this time will be different.

I call her when I get home, tell her I managed to get through four hours without sneaking out, talking out, antagonizing the instructor, or creating a scene. Evelyn says, "Keep it up, kiddo; you'll do all right." She sounds tired, so I let her go. I read part of a chapter in *Emergency Medical Management,* then go to bed early. I have to work with Andrei tomorrow, and that's never easy.

Alecki engineered it; my unemployment was about to run out. Alecki's not quite trusting this AA way of life just yet. He has been working for Andrei for over six months. He says it's not that bad, but Alecki is more easygoing than I am. Dre's threatened by women, especially intelligent women. Around lesbians, he tends to grasp his crotch periodically.

Like Marius, my oldest brother, Andrei resembles Pop—short, barrel-chested, with thick wavy black hair. Furry—hairy legs and forearms, hairy hands, thatches of curls hanging over collars. Marius took a job where he wears a suit and tie; it hides most of that hair.

Andrei looks like Marius, but he lacks our big brother's fine sense of complacency. Marius is a brain, Alecki a poet, I'm an athlete, Andrei is . . . the baby. He paints houses with Pop, he's a good worker. Built, too; with no more effort than hauling around ladders and cans of paint, he resembles a hairy bodybuilder—slim muscled waist, chunky biceps and deltoids and pecs. But he's irritatingly unsure of himself, especially around the family.

Andrei likes to point out that he's the one who'll keep the family business together. He gloats that despite our years of college, neither Alecki nor I have had a steady job for more than five or six months at a time. This thrills him: in a good year, he grosses more than Marius, who has a master's degree in chemistry. Even with all his tally marks, Dre still needs to put someone down.

Now both Alecki and I are working for him. The Seventh Step is all about humility. I ought to get credit for that, just by virtue of this job.

I get to the job site by seven. Painting interiors sucks, especially residential. You have to be careful about drips. I don't use masking tape; I could cut a good edge even when I was drinking. You have to move furniture, though, and cover stuff, and take down the fixtures, and make sure the drop cloth is tight to the wall. And homeowners: the women hover, fret about color choices and the potential havoc you may wreak. The guys are sheepish, compelled to tell me why they couldn't do it themselves. "Bad back; I can't stand on a ladder anymore," or "I just had hernia surgery." Spare me—I'll paint; you pay when I'm done.

Interior paint stinks, and the rooms get stuffy and humid as it dries, and close to the ceiling it's hot. The worst part will be that I can't avoid Andrei.

I should be grateful that I have a job, grateful that there are interiors to paint in January, because there's not much work I'd want to do outside.

This house is big. Dre's truck is here, but not yet unloaded. Seven is early for working in someone's home. The garage is open, so I haul in the paint buckets and sawhorses and set them by the door to the inside.

Andrei starts out, then halts. "Hey, Terry. Thanks." He stands just inside and I pass everything rapidly through the doorway. It is a cold damp day—this way we won't let out so much heat as we bring in the equipment.

The upstairs rooms are cleared of furniture already. I spread the drop cloths, then remove the switch plates and outlet covers with my Swiss Army knife. Andrei brings up the paint. He pops all the cans and checks for uniform color. His radio, a disreputable jam-box spattered with every color of pastel, is permanently tuned to "The Home of Classic Rock."

Dre's got his industrial-sized coffee thermos, too. He pours some into the cap and offers it with a grin. "You look like you could use a little."

I accept, surprised, and savor the warmth as I ready my bucket and brush. Dre's the only guy I know who drinks coffee as rot-your-teeth sweet as I do. So far, he's on good behavior. It's just the two of us today; Alecki and Derrick are finishing another job. They might come here tomorrow.

I stir the "Desert Sand" and cut in around the baseboard. Andrei hops onto the sawhorse and begins to edge the ceiling in white. He sings softly in his raspy baritone, a voice that sounds strained unless he's approaching full volume. Occasionally I catch him watching me, but I just keep painting. When he slops a big drip down the wall, I refrain from comment and toss him a rag.

"Thanks," he says, and wipes away the worst of it. "Hey, Terry, you remember painting at Mrs. Porter's?" He smirks.

I laugh. "The job that wouldn't quit." I was eighteen, just out of high school; Andrei was only fifteen and a half. He looked older, not as thick through the chest and shoulders as now, but sturdy, and already sporting a ratty mustache and a little patch of hair on his chest. Between us, though, we had eight summers of experience in painting. Pop got us started, then talked to Mr. Porter and left us to work alone.

The job was supposed to be only the kitchen and the bathroom. We ended up spending six weeks; we painted some rooms twice. By the second week, Mrs. Porter answered the door in a towel every morning. "You caught me getting ready for the shower again." We'd blush and apologize, snicker to each other as we set up.

By midmorning Tuesday of week three, I was zipping up the dress she couldn't quite reach. She began to show up in the towel on her way out of the shower, too. By week four, she'd had us each alone in her bedroom.

We'd come home and say, "Pop, she changed her mind again. Now she wants us to go back and do all the closets, and the inside of the garage."

He'd shake his head. "Whatever you guys are doing, keep it up."

I think Dre had it up all summer. We did have a good time, before Andrei got his own crew and became the Prince of Painting.

"I wonder about her," Andrei says. "If things ever get slow, I figure I've always got a job somewhere."

"I wonder if she's settled down."

"She's probably doing the cable guy," he says.

"Or girl."

Once the prep work's done, Andrei sets up in the next room. He's got only three drop cloths on this job, so he cuts in one wall at a time while I roll the ceiling and walls of the first room.

We work steadily all day and finish the upstairs. Maybe Dre's grown up a little; I can handle him like this. We're both trying so hard, though; I'm not sure it can last.

Every other Saturday, Holly works the desk at Dynamo until closing. It sucks, but I need to study anyway. I'm highlighting the handout on "Diabetes: Insulin Reaction vs. Hyperglycemia" when the phone rings. I hope it's Holly.

"Fucking cop! I hate that fucking bitch."

I look at the phone, as if it could explain. "Uh . . . Jeri?" Sounds like her, but the words are wrong.

"Terry. I have never been so pissed off." It's definitely Jeri. "The fucking bitch—She—I should just—"

"You want to come over?"

"If it's OK," she says. "I'm not drunk, but I've had a couple."

"No problem, Jer. Just don't bring it with you."

"Course not." The phone clatters, then goes dead.

I put on some coffee, rake my papers and notebooks into a pile, run the vacuum through the middle of the room. Whacker, big-eyed, watches that noisy beast from the back of the couch.

Jeri storms into the room and slings an arm around my waist. "Terry," she breathes, "so glad you're here."

She's red-eyed, maybe from crying, and a touch unsteady. "Hey, girl. What happened?" I extricate myself and lead her to the sofa. By the light of the lamp, three parallel welts show dark on her cheek. "Rita slapped you?" I'll kill her.

"Fucking cunt," Jeri snarls. This got ugly. "Yeah, the big cow smacked my face." She jams her hands in her pockets and slouches, legs straight out and crossed at the ankle. Her right foot jerks to the rhythm of her fury. I see her at seventeen, sulking outside the principal's office.

I get Jeri a black coffee, pop a Coke for myself. A rage boils within me; I can barely contain the urge to put my fist right through the wall. Before I go off, though, I should get the whole story. I owe Jeri that. After a deep breath, I ask whoever I've been praying to for a little help.

When I come back from the kitchen Jeri's head is down, her hair hanging. I can't tell if her eyes are open. I drink my soda and wait. The Serenity Prayer runs through my head: pleas for courage, acceptance, and wisdom compete with fantasies of beating Rita bloody.

Next to me, Jeri is breathing hard. A faint disturbance of her bangs echoes the furious movement of her foot. One hand finally pulls free of her pocket and takes the coffee, and Jeri's dark eyes lock on mine. "You're taking this calmly," she says.

I shrug. "Tell me what went down."

She sips her coffee, shakes her head. "It was stupid, really. There's not much to tell. I just wanted to go out."

"Go out? Where?"

She sits up, sheds the attitude for real frustration. "That's the thing—I didn't even care. Just to get out of the damn apartment and spend the evening with someone besides Rita and the dog. I told her pick somewhere.

"She couldn't do it. Her family might see us at a restaurant, or her cop friends might see us at a club, or she could run into some kid from the DARE program if we went to the movies and then her career would be over."

"And you guys fought?" *God, grant me the serenity to accept the things I cannot change—*

"I yelled at her." A grin flickers across her face. "Got kind of personal; I said something about if they couldn't ID her big butch ass by now, then going out with me wasn't going give it away. Rita looked all shocked, and then she slapped me."

"You called her butch, and it hurt her feelings?"

Jeri smirks. "And she's a goddamn cop!"

"Got her a badge, a gun . . ."

"Big old nightstick!" she says. "Scared me the first time I saw it. I was hoping she wouldn't have any funny ideas about that, or the handcuffs."

Pretty soon we're both laughing, and I can see the welts will fade from Jeri's cheek without a bruise. I'm not going to have to go after Rita with a baseball bat after all.

"My woman's not much better," I tell her.

"Holly? You guys go out. She'll go to the bar."

"And movies, and restaurants. She's not like Rita; I don't know how you could stand that. And Holly's fine, too." I pause, rub my forehead. I couldn't say this to anyone but Jeri. "The only real problem is she's straight. She knows it. There's no risk for her in going to the bar; everybody just wonders why that straight woman is there."

Jeri's brow furrows. "You know, I wondered . . . You think it was the divorce?"

"I don't know. Holly has a thing for girls, but I think it's mostly fantasy. She had a crush on me in high school."

"She hid it well."

"I wondered, back then, but I never could believe it. Maybe she was attracted to my attraction. That happens."

Jeri stretches. She turns so that her head's propped on the arm of the couch, her feet are on my leg. I strip off her shoes and socks. "Put on some music," she says. "Got any Sinéad?"

"Lex does." I rummage through his CDs, find *The Lion and the Cobra*.

"So what's up?" she asks. "I know she likes you."

"Holly's just playing with me. She won't admit it. We have a good time. The sex is decent; she caught on to that, and her body makes me crazy. But when we're done, we're done." I look at Jeri, and she nods. "I feel like a serial one-night stand."

Jeri chuckles. "You used to aspire to that. You've changed."

Whacker rubs against my shins; I stroke him from head to tail, the way he likes. He sniffs Jeri's shoes and makes a face at me, then turns his backside to them. His tail stiffens and trembles.

"I don't think so!" I boot him gently away, and set the shoes on the coffee table.

"He must have smelled the dog," Jeri says. "You really have changed, Terry. At first I didn't think you were going to make it in AA. When you were drinking, you seemed like you had your act together, even if it was an act. You were too cool to be real; I guess that's why you blew up every so often. Then you quit, and you were just raw. Transparent, almost; I could see every piece of you, and I thought it was going to be too hard. But now you're more together again."

I consider this. "For awhile it felt like that. Raw, or like I was stripped, and I didn't have alcohol to put that cloak back on me. Vulnerable." I grin, a little self-conscious at Jeri's acknowledgment. "It is starting to get easier, though."

"Look at you. You're in school; you've got a job. You've never been able to do both. And you're just . . ." She pauses. Once more I see Jeri as she was in school: poring over a book, dark eyes glittering in concentration. "A year ago I could see you with Holly, no problem. But a year ago I wouldn't have called you up about Rita. You're my best friend, always, but I wouldn't have been able to trust you with that. Tonight I needed somebody to listen to me, or just to be around. When you were drinking, it would have all been about *you*. You would have been drunk, and driving when you shouldn't, and going out to kick butt, and I would have spent the whole night trying to keep you out of trouble."

I guess that's a compliment, but it stings. I gulp too much Coke and swallow hard. "So I haven't been much of a friend."

Jeri's eyes go wide. "No, Terry, you've been a great friend. You're fun, and you're smart, and generous, and you're loyal to the death." She holds up her left palm. "Blood brothers, right? You're just a *better* friend now." She gets up and gives me a quick hug, kisses the top of my head.

Alecki comes in the front door. His eyebrows lift. "Jeri! Haven't seen you in a long time."

"Alecki." She sits back down. "Your sister was just trying to sober me up."

"She'd be the one to do it." Alecki hurries to his room, obviously reading way too much into the situation.

Jeri picks up her shoes and socks, then sighs. "Girl, I'm beat. Would it be all right if I stayed on your couch tonight?"

"You've never spent a night on my couch before. Come on."

In my bed, warm against me, Jeri snuggles as softly as she did when we were twelve. God, I love this woman.

Ever since I started the EMT training, the days rush by. Saturday morning at 7:30 I have a midterm, then after the test I have to paint with Andrei until 5:30. It's a rush job, so we have a full crew. Pop even comes to help, and we get the job done by dark.

To celebrate our timely finish (with an unusually large payoff) Andrei and Derrick are going out of town for a few days. My classes are canceled until Thursday—I have four days off.

Sunday I sleep half the day. Holly's working at Dynamo. I'll go work out later, then we'll get together. After setting up the date with Holly, I give Beryl a call. She says the ambulance service at the hospital will be adding some positions this summer. She had mentioned me to her supervisor, and he invited me to fill out an application.

Beryl suggests that we meet at The Coffee Grounds for a couple of hours, until the seven o'clock meeting. I dress and drive down to Grand, where Beryl is at the coffeehouse with Annie.

"Look who I scared up," Beryl says.

Annie asks how I'm doing; she hasn't seen me much since I've been in school and working. Even when I get to meetings, I have to get home right afterward to study. School's only for six months, though, and that's half over.

"I'm glad I took EMT training," Beryl says. "I'd never make it through college. Tried it for a year, but all I did was drink and puke."

Annie says, "I never threw up, no matter how drunk I got. I don't know why."

"Control," Beryl says. "It's because you're such a control freak."

"I never thought you were really a drunk," I tell Annie. "When I first saw you with Bill, I thought you were a plant."

"A plant? You mean an impostor?"

"You're a grade school teacher."

"I'm a real alcoholic," she says. "I just always passed out before I got the opportunity to vomit. I didn't go out much. Just watched TV, lay on the couch, and quietly drank myself into a stupor."

"I was never a quiet drunk," Beryl says. "Everybody knew it when I got drunk. There's pictures out there I wish I could get my hands on."

"Such as?" Annie says.

"There's some bad ones." Beryl hesitates, gets a little red. "I know too many women with Polaroid cameras. One time I was at a party at my friend Jenny's. I got just stupid drunk, so somebody took me to Jenny's room and I passed out on her bed. I don't remember any of this. Apparently I got up a couple hours later, walked right past everybody and into the kitchen. They heard me open the oven door and came in to see what I was doing. I'd pulled open the door, sat down on it, and peed."

Annie groans. "A real Kodak moment."

"I didn't ever do that, but when I first started drinking I got sick all over this guy I was seeing," I say. "It's no way to impress your date."

"That's the truth," Beryl says. "I doused I don't know how many cars. The worst, though, was when I was a freshman at MU. I was mad about something, I think, or just being an idiot. Anyway, I drank a whole quart of Southern Comfort in my dorm room. Didn't mix it or anything, just drank it straight down.

"It didn't stay down. It was Puke City in my room that night. My roommates were ready to kill me. I barfed in the trash can, on the throw rug. They left me on the bathroom floor; I remember someone coming in from the other side of the suite and wanting to use the john. I was trying to hit her, to get her to leave, but all I could do was punch at her ankles. I couldn't even raise my head.

"Somehow I got myself into bed later that night. I wake up the next day with the hangover of the century. The room reeks like peach and puke—horrible. I take out the trash can, put the throw rug, the towels, my clothes out on the landing, go to take a shower.

"I get out of the shower and the room still reeks. I can't figure it out. I go to my dresser, which is right next to the bed, open my underwear drawer—"

"Oh, no!" Annie's got the picture.

"Yes. Middle of the night, I must have just leaned over, opened the drawer, shut it all up when I was done."

"That is gross, Beryl. Really gross."

"I've got a worse one," I tell them. "It was when I was up at Kirksville. I was a PE major. Never went to class; I just partied all the time.

"It was the end of the semester. Almost everybody was done, but I had this one last Saturday morning final in kinesiology. I'd missed most of the labs—I had to get an A on this final to pass the class. There were parties going on, though, because everybody else was finished.

"Day of the final, I slept through the alarm. Woke up ten minutes before the test. I was still half-dressed from the night before, so I pulled on my jeans and sneakers and ran like hell.

"I got there just as the teaching assistant handed out the test. Took my final; everything was cool. Went back to my apartment to take a shower. Looked in the mirror—one side of my hair was completely plastered down with dried vomit."

Annie's hand flies to her mouth, then she and Beryl guffaw. "That's the worst," Beryl says. "No shit."

"It was bad. Looked like I'd styled my hair with oatmeal mousse."

We swap war stories until it's time for the meeting. I've missed these guys; it's nice to have a chance to get together.

Evelyn's at the Lambda Club. After the meeting, I get a Coke from the machine and join her in the lounge.

"How did the midterm go?" she asks.

"Aced it. Ninety-nine percent."

Evelyn smiles so big that her denture slips a little.

"The coursework is easy," I say. "I've always been interested in the body."

She laughs. "That's half your problem, Terry."

"I'm serious. The human body is a fascinating subject. I was a PE major for awhile, and I've had courses in first aid and kinesiology, so the academic work isn't completely new. The medical terminology is new, but I had six years of Latin in school, and some Greek in college. Really, the only hard thing has been switching my meetings. But I'm at home group on Wednesday night and I hit a meeting or two on the weekends."

"Do you feel like that's enough?" she asks.

"I'm OK with it."

"How's the house painting?"

"Andrei lets me work around the school schedule. Now that the days are getting longer, he works into the evenings, but I knock off at three o'clock so I can get a shower and grab some dinner. I put in extra hours on Saturdays, if I need the money. Andrei knows I do good work; it's my personality he doesn't like."

"Usually it takes families the longest to notice any changes. He'll come around."

"I'm not holding my breath. If he wasn't my brother, I would have no use for him."

Evelyn scrutinizes me for a long moment, then grins and slaps my shoulder. "You know what? You look happy."

I shrug, then grin right back. "Yeah, I guess I am. Busy, but happy."

"Are you still seeing Holly?"

"Since school started, we've only gone out a few times. I see her when I work out, which isn't that much, but I am going to drop by the gym tonight. Actually, I should be going now."

Evelyn gives me a quick hug. "Take care, kiddo."

When I get to Dynamo, Holly is at the desk. I run my driver's license through the scanner; it just beeps. "Not working?" Holly asks. I hold it out and she palms it, enters someone's code into the computer. "Maybe we should just make you a new card, Terry."

Excellent. She's got me in the system. It's the only way I'll ever belong to Dynamo. Holly's been letting me in with the driver's license ruse, or sometimes I'll say I forgot my ID. It's risky, though; she could lose her job if she gets caught. We talked about making me a fake ID, but couldn't figure out how to falsify the payment. I hit on a plan: Holly goes through the attendance records, finds a woman with a lifetime membership who hasn't been in for a few months. She'll make a new ID for that account, but with my name and picture on the card. The time is paid for, no one is using it; nobody loses.

I pose for my picture with a big victorious grin. "I'll have this ID for you by the time you're done with your workout," Holly says.

Dave, the beefcake trainer, says, "I'll do it. You're closing; I don't mind." This is great: Holly doesn't even have to make it herself.

Before I change into my workout clothes, I take a quick shower. I want to be relatively fresh when Holly gets off. She leads two aerobics classes four evenings a week, and lately she's been working the desk until closing. If I didn't lift, I'd never see her. It's been nearly three weeks since we spent a full night together.

Hot water flows over me, the evening's first caress. Holly and I took a shower together at her place last Sunday. I ended up on my knees in front of her. She pressed her shoulders against the tile wall, arched her hips forward; by the time she was done, the water on my back had turned cool. I shiver, in memory and hopeful anticipation.

Someone's humming over by the sink, a sweet familiar song that I can't place. When I emerge from the shower in my towel, though, I find only a flushed young woman, sweaty from her racquetball date, and generic jazz through the sound system.

I put on my shorts and tank top, go upstairs to the weight room. Two Herculean red-faced men are at the squat racks. They bellow and exhort each other through "one more; push it!" The inclined abdominal board is hooked on the third rung; I climb onto the pad, secure my feet under the strap. The behemoths are reflected in the mirror, rising and falling as I curl my trunk, raise my torso again and again until the muscles burn and sweat gathers behind my knees. I fall back, take a few slow breaths. By the time I'm through with my abdominals, the guys are gone. I'm the only person here.

The lat pulldown machine has the wrong attachment. Since I'm short, I have to stand on the seat to undo the clasp and suspend the longer bar from the cable. I hop down, take a wide grip, and sit. From arm's length, I draw the bar slowly down, working the broad muscles of my back. I've always liked this exercise, the deep stretch as the weight pulls my arms overhead. Between sets, I find Holly's reflection in the mirror before me. She's still at the desk, flipping through an aerobics schedule. Bored; I'll take care of that soon enough.

Bar dips next: I hoist myself onto the parallel bars of the rack, my body suspended between extended arms. Lower myself, controlled, then exhale and press up. Most women can't do dips. I crank them out like push-ups; keeping time with the canned music, not bothering to count. Panting, I jump down, wipe my sweaty forehead with the back of my hand.

Holly's reflection again, this time close. "Hey, girlfriend," I say, and turn the wrong direction, disoriented by the mirrors. "You here by yourself?"

"Yeah," she says. "I'm closing, but I'm almost done. Hey, did you see those guys doing squats?"

"Couldn't miss 'em."

She tells me that they're linebackers; they play for the St. Louis Rams. Holly loves football, a carryover from her days at St. Thomas.

"Looks like it's been busy," I say. "The windows are completely steamed up."

"It was a total zoo, all afternoon. Everybody came in at once." She snags a leather jump rope from the floor, hangs it from the proper hook.

"You want to go out?" I ask.

"I don't think so; let's just go to my place and chill."

"Fine with me." I'll show her a better time that way. "Hey, can you spot me on the bench?"

"As soon as I get done."

I grab a pair of dumbbells from the rack and face the mirror. Curl the weights to my chest and lower them slowly, keeping my elbows tucked to my sides. My biceps bulge, then lengthen. The sound system goes off; the sudden silence is eerie. My breath becomes loud, I can hear the switches snap as Holly turns off the overhead lights by the cardiovascular platform. I set the weights down as if they're made of crystal.

That tune is in my head still, the one from the locker room. I do another set of curls to the slow meter, try to put words to it. *Amazing Grace, how sweet the sound/ That saved a wretch like me* . . . That's it. Haven't heard it in years; I don't know if I could remember the words. The melody permeates my brain; I'm in for an evening of it.

My workout is done, except for bench presses. An Olympic bar sits on the two uprights that form the rack of the weight bench. The bar alone weighs forty-five pounds. I thread a ten- and a five-pound plate onto each end of the barbell, then sit and wait for Holly, feet up on the bench and my arms across my knees. A glance in the mirror confirms that the position displays my deltoids admirably.

Holly surveys the room. I picked up weights as I went, so it's already straightened. She shuts off the lights at the near end. "You don't mind, do you?"

"No, I can see." Emergency lights hang by the exit.

"All right, let's get these done." She takes her place at the head of the bench. I lie down, whip out a quick set of ten. Holly scoffs. "Intensity, girl! You're working too light."

"I'm saving my energy for later."

She laughs. "How much can you bench?"

"More than this. Put twenty on either side." I hook my wrists behind the uprights and let gravity stretch my pecs. My legs fall to the sides, a provocative arrangement. I've always had a fantasy of making it on a weight bench. Sprawling on the narrow support, legs spread, the grunt and thrust and sweat; it gets me hot.

Holly slides forty pounds of plates onto the bar, then steps close. The hem of her gym shorts just touches the top of my head. I wrap my fingers around the knurling, a little in from my normal grip. Tighten the muscles behind my shoulder blades, take a big breath, and lower the bar to just above my nipples. Thrust it up with a grunt.

Holly helps position it on the rack. "Damn, Terry! That's more than I weigh. That's way over what you weigh."

"I weigh more than you'd think, for being short. We're probably about the same."

"Little as you are?" She looks dubious, but I'm not going to get into an argument on weight.

"Put on thirty more; I'll try again." That will be one hundred seventy-five, more than I've ever done. Can't hurt to try it with a spotter.

Holly puts on two ten-pound plates. "Try this first. You want a lift-off?"

"Please."

She steps up to the bench. My attention is diverted—what I'd taken for a leotard is just a Spandex top, tucked into shorts so loose that I can see they appear to cover nothing but flesh. I wasn't the only one thinking ahead. Holly grips the bar and tenses. "Ready?"

"Not yet."

She nods, eyes on the bar. My hand on her thigh startles her. Holly's definitely not wearing panties; curls brushed against my knuckles when I reached. "Shit, Terry, what are you doing?" Her voice is edged with panic, low, but she doesn't move away.

"There's no one here." I cup my palm over that provocative little juncture where all the seams of her shorts converge, press gently upward.

"We're right in front of the window." Now she's whispering.

"No, we're not. Besides, it's steamed up. Nobody can see in." My thumb strokes the seam, persuading. "We can both get a workout."

Holly leans on the bar, takes a wide stance that brings her tantalizingly near. I slide my hand to her hip, draw her closer. Propped on my elbow, I can barely bring my face to her. I breathe against her shorts, then draw the cloth away and kiss the soft inner thigh. I reach for her breasts. Spandex restrains her nipples; a light persistent circling of fingernails brings them forth.

Half-reclining is a strain right after a workout. I hate to stop, but a tremor of fatigue racks my left shoulder. I fall back onto the bench. "Come around to this side. I can't reach you there."

Holly looks to the window again. "You're crazy. I'm going to lose my job."

I knew she'd be like this. "Holly, we can't stop now. If I'm crazy, it's because of you." Holly gives me an "Oh, please" look, but I'm not giving up. She's stalling, twirling a lock of red-gold hair around her finger. "Just sit here in front of me a minute. At least give me a kiss." I sit up and lean back against the cold barbell.

Holly straddles the foot of the bench, places her hands on my shoulders. Is she going to reason with me, kiss me, or just hold me at arm's length until my passion falters? A drastic response may dispel her doubts.

I stand, step close. Holly's hands fall to my waist. I entwine my fingers in her hair, dig my nails into her scalp until she shivers. Holly sits down and I nip her neck, tarry at the soft spot behind her ear. Tip her head back, kiss her until her lips soften and her hands knead my hips and neither of us can breathe. Ardor prevails.

She lifts my shirt. Warm lips caress my nipples; her soft touch brings a sweet ache to my groin. I take her hands. "Stand up."

She does, and I kiss her once again, slide down to the bench beneath her. Caress her thighs, urge her closer. Holly grips the barbell; I hope it is secure.

Her musky scent compels me. I slide two fingers inside her, curl them slightly, nuzzle the front of her shorts with my lips. "Wait," she says. She steps over me, takes off her top, her shorts and sneakers. Gloriously nude, she straddles the bench again, shifts her stance to meet my eager tongue.

Her labia glisten, rich and swelling. I part the lips, point my tongue, find her clit. Her knuckles are white; she's gripping the uprights, her triceps taut. I relax my neck, the muscles of my jaw. My rhythm is established now; I realize that song is still in my head. *I once was lost, but now I'm found. . .* It almost makes me laugh, but that would be a crime right now. No point in fighting it; the tempo is right.

Sweat from Holly's thighs wets my shirt. Her breasts obscure a full view of her face, but I can tell she's looking up. Watching herself in the mirrors, I think. Ex-cheerleader, aerobics instructor—what else would she be doing? Back in high school, the cheerleaders sometimes practiced at the same time as the girls soccer team. I saw them there, and dreamed of doing this very thing, even before I knew the finest feeling in the world is to have some sweet woman about to climax against my upper lip.

I can't stand it. I reach beneath my shorts, match the stroke of my finger to that of my tongue. *How sweet the sound . . .* Holly's breathing hoarsely. Each caress elicits a jerk of her hips. I try to lighten my touch, diminish the pace, but that crazy song compels me . . . *the hour I first believed . . .*

The weights rattle on the barbell; Holly shakes from her foundations. Her hips grind into my face. A spasm rips through me, but when her left knee buckles, my hand gets pulled away and I have to grab Holly to save myself. We tumble to the floor, me on top. She clutches my shoulders and bursts out laughing, tears rolling down her face. "Holly?" Now I'm whispering. "Are you OK?"

She wipes her eyes and laughs again. "You sucked the sense right out of me," she says. She's limp now, sprawled, arms outstretched. I curl against her side, stroke her beautiful bare torso, soothe her until her swollen eyelids flutter open. She smiles at me and starts to speak, then shoves me away. I hear it, too—the elevator's moving. It stops at the lobby. In the mirror, I can see the doors slide apart. A faint sweet song emerges, the same voice I heard in the locker room. *"When we've been gone ten thousand years/ Bright shining as the sun—"*

Holly leaps to her feet, then crouches. I grab her tangled clothes, throw them at her, untie the laces of her sneakers so they're ready to slip on. A middle-aged woman is pushing her cart of cleaning supplies into the lobby. By the time the woman shakes out a new trash bag, Holly is disheveled but dressed. Her eyes are huge, and her weird smile is just this side of a grimace.

"Lie down," she whispers.

"What?"

She shoves me onto the bench, repositions herself as spotter. "Ready?" she says loudly.

I start to laugh. Her glare pins me to the bench. I grab the bar, but there's no way. I wasn't sure I could lift this much the first time. "Holly, for crying out loud, I just got off."

She starts a lift-off. I tighten up in self-defense and manage to lower the bar to my chest without killing myself. Limp with laughter, I can't budge it. I can barely breathe. Holly's ineffectual jerking bounces the one hundred sixty-five pound bar on my sternum, squashing me.

The cleaning woman runs past Holly, yells, "Grab onto the end of it!" Together they raise the bar to the uprights. I sit up, rub my chest, and erupt in another surge of giggles.

"You was lucky, miss," the woman said. "I come in a little early tonight."

"We were just going," Holly babbles. "I didn't think . . . I was closing tonight, but we were just . . . Thanks so much."

"Yes, ma'am," she says. "You're welcome." She squats and reaches beneath the bench. Retrieves my new ID and Holly's car keys. She looks at the picture, then holds the card and keys out to me. "Here you go."

Holly grabs them before I can react. "We appreciate that, Irene." The woman's name is on her badge. "We've always been happy with your company. Thanks again. I'll write a note to your supervisor, tell her what a help you were." I've got to get her out of here; she's trying to stuff everything into the pocket of her shorts, but they're on backward.

"You was lucky," Irene repeats. "God was looking out for you tonight."

"Saved a wretch like me." I need to get my giddy self out of here, too; the giggles overtake me once again. "Good night, Irene," I say, then wish I hadn't.

Holly's hand tightens on my shoulder, and she practically shoves me to the door.

"That was fun."

"You are a goddamned lunatic, Manescu!" Holly walks to her car and I trail behind, uncertain. "Listen," she says, "I don't think I can take much more of you tonight. I'm going to go home. I'll call you."

After the Wednesday meeting, Evelyn corners me. She is amused by the gym escapade, but also concerned. "Do you love Holly, or is she just a piece to boost your self-image?"

"I don't think I love her. I care for her. We have fun, sometimes." I fiddle with the laces of my boots, knee tucked to my chest. "In high school, I had a big crush on her, and Holly had kind of a secret thing for me, too."

"Terry, this isn't high school. Do you think she loves you?"

"No. I doubt it. I think she wants me, and she's curious about girls, and she thinks I'm hot. I don't think she's even really gay, though. I don't think she'll stay with women."

"Are you being safe?"

"What?"

"Safe sex. Gloves, lubricant, dental dams. You know what I mean."

I shrug.

"Why not? Couldn't happen to you?"

"I don't know. I just never think about it. I don't like it."

"I don't like being an alcoholic, either, but I am." She jerks a cigarette from her pack, taps it on the arm of her chair. "I can't tell you what to do, but I'm telling you this—if you're not practicing safe sex with a straight woman, or any woman, you are a damn fool."

I shrug again, accidentally squeeze a dent into my can of Coke. Evelyn is right. I know it, she knows it, but I don't like to lick Saran Wrap and I've never even seen a dental dam. "Do *you* practice safe sex?"

She laughs. "Can't get any safer."

"Well, yeah." Stupid question. "You know what bothers me most? The fake ID. We brainstormed on that for months, but now that I got it, I don't really want it. I sure don't want to make amends for getting it."

Evelyn nods. "It's the petty stuff that gets to you. But Step Nine says 'Made direct amends except when to do so would injure us or others.' Holly's involved in this, too. Jeopardizing her job to save your conscience is not called for."

"What am I supposed to do about it, then?"

She fixes a stern look upon me. "Why don't you write about that, and we'll talk it over with your Eighth Step. In the meantime, grow up a little."

"Ouch."

"You're getting better, Terry. Don't think you're not." She pauses. "You're miles ahead of where I was at five months sober."

Alecki calls me to the phone. The voice is familiar, but it takes me a minute to catch up to the words.

"Terry? I got your number from Angela. I'm sorry to call, but I didn't know who else to talk to, and I've got to do something. She's crazy, and she's sick, and I don't know what's going to happen next. I keep thinking that this can't get any worse, and then she does something even crazier."

"Who does?"

"Erica! Yesterday was her court date for the DWI, and I reminded her, and she just told me to shut up, she didn't want to talk about it. She got drunk from noon until she passed out at seven, and she didn't go to court."

Apparently I am talking to Willow. "She didn't show?"

"No. Her lawyer called and she wouldn't talk to even *him*. He'd already told her that she ought to go to treatment for a month, that if she was in treatment when the case came up she'd just get a suspended sentence and a fine. She told him she was going to go. I thought she was. She needs help. I called some places, but Erica wouldn't talk to the people on the phone. I can't get her to go for an intake; she just laughs at me and says I'm not her mother."

"You won't get her there if she doesn't want to go."

"Terry, she has to go! She could lose her license!"

No shit. "She'll go to jail if she keeps blowing off court."

"Oh my God, I know. That lawyer was so mad when he called yesterday. He said he couldn't work with her if she won't work with him."

"Sounds reasonable."

"But Terry, she wouldn't even talk to him. I had to do it."

"Willow, you don't. The only thing you need to do is take care of yourself and stop trying to take care of Erica. She's a big girl and she's got enough of Daddy's money to keep a lawyer happy for a long time. Taking care of Erica is too big a job for Erica; you're not going to be able to do it."

Willow doesn't even slow down. "That's why I called you. I was hoping maybe you would come over and talk with her. Maybe together we can take her to one of those treatment places."

In your dreams! I choked on my Coke when she said "come over." It takes a moment to stop coughing and wipe up. "Jesus, Willow! Erica's not going to talk to me. She hates my guts."

"No, she doesn't. That's the thing. I think you could really get through to her. I used to think that, too, that she hated you, but that's just Erica. She talks about you a lot, and what she says sometimes isn't very nice, but I think it's because she's jealous."

"Jealous! Of me?"

"Erica has a lot of respect for you, Terry. She just won't let it show. She's always saying how she can't believe you're still in AA; she gave it about two weeks. See, she thinks about you."

And I try *not* to think about her. "Willow, Erica and I go back a long way, and she has done nothing but fuck with me since we broke up."

"I know. I've seen it. But she's always been jealous of you. She talks about you all the time. Whenever you turn up—well, you know how she gets. I think she was jealous the first time you met, and that's why she's always tried to manipulate you."

What do I have that Erica could want? "Willow, I don't think I can help Erica, regardless of what she thinks of me. Erica doesn't want any help. She's not willing to do anything for herself. I can see that because that was me, too. Until I was ready to make some changes, nobody could do anything for me."

After a pause, Willow says, "So you won't talk to her?"

"Only if she asks me to." Maybe. "Willow, you might need some help, too. You need to get away from her."

"Oh Terry, I couldn't. I don't know how she would get by; you haven't seen her."

I've seen enough of Erica to last me for my whole life. "Tell her to call me if she wants to go to a meeting."

"Yeah. Thanks." She hangs up.

After my home group, I ask Evelyn what she thinks. She tells me I did good, that you can't help someone who doesn't want it. She suggests I reread Chapter Seven of the Big Book, "Working with Others."

Chapter 8

Sobriety is like two dogs fighting. The one you feed is the one that will win.

overheard at an AA meeting

Holly and I had a Rollerblade date at Forest Park on Sunday, but one of the other aerobics instructors at Dynamo quit without notice. Holly taught two classes Monday, four classes a day on Tuesday through Friday, three on Saturday. She's a little stiff through the quads and back, so a gentle walk seems more in order. I reach for her hand, but she looks at me from the sides of her eyes, and I stick my hands in my pockets. Maybe not in Forest Park. "You want to walk down Lindell and look at those houses?"

"Sure." Holly seems distant. She looks at the ground as much as anything. We walk in silence, stopping once to admire a huge home with a colored slate roof.

Farther down Lindell we find a series of booths; a banner says "Art in the Park." Tapping noises come from the nearest tent. Inside, school-age kids kneel on the ground, pounding nails into scraps of wood, driving screws into Styrofoam packing blocks. A lanky redheaded girl twists her screwdriver fiercely.

"She looks like me when I was a kid," Holly says.

"Yeah." The kid actually reminds me of Cole, scowling at a sketch. We watch her for a bit, then stroll through the rows. Holly pauses at a photographic display, large pictures of Southwestern mountains and chasms and canyons in dramatic contrasts of light and shadow. Next are oil paintings of wildlife. A couple of booths feature ceramics of every dimension, from lapel pins and earrings to sculptures as big as me. Most of the artists are local, but some come from Granite City, Springfield, Cape Girardeau.

Holly excuses herself and joins the long line to the bathroom; there's only one in this part of Forest Park. Usually they bring in Porta Pottis for festivals and fairs, but if such a thing's around here I don't see it.

Next to one of the exhibitor's booths a five-gallon plastic drum lies on its side. I upend it and take a seat. The radial fins on the bottom cut into my rear, so I fold my jacket for a pad and sit back down.

From the parking area comes a lanky figure with a familiar lope. It's that newcomer from the lesbian AA meeting. Indigo is supposedly her singular name. Today she looks like a Civil War reenactor, with boots, khaki pants, an olive shirt, and leather suspenders that just barely show under her khaki-colored duster. I don't know what you call that hat; it's not a cowboy hat, more like some Aussie expedition thing that's pulled low enough to obscure much of her face.

She saunters down the hill. I can't catch her eye, only a glimpse of mouth and cigarette. A huge pouch hangs from her shoulder; it's made of heavy woven cloth, like a saddle blanket. Indigo is flanked by two big dogs. One's a shepherd mix with a clouded eye, the other looks like she's mostly black Lab. The woven pouch and the animals give Indigo a vaguely mythological appearance, as if she is some ancient hunter-goddess.

I'd say "hi" if she met my eyes, but it really would be hard to tell. She's more persona than person, walled up in all the gear. How could someone be so shy that she'd need two big dogs to walk around at an art fair? The dogs probably wait in the truck while she goes to meetings.

A savory aroma diverts my attention. A Greek man is selling skewered chunks of pork, grilled and seasoned, with plastic cups of peppercini and olives on the side. I get a couple kebabs and one Coke, one diet. Holly joins me under a big old sycamore.

"Thanks, Terry. These are good." She laughs. "I've been eating like a pig all week."

"No wonder. You probably burned seven thousand calories a day."

"Probably," she agrees. "Sandy's replacement is starting tomorrow; she trained with me yesterday."

"I don't know how you did it. Did you get paid double?"

"I got regular pay for the extra hours and a bonus every time I went over three classes a day."

"That's cool." I gather the napkins and skewers, stuff them into the empty cup.

"Let's look at the tents on that side." We wander around until Holly stops before some sketches. A couple of muscular black women are approaching. I watch, wondering if they are lovers, sisters, just friends. The shorter one is fine. She sees me looking, smiles.

"Terry, that looks just like you."

"Who?"

"This." Holly indicates an India ink drawing of two softball players on the tailgate of a pickup. The blonde resembles Jane, second baseman on the DC team at Weston. The dark one looks like me. I back away from the sketch, look around the booth. My heart is pounding.

"Look, this one does too. You and Whacker."

Me and Whacker. The title is "Best Friends: II," signed by Cole Rankin. The tailgate picture is "Best Friends: I." I break into a sweat.

"She just stepped out."

I start at the voice. The artist is seated in a folding chair, by some large landscapes in acrylics. She frowns at me, looks at the picture. "That does look like you. You got a twin sister in Weston?"

"I don't have any sisters." I'm edging out of the tent, my jersey clammy against my back.

"You lived in Weston," Holly says. "Didn't you go to school up there?"

"No. Here and Kirksville." I hope I don't look as weird as I feel. Didn't I tell Holly that Cole was an artist? Is she playing with me? I want so much just to run. "Let's go get something to drink."

"Drink?"

"A C-Coke." Now I'm stuttering.

"Terry, you just had one. Look at these pictures; I can't get over it."

They aren't all of me, only about a quarter of them. This is too weird. The artist in the back is telling Holly that she and "her friend" split the booth. They drove in together to share expenses.

"I've got to have a drink, Holly. I'll meet you down there." My mouth is dry, for sure. I buy another soda from the Greek and sit on a bench. Try to slow my breathing, stop the trembling of my hands and body.

The crowd is suddenly full of auburn-haired woman. I don't want Cole to spot me, but I'd give a lot to get a look at her.

Holly finally joins me. "You must have a double. Joanne, that painter, she couldn't believe it either."

"Is she from Weston?"

"Jefferson City. The one that did sketches is from Weston. She's good."

"They both are."

"Yeah, but those drawings are totally realistic." Holly takes my Coke, drinks a little. "Are you OK? You look pale."

"That meat made me feel funny. I broke out in a sweat."

She rubs my low back. "Terry, you're soaked. Do you want to go?"

"I think I better. Maybe I need to lie down awhile."

"OK. Let's go to your place." She frowns at me. "I'll drive."

I look straight ahead, to keep from checking every passing face. A doggy snort warns me away from the saddle-blanket pouch. The black dog and the part-shepherd with the rheumy eye lie close together, under a vast elm. Indigo's hat is slung on the pouch, the duster folded beside it. That's odd; she wears those even in the AA meetings.

We're approaching a drum circle, near the parking lot. A long-haired guy with bowed legs and multiple facial piercings taps a silver drum with one hand. He's talking to two teenage girls, the drum more of an accessory than an instrument. Most of the drummers are real musicians, though. Holly and I stop to watch. "How are you feeling?" she asks.

"Better. Let me just sit here a minute and finish my Coke. It might help settle my stomach." She nods and sits down close, not touching.

I spot Indigo, dead center in the circle. She has hair, a long dark braid well past her shoulders. It's usually hidden between her hat and coat. She's playing a mahogany-colored drum with white inlays. The drum is strapped to her waist, the body of it between her knees. Her mouth is slightly open, tense, tongue at the corner of her lips. Her eyes are half-closed, as if she's bearing down.

Her suspenders loop loosely below her waist. The sleeves of her shirt are turned up, revealing pale, sinewy forearms with prominent veins. Eight other drummers play, plus the poser, but Indigo guides them. One foot is forward, her knees bent. The cadence rocks her back and forth, sometimes she lunges with the changes. Total transformation: Indigo, with face and hair, gear discarded, laying down this trance for the partisans of rhythm. Humbly I witness this; all I knew of Indigo was the weirdly irritating facade that she brings to meetings.

We listen until Holly gets restless. The music gets me out of my head, helps me calm down. Still, I don't think I could stand to be touched right now. Holly drops me off and goes home.

Alecki and Whacker are playing in the living room. Alecki bought a Snoopy fishing pole, kid-sized, and tied a rabbit-fur mouse to the end of the line. He sits on the couch and casts the mouse, reels it in slowly. Whacker's eyes are huge. His hind end wiggles. He pounces theatrically; he's fond of my brother. Not fooled by catnip mice, Whacker really likes the fishing line. He traps the mouse in both front paws, then tries to snap the line between his teeth before Alecki tugs the mouse free.

Watching them helps me shake the remnants of brittle shock that messed me up at the park. I'm waiting for a call back from Evelyn. When the phone does ring, I start up with such vigor that Alecki jumps and Whacker drops the mouse. "Damn, Terry," Alecki says. He winds the line furiously, retrieving the mouse before Whacker grabs it.

"Terry? What's up?"

That gravely voice; I relax a little just to hear her. I take the phone to the kitchen and spill the story, stuttering again in my urgency.

"You never saw her, though?" Evelyn asks.

"No, but I couldn't stop looking. I felt so weird. I was dying to see Cole, but I didn't want her to see me. I haven't seen her since August, and she probably hates me, but God, I'd give a lot to lay eyes on her again. It was strange having Holly there, though."

"I imagine," she says. "Probably weird for her, too."

"I don't think she made the connection. It's not like I talk about Cole all the time."

Evelyn snorts. "What the hell, Terry? Some days you don't talk about anything else."

"You mean Cole? Nicole? I talk about her a lot?"

"I don't know if you talk about her to Holly; I hope not. But Cole is taking up a whole lot of space in your head, kiddo. She's been living there rent-free since August, and I'd guess for a good long while before that.

"As far as Cole hating your guts goes, I kind of doubt it. You're the one that's done that. How many pictures of you were in her display?"

"Half a dozen, at least."

"Had you seen any of them before?"

I think back. Cole did one of Whacker and me when I was in Weston, but it was smaller. "I don't think so."

"I don't know how Cole is feeling, but if she's drawn half a dozen or more pictures of you in the last nine months, I'd say you are still very much in the young lady's regard."

I slide down the doorway, sit in the floor. Cole *has* to despise me . . . What if she doesn't?

"Terry?"

"Yeah?"

"Just checking."

"I'm here. I just . . . uh, just . . ."

"I know. Let's get you on track. I'm not so concerned with what Cole does or doesn't think of you. You won't know for sure until you talk to her. What I'd like to see you do is clean up your side of the fence. How are you coming with your Eighth Step?"

"She's on it." I swallow hard; my mouth has gone dry again.

"I gathered. Maybe it's time to get into action with your Ninth Step. You've been hung up on this thing for a long time, and it's not going to go away. The Steps are there to help us deal with the past and get on with living."

"Yeah." Confusion and doubt drown out Evelyn's words. Cole might not hate me. Would she want to see me again?

"Are you coming to the meeting Wednesday?" Evelyn asks.

"Yeah."

"Pick me up?"

"I think; I'll call if I can't."

"Good enough. See you."

Cole's still sketching me. She might not hate me. What if she doesn't? I sit on the floor, consumed by questions, afraid to hope, until Whacker runs across me with his wild trill and Alecki invites me to join him for a burger.

I go out with my brother, grateful for the distraction, but all that night I dream of Cole at the easel, sketching. Over and over I wake myself up by reaching for something that isn't here.

When Holly asked me to meet her at Minerva's, I started to say something. Pull out my six-month coin—"Remember?" Really, I don't mind; I don't feel like drinking anyway, and tonight I'd rather be there than at a meeting.

Since I will miss my regular Friday meeting, I should do something related to recovery. After work I shower and change, then review my Eighth Step. *Made a list of all persons we had harmed, and became willing to make amends to them all.* The persons I had harmed are listed in my Fourth Step inventory already.

Mom, Pop, Angela, Erica, Nicole. Meredith, Melissa, and scads of nameless rugby players. Andrei—I bullied him. None of this appeals to me; even when I was sorry, I would never say it. The list is done; Evelyn says the willingness comes with time and prayer.

Some of these amends aren't ever going to happen, but I can be willing to return the Harley T-shirt I stole from that speed freak if the circus ever comes through town again. That reminds me: I took those books from the used bookstore on Euclid. I write that down, then put the list aside and grab my jacket.

I get to Minerva's early, shove into the crowd and take a table by the dance floor. My mind quiets immediately, though I'm only drinking Coke. I can be calmer in a bar than in the solitude of my head. I can be more tranquil bashing a soccer ball down the field and slapping palms with Jeri than I ever could be in church.

Jeri's in here, with a woman I don't know. She hasn't seen me. A lot of these faces I know, some of the names. Holly likes it here because she's just another face in the crowd. She's not, really; that face stands out anywhere. But Minerva's is only a bunch of dykes, and Holly doesn't care who sees her here.

I want to sit here and slow down. When Holly arrives we can dance. We'll dance, and not talk. I'll get close, smell her perfume, her body—

faint sweat and the clean scent of her hair. Touch her damp skin, feel the senses sharpen within me. Fall into focus. Take her home, not speaking, touch her, taste her. Watch her eyes dilate, feel her grip my wrists, pull my hair. Find my power, find control, give what she wants and make her mine for one more night. I'll bend my head to the task and concentrate, fervent as prayer, her excitement driving mine. The panic and the power—we'll merge and move through night, until morning comes and once again our vapid conversation blows us gently, steadily apart.

Talk about bullshit. What I really need to do is get honest. I don't love Holly, she doesn't love me, and lately we're not even good company. The sex is hot, but any more it only gets me high, then leaves me empty. What I need to do is get out, live my life with some kind of integrity.

There's a quarter in my hand, I've been tapping it on the table. I don't remember grasping it. Should I call Holly? Evelyn? I finish my Coke and go to the pay phone. The number I dial doesn't require coins; I charge the call to my card.

"Hello?"

Her voice vibrates through me like a bass chord. "Cole? Hey. It's Terry."

"Terry! What are you doing? Where are you?"

"St. Louis. In a bar, actually. Drinking Coke."

"Playing pool?"

"No. Not tonight. I was just thinking about you. I need to talk to you. The way I left—" I breathe in, try to keep the shaking from my voice. "I just need to tell you some things. In person."

Long pause. "I would like to see you," Cole finally says. "I could maybe come to St. Louis. My car's not running very well, though."

"Mine is," I blurt. "I got my Mustang back. I could come up. Or tell you what—I'll send you a bus ticket. What's a good day for you?"

Holly's approaching, looking fine in a navy dress and a sexy smile. Cole says, "I'll have to check at work."

Adrenaline surges through me. "Think about it," I tell her. "I'll call you back in a couple days."

"Sure," Cole says. "Thanks for calling, Terry. It was good to hear your voice."

I hang up, shaking, feeling like a fraud, and turn to Holly. "I couldn't remember what time you wanted to meet." I lead her to our seats, pull out the chair for her. Under the table, I grind a fist into my palm.

"Looks like you've been here awhile." She indicates my empty glass.

"Just twenty minutes," I say. "Do you want to dance?"

Holly glances at her beer, barely touched, then meets my eyes. Doesn't answer, but really looks at me. She nods, drains off a quarter of the glass and follows me to the floor.

We start off easy, moving with the tempo. I avoid her eyes and watch her body—swaying hips, the roll of her shoulders, the swing of hands and arms. She dances well; her work attunes her to music and her body. She must have the endurance of a marathon runner.

My body feels stiff today, my dance constrained by the tension of my awareness. I follow Holly, move up close enough to feel her heat, almost touching.

The music ends. Holly searches my face again, but I look down. "Be right back," she says. She returns just as the next song gets going, with her lips red and wet, a whiff of beer on her breath. This time our dance is seamless, relaxed, yielding to the rhythm. Holly gets a flirty grin that goes straight to my groin, and I wonder where this night will take me. I know what I want, I finally know what I have to do, but there's something in me that can't resist a smile like that.

I shift out of my head and back into my body. We dance like we're bound by invisible threads, interwoven. Neither of us leads, but somehow we move together.

When the song is over, Holly puts her hands on my shoulders. "I love how you dance," she says, then kisses me, long and deep. It's a passionate kiss, more body than soul; I surrender to it. The woman has never kissed me anywhere but in her bedroom or mine. The music crashes back in a pounding techno beat that lifts me right into the air. I dance my frustration, kinetic savage moves. A fine fringe of sweat flies from my bangs. Holly's flagging, just a little, but the beat bashes into my chest and comes out my feet. Not too many dancers are left at the end of this song, but a few onlookers whoop and clap when we're done.

My chest is heaving, and I'm drenched, lightheaded, high. Holly's gasping. "Too fast for me. I've got to have a break."

"OK," I say, but I don't want to quit. A peppy hit of pop comes on, and Jeri stands before us.

"Can I borrow Terry?"

"Have fun," Holly says. "I'll be back."

Jeri starts with a familiar step; we've danced to this before. She stares at me. I focus over her shoulder. All I want to do is move; if I stop I might shatter.

When this song ends I look for Holly, but she's not at our table. The next one is a soft, sexy number. Jeri moves in, rolling her narrow hips.

"Don't fuck with me, Pan," I warn her.

She looks surprised at the old nickname; no more than I. "Where you at, my friend?" she says. "You look like you're cruising the edge of a nightmare."

"I'm not." I wipe sweat from my face with both palms. "It's not even a bad dream, just an old one that I need to let go."

She frowns. I must look strange tonight, to elicit these searching gazes. "I thought you were high," she says. "You're not."

I push back my damp hair. "No. I'm OK."

Another of those looks.

"I'm cool, Jeri. Really."

She puts me in a headlock, kisses me over the left ear. "You're always cool," she whispers. "Holly's coming back." She walks away, toward a table where a lone woman is looking our way.

Holly smiles at me. "You're dripping. You still good to go?"

"Always."

"Why didn't we do this more?" she asks, and I wonder at the "didn't."

Loose and free, we dance three more times, abandoned to the rhythm. I can't watch Holly without a surge of hormones burning through me, but I refuse to think ahead. Present in our bodies, connected to the moment, we move without expectation.

The movement energizes me, but Holly taught consecutive one-hour classes today. "Let's go to my place," she says into my ear. I need to talk to her, but it's too loud in here, so I drive behind her taillights to her apartment.

At the curb I pause a moment, watching Holly go up the walk. Why did we wait so long to dance? This all could have been different.

I come inside to candlelight and smoldering music, k.d. lang's sultry sound. Holly takes my hand, pulls my hips against her. I breathe in Obsession, a little sweat, and beer. "We need to talk," I say. My voice is low and faltering.

"Not yet," she whispers. "Be with me, Terry."

I surrender once again, my body hot and wet on hers. We dance, on and on. Desire scorches my skin, Holly feels as ripe and bursting as a plum under my hands. We kiss, still swaying to the music, until my lungs burn and I have to break away for air. Holly peels away my sweaty shirt, strips me to the waist. Runs her tongue from my throat to the top of my jeans, and I'm witless, stoned.

There's a blanket folded on the couch. Holly shakes it out and spreads it on the carpet. I unbuckle my belt, kick off my shoes, slide my pants to the floor. The candles flicker with the stir of our undressing; Holly's body glows surreal and radiant. She lies upon the blanket, and our full contact shocks me like a dive into an icy spring. Holly rolls from under me; her hands and lips travel my length. She trails her fingers over my flesh until I become liquid, makes love to me with aching sweetness and attention. I come slow and full, waves surging and ebbing until ripples die away and tears spill down my cheeks.

Alongside me, she pulls my head to her shoulder. Wipes my tears with a gentle hand.

I wake with a start, sweat cooling on my legs and back. "Holly! I—"

"Hush. You went to sleep."

"Oh my God. I'm sorry. I never do that. I—"

"It's all right, Terry. It's enough. What we did was enough." She kisses my forehead, then gets up. Comes back with some pillows and a sheet, arranges herself on her side. "So you need to talk?"

I'm so confused: mortified, sorry that I didn't make love to her, but I had already decided I wouldn't do this tonight. I roll to prone, clench the pillow under my chest. "Yeah. This isn't going to be easy. I have never had a nicer evening with anyone."

"But?"

I drop my head to the bunched pillow; it muffles my voice, and Holly leans closer to hear. "God, Holly. You're about the most beautiful woman

I've ever seen. I've wanted you forever. But we just don't seem to connect." I look back up. "Until tonight, we didn't."

"I know." She sighs. "I knew that this is what you had to tell me. It's me. I just don't think I can do this with a woman. I was going to say the same to you. For once, I dropped my guard tonight, but Terry, I can't keep this up. I think you're a great person, and you do things to my body that turn me inside out, but I don't think I'm gay."

I almost laugh. "I don't think you are, either. Too bad." There's not much left to say. There is Nicole, but she never was the trouble between me and Holly. I'm surprised to find myself crying.

"What's wrong?" Holly asks. "I thought I'd make it easier for you."

"You did," I say, and swallow hard. "But you made it harder, too. When we danced tonight, it felt so different."

She slides closer and reaches for me; I rest my head on her shoulder once more. "It did, I know," Holly says. "I can't do it, though." There's a catch in her voice; I think she's crying too. We lie there for a long time, not speaking, growing calm.

When I sit up she asks, "Do you want to stay tonight?"

I'm tempted, and I am worn out. "That would make it harder. Thanks, though." I gather my clothes, dress slowly. A candle gutters out, and my eyes flood with tears at the finality. I've never left anyone with mutual regard.

Holly sits on the couch, wrapped in the sheet. "I'll see you around," she says. "I don't think I'll go back to Minerva's. Not for awhile. But I'll be playing soccer in the fall."

I go to her one last time, thinking of the school-kid that taped a poem to her locker door. We press wet cheeks together, and I leave. The cool night air feels good on my flushed face; I roll down both windows before I drive off.

I wait a couple of days to talk to Evelyn. I know she's not like that, but a persistent thought nags me: that she'll be sitting there thinking *it's about time*. After the meeting Wednesday, I ask her to join me in the smoking lounge. "I did it," I tell her. "I broke up with Holly."

Evelyn raises her eyebrows. "When?"

"Friday night." She looks at me, no comment. "The funny thing is, she was getting ready to dump me. She said she doesn't think she's gay. I said if I can't convince you, girlfriend, then I know you're not."

Evelyn's steady gaze cuts through my bravado. My grin fades; I drop my eyes. Her voice is gentle, though. "I know it hurts, hon," she says. "You made a tough choice, but it was a good one."

I dig the heels of my hands into my eyes and take a long breath. "It doesn't feel that great."

"It may not, for a while. Sometimes the best choices are painful." She leans close, takes my wrists and pulls my hands down to my lap. "You have made some huge changes in your life. You're sober, you're working the Steps, you're going to school, making friends outside of the bar. You're finding out how to live as a responsible human being. It's not easy; takes a whole lifetime to get it figured out, if you ever do. The good news is that all you have to do is try to make the best choices you can, one day at a time."

I lift my head, wipe a stray tear that sneaked out. "I didn't think doing my best would feel so shitty."

"Sometimes it does, kiddo." Evelyn smiles at me, squeezes my hand. "You *are* doing the right thing. You're not hurting yourself or getting loaded. When you get upset, you cry. That's how it's supposed to work. You feel the pain, don't drink, talk to somebody; eventually you will feel better. You're making good choices, even when they don't feel good. You're doing OK."

"Thanks."

"You are. I mean it. Matter of fact, you're doing so well I think you're ready to move on. Put the pain to some use. If you're hurting, let that emotion lead you to the Ninth Step."

I wish I had a cigarette, something to do with my hands. "I've been thinking about it. I've got my Eighth Step list—Angie, Andrei, Cole, Melissa, Erica. Those are the main ones. The tough one will be Cole."

She nods. "Cole, or Erica. The toughest ones provide the greatest healing, though. Remember that the Twelve Promises come right after the Ninth Step in the Big Book." She takes out her cigarettes, tempting me further. "I think Cole will be open to what you have to say, Terry. She's been in touch with you, at least."

"That's the other thing I wanted to tell you." I take a deep breath. "I've talked to Cole, twice. I sent her a bus ticket for next weekend."

Evelyn fumbles her lighter, nearly drops it. "Well. You have been busy."

"I didn't think I could do this by letter."

"No, you're on the right track. Pray about it. You'll know what to do when the time arrives." She taps a cigarette on the tabletop, lights up. I'd better get out of here before I relapse on tobacco.

Chapter 9

When I was new, my sponsor volunteered me to come in early and make coffee. People would talk to me as they got to the meeting. Made me feel important, like they needed me. Actually, they needed coffee.

overheard at an AA meeting

"Morning, Terry." Alecki is already up and in the kitchen. "Did you kill anyone in lab last night?"

I pull out a kitchen chair. Whacker's in the seat; he lifts his head and glares, so I take the one to the left. "Just the instructor. What are you baking?"

"A lemon poppy seed loaf. Thought since I was up, I'd fix breakfast." He pours coffee, sets it before me.

"What a man."

"I'd make someone a wonderful wife."

"You do look lovely in an apron."

I drink half the coffee, then open the back door and check the temperature. The morning is cold, but not cool enough for coveralls. I excuse myself, change into some paint-stained jeans, wash my face and comb my hair. The bread is cooling on a rack when I come back.

"It's almost ready." Alecki sits down across from me. "Seriously, how's school going?"

"It doesn't quite seem like school. It goes fast. Every other Tuesday we start a new unit, and every Thursday we're in the lab."

"You like it, though?"

"It's interesting. I like the lab objectives; it's all fairly physical. I already turned in my research paper, so I never have any homework except the weekly reading."

"That's cool," he says. "The hours work out well."

"Yeah, except I don't get to as many meetings."

Alecki hops up and saws off steaming slices of the poppy seed bread, his back to me. He asks, "So you think you still need to go to the meetings?"

"Definitely." Is he ever going to get it? "It works, Lex."

"You're talking total abstinence, the rest of your natural life?" He sits down and passes me the bread, but still won't meet my eyes.

"The rest of my life, one day at a time. In AA, you don't stay sober forever, you just stay sober today."

"As long as it's today, then you'll be OK. I mean, you'll be sober. You were OK anyway."

"That's debatable." I get some more coffee. "You working in Kirkwood today?"

"All of us are, I think. It's a big job, bunch of rental properties. Want to ride together?"

"Sure, if you'll drop me by a meeting when we're done; I can get a ride home."

A slightly off-center skunk stripe marks my hair, from leaning into the edge of the fascia. The afternoon has turned warm, with an oppressive humidity weighing on us, and Andrei and I are about to get on each other's last nerve. He insists that I carry my paint every time I descend the ladder, even though the bail of my paint bucket is secured to a rung with an S-hook. It's a handy gadget: the bucket handle fits into the bottom curve of the hook and the bigger curve hangs on the rung of the ladder. I had been leaving the bucket suspended at the top when I moved the ladder, but Andrei yelled, "You're gonna spill your paint. Are you stupid?"

A lot smarter than you, boy. "You're the boss." I climb down, set my bucket on the ground, tip back the heavy wooden extension ladder and move it over six feet so I can paint another stretch of gutter. The gutter and fascia are white, but the soffit is dark brown, so I have to pay attention.

The ground drops off as I approach the corner of the house, causing the ladder to tilt. Around the back of the garage, I score a concrete block and an eight-foot two-by-six. I set the block on the downhill slope and lay the end of the board across it, creating a raised, level platform.

I'm jumping on the board, setting it into the soft earth, when Andrei comes around again.

"Terry, don't put your ladder on that," he says. "Let me do that part; I'm taller."

I'm not an idiot. I step away from my creation; Andrei just shakes his head. "Get the soffit on the back side of the house; my roller's over there."

I get started with Andrei's three-inch trim roller. The yard is level in the back, so this part is easy. But how is Andrei painting that downhill stretch? I peek around the corner; he's got the ladder on my makeshift scaffold after all. "How's that platform working for you?"

He shrugs. "Clean up your tools as soon as you finish that west side."

I knock off the last bit of soffit, use one of Dre's curved plastic roller scrapers to divest my roller cover of most of the thin brown latex, then seal the roller in plastic wrap. Derrick and Lex are cleaning up, too, and Andrei's hauling the ponderous sections of extension ladder to his truck. He could just leave them behind the house overnight; nobody's going to steal something that awkward and heavy.

He sees me wrapping the roller. "Terry, wash that out. It'll get hard."

"We'll be back in the morning, Andrei; it's not going to dry out that fast. I need to get to a meeting."

"Wash it out or give it to me," he says. "I'm not paying you to argue. You'll get to your damn meeting."

"Like this?"

"So, you look like a painter. You ashamed you've got a job? They'll probably give you an ovation."

In the meantime, Alecki has dropped his roller and mine into a bucket of water. I hear the spinner too late; he slings a wash of brown stain across my torso and right arm.

"Lex!"

"Sorry, draga," he says. "You really look like a painter now."

Alecki takes me out for a burger and fries as consolation. He gets two bacon double cheeseburgers and some super-sized fries. I thought I ate a lot.

"Is Dre always such a dick?" I ask.

"Don't be sexist."

"Excuse me. Is he always so fussy?"

"He was with me, too." Alecki slumps sideways on the fiberglass bench, stretching out his long legs. He looks tired. "After awhile Dre will lighten up. At least he's letting you work with Derrick and me now. He did the same thing when I started—we were doing interiors, and he kept me right under his nose until he was sure I wouldn't embarrass him in front of his crew."

"But I've been painting houses since I was twelve years old. You probably started with the roller when you were ten."

"It's not your work he's worried about. It's your mouth." Alecki smiles. "You're older than Andrei, and smarter than he is. Hell, Terry, you're better-looking. You've had more girlfriends than Dre. He wants you to know who's boss. He wants me to know it, too. You and me together, baby; he's scared of that."

"Is he that insecure?" The business belongs to Andrei; he's been on his own almost three years.

"He's unbelievably insecure. Boundlessly insecure. And he cares what his friends think, he cares what his crew thinks, he cares what you and I think. Above all, he cares what Pop thinks." He mimics Andrei's affected, too-deep baritone. " 'Right, Pop? Right, Pop?' "

I snicker; he can even wrinkle his forehead like Andrei. "I'm surprised he's letting us have dinner together."

"It worries him," Alecki says.

Kirkwood has three AA meetings on Fridays; Alecki drops me off at a club. I'm a total mess: white stripe on top of my head, little white and brown speckles on arms and face from the rollers, and that splash of brown across my shirt, courtesy of Alecki. I spot the coffeepot and pour a cup, load it with sugar. A thin, well-dressed woman is watching me; I get a little twist in my guts when I realize it's Laura. I haven't talked to her since she canned me.

She waves. "Terry," she says. "How are you?"

I walk to her, reluctantly; she's surrounded by empty chairs. "I'm doing all right. Just got my six months."

"Congratulations." She rifles through her purse. "I got my two-year coin in March."

I finger the medallion. "That's a long time." A long time to go without a drink, but it's not such a long stretch of recovery. When she sponsored me, I thought Laura had been sober forever, but she just had a little over a year. No wonder we couldn't get along.

I give back the coin with my congratulations, take the seat beside her. She eyes me, says, "Looks like you're working."

"Just down the street. I didn't have a chance to clean up." I look down at my spattered clothes. "At least it's not a gay pride T-shirt."

Laura frowns down at her coffee. She starts to speak, but she's interrupted by a chunky teenage girl who flops into a chair across the table from us. The kid grins at Laura, craving attention. "Hey, woman," she bellows.

Laura says, "Hi, Tiffany." They talk for a moment, then Laura introduces me.

"My next-to-last boyfriend was a painter," Tiffany says. "I was working at Dairy Queen and he came in and ordered an orange shake. He had little speckles of paint on his nose just like you, and I thought it was the cutest thing."

Dubious, I brush my palm over my face.

"I wanted to lean over and kiss his nose," she says.

At this particular meeting, no smoking is allowed. I'm glad; I get so sick of coming from an AA meeting smelling like I've just been at a bar. It's a small meeting in a storefront shared by AA and Al-Anon groups. Most of the people here are under forty. I take the preamble to read; I could do it from memory by now.

The topic is the Ninth Step. I pass, since I'm not quite there yet. The guy next to Tiffany talks interminably about amends to an old boss. I listen for a while, then get lost in a daydream, musing about amends to Cole and possible fortuitous outcomes.

Chairs scrape back as people assemble into a circle. I join hands with Laura and a shaking middle-age man who smells of smoke and sweat; we recite the Lord's Prayer. The sweaty guy smiles at me. I've seen him at some other meetings; his name is Al. He says he can give me a ride home.

Tiffany rushes Laura as soon as the meeting ends. I throw away my plastic cup, tap Laura's shoulder and give her a silent wave, not wanting to interrupt. She grasps Tiffany by the forearm, halting her midsentence. "Excuse me. Terry, can you stay for a few minutes?"

Al's outside, smoking and talking to some of the men. "Sure." I help put away chairs and discard empty cups, then stand against the wall, arms folded across my chest, until Laura and Tiffany are finished. Laura gives the girl a quick hug, then strides toward me.

"What's up, Laura?" I uncross my arms, my hands uncomfortable by my sides. I'm not sure where to put them.

"I need to talk with you a minute." She jams her hands into her pockets, as tense as I am. "Let's go outside, so I can smoke."

The humidity feels soft as a blanket now that the sun has set; it's pleasant after the hot afternoon. Laura sits on the hood of her car, lights a cigarette. "Sit down, if you want."

I perch on the right fender.

"I've been thinking about you, Terry. About how I sponsored you. You were the first person I sponsored, and I had no business doing it. I hadn't even finished working through all my own steps yet, but the woman who was my sponsor was big on service work, so she wanted me to try." She looks at me. I just return the look. I'm not going to take her off the hook. She puffs her cigarette and shakes her head. "I'd forgotten about those T-shirts. I don't know why I made such a deal about it. People wear all kinds of stuff to meetings.

"I don't know any lesbians except for you. I guess you made me nervous. When I get nervous, I try to fix things. The only thing I knew to do with you was give you rules to follow."

"That's not my specialty," I admit.

"Well, no, you're an alcoholic. I guess what I want to say is that I'm sorry that I didn't listen to you more and try to get to know you instead of just throwing rules and slogans at you. I got angry because you didn't do what I told you to, and I just didn't think I could deal with you." Laura attempts a strained smile. "You wouldn't do it my way."

"I was no angel," I say. "It worked out for both of us. Now I've got a home group where I'm comfortable, and a great sponsor. I'm crazy about her."

"I'm glad," Laura says. "I worried a lot about it. I've prayed for you, that you would get the program. I was afraid that I had run you off from meetings." She laughs nervously. "That was just me being grandiose. Anyway, I wanted to make amends."

"I accept." I tell her about EMT school, and Vocational Rehabilitation, and house painting, and that I'm working the Steps. I'm surprised to hear she prayed for me; I thought she had tossed me aside like one of her crumpled cigarette packs.

I hop down from her fender. "Tell Richard I have six months."

She brightens. "I will. He'll be thrilled." She gives me a quick, awkward hug, then flees in her Accord.

This should be our last day of painting at the rental properties in Kirkwood. Dre's struggling to get his ladder placed on a sideways slope. He sets it firmly in the dirt, then jams the high side down hard. By the time he's four steps up, the ladder tilts sharply and slides. Andrei jumps to the ground. Paint sloshes from his bucket at the impact.

"You want me to show you how I do it?" I try to interject a sincere and helpful note, to protect his fragile ego.

Andrei frowns. "You mean that little ramp you made out of boards?"

"Yeah. There's some blocks by the garage." I run and get a couple. Dre pulls a short length of two-by-six out of the truck.

I start to arrange the blocks on the low side. "That's OK," Andrei says, "I remember how you did it." I shrug, get my bucket. He says, "Thanks, Terry."

Oh my God, he thanked me. "Sure."

I work on the siding with a combination of roller and four-inch brush, a sloppy but rapid technique that spreads a heavy coat. I hit the crevices with the brush, left-handed, pass the roller over the siding with my right hand. The paint doesn't drip or run, but I do fling it all over myself.

Dre's working above me. He's fast, considering he has to keep moving the ladder; he almost catches up to me at one point. Not wanting his paint flecks in my hair, I speed up and move around the corner.

Like the last house, the front and back yards are level, but the sides slope steeply toward the back corners. I go get the sawhorse and work from the top of that to extend my reach a bit. Dre's trying to set up the ladder on another "cheater" of boards and blocks, but he has to build them up so high that it's starting to get unsteady. "Terry," he says. "Bring me that sawhorse."

"What for?"

He scowls at my challenge to his authority. "Just bring it." He sets the end of one board onto the top of the sawhorse.

"I don't think it'll stay. This dirt is too soft."

He ignores that. "The board's too short. I just need a longer one. Get me one out of the truck, will you?"

I get the board, a hammer, and some nails. We tack the longer board to the top of the sawhorse. It's still wobbly, so I stick some broken bricks under the legs of the sawhorse to level it. One end of the board is on the sawhorse; the other, on the uphill side, is in the dirt. We set the ladder in the center of the board, which bows in the middle.

"That's good enough; the weight of the ladder will hold it." Andrei starts up the rungs. The board bends further under his weight. It looks precarious, but I've done worse.

I pick up my bucket, resume work at the corner. A few minutes later, I hear a short squeal. "Dre, there's a nail pulling. I'm going to put in another one."

"It's OK. I'm done. I'm coming down." He lifts his bucket from the S-hook. The bail catches on the hook; he jerks it. The nails let go with a shriek, and the board holding the ladder tilts wildly. The sawhorse slips from the bricks and tumbles to its side. Andrei rides the ladder down as it turns and smashes into the ground.

He's face down, still. White paint drips from his right arm and shoulder. Alecki and Derrick tear around the corner, gaping at me as I rush straight into the house. "Don't let him move!"

I gasp "Sorry," at the astonished woman washing dishes and run to the phone on the wall. I call 911 and report the accident. The dispatcher says she'll send an ambulance. She says don't move him; don't let him get up.

Outside, Andrei is moaning, trying to pull his left arm from beneath him. Alecki is pale; even his lips are white. I push Alecki back. "Derrick, wait in the street for the ambulance."

Dre's eyes are open, but they don't appear focused. He's ashen, and his face is streaked with blood. "The ladder fell," I tell him. "There's an ambulance coming. Don't move; you're going to be fine." He groans, tries to lift his head. "Keep still, Dre; just keep still." I move closer, lie down behind him so that he can feel me there. "Keep your head down. Try to relax." The knuckles of his right hand are white where he still grips the bail of his spilled paint bucket. His breathing is shallow and fast. I stroke his thick black hair, rub his back lightly. "Breathe, buddy. Lie still and breathe."

Alecki is still crouched with his mouth open. He starts when I speak. "Go wait for the ambulance. Tell Derrick to start cleaning up. You help him when the paramedics get here."

"What happened?"

"The ladder fell. Go, Lex. We'll talk later."

Dre's body shudders. "Oh, shit," he moans, as he jerks his left arm from beneath and tries to push himself up.

"Andrei, lie still. You're hurt. Don't move." I scramble to his head, press my knee against the back of his neck and cup my hands at the base of his skull and his forehead. When he pulls his arm free again, I trap it under my other knee, straddling his head. "Don't move, buddy. The ladder fell. You need to keep still until the ambulance comes." The muscles in my low back burn, but I'm afraid to shift my weight. Dre's trying to look around. I grasp his head firmly, keep it stabilized against my leg.

He draws a shaky breath. "Get off," he whispers. "Let me go."

"No, Dre. Lie still. You're hurt." He tries to pull his arm from under my knee. I lean harder on his wrist, see the old scar by his thumb.

I never was sure how Andrei got the hook in his hand. We had gone fishing in the pond at the golf course. Andrei was seven, I was about eleven. I was peeing behind a tree. When I heard him scream, I ran out with my shorts half up and tore across the manicured grass to my brother.

Andrei had stuck himself in the left hand, in the web between the thumb and forefinger. The barb was under the skin. I bit down on my lip.

Andrei was flapping his hand, shrieking, "Get it out, Terry! Get it out!"

"Be quiet, Dre." I made him sit down and cross his legs. He rocked back and forth, gripping his wrist and wailing like a fire engine. In the tackle box, I found the little pair of pliers. Grandpa had told me what to do if a hook ever impaled me.

Skin is tough. It was like pushing that hook through the trunk of a tree. I had to put my knee on Dre's wrist to hold him still. He wouldn't stop screaming.

Two golfers ran to us. The skin of Dre's hand stretched, taut and white, until the little point showed and slipped free. One of the men took the pliers from me and snipped off the barb, slid the hook out. I watched as if through a veil, trying not to gag.

The other golfer asked my name. He squatted before me, touched my bitten lip, and brought away blood that he wiped on the grass.

"Terry," he said, "you're one tough little kid."

No wonder Andrei doesn't want me to hold him down; I'd forgotten. I shift my weight slightly and keep a firm grip on his head, praying for the ambulance to arrive. Andrei has passed out again, thank God.

Finally the siren blares down the block. Alecki races up, an EMT and a paramedic at his heels. Gingerly, I release Dre's head and back away. The crew starts the ABC scan: airway, breathing, circulation; I recognize it from my classes. The paramedic is a woman, Sarah; she takes vitals while the EMT runs to the ambulance and returns with a backboard. They log-roll Andrei onto it; I help with the legs. Sarah secures Andrei's head and neck, the EMT begins to cut away his clothes.

Now that someone else has taken over, I realize how much my back hurts. I could go help Alecki and Derrick clean up, but instead I stretch, then sit against the wall and watch. Sarah asks me what happened. I indicate the makeshift scaffold; the sawhorse is upended next to the foot of the ladder. She just says, "Damn."

"I think he hit his head on the ladder," I tell her. "He was unconscious initially, then he kind of came around and kept trying to get up."

"I saw that you were stabilizing his neck," she says. "That's good. He looks like he landed face first."

She asks me about medications; I don't think Andrei takes anything. His pupils constrict to her penlight; he withdraws his arms and legs from a painful stimulus. The EMT gets the stretcher, and they load Andrei onto the ambulance. His face is white through the blood. He's moaning, trying to look around now, but his head is strapped down. I ask Sarah if I can ride; she says OK.

Alecki follows in the truck. Sarah moistens gauze with saline, gently wipes some of the blood from Dre's face. His eyes track her hand briefly, then dart away. The pupils are huge, black.

"He's in shock," I mutter.

She nods. The gauze uncovers a deep split above the bridge of the nose; he's bleeding from there and his nostrils. There's a pale bluish knot coming up on his forehead where he caught the rung of the ladder. "His pupils are equal," she says. "That's a good sign." She notes the time, jots something on a form. The driver is talking to the dispatcher.

I look through the back window at Alecki, give him a thumbs-up. Andrei doesn't look too great, but he's hanging on. I tell Sarah that I'm in the EMT training at the community college; she says that's where she went, too, six years ago. I ask if she knows Beryl, but she doesn't.

The ambulance backs into the emergency bay, and Sarah throws the door open. They whisk out the gurney, then I hop down and follow. Dre's mumbling, unintelligible. I let Alecki go in with him.

At the admitting desk, I tell the guy, "I need to call my parents. That's my brother." He nods, indicates the bank of pay phones on the opposite wall. He's already assembled a clipboard of forms.

Mom answers, thank God; I didn't want to leave a message. I tell her that Andrei fell, I don't know how bad he's hurt, and that I think Pop is at the site on Clayton Road today.

At the desk, I answer all the questions that I know, and when Alecki comes out he gets Andrei's wallet from the truck and does the rest. Dre's lucky—Pop insists that he carry insurance. Most painters are hourly, paid in cash.

Alecki joins me in the waiting room.

"How is he?"

"Not fully conscious, last I saw," he says. "His right arm might be broken."

I grimace. "He hit his head hard. Rode the ladder down and slammed his face into it. But his eyes looked OK—pupils were equal and reactive, and he could feel his hands and feet, I think. I'm sure he has a concussion, but maybe it's not too bad."

"It rained Sunday; the ground's still soft. Maybe he didn't hit that hard."

A few minutes later, Mom and Pop come blasting through the door. I don't know how they rode together and got here so fast. Pop keeps wiping his hands on his pants. He smells like oil paint, and it's still sticky on the sides of his hands. Mom is pale; she has a cigarette. The admissions guy asks her to put it out. She hits it so hard the tobacco crackles, then crushes it out on the chrome door of the trashcan.

"Alecki!" she moans, enveloping him in a cloud of smoke.

He stands, and Mom falls against his chest. He pats her back. "Let's sit down. We haven't heard anything yet."

"They're probably taking him up to X ray," I offer.

Pop sits down heavily beside me. "What happened?" he asks.

I tell him about the scaffold, and that I warned against it, then I confess that I had shown Andrei how to put one together. "But the nail was pulling. I told him to wait until I drove it back in, but he kept going."

"He's hardheaded," Pop says. "He never would listen to you."

I blow out a deep breath; I was expecting to get blamed for this. The EMT is coming down the hall. "Excuse me," I say.

He comes right over. "They're taking him to X ray," he says. "They'll know more after that."

"Is he going to be all right?" my mother asks.

"He's in and out," the EMT says. "His eyes look OK, though, and he answered a few questions. Sensation appears intact in his hands and feet; those are all good signs." He crouches in front of my chair. "Listen, I wanted to tell you that you did a nice job stabilizing that neck. He's restless, and he's a strong guy. It's a good thing you acted so fast, and that you stayed with him."

"Thanks," I say.

"Sarah tells me you're taking EMT training."

"That's right."

"You'll be good," he says.

"I hope so," I tell him. "I want to be."

He stands up and nods to my father, then leaves.

"That was nice," Pop says. I don't think Mom noticed; she's too worried about Andrei.

"This could be a while," Alecki says. "Derrick's cleaning up, but I brought the truck in. Maybe I should go pick up the stuff."

"You stay with your mom," Pop says. "Terry and I can go." Alecki hands me Dre's keys. Outside, Pop asks, "Are you OK to drive?"

"Yeah. I'm all right."

Pop nods. He shakes a cigarette from his pack, offers one to me.

"I quit."

"I know," he says. "Just thought today you might need one."

"No, I'm OK. I could stand a Coke, though. My mouth is dry."

"Pull through McDonald's, then; I could use one, too."

Derrick's already gone. He did what I would have done: chained the ladder and sawhorse to the gas meter behind the house, put the paint cans next to it, and stacked the cleaned tools and buckets and the folded drop cloths on the front porch. Pop's in no hurry to rush back to the hospital. I show him the sawhorse, how the board pulled away from it, where it dug into the mud as the ladder fell. Then we walk around the other three houses. Pop inspects our work with an occasional nod, his highest form of praise. He finally meanders back to Dre's truck.

"I'll see you at the hospital." I start toward my car.

He beckons me back. "How bad you think he is?"

"I don't know, Pop. He hit his head. I don't think he's paralyzed, but he might have an injury to his brain. He wasn't really conscious when I saw him."

"So you think he's pretty bad off?" His gaze is level, demanding the truth.

"He could be, Pop. He's not coming home tonight. Beyond that, I can't say. By the time we get back they should know more."

"Right." He hesitates. "And you're OK?"

"I'm fine. I was shook up in the ambulance, a little, but—"

He stops me with a dismissive wave. "Alecki tells me you've gone six months without a drink."

"Oh. Yeah, I have." I feel my face go red. "I'm not going to get drunk over this, Pop. I was thinking that I might go to a meeting tonight, but I want to see how Andrei's doing."

"You go." His voice is firm. "You do whatever you need to do."

"Thanks, Pop." I hesitate, wondering if the time is right. We don't talk much, ever. "Listen, Pop, I want to tell you—all those years I was in school, I was drinking a lot, messing around, getting in trouble—I want to say I'm sorry. I wasted a lot of your money. You believed in me enough to send me to school, and I'm sorry I didn't amount to anything." My voice cracks, and I look off to the side, blinking away the tears.

He scowls, looks away. "I don't know that it was a waste. I wanted you to go to school, all of you. And especially my girl—you've always been so smart. You just weren't ready for it."

"I guess not." There's a knot in my throat, and my Coke is all gone. "I don't think I can make it up to you and Mom. I am sorry, though."

He shrugs. "You're in school now, and you haven't asked me for a dime. You're going to that group, straightening yourself out." He clasps a rough, stained hand on my shoulder. "You're all right."

My voice fails altogether this time, and Pop just smiles. "I'll see you at the hospital," he says.

Alecki and Mom are smoking outside the emergency room doors. They must have heard something, or they'd be inside still.

Alecki walks to Pop. "They're taking Andrei to surgery," he says. "He's got a broken neck, but they don't think there's any damage to his spinal cord. They're going to put something on him, some kind of thing to keep traction on his neck until it heals."

"A halo."

Mom glares, as if I'm joking.

"A halo is a kind of splint that attaches your head to a body jacket. It keeps your head still, but you can get up and move around." I decide not to mention the bolts into the skull.

The surgery doesn't take long. They don't even shave his head. The doctors just fitted Andrei with a plastic jacket, screwed four pins through the metal headband into his skull, and fastened everything together. The surgeon said Dre had no evidence of neurological impairment. That could change if local swelling impinged the spinal cord, but he didn't foresee any permanent disability other than decreased range of motion in his neck.

"His fractures are at C4 and C5." He points to an X ray that doesn't mean a thing to me. "The facet joints snapped at both sites, and there is a transverse fracture through the vertebral body here. The displacement is very slight, so we're not looking at a bone graft. He was lucky." Then he shows us a picture of the halo, a pamphlet with a drawing of a contented-looking woman in a metal and plastic exoskeleton. "This explains issues of care," he says. "Your son will be here about three or four days; he has a concussion, and we're monitoring that. If everything goes well, the halo can come off in three months."

Andrei didn't go to the recovery room; they took him straight to Neurological ICU. They only permit two visitors at a time. Alecki and I go first, since Pop wants me to make it to a meeting.

Dre looks rough. The upper half of his face is swollen, and the blue pouches under his eyes are going to bruise dramatically. Steri-strips clasp together the bridge of his nose. A metal band is screwed to his head above the outside corners of each eye and right behind either ear. Adjustable metal uprights attach the halo to his body jacket at the shoulders and in the back. The jacket is shaped like a vest, mostly plastic, with a fake sheepskin liner.

Alecki says, "How you feeling, Dre?"

Andrei rolls bloodshot eyes toward us. Shifts his torso slightly to the right, and licks his lips. I look for a water pitcher, but there isn't any. He's probably on a reduced intake, because of the concussion. A saline IV drips into his left arm; a plastic splint covers his right forearm and hand. I'm startled to finally hear his voice, faint and hoarse. "Man, you don't want to know."

"I know that's right." Alecki takes his hand. "It could have been a lot worse, though."

Andrei stares at nothing, his puffy eyes half-closed. The bed is cranked up at a sixty-degree angle; his head looks like it's inside a birdcage. It can't be a comfortable position for sleeping.

"Dre, take it easy," I say. "We've got to go. Mom and Pop are waiting."

He responds with another bovine roll of his dark eyes. It's an eerie expression, but he can't move his head and torso. "Mom's here?"

"Yeah, and Pop," Alecki says. Andrei appears more stuporous by the second, though his body is held at attention. Alecki squeezes Dre's hand again and we go out. Marius and his wife, Julia, are in the waiting room with Mom and Pop. I haven't seen my big brother since Christmas. He gives me a stiff hug, says, "I hear you were the hero."

"I just held him down," I say.

"This hero's got to go," Pop says. "You two can talk later." Marius nods, and I take my leave.

Alecki calls and checks on Andrei every day. I haven't been to see him; I've been busy with meetings and school this week. I can't get used to the idea of visiting Andrei; it's not like we ever visited before.

Alecki and I finished up the site in Kirkwood, then broke down Dre's equipment and put it in storage. We had two more jobs lined up, but Andrei said to turn them over to Pop's crew. Alecki is going to work with Pop. I'm going to coast for a month or so, only work on weekends if they need me.

Pop offered me a little money while I'm in school. I didn't take it at first, but then I talked to Evelyn. She thought it was OK: he wants to do something for me and I can allow him that. Funny way to make amends, letting Pop pay my part of the rent and give me gas money until I finish school.

Dre's improving fast, according to Alecki. He revels in all the attention, but he's also restless, feeling confined. By the end of the week, he's been to physical therapy three times. At first he walked the short wooden staircase in the department, but now he's graduated to the hospital stairwell and the outside curbs.

Alecki tells me this, then puts our phone on speaker, so that Mom can talk to both of us. She's in the room with Dre. "Andrei has to take it slow, because he can't see his feet," Mom reports. "Besides, he's so stiff with that thing around him. A doctor came in today and tightened the screws in his head with a—what was it?" There's a muffled reply from Andrei. "A torque screwdriver. Isn't that awful? Tightened him up all around. And the woman comes and helps him put on his clothes, she gave him a big long shoehorn and some bathroom thing. He's wearing your father's shirts. Tomorrow she's supposed to show me how to wash his hair."

"When does he get to come home?" I ask.

"Day after tomorrow, I think, but I just don't see how I'll be able to take care of him. There's so many things—we'll need a hospital bed, I guess."

I consider. "No, you won't. He could sleep in Pop's recliner."

"Oh, that might work."

"You ought to get Internet access on that old computer Marius left. Let Andrei do something constructive."

She sighs. "I don't know anything about that. I wouldn't know where to start."

"You just need a modem and the software. I can help you find something, or Marius can do it. Can Andrei use the phone?"

"No, he can't get it around that thing."

"Then get a speaker phone. That's what we're using right now."

"I thought you sounded funny," she says. "It's like you're in a garbage can. That's a good idea, though. Terry, I'm writing all this down, I want you to know."

I almost thank her. "I'm glad I can help. Tell Dre I'll come over this weekend. We can take a walk."

"Oh, Terry, I don't think he's going to want to walk."

"He's going to need exercise, Mom." I hear a baritone rumble of protest; she's getting it from both sides. "I have to go; I have class."

"Andrei says to thank you for calling."

"Tell Dre to take care. Bye, Mom."

Chapter 10

You know HALT: don't get too Hungry, Angry, Lonely, Tired. There's CRAP—Carrying Resentments Against People. The best one is RELATIONSHIP—Really Erotic Love Affair Turns Into Our Nightmare, Sobriety Hangs In Peril.

overheard at an AA meeting

My tires mutter on the highway, a thin anxious sound. I don't remember if the bus station is on Twelfth or Thirteenth Street. It has only been two weeks since I first called Cole, but between Andrei's accident and school I haven't had time to worry. Today I took the time; all day I have been plagued with fears ranging from probable to completely implausible. What if Cole is still angry? What if I hurt her, broke her nose or something, and she never told me? What if she is only coming here to tell me how much misery I inflicted upon her?

What if she couldn't stand to face me? What if she changed her mind, and never even got on the bus?

I tune the radio to a classical station. Cole likes piano music, Rachmaninoff and Chopin. A fast piece plays, brassy and dynamic, maybe Tchaikovsky. The music breaches my preoccupation, clicks my barely contained fear a notch higher. A jab to the power button shuts it off.

Why did I send the bus ticket to Cole? It would have made more sense for me to go to Weston. A light rain is falling, just enough to dampen the windshield. The wipers catch and flutter across the glass. My armpits sting with sweat, prickles of fear at the Greyhound sign down the street.

I'm a little early; the lady at the counter says the bus will be right on time. I pop into the rest room, pee from sheer anxiety, then comb my hair, put on lip balm and some patchouli. I take my six-month AA chip from my pocket and clench it in my fist, take a deep breath and reenter the station. The cracked green vinyl seat sags. I perch on the edge of it and silently recite the Serenity Prayer.

Big wet tires roll in and the air brakes squeal. Not many passengers are on this bus; Cole's auburn hair gleams with faint luster through panes of dirty glass. The breath catches in my chest, as if the wind had been knocked out of me. I find myself gasping.

At the door, Cole looks at me and smiles. I bite my trembling lip, force my gaze to hers. "Hey, Terry," she says. She hugs me hard, almost lifting my feet from the floor. My fingers clutch a wad of her shirt. Cole steps back, wet-eyed. "God," she says, "you smell just the same."

"I *smell* the same?"

She grins, reaches for my hand. "Better. You don't smell like beer."

Cole's a head taller than me, standing close enough that we could kiss. Not here, though, in this grimy old station. And not before we talk. "Is that all the luggage you brought?" I ask. She has an overnight bag, a book bag, a cardboard mailing tube. I take the suitcase, and she follows me out to the Mustang.

"Nice car," she says. "This is yours?" Cole's never seen me drive.

She looks different, as if she'd gotten taller. Her face is more open, her smile less tentative. Her bangs aren't half-hiding her eyes. She pushes the car seat back, stretches out her long legs. The window is slightly open; she rolls it down and takes a big breath of rain-scented air. "Want a piece of candy?" She holds out a handful, foil-wrapped.

"What kind?"

"The blue are vanilla, the tan ones taste like coffee."

"Trying to get your cappuccino fix on the bus?"

"Exactly. Damn, Terry, it's good to see you. I couldn't believe it when you called. It seems so long . . ."

I suck on a vanilla hard candy, thinking. "Eight months next week," I finally say.

"It's good to see you sober," she says. "How's that going?"

"OK. That's why I wanted to talk to you."

Cole stares past the wiper blades that streak the window. Streetlights cast raindrop shadows like a veil on her fair skin. I keep glancing over. How many times did I imagine her in that passenger seat, or sliding between me and Holly in a restaurant, or lingering in my doorway when I woke? I hope this weekend sets me free of the wounded specter of my guilt.

"How was the bus ride?"

"Long." She stifles a yawn. "I can't believe that we only went one hundred fifty miles. I left Weston right after lunch, and it's already getting dark."

"That's partly from the rain. Buses wear you out, though. Would it help if I got you a cappuccino?"

A shy grin lightens her fatigue. "You bet."

I fell in love with a gorgeous woman, then lost her beauty in a memory of blood and tears.

I turn down Euclid and find parking by the coffeehouse, then kill the Mustang twice as I parallel park. My face gets red; I tell Cole, "Mustangs only like to go forward."

"It's a great car," she says. "Well maintained."

At the cafe, we face each other over a little round table. Driving was easier—I can't meet her eyes for long. "You look great," I tell her. "Still swimming every day?"

She shakes her head. "I swim once in a while. I've been taking kickboxing lessons four times a week, though. It's a great workout."

"Kickboxing! Do you spar?"

"Some. Mostly we work out with pads, or with the heavy bags. A lot of it is training—skipping rope, footwork, drills for kicking and punching."

"You like that?"

"Uh-huh. We learn jabs, crosscuts, uppercuts, hooks. I like to punch the heavy bag."

"Really?" Cole always seemed too passive for martial arts. The onset of this new interest dawns on me; that erodes any remnant of my assurance. I take a drink of Coke, feeling weak.

Cole is silent for a moment, too. Then she says, "Never again, Terry."

I nod, looking at the wood grain of the table. Cole fiddles with a stirring stick. "I've waited nine months to say that to you," she says. "It sounded melodramatic."

"I want to talk about it, but not here," I say. "Alecki is fixing us dinner. When you're done with your coffee, let's head to the apartment."

With a mutual effort, we guide the conversation to neutral territory—AA, EMT school, Cole's artwork—and maintain that all the way home. Alecki greets us with vegetarian lasagna, cheese bread, salad topped with roasted garlic cloves and kalamata olives. Dinner is an odd suspension of reality: pleasant and uneventful, as if time had turned back.

Alecki charms Cole, asking about her art, tarot, and her plans. She says that she wants to give more time to her art, and that she's getting tired of Weston.

My breath catches; will this be the last time I see her? If so, it's still more than I deserve.

After dinner, Cole asks Alecki if he wants a card reading. He brightens, then catches my eye. "Maybe tomorrow, if you have time. I've got to meet some friends in a half hour."

The two of them clear the table and stack dishes in the sink. I fix a pot of coffee. I bought some Sumatra, Cole's favorite; she sees the bag and smiles. By the time the last drop drains into the carafe, Alecki is out the door. I pour two cups and bring them to the table.

"Thanks, hon," Cole says.

That sounded strange; I almost thought I misunderstood her. I wish she wasn't sitting so close. I'm about to vibrate with anxiety, and Cole has moved her chair until her leg is almost touching mine. I can't talk to her like this. "Let's go to the living room."

Cole takes the sofa. I start to sit in Lex's armchair, but that puts the lamp between us. That will make it hard to look directly at her. I turn off the lamp and light Lex's candles: one by Cole, two on the coffee table. They are scented, cinnamon and vanilla. The room starts to smell like pumpkin pie. I need to sit down, quit procrastinating.

Cole watches this frantic preparation without a word. The candlelight strikes sparks in the waves of her hair; shadows deepen her pale eyes.

I sit, wish briefly for a beer, then force my gaze to hers. "This probably won't take long." My voice is thin and shaky. "I just have to get started. When I told you—"

Cole scoots to the edge of the couch. She leans forward, props her elbows on her knees.

"That night, I was going to meet you after I went to the bar. I got there early and shot some pool with Jane. I didn't think I'd be too long. I was excited, Cole. I couldn't wait to see you." My hands are cold and sweaty. I glance at her, she nods encouragement. "Some girls I knew from St. Louis came in. We weren't really friends; I knew them from Minerva's. I was glad to see them, though. I was kicking ass at pool. Afterward, we all danced. You know what happened then—I did the coke; I got sick. Jane took me home."

My heart is pounding. Cole can probably hear it. Everything looks bright and sharp—the outlines of the coffee table, pattern of the sofa, Cole's eyelashes and lips. Her steady gaze bears upon me.

I swallow some coffee, release my dry tongue. "I don't want to drag this out. I need to make amends to you, but I'm not sure how. What I'm trying to say is, I'm sorry that I didn't call that night. I had a seizure at the bar. I hadn't been drinking that much, but after the seizure I was kind of out of it. I fell asleep. When I woke up at Jane's the next morning, I felt awful about it. I guess I called you."

"You did."

Her voice is hoarse, so soft I nearly missed the reply. Sounds like she might be crying, but I'm afraid to look. "I felt so shitty, Cole. Physically I felt like crap, and I knew I had stood you up. I was mad at myself for doing the dope—I could never turn it down. I felt so bad, and you had to work; you weren't going to be home until that night. Jane gave me a beer for breakfast, just to help me get going.

"I don't know why I got so loaded. I stole that gin from her cabinet, right before she dropped me off at your place. I just pulled the blinds in your living room, sat there all afternoon in the dark and drank. I think I was, you know . . . I was really sorry. I felt terrible about the whole thing, but it was hard for me to say that."

"You were afraid." She isn't crying. She's still leaned forward, hazel eyes burning into me.

"Yeah, I was. I am." I take a deep, shaky breath. "Cole, I don't have any excuses. I stood you up. I didn't call. I got drunk at your house. I knocked over the furniture. I hit you." That last one trailed off. I sit up straighter, face her. "I beat you. Then I left town and never said a fucking word to you. Cole, I am so sorry." That's it for eye contact; I stare at the candle flame. "I'm really ashamed of how I acted. I can't take any of it back; all I can tell you is that I am sorry."

Cole is quiet for a long time. When I look up, though, she's got a funny little smile. "You've changed," she says. "I don't know what you thought, Terry, but I have never hated you. Mostly I'm just glad that you're not drinking anymore." She stands and puts her hand on my shoulder. "Let's take a walk."

"OK." Relieved to be moving, I get my jacket. Is it over? I think I said what I was supposed to. I didn't cry, either; I was so blocked with fear that I couldn't.

Cole switches on the lamp and blows out the candles. "Ready?"

The rain has stopped; it washed the streets, left the air clean and fresh. Cole sticks her hands in her pockets and sets a brisk pace. "I never hated you," she says again. "I was upset that you left, but now—I don't know, it was probably good for me." She glances sideways at me and smiles. "When I first met you, I could just sit and watch you play softball or shoot pool or dance. I didn't even care if you knew my name; looking at you was enough. When you got interested in me, I was shocked. I didn't think you would ever notice somebody like me. You're so hot, Terry; everybody wanted to talk to you. Everybody wanted to be with you, but you chose me. I never understood it. I couldn't believe that I could get so lucky."

Lucky—I took care of that.

The toe of her shoe catches a tilt of sidewalk and Cole stumbles against me. I steady her with a hand on her waist. Those big feet; Cole always was a little clumsy.

Cole is broad-shouldered, not quite as tall as Holly. Not brawny; smoothly muscled, a swimmer's build. Gorgeous firm breasts. She's still going on about how overwhelmed she was. Her hands describe a circle, and she frowns earnestly. My palm is warm from touching her.

"—but really, all I hoped for was to find you sober, and happy." She pivots to face me, shoves her hands back in her pockets. "Are you happy?"

"I'm happy tonight." My body shifts, relaxes. "I'm happy that you're here, and I'm glad we talked."

"I am, too." Cole smiles again, those full, soft lips. "I feel so much better since we talked. This is part of AA, right? Making amends?"

"That's right. It's the Ninth Step."

"I don't know if you've thought about this." Cole starts to walk again, slowly. "I don't know if it's my place to bring it up. But she would never say anything to you, so I will.

"I've talked to Jane a few times since you left. I see her every so often. She doesn't have a lot of friends, Terry. She doesn't have much of anything, really." She pauses; confronting people isn't easy for Cole. "Jane thought the world of you. She would have done anything for you. When you left, you never said a word to her."

I suck in air, try to blow out some tension. "I didn't say anything to anybody. I was blind drunk."

"I know that; I know. But you've never spoken to her since. I don't know what it meant to you, but you were the best friend Jane's ever had. She still misses you; it hurt her when you left."

How can I explain? "I thought I was doing everyone a favor by getting out. I thought you would all be better off without me."

Nicole stops. She casts a quick glance at me, then looks down. "Seems like you thought of you, and not of anybody else."

"Later I did. I've thought of you a thousand times since then. I thought about Jane, too. I was just so ashamed." I shrug. "I couldn't even hope that anyone there would want to see me again."

A smile of disbelief plays across her face. "I did," she says. "Every damned day, I wanted to see you again. See, you think it's all about you. It's not. You hurt, I hurt, Jane hurts—nobody hates you; nobody wanted you to run away."

"Everybody just wants me to confront this massive ego and take responsibility, I guess."

"That's it. That's about right, you worthless shit." Her smile is genuine now. "Is that what you want to hear?"

"No. Not anymore, Cole. I'm glad you told me about Jane. I'll give her a call."

"I hope you do," she says. "Damn, I missed you."

Relief at having done the amend is beginning to seep into my consciousness; it lightens my step. A little wind is blowing. Ragged clouds scud across the sky, and I glimpse some stars in between. "I missed you, too."

She sees me looking up, and does the same. "Pretty night."

"Gorgeous." We're approaching a corner. "Are you ready to go back?"

"No, it feels good to move after that bus ride. After Lex's lasagna, too; that boy can cook."

I turn north; that will take us up by Forest Park, in a big loop. "Alecki loves to cook for company. If he's not out too late tonight, he'll probably make some coffee cake for breakfast."

"Sounds good. I need to ask a favor, Terry. Can I stay until Monday afternoon? I have an appointment that morning."

"That would be great. I don't have class until Tuesday evening, and things are kind of in limbo at work." I fill her in on Andrei's accident, only slightly inflating my role in saving him from certain paralysis.

"He's lucky you knew what to do." She's agreeably impressed. "What have you been up to, Cole? Still at the bookstore?"

"I've been working part-time. Still sketching; I had a few small exhibits in shows. I had a booth at a park here, not too long ago. I want to move on, though. There's not that much going on with art in Weston."

"Just the college, I guess."

Her eyes flare. "I'm *sure* not going back there." She'd had a bad experience, an affair with a professor her first year, and had never returned. "I would like to take some classes, though. I'm not sure if I want to go full-time again or not. If I do, I'd qualify for financial aid."

"That might ultimately be easier than taking a few classes. Where do you think you would go?"

She ducks her head and grins. "I've been thinking about Washington University. I talked to a professor from there at the art show in Forest Park a few weeks ago, and we've kept in touch. Sounds like a great department over there."

"It's a prestigious school." It's also three blocks north of Lex's apartment. Giddiness bubbles within me.

Cole's smile broadens. "I have an interview there Monday. I've already applied for financial aid. I just wasn't sure I wanted to move to St. Louis, but I like it here already."

My mind races—Cole's moving here? When? Where will she live? Does she want to get together? Will she stay? I muster a reply. "You'd like it. St. Louis is a great place."

"It's a lot bigger than I'm used to. Weston was a big city to me."

"St. Louis isn't that big once you get to know your way around. When you find your niche, it's just another little community with a lot of things to do." An urge to giggle almost overcomes me, but I stifle it. I can think of some things for her to do.

Cole grins again. "Maybe you could show me around? It would help if I had some connections here."

"I could help you out." I'm practically bouncing with excitement. I tell her about the art museum, just a few streets north of here, and the galleries around the Loop and in Clayton. Then I tell her about all the dyke teams: softball and soccer, rugby and basketball and volleyball, touch football in the fall, and all the old friends that I want her to meet.

Cole lopes alongside. She smiles and nods, watching me. By the time we get to the apartment, the clouds have dissipated into sparse shreds, and stars gleam bright above us.

She gets her travel bag and goes into the bathroom. Unable to contain my glee, I grab the phone. "Hey, Evelyn, this is Terry."

"Hey, kiddo. How did the amends go?"

"Cole's moving to St. Louis. She's going to go to Wash. U."

Long pause.

"Cole said she never did hate me. She missed me, but she was just kind of afraid to get in touch. She's shy. She thought I didn't want to see her, like she would be some kind of a bad reminder or something."

"Some amends," Evelyn finally replies. "So Nicole is moving to St. Louis?"

I'm struggling to keep my voice down. "She's going to study art at Wash. U. She might go full-time, or she may just take a class to see how she likes it."

"Where is she going to stay?"

"Tonight she's staying here, on the couch. If she moves here, I think she'll get her own place. She will if she can afford it."

"That's good," Evelyn says. "It's a little premature for the two of you to jump into anything."

"I know; I thought about it. This place isn't big enough for three of us, anyway."

"You did some good work tonight, Terry. I'm glad it turned out so well. But before you make any promises, pray about it. Ask your higher power for guidance before you move on."

"I will. I'm trying to slow down here." I giggle then, like a kid. "I'm so excited!"

Cole comes out of the bathroom. "Terry, is this where I—oh, sorry."

"Gotta go; I'll talk to you tomorrow."

"Take care, hotshot," Evelyn says. "Take it easy, and I mean that."

"Right."

I get Cole set up on the couch. I can tell she doesn't like the idea of sleeping there, probably because Alecki is still out. I hope he remembers to come in through the kitchen.

I undress and stretch out with my hands behind my head. I'm way too excited to sleep. My happy mind plays with possibility: Cole and me, in St. Louis, checking out coffeehouses, getting our own place, strolling in the Botanical Garden.

No relationships for a year. I can see why; forget "One Day at a Time," I want to have fun with my fantasies.

The occasional doubt tries to creep in, too; what if Cole wants to be just friends? What if we have grown too far apart in the last eight months? I'm feeling too good to spend much time with this stuff, though.

There's a tap at my door; it opens, hesitantly. I sit up.

"Terry?" The dim light from the kitchen outlines Cole's silhouette.

"Yeah?"

She eases the door shut. "Would it be all right if I just . . ." She pushes back her hair, her face shadowed.

"You want to lie down?" I scoot over to the far side of the mattress.

Cole stretches out next to me. I turn on my side and regard her with wonder. "I don't want to do anything," she says. "I'd like to lie here with you, though. If it's all right."

"It's all right." I slide close; reach across her belly and take her hand. "I'd like that, too." I'm calm now; I go right to sleep.

"Some amends," Evelyn says. We came to the clubhouse early, started the coffee and then ducked into a side room.

"Yesterday we just had time for breakfast. Cole had an interview at eleven, then I took her to the bus stop."

"And she slept on the couch."

"She started on the couch." I can't repress a smile.

"But ended up in your bed. Well." Evelyn smirks.

"Really, all we did was sleep."

"And how was that?"

"It was . . . nice. Comforting. I slept great."

Evelyn nods. "I believe that. Amends are a powerful thing."

"That's no lie. Tough, though. And then when Cole said she might be coming to St. Louis, my brain really took off."

"I'll bet."

"I tried not to get too caught up in it. Cole's still not sure what she's doing. She said the interview went really well."

"Sounds like she's been waiting to hear from you before she decides."

"I think so. Anyway, yesterday I just let her talk. Any questions I had, I wrote them down."

"In there?" She gestures to my spiral notebook.

I flip to the page: "'Will Cole move to St. Louis? When does the fall semester start? Will Lex care if I move out? Will Cole want to get a place together? Does she want to touch me as much as I want her? Is she afraid that I might start drinking again? Is it too soon for me to get into a relationship? Can I visit her in Weston? Has she dated anyone else? Should I tell her about Holly? Should I tell her about Pat?'" I toss the notebook on the table. "That's about it."

Evelyn grins. "Good start. What is that, a dozen?"

I turn the list. "Eleven. Wait." I take out a pen and add, "Is it completely insane to resume a relationship with someone whom I have beaten to a pulp?"

"That one I can answer," Evelyn says. "In general, I wouldn't recommend it, but sobriety changes everything." She lights a cigarette and blows the smoke away from me. "People tell you to wait until you have a year sober. Obviously, it's too late for that. I think you're doing all right. For now, you're keeping your pants on. Put your sobriety first, keep making good choices, and most of your questions will work themselves out." She winks at me. "If you knew ahead of time what was going to happen, it would spoil half the fun."

Chapter 11

Sure I was suicidal, but I was never dirty.

overheard at an AA meeting

"I know you said you wouldn't talk to Erica unless she asked. I called to let you know that she did say she wanted to talk to you."

This time I recognize the voice, or at least I recognize the urgency. "But Willow, she didn't say it to *me*."

"I know, but I think she will talk to you when she gets up. She's taking a nap right now."

No answer will satisfy the wired desperation of a woman trying to control someone else's drinking. "Is Erica sleeping, or did she pass out?"

"I don't know, she came over to my place and said she was ready to talk to you, then she went to sleep on the couch. I helped her to my bed later. If you come over in a little bit, you could be here when she wakes up."

"Before she starts drinking again."

"Right."

"We've been over this before—Erica doesn't want to stop drinking. She doesn't want to quit using coke; she doesn't want to talk to me; she doesn't even *like* me. *You* want me to talk to Erica. I understand you're scared, that you want her to stop, that Erica's making your life a living hell, but there's nothing I can do about it. The only thing you can do is get away from her."

"I did," Willow says. "I'm staying with my cousin, at her place. But Terry, you can't believe how much worse she's gotten since I moved out. She won't even let me come over to the apartment. She says it's trashed, and half my stuff is still there." She blows her nose. "If she didn't have somebody to help her, she'd probably be dead by now. You don't know what she's like. I can't just leave her. I promised."

"You said that before. What was that, eight weeks ago? So you've been miserable for eight more weeks, and Erica's been loaded; you aren't improving the situation any."

"I know what you're saying," (more sniffling) "but I really do think she meant it this time. She knows she's going to go to jail unless things change."

"At this point, Erica might be better off in jail. You tell her she can call me when she gets up. If she calls, I'll come over," I say, confident that she would not.

I didn't hear the phone when it rang; the message came at 2:43 a.m. It was after eight the next morning when I noticed. "Terry, this is Erica. I'm at my apartment. I want to talk to you." God damn it. No way out.

I call Evelyn first. She mulls it over, speculating that this may be an opportunity to perform a Twelfth Step call as well as a chance for me to make amends. "Pray for willingness," she says. "Then pick me up. I'm coming with you."

Erica doesn't answer her phone; she's probably passed out again. After leaving a message that I am on my way, I pray for the best possible outcome, then pick up Evelyn.

Evelyn lights a cigarette and cracks the window. "Your streak is still going."

"What streak?"

"Well, it's not exactly a winning streak, but you certainly take the prize for the most dramatic series of amends I've seen lately. I can't wait to see how this one turns out."

My tap on the door goes unanswered, but the door is slightly open. I step inside and call, "Erica!" No reply.

Evelyn motions me through. I've never seen anything so squalid; every inch of the apartment is trashed, and the place reeks. Erica's not around.

I cast about for the telephone, unearth it from a litter of plastic cups and soiled paper napkins. Erica got my message; the answering machine is rewound. There's no answer at Willow's. I call home, find out from Alecki that Willow had just phoned to say she's taking Erica to St. Anthony's for treatment.

"Shit. This is crazy," I tell Evelyn. "I'm sorry I dragged you over here."

"What's going on?"

I tell her we must have just missed them; Erica's gone to treatment. "I don't think there'd be any point in talking to her there."

"No; she'll have plenty on her mind for now." Evelyn frowns at me. "Are you serious about making amends?"

"Sure."

She looks around and shakes her head. "If I was Erica, I wouldn't want to face this shit. I don't know if she wants to stay sober or not, but I'm willing to bet there's dope stashed here somewhere. She wouldn't stand much chance, coming back to this. You want to clean it up?"

I shrug. "It would be better than talking to her. Probably would mean more to her. You don't mind?"

Evelyn scans the room again. "I started to say I've dealt with worse, but maybe not. Let's see what we can do in an hour and a half; it's not that big a place."

Six bags of trash out of a two-bedroom apartment. I'm talking big black plastic bags, full of cigarette butts and ashes, paper carryout bags spilling shriveled fries and dirty napkins, big paper cups with an inch of watery dregs. More than anything, there are bottles. Pints, half-pints, Jim Beam and Gilbeys and Smirnoff, an empty quart of Ten High, even some Everclear nestled among a pile of Mountain Dew bottles. I find Coke bottles, Pepsi and 7UP, Diet Wild Cherry Pepsi. Seven empty pint-sized chocolate milk cartons line up along the counter: last week's breakfasts.

Once I take out the trash, empty the ashtrays and collect the glasses, the place looks better. It still smells, though. Evelyn's washing dishes, so that's not where the stench is coming from. I start scouting.

The trash can's an obvious culprit. Erica did fill two black trash bags, but eventually abandoned any pretense of picking up. The wastebasket has no bag in it. It's full of half-eaten food. She'd emptied ashtrays over that, then vomited into it.

I haul the reeking mess out to the Dumpster and throw the whole wastebasket in. Erica can afford a new one. I line a paper bag with a plastic one and stand it where the trash can had been.

A wretched odor emanates from the bathroom; I stand back and flush the toilet, largely abolishing the problem. I've never been too drunk to flush a toilet.

Evelyn's finished the dishes; she starts wiping cigarette ash from all the horizontal surfaces in the kitchen and living room. I open windows, but the back of the apartment still stinks. In desperation, I place a scant smear of patchouli on the bulbs of the two table lamps and turn them on. By the time I'm done vacuuming the front room, the smell is penetrating the foul miasma.

I join Evelyn in the bedroom. "Smells like patchouli and shit in here."

"You got a good nose, kiddo. I tried to pull those sheets off and they were stuck."

Too much for me; I gag. Evelyn takes me out to the front steps. I crouch with my head between my knees, gulping fresh air. She brushes by with another bulging trash bag, headed for the Dumpster, then nudges me on the way back. "I found some fresh bedding. Help me make up the bed and we'll get the fuck out of here. You've done your amends and more."

The next week flies by. I interview at the hospital, and Beryl's supervisor Mike tells me I have the job, contingent on my successful completion of the EMT program. The semester is about to end, and I have finals. The last one leaves me with an oddly empty feeling. I talk to Alecki about it, then give my sponsor a call. "Evelyn? Lex and I are going to bring a pizza over to Andrei tonight. I wanted to let you know I won't be at the meeting."

"How is Andrei?" she asks.

"In terms of healing, he's doing great. He's a little depressed, though. One of his pins came loose last week, and he had to go back to the doctor and get the pins over his right eye and behind his left ear replaced. They place them in pairs, to keep the tension even."

"Dear God," she says. "This sounds like such a nightmare."

"Evidently it's pretty common for pins to loosen like that. He said they just tell him to close his eyes. There's a local anesthetic, I guess, but he can hear the pins go in."

"That's enough," she says. "More than I want to know. You go cheer up your brother; the meeting will get along without you for tonight."

On the porch, I wait for Alecki. He'd gone to rent some movies and pick up the pizza.

Andrei looks almost as bad as he did in the hospital. Sunk into Dad's recliner, he doesn't appear to have moved from it in weeks. He's wearing an old baseball jacket, open over the plastic vest, and a ratty pair of sweatpants. The bruising is gone from his face; the laceration on his nose has closed except for a central scab, but it's a livid pink. There's a small bandage next to the new pin. He's going to have a lot of scars.

"How's the halo, Dre?" asks Alecki.

"At the moment, solid. Mom told you about the pins, didn't she?"

"Yeah. That's too bad."

"It's disgusting. They give me a little shot, tell me to close my eyes, then I hear bolts crunch into my skull."

Alecki shudders.

I open a pizza box on Dre's lap. "Maybe some sausage, green pepper, and onion will help."

He smiles, halfway. "Hey, that's your favorite."

My face gets red; Alecki says, "I picked it out."

"That's OK," Andrei says. "I've never had pizza I didn't like. The doctor said I'm losing too much weight, so bring it on."

He does look thin. "You'll put it back on once you get back to work."

"That's not the problem. It's the vest. They'll have to redo it if I gain or lose much weight. But all I do is lay around and get skinnier and flabby."

Alecki is setting up TV trays for all of us. Mom brings in a two-liter Coke, then leaves us alone. She needs a break from Andrei, and vice versa. She and Pop are going out to dinner.

We're all serious consumers of pizza. Andrei turns on MTV, and we eat. "This is great, you guys," he finally says. "Thanks. I haven't had pizza in over a month."

"We got some movies," Alecki says. He hands the boxes to Andrei.

"I've probably seen them. That's what I do all day—watch videos."

"What do you want to do?" I ask.

"Nothing I'm allowed."

"Dre, there's a lot you can do, especially with Lex and me here. What would you like? Let's take a walk—it's a gorgeous day. We could go play darts somewhere, or get some ice cream."

He hesitates.

"What?"

"The one thing I would really love is if you guys could help me wash my hair. It's a total project, and Mom hates it, and I hate to ask her, but it itches and it feels sticky." He scratches around the metal band. "This fucking halo."

"You do make a pretty mangy angel," Alecki says. "You need a haircut, too, but you wouldn't want me to do it."

"So you guys will wash my hair?"

"Sure," I say. "As soon as they leave for dinner."

It is a project; we have to keep his body jacket dry. I take the roll of bisqueen from the garage. That's the plastic Pop uses to mask fixtures and counters, especially if he's spraying. I drape and tape Andrei, then secure a rolled towel around his neck. He kneels on a couch pillow, leans over the edge of the tub. Alecki douses his head with pitchers of water.

Dre's hair is black, much curlier than mine or Lex's. Marius has curly hair but not to this degree. Andrei hasn't been able to brush it very well, and it's started to mat. Despite the grease, I have to work out the tangles with a handful of conditioner before I use shampoo. The third time I soap him, I finally work up some lather. No wonder he was itching. I dig in with my fingernails, and he groans like an old dog.

It takes a good forty minutes to get his hair clean. My back is stiff by the time we're done. Alecki puts his hands behind his hips and stretches his spine, then twists sharply to the side. His low back pops audibly.

I can't imagine what leaning over the tub felt like to Andrei; he was really in an awkward position. By the time we finish, he's trembling with fatigue. He sits on the toilet, toweling gingerly, as Alecki liberates him from the plastic cape and I mop the pools of water from the bathroom floor.

"You smell pretty," Alecki tells him, and Andrei grins for real. They go to change his sodden pants. From the bedroom, I can hear the two of them singing "I Feel Pretty," from *West Side Story*. Alecki was in the production in high school, though I don't recall him playing Maria.

Andrei is exhausted; Mom said he still takes pain meds in the evenings. We reinstall him in the recliner and throw the towels in the wash. He's sound asleep by the time Mom and Pop come back from dinner.

Mom gives Alecki a hug, says "I'm glad you spent some time with him. He's bored to death." She looks at me, falters, then hugs me too. "Thanks," is all she says, but it's enough.

Rain washes the sidewalk, tepid in the heat. When the warm rains of last summer swelled the humidity, Cole would say it smelled like Texas. I called her over the weekend; she'll be moving here in August.

Beryl leans against the brick wall next to the ambulance bay, smoking. This is my third shift at the hospital, and it's slow. This morning we transferred a patient to a nursing home, but we haven't had any calls in over three hours. It's a gray and rainy day. Visitors meander into the hospital under umbrellas.

"Everybody's too lethargic to get sick."

Beryl nods. "We'll get something soon, I bet. But it's a lazy day, for sure. I'd just as soon stay here."

I crouch, my back against the warm bricks. The overhang keeps off the rain, but a fine spray mists my face in an occasional gust of wind. Puddles are growing in the parking lot, even in the grass, and there's a dull roar of water washing into the storm sewer.

Beryl stubs her cigarette out against the wall. She yawns. "I'm about half asleep. Think I'll get some coffee. Want something?"

I fish out some change. "Get me a Coke. Thanks." Now she's got me yawning. In the ambulance bay I spot the open rolls of tape stacked on the counter. I haven't juggled much lately, but I get three of them in the air with no trouble at all. I work with those a couple of minutes, until my rhythm's going, then I pick up two more. I have to concentrate to keep five in the air. I consciously relax my shoulders, breathe evenly.

"Nice hands; you're very deft." Beryl sets my Coke on the counter, and I drop two rolls. One eludes me, rolls under the ambulance. "Maybe I spoke too soon," she says.

"No, I can do this. I'm out of practice." I fall to my stomach, retrieve the tape from behind the front tire, then hop to my feet and start again. Beryl counts sixty-two passes before I drop another.

"That's cool. I never tried to juggle."

"It passes the time. Just takes some repetition. Hang on." I run out to my car, bring back the little hip pack that holds my assorted footbags. I start her off with just one ball, passing high from the right hand, low from the left.

"No problem," she says. "Give me two."

"Not yet. You want to be steady—think metronome. And get the right-hand one a little higher."

"OK." She watches the footbag lift and drop, adjusting her position to its fall. "How's your sweetie?"

"Which one?"

Beryl chuckles, missing a catch. "Get over yourself," she says. "Have you heard from Cole?"

"I have." I pick up her footbag and demonstrate the two-ball pass. "High to the right, low to the left, same as before."

Beryl throws the balls jerkily, but catches both. "OK, I got it. So, what's up?"

"The young lady is coming this weekend," I say. "She's got a meeting with her advisor, and I offered to show her around the campus."

"You never went to Wash. U., did you?"

"No," I say, "but I have spent the night on the campus."

"You're a *hound*," Beryl says. "Is she going to stay with you?"

"I offered her the couch, but she may go back that night. Weston is not that far."

Beryl looks skeptical.

"We are actually, genuinely taking it slow. Our plans are for dinner and dancing." Dancing was Cole's idea, and a surprise to me. All the time we were together, she never even tried it. At Weston's only gay bar, Cole always stood against the wall and stared, her hazel eyes dreamy, and I'd get with one woman after another before going home with her.

A footbag whacks my left ear, dispelling my dance-as-foreplay reverie. "Sorry." Beryl smirks. "I want all the details Sunday afternoon."

"I'm telling you," I say, "we're going to take it slow. Just campus, then dinner and an early night at Minerva's."

By the time we finally get a call, the rain has slackened to a drizzle. There's a two-car accident at Highway 40 west, on the overpass right before the exit from 40 to 270.

A single patrol car is on the scene; the fire department has not yet arrived. The cop runs up and fills us in: the driver had started to exit, then changed her mind and tried to pull back into a driving lane. The car on the overpass is a Ford Taurus, two-door, not new. The truck that sideswiped them is pulled off the road, farther up.

The driver's side of the Taurus is creased, the door jammed shut. The driver can't get the window down, either. The passenger is penned in by the guardrail, though she can open her window. It doesn't look like anyone's hurt, but the two ladies are panicky.

"The driver's-side airbag has deployed," says the cop. "The passenger's in labor. They were on their way to St. Luke's when they got hit."

The cop has secured the area with cones and flares. Still, the noise and rush of traffic is unnerving. I pray that no one disregards the flares because they are too busy looking for the exit. This is the most heavily traveled intersection in the city.

Outside the driver's window, Beryl shouts, "We're going to get you out of there. Try to stay calm." The driver turns up her hands, shakes her head, then indicates the passenger.

"They can't hear you," says the cop. "Traffic's too loud."

I whip out my notebook and jot *Stay calm. We're going to get you out.* I hold it to the window; the driver reads it aloud and nods. I flip to page two and write *Are either of you hurt?* She shakes her head, then points to her friend and starts yelling again.

Beryl is pulling the ambulance up closer; she edges it around the patrol car. "Tell them we're coming through the back window," she yells. I relay the message. The driver shrugs and nods. The passenger draws up her knees, grabs the armrest and grimaces. We've got to move on this one.

Beryl tosses me a blanket. "Hand it in and tell them to cover their heads."

I hop onto the hood; it's a little slick from the rain. I have a wonderful view of the traffic on I-270, far below. Holy shit; I didn't think I'd have to get so close to the edge.

The passenger is panting now, pale and sweaty, her eyes half-closed. I slap the windshield to get her attention. "Put your hand out the window." I yell for all I'm worth, and pantomime stretching. She tries, but her belly's so big she can't get very far forward. I sprawl across the hood, hook my fingers under the edge of it for a simian sense of security. With my left hand, I give the blanket a hard fling. The corner goes into the window but slips back out before the passenger can grab it. She secures it on the second try.

I scoot back, sit up in the middle of the hood, and pantomime holding the blanket over my head. They misunderstand, put it up like a curtain behind them, all four arms stuck straight up. Beryl releases the impact tool and the back window shatters. "Got it!"

The women drop the blanket, and the passenger has another contraction. That's two in under five minutes. She grabs the armrest, hikes a foot up onto the edge of the seat, and lets out a roar that even I can hear.

I run to the rear of the car. Beryl is in; she's already cut the lap belt from the driver. I brush away sparkling crystals of safety glass, help the woman climb through the window. She's babbling, "Her water's broke! Any second now! Jesus Christ, get in there!" The cop leads her to the patrol car.

Beryl pops out right behind. Her gloves betray a smear of blood. "You're up," she says. "She's not quite crowned, but I could feel the head. I'll get the kit."

I'm through the window before it registers. Crowned? We're going to deliver it here? "Are you in pain?" I ask the passenger.

She looks at me as if I am insane. "I'm having a *baby*," she snaps.

"I mean, are you hurt?"

"No. Not that I can tell." She grits her teeth and rises halfway off the seat, then lifts her knees and braces them against the dashboard. Her face goes deep red; looks like she's holding her breath.

"Breathe!" I tell her. She starts to pant, drops back into the seat. Her face goes pale again. Sweat beads on her upper lip, trickles down her temple. "Don't hold your breath like that. Your blood pressure will go up."

"I know," she says. "I'll try."

"We're going to have you deliver here, then we'll get you to the hospital."

She nods, eyes closed. "Your partner told me."

I get her to recline the seat a little, and to shove it back as far as she can. She scoots her hips to the edge of the seat, braces her feet up on the dashboard. I slide my seat back, too, and tilt the steering wheel as high as it goes.

Beryl tosses in a couple of chucks, sterile absorbent pads. I tuck one under the woman's hips, lay another on the floorboard. I'm not going to be able to get in front of her; I'll have to do this from the driver's seat, on my belly. My legs are drawn up under me, and I'm breathing almost as hard as the patient. I remind myself of what Mr. Carr told us: "Birth is not an emergency. They're going to come out whether you are there or not."

"My name's Terry. I'm an EMT." I unroll a blood pressure cuff, begin to take her vitals.

"Paula," she grunts.

I check her blood pressure, respirations, heart rate, then assume a horribly awkward stretch to check the fetal heart rate. I find the fetal tones in the left lower abdominal quadrant, ticking away like a muffled watch. "Is this your first baby?"

"My third."

Shit, this ought to be quick. "When did your labor start?"

Another contraction; I get out of the way. Beryl has the backseat spread with chucks. She's laid out hemostats, a bulb syringe, an adult airway, an infant endotracheal tube and laryngoscope, several sanitary napkins. I grab two of those to capture blood loss and hope the rest will prove superfluous. "Doing OK?" Beryl asks.

"Her vitals check out, for being in labor. Fetal heart rate was 156."

"I meant you."

"Me? OK? Yeah, but shouldn't you—"

She shakes her head. "My legs are too long. You're perfect for this."

Paula's fallen back against the seat. I don a mask, goggles, gloves. Beryl takes over the history—term pregnancy, no prior complications, no significant medical history, no medications, "but I'll take some if you've got 'em."

"Sorry."

"Terry," Paula says, "do me a favor."

"What?"

"Get my purse," she says. Beryl stretches in and pulls it from behind the seat.

Paula digs around, produces a cassette. "This is my birthing music. Would you put it on?"

I look at Beryl. She shrugs. "I don't see why not."

The front speaker on the driver's side is blown from the impact. I adjust the tape player so the music comes through the back speakers alone, and it sounds fine. The tape is one that Paula put together; it starts with a song by Enya.

"That'll help me relax," Paula says.

"I'm all for that."

"Also, I don't want an episiotomy."

Beryl tells me to apply counterpressure with two fingers against her perineum once the head is crowned. "If you give some support, she's less likely to tear." I cut away the gauzy maternity underpants; Beryl had only snipped through the crotch. She's still talking to Paula, reminding her to breathe through contractions and to go ahead and push. She gets the name of the obstetrician and radios the hospital. "They're sending an obstetrical nurse," she says, "but I think she's going to miss all the fun."

I think so, too; the baby's head is visible, though it slips back between contractions. I get as comfortable as possible while balanced on my abdomen with my left hand pressed firmly to Paula's crotch. I can't draw a full breath. My left knee is on the floor board, the other crunched into the driver's seat, my weight is on my stomach and my right forearm. It's so tight in here, the baby may hit me in the face when it comes out.

Beryl asks, "Is it a boy or—"

Paula's bellow drowns her out. Beryl yells "Breathe!" Paula pants and strains, and the head crowns. My breath feels moist under the mask, a vaguely choking sensation. The whole car is damp from rain and condensation and sweat.

"What are you having?" Beryl asks again.

"A girl," she says. "I'm excited. I've got two little boys already."

It's so close down here. My goggles are steamed, my belly clenches against the seat. Between my thumb and forefinger, the top of the baby's head looks big as a moon. Softballs fill my field of vision like this when I'm at bat.

Paula's frantic hand lands on my hair and pulls, nearly lifts me from the seat. She squeezes, then relaxes; the baby's head slides out. "Sorry," she gasps, then strokes my head, as if I was one of her kids. I slip from her grasp before she tightens up again.

The baby's head is in my left hand. Blood surges from underneath, I can't see where it's coming from. I catch as much as I can on a pad. Paula might have torn a little; I keep pressure on the perineum with my right hand.

"The fire department's here," Beryl says. "They've got the Jaws of Life. You want them to wait?"

"The head's out; they'll have to wait." I don't want to lose my balance now. I cradle the little face, try to breathe with my diaphragm jammed into the edge of the seat and the steering wheel in my butt. Thank God this is not a five-speed.

The baby's trying to turn its head to the left, rooting against my palm. One eye is visible, barely open and unfocused. The head is kind of flat on one side. We wait, Paula and I, and this little head. Beryl says, "Keep breathing." She's talking to Paula, but I set the knuckles of my right fist into the floor and lift up, expand my chest for one good breath. My butt hits the steering wheel. My ribs are assaulted by the buckle of the lap belt and my right hip is cramping, but this won't be long.

Paula bears down, her legs draw up. The top shoulder slides out. I shift my weight, bring my right hand up. As soon as Paula relaxes, a baby girl slithers into my grasp.

I lower her to the chuck, just for a moment, and let out the breath I was holding. "She's here," I call to Beryl. "Check the time." The baby jerks all over at my yell. She gasps her first breath.

"Four thirty-six p.m."

Paula reaches. I lay the baby on her belly, and she smiles, and laughs, and starts to cry.

"We need an APGAR," Beryl says.

"Hold on." I twist myself upright, into the driver's seat. The umbilical cord is pulsing across Paula's thigh: coiled like a phone cord, bloody and visceral. Paula's saying "You're so pretty" to her little girl.

I score the APGAR: two points each for heart rate, breathing, movement, reflex, color. Except for bluish hands and feet, she's good. "Eight of ten, cyanotic distal extremities."

"Probably cold," Beryl says. "I'll tell these guys to come in."

"This may be loud," I warn. Paula gently covers the baby's ears. There's a bang, a horrible metallic shriek, a rush of air that smells like wet roads and car exhaust. The traffic's loud and close. The baby is in such a rage by the second APGAR check that she gets the full score.

"You're a perfect ten already," Paula tells her.

Beryl comes around with the stretcher. The cord has gone limp, so I clamp and cut it. The baby catches my finger and grips. I stop, look at this human being that was not in the car ten minutes ago. "Good luck," I say.

A sudden gush of blood hits the chuck. I hand the baby out to Beryl and wait for the placenta. When that is expelled, I bag it for transport and help Paula out of the car. She has to scoot sideways across the seat; it looks like an effort. The nurse has arrived; she checks out the baby, says she looks fine.

Traffic still roars by; it's rush hour now. The rain has stopped. We get Paula and the baby in the ambulance. Beryl drives; I radio the hospital that we are bringing in a thirty-three-year-old woman and her fifteen-minute-old daughter.

Beryl and I are off shift by the time we get back, with an hour's overtime. "Will I see you at the meeting?" I ask Beryl.

"Definitely. I was going to make sure you'd be there. This stuff is like drugs; you get a big rush from it, but then you have to come down. You'd be better off at a meeting tonight."

"I'm OK."

"Sure you are. You're buzzed. You ought to see your eyes." She laughs. "That was pretty cool, though. You jumped in there like you deliver kids every day."

"Scared the shit out of me."

"It's supposed to. You did OK, though. You got confidence, and good hands, and you can fit into tight spaces. Who knows, in ten years maybe you'll be a gynecologist."

"Let me run that by Evelyn."

"Take it easy; I'll see you tonight."

I go home and soak in the tub, then catch a nap before the meeting.

I just broke a boot lace. It's the last Wednesday of July, the monthly birthday meeting at my home group. Beyond that, it's *my* birthday—I had nine months on the eighteenth. Indigo got six months a week ago, too. I have anointed myself with patchouli, put on my black jeans, ironed my blue-and-black pinstriped shirt and polished these boots to a mirror shine. Then I broke my lace.

My hand aches where I yanked the lace. It's been raining all day, and the fracture still throbs when the weather's wet. I wonder how Pat, the waitress, is doing. Beryl had a call on Shenandoah a couple weeks ago, on my day off.

The front door was standing open. Whoever had called 911 was gone. An emaciated white woman with short dark hair lay naked and unconscious on her bedroom floor. Beryl said the woman was young, but in bad shape: a probable stroke or head injury. There appeared to be cocaine or heroin in her nasal passages; she was bruised around the head and face. Old bruises covered her torso and legs, Beryl said.

Sure sounded like Pat, but I didn't pursue it. Beryl was kind of down about it; there's something eerie about a transport who's your own age.

Alecki is in the kitchen, drinking wine and writing furiously. I take the boots from his closet and pull out the laces. They're too long, but I double-knot them. My jeans will cover it.

"I'm out of here," I tell Lex.

He looks me up and down. "What did you get from my room?"

"I owe you a pair of boot laces." I pick up his cigarette, but he grabs my wrist before I get it to my lips.

"Give me that. It's a filthy habit," he says. "And you stole the laces from my shoes! You're a scab."

"You're a selfish bastard."

Alecki stubs out the butt. "You do look sharp, draga. Nine months." He wraps his arms around my waist. "I'm happy for you."

"Thanks, Lex," I say. "It doesn't seem like that long. A lot has happened, though. I'll be out late, probably; I'm not working tomorrow."

Indigo is in front of the club when I pull up. Tonight she's wearing the Aussie hat with boots and suspenders, but she ditched the duster in late spring. She is definitely eccentric, but then I used to wear my gay pride T-shirts to mixed meetings. "Hey, Terry," she says. "I wanted to be the first one to congratulate you tonight."

"Thanks, Indy. Congratulations back at you. Coming in?"

"Not yet. My sponsor will be here to give me my coin. I told her I'd wait outside for her." Indigo's sponsor, a straight woman, has never been to the club.

Annie's leading the meeting tonight. She talks about serenity, how good her life is today: no longer a series of self-created crises, just living in each moment and mostly enjoying what comes along. She reads from page 449 of the Big Book: "And acceptance is the answer to *all* my problems today.... Nothing, absolutely nothing happens in God's world by mistake. Until I could accept my alcoholism, I could not stay sober; unless I accept life completely on life's terms, I cannot be happy. I need to concentrate not so much on what needs to be changed in the world as what needs to be changed in me and my attitudes."

Camille talks next. She reads the AA Promises: "If we are painstaking about this phase of our development, we will be amazed before we are halfway through. We are going to know a new freedom and a new happiness. We will not regret the past nor wish to shut the door on it. We will comprehend the word serenity and we will know peace. No matter how far down the scale we have gone, we will see how our experience can benefit others. That feeling of uselessness and self-pity will disappear. We will lose interest in selfish things and gain interest in our fellows. Self-seeking will slip away. Our whole attitude and outlook on life will change. Fear of people and of economic insecurity will leave us. We will intuitively know how to handle situations that used to baffle us. We will suddenly realize that God is doing for us what we could not do for ourselves."

Next is Evelyn. She congratulates Indigo and me, then tells of how her intuition developed along with her faith.

The warmth and camaraderie of this meeting impress Indigo's sponsor, Tina. "My home group has about forty members, and I like it, but I miss the closeness of a smaller meeting. You gals all know each other; you care about each other," she says.

Beryl is sitting by me. She says, "My name's Beryl, and I'm an alcoholic."

"Hi, Beryl."

"I want to talk for a minute about my friend, here." She grasps my shoulder. "Talk about the Promises—I remember when she came in here. She had a cast on her hand; half the time she was Billy Badass and the other half she was trying not to cry. This woman has seriously made some changes—she's not such a badass anymore. I kind of like who she is. I get to see her at meetings, and now I even get to work with her, and that's pretty great.

"Terry's at the meetings, she works the Steps, she's got a sponsor, and she tells us when things are messed up and when they're going good. Turns out there's a real human being under all that attitude.

"And you—" Beryl turns to Indigo. "Girl, you were scary. I wasn't even sure you could talk. Turns out you've got some things to say. I want to tell you all that I am proud to be sober and to have the privilege of watching these women come in here and get sober and sane." She shakes her head. "It's a miracle, man. A fuckin' miracle."

Tina gives Indigo her coin, and Evelyn gives me mine. Annie brought in a big spice cake; we adjourn to the smoking lounge for coffee and cake. Since it's Wednesday, nobody wants to go out. Annie and Camille have to get up early for work Thursday; Evelyn's meeting with a newcomer. Beryl won't say where she's going; I'm sure I'll hear about it later.

"I don't feel like sitting," Indigo says, "but I'll take a walk if you want."

"Sounds good."

We take the Mustang down to Kingshighway, stop on Lindell at the edge of Forest Park. The clouds have passed. It's a gorgeous night, stars shining even through the city lights. We walk into the Central West End.

The drugstore on Euclid is open late; Indigo follows me in. By the yellow Dr. Scholl's display I find replacement laces for Lex's boots and a tin of black paste polish.

Indigo gets a roll of Butter Rum Life Savers. I pay for her purchase along with mine, and she dumbly grins her thanks. I can tell she mostly hangs out with dogs.

We walk south, toward Lindell. "I took the laces out of my brother's boots tonight," I tell her. "I used up his polish, too."

"So you're practicing Step Ten," she says. "Making amends promptly."

"I'll see your Ten and raise you two. When I get home I'll give him the laces, then tomorrow I'll polish his boots."

"Practicing these principles in all your affairs? You're on Step Twelve?"

"Evidently."

"So you're available as a sponsor now?"

Indigo had asked me to be her sponsor last spring, but I told her I wouldn't sponsor anyone until I had worked all twelve steps. "Why, are you looking? What about Tina?"

"Are you available?" she repeats.

I can't tell if Indigo is serious because she's smiling. "I hadn't given it any thought. I guess I am."

"Cool," she says. That's all.

We turn down Lindell. The 4522 Club doesn't have late meetings tonight, so we can't get in. Unlike the Lambda Club, nonmembers can only enter 4522 during meeting times. A couple of guys I recognize are in the back lot, sitting on the fender of a car and smoking, but Indigo and I go back toward Forest Park. I'd rather walk with her silence than talk bullshit in a parking lot.

When we get to the Mustang, Indy surprises me with a hug. "Thanks for taking the time," she says.

"Sure. I enjoyed it." I take her back to Lambda, where she left her truck, then I head home.

There's a note on the kitchen table: Alecki went out with some friends. Next to the note, a large brownie bristles with nine pastel birthday candles. The rest of the pan is cooling on the counter.

This birthday-candle brownie can remain for a celebration with Lex. I cut a smaller brownie from the pan and pour a glass of milk. Whacker jumps onto my lap and pounds my thigh with his paws. I push him into a purring heap, give him a little chunk of brownie. Pecans and no icing: my favorite kind.

I wish Alecki were here. It's too late to call anyone. I was excited before the meeting, but this is starting to feel like another night alone. It's ten twenty-five; Cole is probably sleeping. I left her a message that I got my nine months, but my voice mail has no reply. Cole and I have been talking once or twice a week, but we don't get to see each other much. She's dragging her feet on the move to St. Louis. I think she's waiting until we are ready to get an apartment together. I wish she could have come tonight, though; I miss her.

I must be getting tired. I ask Whacker if he would care to join me in maudlin reminiscence, but he only wants my glass of milk. I pour a little into the dessert plate and set it on the floor for him.

The doorbell sounds—Alecki must have forgotten his keys. I open the door, yawning hugely.

"Hey, Terry." It's Cole. I shut my gaping mouth and stare a moment. She laughs, blushing, and extends a bouquet of white carnations.

"Cole. I'm sorry, come in."

She ducks her head and grins, then grabs me in such a hug that my feet come right off the ground. Carnation leaves tickle my right ear.

"There's nine of them," she says.

Released, I take the flowers. They droop a bit from the long ride, but they smell great. "I'll get a vase." Alecki has one stashed under the kitchen sink. It's dusty and spattered; I give it a quick soaping.

Cole follows me into the kitchen, still beaming. An overnight bag is slung over her shoulder.

"I can't believe you're here," I say. "Did you get my message?"

"Well, I . . ." She steps back. "Not exactly. I just happened to call a couple hours ago, while you were at the meeting."

Carnations—my favorite flower. "You talked to Lex."

"I know you don't like that." Cole steps back again, crossing her feet and almost stumbling. "I thought about it when I was driving down, how much you hate people talking about you. I was just excited, Terry. I wanted to tell you how proud I am of your—birthday? Anniversary? Anyway, your nine months."

I *don't* like people talking about me but worse than that is watching Cole back away. Her bag is clutched in front of her now, the canvas strap wadded in her hands.

"Alecki does it all the time," I tell her. "Now that I'm sober, it's not as bad. I'm excited, too, Cole. You drove down just to congratulate me?"

She smiles.

"You look like you're planning to stay the night."

"If it's OK," she says. "If you want me to, or else I could—"

I catch a loop of the shoulder strap, tug her gently forward. "You're not going anywhere. We've got some celebrating to do. Unless you're tired . . ."

"Driving down, I was a little—" We turn the corner; I pull her down the hall. "Well, no, not *that* tired."

I fall across my bed and Cole lands on top of me. The bag is still wedged between us. "I could massage your shoulders," I say. "That might revive you."

For an answer, I get a kiss. Squashed, breathless, I extricate the overnight bag. The next few kisses are full contact, warm and lingering; they leave me even more breathless. "Shoulder massage," I finally repeat. "Sound good?"

Cole rolls over and stretches out.

"I'd do a better job without that T-shirt in the way."

The T-shirt sails across the room, followed by her bra. Cole shakes out her long auburn curls and grins. "I feel better already."

She looks glorious. She'll get a massage later; right now we have some celebrating to do.

ABOUT THE AUTHOR

Bridget Bufford, a St. Louis native, now lives in mid-Missouri. An Amherst Writers & Artists Affiliated workshop leader, she facilitates writing workshops for established and aspiring writers, children, and individuals with special needs. Her writing has appeared in the *Harrington Lesbian Fiction Quarterly* as well as the anthologies *Pillow Talk II* and *Body Check* (Alyson Press) and *The Use of Personal Narratives in the Helping Professions: A Teaching Casebook* (Haworth).

SPECIAL 25%-OFF DISCOUNT!
Order a copy of this book with this form or online at:
http://www.haworthpress.com/store/product.asp?sku=4927

MINUS ONE: A TWELVE-STEP JOURNEY

_____ in softbound at $13.46 (regularly $17.95) (ISBN: 1-56023-468-7)

Or order online and use special offer code HEC25 in the shopping cart.

COST OF BOOKS_____

OUTSIDE US/CANADA/
MEXICO: ADD 20%_____

POSTAGE & HANDLING_____
(US: $5.00 for first book & $2.00
for each additional book)
(Outside US: $6.00 for first book
& $2.00 for each additional book)

SUBTOTAL_____

IN CANADA: ADD 7% GST_____

STATE TAX_____
(NY, OH, MN, CA, IN, & SD residents,
add appropriate local sales tax)

FINAL TOTAL_____
(If paying in Canadian funds,
convert using the current
exchange rate, UNESCO
coupons welcome)

☐ **BILL ME LATER:** ($5 service charge will be added)
(Bill-me option is good on US/Canada/Mexico orders only;
not good to jobbers, wholesalers, or subscription agencies.)

☐ Check here if billing address is different from
shipping address and attach purchase order and
billing address information.

Signature_____

☐ **PAYMENT ENCLOSED:** $_____

☐ **PLEASE CHARGE TO MY CREDIT CARD.**

☐ Visa ☐ MasterCard ☐ AmEx ☐ Discover
☐ Diner's Club ☐ Eurocard ☐ JCB

Account #_____

Exp. Date_____

Signature_____

Prices in US dollars and subject to change without notice.

NAME_____
INSTITUTION_____
ADDRESS_____
CITY_____
STATE/ZIP_____
COUNTRY_____ COUNTY (NY residents only)_____
TEL_____ FAX_____
E-MAIL_____
May we use your e-mail address for confirmations and other types of information? ☐ Yes ☐ No
We appreciate receiving your e-mail address and fax number. Haworth would like to e-mail or fax special
discount offers to you, as a preferred customer. **We will never share, rent, or exchange your e-mail address
or fax number.** We regard such actions as an invasion of your privacy.

Order From Your Local Bookstore or Directly From
The Haworth Press, Inc.
10 Alice Street, Binghamton, New York 13904-1580 • USA
TELEPHONE: 1-800-HAWORTH (1-800-429-6784) / Outside US/Canada: (607) 722-5857
FAX: 1-800-895-0582 / Outside US/Canada: (607) 771-0012
E-mailto: orders@haworthpress.com
PLEASE PHOTOCOPY THIS FORM FOR YOUR PERSONAL USE.
http://www.HaworthPress.com   BOF03